TIMEKEEPER

THIREENA YUKI

TIMEKEEPER

THE SAGAS OF ALERIA

First Printing, 2021

ISBN: 979-8-9853677-0-6

Cover Illustration by Alex Gavrilas

To my kids,

This would have gotten finished way faster without you guys.

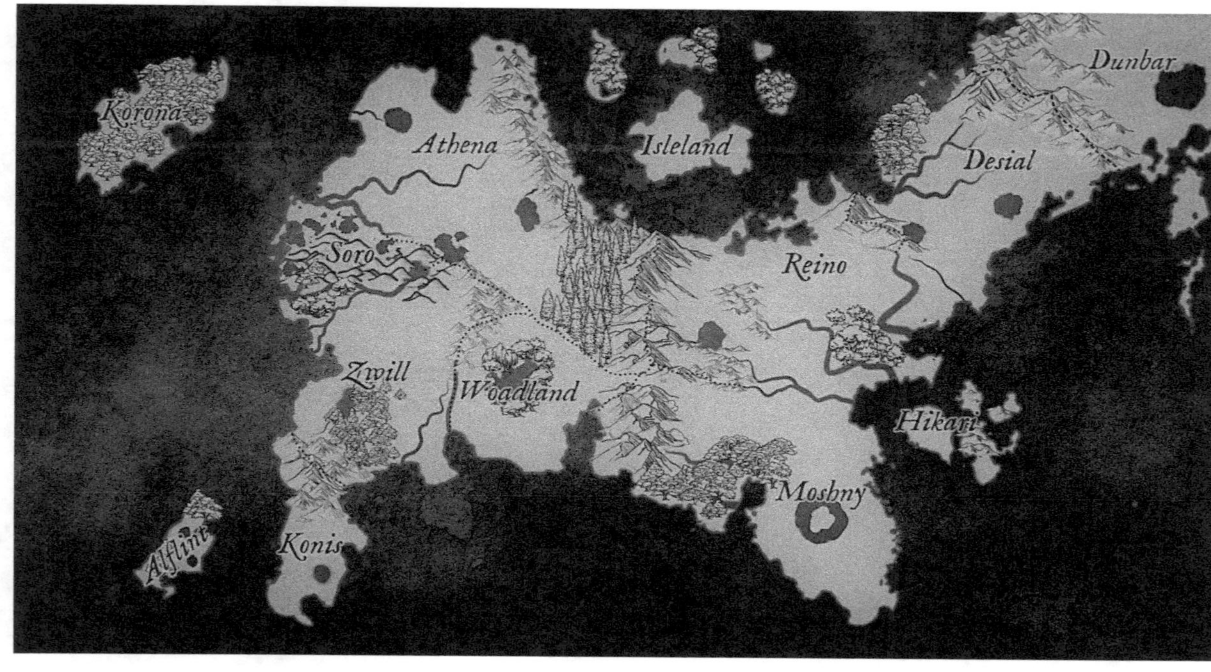

Korona
Dunbar
Athena
Isleland
Desial
Soro
Reino
Zwill
Woadland
Hikari
Moshny
Alflint
Konis

TIMEMAKER

Come.

The ghostly figure was turned away from him as they walked through the moonlit woods. The slender and towering trees were swaying back and forth, sprinkling light snow over their fresh footprints.

Closer.

The pair made their way along a path that he had traveled on many times before. Her glimmering white gloves made of fine fur were delicately holding his hand as they passed centuries-old stone monuments hidden within the mass of Desiali trees. Everything was a soft blur, as it always had been. The monuments with crumbled etchings weren't legible and every time she turned around, he couldn't make out her face.

Almost.

The forest was thickening as she gripped his hand harder with every step they took. Their pace grew steadily until they were almost running. Suddenly, she stopped and turned towards him. Her face was still blurry and unrecognizable.

We're here.

A hoarse young rooster crowed in the distance, accompanied by faint shuffling feet and the voices of villagers outside trying to strike up bargains. Leon was surrounded by the harsh morning sunlight as specks of dust floated across his scope of vision. His cracked window let in rays of light that streaked onto his face. The room was small and uninviting, but this had been his room for as long as he could remember. Even though one would say he had outgrown it, he loved the comfort of being surrounded by familiarities. He certainly could afford to live in a larger house but he had always seen his frugality as a virtue.

Living on a small hill on the outskirts of Vici, the view from his window offered great sights to the city. He had a clear view of the blacksmith, the general stables, and his workshop, but overshadowing everything else, was a magnificent castle larger than any building that most people had ever seen. With a perfect curtain wall and tall spires, the architecture was something to admire. Leon was never told how old the castle was, but with no sign of damage or wear, he wouldn't be surprised if his humble cottage was older than the Desiali castle.

Years ago, his grandfather had sat Leon down on his lap and looked out of his bedroom window with him. With an unobstructed view of the castle, he had explained that things look smaller, the farther away they are. He had also explained to Leon that the most important and magical people in all the land, lived in that grand castle. The boy's eyes grew bigger every time he heard about the people who had the luxury of living in a building so extravagant. Leon envied those magical people, as did the rest of the folk in the country, he supposed.

His grandfather's stories had also convinced Leon that they were the greatest rulers that the country had ever seen, yet suspiciously, he had actually never seen them with his own eyes. Leon was always taught that the Minet family and all their neighbors were better off than any of the surrounding countries because of The Vasili. Leon would bombard his grandfather with questions about The Vasili and their history but was always disappointed in the brief and limited answers that he received all too often. The enthusiastic young boy wanted to know all the details about them, but his grandfather always seemed to be hesitant.

"In time, you'll find out," or something vaguely similar was always his answer.

Leon was surely not the only one who wanted to know more. The Vasili were so secretive that he suspected even his grandfather knew little about them. Nobody even said their names, they were simply called "The Vasili". After a while, it seemed as if all the children of Vici would give up asking about the royal family and would accept things the way they were.

Leon looked out of his window. The castle looked exactly the same as it did when his grandfather had sat the boy on his lap. Sometimes during holidays, the castle would be decorated with colorful streamers or flags and even the gray hues of the stones seemed to outperform those of the simple cottages in the city. On the other side of his bedroom door, Leon heard a deep bellowing laugh. It was so distinguishable that most peo-ple in this part of the city knew to whom it belonged. Leon quickly put on his clothes and headed downstairs toward his grandfather's loud voice.

"They say this year it'll be a bit hot for the Grand Festival," said a small cheerful voice.

Mrs. Potter sat at the small, delicately handcrafted table across from an old muscular man.

"I suppose people will just have to wear less of those fancy underclothes that they have no use for."

Grandfather had caught Leon in the corner of his eye and winked at Leon as if he were thinking the same thing.

Mrs. Potter blushed. She knew Grandfather would spew things like that out of his mouth. Perhaps that's why she enjoyed coming to their house a couple of mornings a week. To Leon, he was just old and didn't care anymore, but anyone who had known Keone in his younger years would say he had always acted like a devious adolescent.

"Good morning, Leon. I just came by to give you and Keone some of my dried apples before opening the shop," Mrs. Potter said as she stood up.

Her graying hair was always neatly styled and her dresses were always clean and freshly pressed. Her proper mannerisms were quite the opposite of the inappropriateness and brutish quirks of his grandfather.

"See you tomorrow," said Leon's grandfather knowing that she most likely would come over again yet another day in a row.

Mrs. Potter hinted a smile as she excused herself and scurried out of the door with a slightly embarrassed look on her face. Mrs. Anjelika Potter had become widowed a few years ago, and it was no secret she was eyeing grandfather. He was a brilliant and quick-witted man and could be easily overshadowed by his looks. His muscular body was still robust as if he had never passed forty, and his bright eyes were as crisp as the sky on a bright and clear day. His thick white hair matched his short trimmed beard. Keone seemed to attract more women than Leon, which was usually quite awkward for him. Perhaps it was the personality that attracted women the most. Keone Minet had the charm that could sweep any girl off their feet. Leon Minet, however, did not possess such ability.

"You're up a bit late," Grandfather exclaimed.

He was leaning back against his chair, as usual. It was a wonder that the chair hadn't snapped yet. His beard was trimmed but his fingernails were dirty, as if he had cleaned himself up, yet forgot what he had been doing halfway through the process.

"Had that weird dream again," Leon said, holding back a yawn.

He grabbed a small loaf of bread off the table, figuring he could snack on it at work before midday.

"The same dream?" said Keone worryingly.

"Yup," answered Leon unenthusiastically.

Grandfather had always been wary of dreams, especially ones that recurred many times. He hadn't always believed in magical powers and spirits but had grown more superstitious after the death of Leon's parents. Dreams, in particular, seemed more important to him than many other superstitions.

Leon grabbed a small bag of Mrs. Potter's dried apples and dashed out the door and onto the cobblestone street, saving him from listening to another one of his grandfather's lectures about dreams. There were people rushing about in every direction in preparation for the Grand Festival. The dust in the air was thick from being picked up by the villagers' feet. Loud housewives were out and about, getting colorful fabric to mend clothing at the last minute for the entire family. Extremely large barrels of rum and beer for the celebrations were being hauled around, enough to make the street lethal if there were to be an accident.

Vici, the largest city in Desial, was a city like none other. Specialty artisans like the Minets were found all over the country, but predominantly in Vici. Desial was the third-largest country on the continent after Reino and Athena. Although a great number of people hadn't stepped foot outside of their own countries, everyone boasted that Desial was the most successful. With abundant natural resources and fertile land, Desial was able to provide for itself and could probably fully support at least two other countries.

This year was the two-hundred-fifth Grand Festival. This year was especially important because The Vasili only came out into public every twenty-five years, but for some reason that had never truly been explained to Leon as to why. When Leon asked his father why the Vasili came out only during specific years, his father would always tell him that The Vasili know if they make a large presence, people will feel oppressed. There was a hint of happiness, but at the same time, sadness in his father's voice whenever he talked about The Vasili; Leon couldn't quite put his finger on it. Even though Keone would sometimes speak highly about the royal family, Leon didn't know if his grandfather's expressions were angry, disgusted, or frightened, but for whatever reason, he had a feeling that his grandfather would rather be inside drinking ale than to be outside tonight to witness The Vasili in public.

Leon quickly ran through the crowds of busy people who all seemed to be in as big of a hurry as him. All his life, he had hated loud and busy. He would rather just stay inside all night during a regular festival, but this Grand Festival was a special event that he was sure not to miss. Some older folks had witnessed the Grand Festival with The Vasili four or five times, but this was Leon's first time. As Leon dodged a stretched-out arm about to collide with his face, he heard a familiar voice calling his name from the crowd.

"Leon! Leon!"

He looked around, almost frantically, trying to spot him.

Jolon was the strongest, fastest, and most handsome person Leon knew, unfortunately not the smartest. Leon had helped Jolon all throughout school and in turn, Jolon's parents would give him exotic gifts and a few silver coins for the holidays. His family was undoubtedly the finest tailors on the continent. They specialized in clothes of fine silk, fur, and fabrics that he had never even heard of. Jolon's mother was occasionally hired by The Vasili and other royal families throughout the continent. Leon was sure that his parents and sisters had been tailoring for the royal family for tomorrow's very special day. Jolon had two sisters, one older and one younger. The older sister, Jarine, had married a talented silversmith who made great antiquities. He had so much wealth that he could stop working and live comfortably for the rest of his life. Jolon's younger sister, Jaora, was small and delicate. Her white skin and light blonde hair would always greet Leon when he would come to their house. Only younger by two years, Jaora and Leon had an attraction toward each other since childhood. Ever since Leon had finished school, he had no excuses for stopping by their house and had not seen her in months.

"Leon!"

He caught a glimpse of Jolon's light blonde hair. Standing half a head taller than most men, he was easy to spot. As Jolon got closer, Leon could see a slender figure next to his side,

Jaora. Her hair was even longer than the last time he saw it His memories suddenly came back to last year's festival. He had been at home, tired from the celebration when suddenly Jaora had walked in and dropped all of her clothes on the floor. Her white skin and long blonde hair had shone in the moonlight. Even though there was alcohol on her breath, Leon hadn't skipped a heartbeat to contemplate any consequences of the opportunity that was set before him.

"Are you ready?"

Leon snapped back to reality.

Jolon was already slightly drunk and in his hands were layers of fine clothing. Jaora met Leon's eyes and blushed.

"Hi," she said quietly and gave a forced smile as Leon blushed.

Jolon would kill me if he knew.

Unaware of the obvious tension, Jolon remarked, "My sister has picked up our parents' craft so well that she was chosen to make outfits for The Vasili"

To take the attention off of her, she added, "Jarine was also hired to make outfits for the handmen."

The word 'handmen' always amused Leon. A smile came across all three of their faces, trying to contain their laughter.

"Congratulations," praised Leon.

Jaora relaxed, "Thank you."

"I've been thinking about applying to be a handman. I'm trying to ask around for more information, but all previous handmen are sworn to secrecy about their duties."

Jolon was serious. The look on his face made him seem slightly more intelligent.

"You should try to apply too."

Leon had thought about working in the castle several years ago, but he was the only heir to the timepiece business and was obligated to carry on the family tradition. Nobody knew exactly what handmen did inside the castle. All anyone ever knew was they would come back with finer clothing and great wealth in five years. The few who served more than five years were given even more luxuries and came back more polished, happier, and looked as if they have never aged in those many years. They were sworn to secrecy, but they always encouraged the men of the city to apply so it must have been grand to work in the castle.

"They only take the best men and I don't want to miss my chance," said Jolon. "I'm definitely at my peak."

He flexed his muscles and laughed. Jolon's build was a perfect image of what Leon would expect a typical woman would crave. Jolon was right; The Vasili only accepted a handful of men and they were usually no older than thirty years old and in great physical condition.

"I have to go get these up to the castle," said Jaora as she eyed the enormous amount of castle steps.

"It has so many steps but once you go in, it's the most beautiful place anyone will ever see, and all of a sudden the steps are worth it," she said dreamily. "I just wish there was an easier way to get there."

"I'll be seeing you soon, Leon," said Jolon. "You really should apply to be a handman too. Great pay too."

As if Jolon needed money. Jaora smiled and rushed away with Jolon. Leon realized the streets were getting even more crowded and started zipping through the Vicians, trying not to trip over the children running about. Finally, he saw it within the haze; the bright red door. His dad would tell him stories about the first clockmaker, his great-great-grandfather starting his shop with the iconic red door.

"Legend has it that Konto not only invented timepieces but also timekeepers," his dad said. "Timepieces tell you what time of day it is, but timekeepers are a truly magical invention. They keep the time for you so you never age. Konto thought it would be a terrible thing if the timekeepers went into the wrong hands, so he destroyed all the work that he had done with his research."

Leon's large brown eyes would light up every time his dad would talk about the timekeepers. Leon had loved the stories of magic and magical creatures living beyond the walls of the city, but like most people in the city, he had never encountered anything that possessed actual magic that he knew of. Stories of unicorns and hinos would be told, but nobody knew if they were even real. Like everyone else, the older he became, the less he believed in any extraordinary magic.

Leon unlocked the red door and slipped inside quickly, trying to keep the whirlwinds of dust out. The musty air and the ticking of timepieces were comfortable for Leon. He had worked in this shop since before his father had passed. Every member of Leon's family had worked in the timepiece business, ever since Konto Minet had invented the timepiece. Konto had taught only his son to make timepieces, and his son after that, and so on. Such was the way of the Desiali Kingdom. The people of Desial, especially the people of the city of Vici, revered family tradition. The children were expected to apprentice, soaking up all their family's knowledge and secrets. Not only would they keep family traditions, but they would also add to what they had learned, making their craft exponentially better. The country of Desial was said to have the most skill in all the continent because of this system. Royalty from other countries frequently requested Vicians for specialized goods. Because of this, the Minets were well known throughout the other kingdoms and would frequently get orders from foreigners.

"Timepieces are what makes us the most mortal, and we keep that secret in our family."

There had been many folks who had come to the shop begging to be an apprentice to learn the art, but they had all been turned away. This was a Minet craft and forever would stay that way. With that in mind, he had to think about how and when he would have children of his own. Leon had no choice but to produce an heir to teach the craft to. The idea would pop up in his mind frequently because timing was something he knew more than anything else. Of course, his grandfather's insistence was also hard to ignore.

Leon glanced at the largest and loudest timepiece standing in the center of the room. Nine o'clock, just in time. Timeliness has always been a strict rule in the Minet household. Leon sat at his work desk with hundreds of scattered metallic parts spread neatly apart. To the untrained eye, one would assume Leon was working on a complicated and ultimately magnificent timepiece, but to people who have been trained to work on timepieces, they would be able to see that this was no ordinary timepiece. When Leon's father had died a few years ago, Leon had made up his mind to continue the legacy of Konto Minet and build himself a timekeeper.

A few years ago, Leon was digging through some books and papers wanting to draw a design that had been floating through his head for days. The design was inspired by a small garden that he had seen and had become an inconvenience while trying to finish another timepiece of a quite contrasting aesthetic. As he was rummaging through his notebooks, a picture of an ancient-looking timepiece was neatly placed in between a stack of books and loose papers. He thought back to all those years ago when he had first put it inside the book. There were three hands and instead of numbers, there were four stones. Symbols were etched around the different stones. Faint lines crisscrossed between different symbols and the stones almost as if it was a puzzle that needed to be solved. He vividly remembered the day he had first found this particular drawing.

His father was putting on the finishing touches of a timepiece that he had been working on for several weeks. The parts on the inside had all been fitted, but it was the exterior that was taking up all the time. The timepiece was to go to a prince in Konis. It wasn't odd for someone of another country to place an order, but the royalty of Konis hardly associated themselves with anyone outside of their own country. Konis was a barren land with mostly desert and mountains. Those who did not know the land would surely perish if attempting to make a trip to the capital. This was beneficial for the Konisi because no other Kingdom dared send their soldiers to war against them. They most certainly had thought about it, too. Numba, a large city in Konis, may seem barren from the outside but deep in underground caverns and mines lay heaping piles of gold and gemstones.

Experienced traders were the only ones brave enough to make the fruitful journey. When they would return home, people would listen to the stories of the great Konis Kingdom. The traders described the city as glittering with gold and precious gems. Large stone walls surrounded the capital built on he banks of a large and almost bottomless river. The women here were tall, tan, slender, and had the most beautiful eyes. The men were also tan but muscular and had pearly teeth. The Konisi were excessively rich and did not have a care in the world. The variety of food was scarce as crops struggled to grow in the sandy and infertile soil. A plain apple in Desial was an exotic fruit in Konisi and could be sold at high prices.

Leon's father had received a shimmering letter from a foreign zanianbird that spring. That particular zanianbird was unlike any that Leon had ever seen. Most zanianbirds were black, white, or gray. Plain-looking birds but sharp and would always know where to deliver. They were, to an extent, magical creatures,. To Leon, they were so ugly, he never grew a fascination toward them. The zanianbird that was sent to his father was worthy of being called magical. Its feathers were dyed with different shades of blue with small intricate silver designs that glimmered so radiantly, Leon was sure that he would be able to spot it in the dark by moonlight. The head was encrusted with jewels, which seemed uncomfortable and heavy, but the bird flew elegantly and delivered with ease. When Leon saw it descend on the timemaker's front perch, he knew it must have come from an exotic land with massive amounts of wealth. The zanianbird rang the messenger bell several times as if it were in a hurry. Opening the door to see what kind of delivery they had received was like a theatre act, as several villagers in Vici stopped to stare at the magnificent creature perched in front of the shop. As Leon's father opened the letter tied to the zanianbird's foot, what seemed like an ordinary letter unfolded into several pages filled with writings and elaborate sketches.

"Konis!" yelled his father. "The Prince of Konis wants me to make a timepiece!"

Leon had never seen his father so uncontrollably excited. Father had diligently worked on the Prince's timepiece for at least five weeks. The design that had been beautifully sketched on the letter was intense and remarkably intricate, but his father had made every detail perfect because it was not just an ordinary timepiece. It was a royal timepiece; a very expensive one at that. His father's reputation in Konis was on the line. Even Leon knew that if his father was able to create this masterpiece for the prince, then he may get more orders from Konis. As the last jewel was placed delicately on the carved surface, Leon slipped a piece of paper that he had found in a book onto the workbench in front of his father.

"Is this your drawing father?" asked Leon.

His father glanced at it and smiled.

"This is my masterpiece, Leon," said his father, holding the newly constructed timepiece.

He motioned to the paper, "This was someone else's masterpiece, and you will also have one, just as all of our ancestors did"

Leon looked down at the paper. The object resembled a familiar timepiece but boasted three hands and no numbers. There was just a face inside with symbols and stones.

"This is the timekeeper," Leon said quietly.

"Ah, that's what the legend is, anyway."

His father did not seem bothered at all by the drawing. It could possibly be the most powerful thing that man had ever invented, and yet he acted like it was just a child's drawing and not one of significance. The young boy quickly pocketed the drawing with nervousness as if he were stealing an artifact and later hid it inside of a book.

The noise outside was not ideal for when Leon was trying to concentrate on his work. A good timemaker could make a very nice and expensive timepiece in a few days, but with all the noise, it would take Leon at least a week to finish a regular timepiece. Thankfully, things would quiet down after that night. This time of the year was the busiest for him too. He would get orders from all seven Kingdoms every season, but during the holidays in Vici, everyone wanted to show off something of value. Since timepieces were both expensive and practical, Leon was one of the most popular craftsmen in the city.

Without warning, the oversized red door to the shop swung open as two burly men walked briskly into the shop. Leon was shocked by the size and demeanor of the two men. Both men seemed to be slightly older than him and had no expression on their faces. The shorter one who was still significantly larger than Leon held a small, plain, but familiar-looking box in his arms. They quickly glanced around the room as if they were looking for something in particular.

"Is anyone else here?" asked the taller man.

Leon hesitated to answer. Surely one of these men could break him in half if they truly wanted to. If he said he was alone, he was terrified of what they might do to him. On the other hand, if he lied, they might kill him too.

Who am I kidding?

"It's only me," Leon forced a smile, trying to brighten the situation.

They didn't answer and their faces were still expressionless. Like soldiers, they posted themselves on either side of the door. The larger man swung open the big red door with such brute force that he could have snapped the door off of the hinges. This time there was one figure. A small figure with long brown hair gracefully poured out of a black hood that covered her face.

"Pardon the intrusion," she said as she swept back her hood. Brown eyes stared at his face.

"Are you Leon the Timemaker?" she asked.

This time Leon wasn't hesitant to answer.

"That would be me," he answered cheerfully, trying to be as friendly as possible.

He glanced at the men.

They look just like statues.

"I have a piece that I need to have looked at. I don't believe it's broken. Just a small part may be needing replacement."

Her expression was similarly lacking in emotion. She motioned to the guard with the box. As he moved forward, he could tell that the box seemed smaller than he had thought, probably because of the man's large and almost daunting hand size. He carefully set the wooden box on the table in front of Leon, spun around, and returned to his post.

"It might just be cosmetic damage. I'm pretty sure Keone will know what to do," she said.

Despite her words, she seemed nervous to leave her time-piece there.

"Keone?" Leon said surprisingly. "You know my grandfa-ther?"

"He is a unique character," she glanced at his workbench full of parts. "I have heard rumors that you are a better timemaker though."

"I can ask my grandfather tomorrow about the piece if you would like."

"Actually, no," she said abruptly. "Please look for yourself first. Maybe you can surprise me."

She forced a small smile. "And please do not show it to anyone else."

Leon smiled back awkwardly, not knowing if her facial expression was genuine or not. He caught her gaze for a few moments before the red doors opened again, breaking the awkwardness. This time there stood two familiar figures. Jolon and Jaora looked shocked as they stopped right in between the two men guarding the door causing Jolon to almost drop the linens he was still carrying. The men just slightly moved their heads, already determining that the two other intruders were not threats. They had hardly even blinked since they had burst into his shop. The woman slowly put up her hood, flashing sorrow-filled eyes at him.

"I will send someone to pick it up the day after tomorrow," she said quietly.

She turned around and headed towards the door. She stopped right in front of Jolon and Jaora.

"I appreciate your hard work," she said to Jaora.

"Thank you," she whispered as she lowered her head.

Quickly, Jolon pulled Jaora out of the doorway. The woman smiled at them and pushed open the heavy door as the two guards followed her.

"What was that?" Jolon asked frantically. "What did she want?"

Leon shrugged, "She wants me to fix her timepiece."

"Let's take a look," said Jolon motioning to the box.

"I actually need special tools from home to open that type of box," Leon blurted.

The lock on the box was indeed familiar. The Fraers made special locks and keys for the Minets. This insured that nobody could open the boxes during delivery and steal timepieces. They also crafted a master key that could open all the different locks for timepiece boxes. He was just as curious as Jolon, but something inside told him to listen to the owner's request.

There was a long pause as Jolon stared at the box in wonder.

"You do know who that was, don't you?" asked Jaora quietly.

I feel like I do.

"No," replied Leon, slightly embarrassed.

"That's Videre, Queen of Desial."

WILD MAGIC

Leon was in shock.

"But she looks so young," he stammered, after a few moments of thinking about what he had just witnessed.

Of course she must have been someone important. Who else would have guards and hide her face in public?

"And get this," Jolon added, "There's no king."

It made sense that Leon wouldn't have known. Nobody talked about The Vasili. With a family that has been so secretive for centuries, villagers were left fascinated and even scared. Primary school students were taught the basics of life; there were no lavish stories about the rulers of the kingdom. Leon recalled asking his third-year teacher the name of the king who had saved the Kiadere during the genocide. The teacher just smiled and said in her usual and absurdly annoying singsong voice that it was not the name of the king that should be celebrated, it was the act of kindness that should be revered. The simple answers that he received all too often had always bothered Leon to a degree of hatred for the educational system.

Jolon smiled deviously and added, "There are also three of them if you can believe that," sticking up his perfectly manicured fingers in Leon's face. Jaora sighed in disappointment as she swatted away Jolon's hand. She had obviously told Jolon to keep quiet about what she had seen in the castle while creating their garments. Now it sounded even more absurd. A country that had three queens and no king. The more Leon thought about it, the more he wanted to know why they were so secretive.

Were other countries like this too, or just Desial?

"They all look the same," Jaora said in her usual quiet voice. "Well, not exactly the same, but the same age and same features. They don't act the same though."

Jaora was not much for rumors or even talking in general, but Leon could tell she was itching to gossip a little.

"There's the one who is really friendly named Valencia and another one that says weird and inappropriate jokes. Her name is Valeria. And you just met Videre."

Videre.

"Videre," yelled his language teacher as he wrote the word on the board. The board was filled with random words from the Olde Language with primary students trying to make sense of why they had to learn something that was hardly used anymore.

"What does Videre mean, Alsy?"

A dark-haired child stood up and responded confidently, "Wild magic."

"She seems really tense and maybe a little emotionless," said Leon, still in shock that he had actually met and talked to a queen.

"She really seems like it," said Jaora, "She almost never talks to me. She seems to have a lot on her mind."

"After seeing her, I'm definitely going to try to get a hand-man position this year," Jolon exclaimed, looking like he was cooking up a devious plan.

In the shop, a timepiece struck 9:30. A few seconds later, other timepieces started to chime, seemingly harmonizing with each other.

"We really need to go," Jaora said suddenly. "We desparately had to stop for food before going up to the castle," she sighed while looking at Jolon, clearly annoyed. "The Vasili need to have all of their final fittings this morning."

"We forgot to give you this earlier," Jaora said while giving Leon a purple and silver handkerchief.

She gracefully smiled at Leon before walking out into the street with Jolon at her heels.

What a day it had been for the timemaker. Leon glanced at the box he had received from Videre. It bore the resemblance of all the boxes that stored precious timepieces, but quite a bit older. It may have just extremely worn like it had been handled numerous times. The inscriptions and designs that once covered the box were hardly visible anymore. He debated on whether to open it in the shop or at home. He looked around nervously as if he didn't remember whether or not there was another person in the room with him.

I don't need anyone to come in and see it.

Leon quickly walked to the door and locked it. Peeking out the window, he could see that people were too busy to bother looking inside a timemaker's shop. If anyone really needed him, they could knock. His heart beat faster as he reached into his desk and grabbed his old brass master key. He unlocked the box slowly as if the lock was made of glass and could shatter if touched it the wrong way. As he lifted the lid, he imagined a flood of light or magical spirits to slither out, but to his disappointment, it was just like opening an ordinary box.

What?

Leon pulled his hand from the box. Inside was the one thing he was obsessed with as a child and even as a grown man. Inside was not a timepiece, but a timekeeper.

A Timekeeper?

Fear. Excitement. Happiness. Confusion. He had no idea what he was feeling. This was it. He knew this was it. He had examined the drawing of this exact thing for hours since he was a little boy. He was looking at one of the most powerful items ever made, a timepiece with magic. He expected that his first encounter with magic would involve spiritual beings or unexplained lights and definitely not something that would just be handed to him. He quickly stood from his desk and went to the bookshelf. With trembling hands, he pulled out an old worn book titled, *The Creatures of Siryl.* He pulled out a piece of loose paper and walked back to his desk. Placing the book carefully down on the desk, he sat down and stared at the paper. The timekeeper and the drawing were exactly the same except for one crack in a gemstone. The label on the paper marked the gemstone as 'DBS'.

A dark bloodstone?

He recognized the reddish color of the gemstone that regularly hung around Jaora's neck.

Does she just want me to replace the stone?

He was a timemaker, not a jeweler. He was certain that gemstones could not be fixed, so he guessed that he had no choice but to replace it. He closed the box and locked it just as carefully as he had unlocked it. He hid the box under his desk and carefully placed the timekeeper schematics back into the thick book. He quickly unlocked the shop door and slipped out into the street, making sure he locked it again behind him filling him with a particular anxiety of leaving the box alone in his shop.

Dust was still swirling in the air as the town bustled. Nobody knew that he had just met a Vasili. Nobody knew that he had one of the most powerful possessions in the world under his desk. Nervously, he hustled down the street and arrived shortly at Mrs. Potter's lavish shop. She made jewelry for several decades from what he guessed. She wasn't the best in the city but she was the only one he knew who dealt with rare gemstones. Leon walked in as Mrs. Potter was rearranging a shelf of display necklaces in a lively manner.

"Good morning again," exclaimed Mrs. Potter in her usual prompt and friendly demeanor. "What can I do for you?"

"I need a dark bloodstone," Leon said quickly.

Her face lit up. Mrs. Potter always had an air about her that he couldn't describe. She always seemed like she knew exactly what type of person everyone was in the city and knew everyone's business. Even though from time to time, she would slip out some gossip, she was good about keeping everyone's deepest secrets to herself.

"I have a couple. Are you looking to give one to a girl?" she asked eagerly.

"Actually, I just need the stone, not set in a necklace or anything. It's for a timepiece."

He felt like Mrs. Potter would ask questions, but she just nodded and smiled.

"Over here" she motioned toward the corner of the room. She hummed quietly as she almost danced to another table. There were loose gemstones placed neatly on black silk, enhancing the brilliance of the gems and freshly polished silver. He scanned all the red pieces, but they were cut in extravagant shapes and not the plain cut as that in the timepiece.

"Do you have one that's cut like this?" asked Leon as he picked up a green gem, the same size and cut as what he was looking for.

Mrs. Potter examined the gem closely. She paused for a moment as if she remembered something important and smiled up at Leon.

"I actually have one like this but it's set in a ring."

She quickly shuffled to the other corner of the shop and scanned the table of rings until she picked out a large silver ring with a dark red gem.

"I just got this a couple of days ago from a man in Konis," she said as she handed the ring to Leon.

The cut and color were an exact match to what he needed. He would just need to pry out the stone from the ring.

"How much?" he asked.

"Don't worry about it," said Mrs. Potter quickly as she gripped his hands. "The girl you give it to will love it."

Leon left it at that. It made his duty of keeping the queen's secret much easier. She brought Leon a small box for the ring and handed it to him enthusiastically.

If only she knew what this gemstone could possibly do.

For a moment, Leon felt like he wanted to share what had just happened. Surely Mrs. Potter would have seen The Vasili at least a few times in her lifetime. After his parents died, he had grown an attachment to her as if she was one of the people he could trust most in this world. He pushed the thought out of mind at the request of the queen. Leon thanked her and turned towards the door. As he reached for the door, he saw a small statue of a cat with two tails and an upside-down crescent on its forehead. He had seen that statue a couple of times before, once in Jolon's home and a one buried deep in his memory that he could not place his finger on. The cat had yellow jewels for its eyes and was deeply mesmerizing almost to the point of hypnosis. Leon snapped out of it and hurried out the door.

The streets were busier than before. The dust was getting into Leon's eyes and lungs as he searched for smaller and less congested roads to get back to his shop. After zipping through the crowd, he turned on the corner behind Sommer's Bakery and headed towards his shop. It was definitely not a shortcut but it was significantly more calm than whatever was going out there on the main roads. Small children ran past him waving the flag of Desial around as if they were cheering on a team. How lucky of them to be able to celebrate this festival so early in life. This would also be Leon's first time attending and inspecting the Vasili. Although he knew that it shouldn't be such a big fuss to see the actual rulers of the country, deep down, he was exploding with excitement and anxiety. He had met one of the queens but for some reason, he had doubts on whether she was the real deal or not. She seemed perfectly plain, enough to be mistaken for a common villager. The only other timemaker he knew about, was at least a week's trek from Vici; an old man named Polne who was a distant relative. Although Leon had met Polne when he was young, he couldn't recall what he looked like. Keone would always talk about him as if he were his best friend, yet, it always perplexed Leon as to why Keone would almost never visit him. Although a timemaker, he had retired and would only agree to be commissioned for repair work

A gust of wind sprayed small rocks into Leon's eyes. A gigantic zanianbird with a decent sized letter flew by him, clearly headed for the castle. The zanianbird had sparkling gold painted designs and jewels adorning its face. It was dressed as elegantly as a prince and with gleaming eyes like a fierce warrior. The powerful wings were strong enough to knock down a small child. Just ahead was his shop and a familiar silhouette of a man was walking towards the door. Leon quickly sprinted to the shop. Keone didn't need to know about what had happened earlier.

The day was going by quickly as Leon tried luring Keone away from the shop as he was excited and antsy about pulling out the timekeeper to insert the new jewel. Keone rambled on about the alcohol, people getting in the way, and all the chatter that he claimed made his head spin. Leon could tell he was bored and needed something to occupy him. Keone, in his younger years, was always busy with projects. After a while of rambling and ranting, his grandfather decided it was time to wander down to a card game where other old men were enjoying themselves away from the ruckus.

The day started fading away by the time Keone had left and Leon would not have time to fix the timekeeper that had been patiently waiting for its new piece. The sky was covered in purple and pink hues and instead of winding down, today was the opposite. The streets were still filled with people and getting exponentially busier now that people had started locking up their businesses and headed to the main roads. The commotion was deafening in some of the more overloaded parts of the city. Children were shrieking while playing nostalgic street games. Teenage boys and girls were holding hands while they chattered away. As villagers started leaving their homes for the festivities, street vendors started setting up on the sides of the roads. Small fireworks were being lit in every direction. The aroma of roasted meats and candies filled the air. There was an aura of happiness and joy and everyone seemed to forget any sorrow or worries. A stench of alcohol was already present in the air as red-faced men would sing national songs. Today was a day for pride, remembrance, fun, and this year, most of all, to see who actually ruled over them.

Finding a spot to see the royal parade proved to be difficult. The streets were lined with flags and ribbons to mark where people were to stand to watch. Even though it was still half an hour before anything would start, Vicians and visitors alike were already starting to form dense crowds behind the lines of ribbon. The children would squeeze in between the adults to get to the front for a better view. Leon spotted Jolon's unmistakable blond hair, and started maneuvering towards him. Jaora was nowhere to be found but their parents were standing next to him.

As he got closer, he could see the bright colors and intricate designs of their clothes. His family had always worn extravagant clothing, displaying their craftsmanship skills. They were always the first to wear something new. A year would pass and half the village would be wearing the same thing. Jolon spotted Leon and waved like an excited young boy. As he got closer to Jolon, the crowd seemed to be thinning out. People were always afraid to stand right next to the fashion icons of the continent. Jolon's mother, Jeela, gave him a familiar constricting hug.

"It's been too long, Leon," she sighed.

Jeela always looked her best but he could see some dark circles under her eyes. Leon had no doubt she had been working hard for this occasion.

"Hasn't he gotten so mature, Jes?" asked Jeela.

Jes smiled slightly. He had always encouraged Leon to be a better version of himself as he had done with his own children. Jes always pushed his children to become successful and took Leon under his wing when Leon's parents had died. Leon was always close to Jolon's family but after the unfortunate accident, he had been groomed to become like one of them. Leon always had a spot at their table if he ever wished to drop by. Even the association was great for his timekeeper business, as they would always introduce potential clients to him. Leon stood next to them, enjoying the personal space. In the distance, he could faintly hear drums and flutes. The parade had started.

"We probably have ten minutes until they'll this part," said Jes looking at the small timepiece he had pulled from his lavish pocket.

Leon had given Jeela and Jes matching timekeepers for their anniversary. He was still a novice at the time but had crafted them all by himself. To have such iconic people wear his timepiece because they wanted to and not because they were obligated, made him feel honored. Even to this day he had never spent such a large amount of time on a set of timepieces.

"Jaora is in the parade," exclaimed Jolon.

You could tell he was proud of his sister for being chosen to make the outfits for The Vasili. As the beating of the drums got closer and closer, the inaudible chattering increased. Leon had always preferred peace and quiet. Loud noises made him uncomfortable and uneasy. Unfortunately for him, his best friend and only relative liked to talk in abundance. Leon could sit in his shop for hours in silence while working on his delicate craft.

The drums were just around the corner and Leon could make out the melody from the flutes. A few moments later, he heard people down the cobblestone road gasping and clapping. In the distance, he saw three horses in shining armor.

No. Two horses and something else in the middle.

The face was broad and it seemed to shimmer in the lamplight. Jolon's jaw dropped. In the middle of its head was a long spiral horn. It seemed to give off its own light. Jes and Jeela smiled as if they were expecting the marvelous sight. Leon's heart started beating faster as he squinted through the haze of firework smoke.

A unicorn. A real unicorn.

Desial had gone to battle with horses wearing helmets with a unicorn horn for adornment but this was the real thing. Across the road, a young woman was crying from shock. All the stories of magic and unicorns that were told to children may have all been real after all. No longer was the unicorn a mythical tale in stories and paintings but an actual living, breathing creature standing before Leon. The horses on either side were the warhorses of Desial, gifts from Korona.

Leon had heard of this enchanted island with strange species and how everything grew much bigger there. Desial and Korona had once fought together in a war long lost to history. Koronians admired Desiali bravery and tactics while Desiali soldiers admired Koronian creatures. As a gesture of friendship, The Vasili were gifted four horses and all their current warhorses descended from those original four.

Leon could feel their hoof beats through the cobblestone. The horses marched in unison without being led by anyone. They knew exactly what to do without any instruction. The warhorses looked elegant, trotting straight ahead with their heads held high. The unicorn, however, was trotting out of step and swinging its head around looking at all the spectators as if it were enjoying all the attention. The light from its horn shimmered and mesmerized all the spectators. The horn's shimmer reminded Leon of the cat's eyes in Mrs. Potter's shop and also had a hypnotizing effect on Leon. After the horses, came the drummers and flute players seated on intricately painted wagons pulled by normal-sized but equally extravagant horses. Their hoof beats pounded in unison with the beat of the drums.

"Whoever trains these horses must be paid a ton," yelled Jolon.

He was almost inaudible with all the noise. The musicians were dressed in matching national colors of purple and silver. Sparkling silver lace adorned their flowing white garments while purple roses were placed in their hair with twine. The national symbol on all the flags featured a broad and majestic silver eagle with an abundance of light purple roses.

Dancers flooded the street behind the rows of musicians. They all moved effortlessly with large fans the size of their torsos. They had been dancing since the steps of the castle and none of them seemed as if they were anywhere near tired. The fans moved to the music as the dancers would glide across he street as if they were skating on ice. Their faces were full of emotion and they intertwined with each other in elaborate formations. All the little girls in the city would be practicing their fan dancing for days to come after watching the perfor-mance.

After the dancers, came a small group of people riding on horses. Jaora was riding close to the front of the group with a gleaming smile. Next to her was Jarine and her husband, Tirin.

These must be the group of people who work for The Vasili.

Jaora was riding on her horse with a sort of smile that Leon had never seen before. Her long blonde hair was also wrapped intricately with purple roses and silver twine. She was gen-erally quiet and always had been sheepish, but tonight she looked happy with all the attention. Jolon jumped up and down waving to both of his sisters as if he weren't already taller than everyone else around him. After a shy acknowledg-ment from the pair, he settled down. Jaora gave a small wave to Leon to which he promptly waved back enthusiastically.

Another set of musicians followed the dancers and the cas-tle workers. They were playing a different tune; one that Leon had heard before but had never known the name of. A group of young men on white horses trotted in front of a woman rid-ing a matching white horse.

Videre? No, not Videre.

"Valencia," Jolon yelled into Leon's ear.

The drumbeats could be felt deep within his chest as he stared in wonder. Valencia was riding on an all-white horse that seemed to have an unreal sheen. Her tiara was almost as bright as her smile. She was no doubt one of the most beau-tiful people Leon had ever seen. She waved to the crowds of people as they screamed in excitement. She looked as though she was overjoyed to be riding through the crowd as if she was born for this very moment. Her pale blue dress matched the elaborate blanket covering the horse. She was riding without a saddle with no lack of comfort. A black cat sat behind her, staring at the crowds of people, almost unbothered by the noise. Even the horse looked extraordinarily friendly as they trotted between the crowd. Two lines of at least thirty men followed behind her. Leon assumed that they were handmen. Valencia was only visible for what seemed like a few moments before she had disappeared around the corner. A new beat and tune could be heard approaching the group. When the drumbeats got closer, Leon felt it more aggressively in his chest than the last tune.

The Tides of War.

The Desiali war song was commonly sung by the men of Desial and more frequently, heard among the Vipole. The tune was strong and forthcoming but was almost drowned out by the vigorous beating of the drums. Warhorses carrying big burly men wearing only pants were riding in front of the largest warhorse Leon had ever seen.

"Valeria's handmen are the fiercest men in all the kingdoms," said Jolon. "That's what I'm hoping to be," he added loudly and eagerly.

Leon was sure that Jolon wouldn't stand a chance against those men if he ever got into a fight with them. Their vein-covered arms were as big as Leon's thighs and each of their saddles carried different weapons, some that may have weighed more than Leon himself. The head of the warhorse in the center of the Vipole group was so big, it almost entirely blocked the view of the rider. The armor was made of dark metals chiseled with intricate designs fit for royalty. Leon recognized some of the designs as Tirin's handiwork.

As the horse drew nearer, Leon could make out the side of the rider's face. She had a scar on her eyebrow that accentuated her uniquely fine face. The crowd stood in wonder at this radiant woman before them. She rode tall and fearless, just like the Vipole surrounding her. Even though it was cool outside, Valeria donned a small leather chest guard with no sleeves and her muscular stomach caught the attention of every man around. Her black leather pants and tall black boots straddled a large saddle with weapons of all sorts strapped onto it. Why one woman would need swords, knives, chains, and a crossbow was beyond Leon. The horse displayed a few red handprints as if it had been prepared to ride into battle that very instant. The look on her face was something to admire. Her expression was strong and confident, yet playful, and had a look of a prankster. Her dark eyes gazed upon all the men as if they were a slab of meat fresh from the butcher. She rode past the city-folk, towering over them with her large and intimidating warhorse. To Leon's surprise, Valeria spotted Jes and Jeela in the crowd and gave them a small nod in acknowledgment. Jeela gave a small curtsy as Jes nodded back with a smile.

The thundering drums started fading away as a new beat sounded. In fact, there was hardly a beat. Light drumming seemed as though it was far in the distance but in the streetlights, he saw two drummers. Compared to the first two spectacles, the band was meager in comparison. The two drummers were beating a steady and modest beat perhaps just so the marching would be in unison. Following the drummers, there were only a handful of flute players. They played a soft and dark-sounding tune. Another song that Leon had heard but could not place his finger on the name of it or where he had heard it before. The spectators were swaying to the music as if they were hypnotized.

A few men on horses emerged from the shadows. Finally, he saw her; Videre. In the center of the four men was the last queen on a beautiful spotted horse. Her familiar face was solemn as she rode through the streets. She did not have the presence of the other queens. Instead of looking like a ruler riding through a celebration meant for her, she looked like a bored child at an adult gathering. Her dress was quite plain and as she got closer, the horse looked different as if it may have been pregnant. Screeches rang out as her horse did the unimaginable. In front of Videre's legs, two large wings were thrown out creating an unexpected windy vacuum within the audience. Jolon stood in amazement unable to speak. A unicorn was one thing, but a horse with wings was another marvelous sight indeed. The horse however, did not fly. It seemed to only be stretching and quickly folded them back to its sides.

Videre didn't seem to be bothered that people were now screaming, cheering, or even crying from joy. She looked as plain as she did when Leon first saw her. Leon caught Videre's eyes. She nodded slightly to acknowledge him just as Valeria had done with Jolon's parents and kept riding to the music. In front of her were two men which Leon had recognized from the shop earlier. The two men behind her had baskets of sweets and coins, throwing handfuls into the crowd. Soon, the music was gone and by that time, people were starting to leave. Vendors would soon be closing and the city folk would have to wait for another 25 years to see another festival with The Vasili.

Jeela turned to Leon, "Spectacular wasn't it?"

Jolon still had a look of shock on his face. He slowly turned to Leon.

"Handmen auditions start next week."

Jes and Jeela laughed as if he were a child saying he wanted to be a dragon when he grew up. Jes patted him on the back and said nothing.

"Take care," said Jeela, "We haven't had you over in a while."

"I promise I will come soon," Leon said with sincerity.

Leon gave Jes a strong handshake and Jeela a hug as if she were his own mother. He turned and started walking home as the atmosphere quickly changed and he could feel sprinkles on his face. Leon welcomed the rain but wished it would have come earlier in the week so he wouldn't have dealt with so much dust that morning. The commotion had died down and slurred words of drunken festival-goers were more noticeable. The air was cool and the smell of alcohol, street food, and fireworks was pungent. He could not stop thinking about The Vasili. He had so many questions; questions that he never even thought to ask.

What was their purpose? Why are there three of them? Why see them every 25 years? How do they rule?

He knew of noble parties hosted by The Vasili, but he questioned if every country was like this. He could not help but wonder if all the other kings and queens of the continent were so secretive.

The street lights were still lit, illuminating the light sprinkling of rain. In the distance, large men with bags were picking up trash in the streets. They looked to be the same men that had been riding throughout the parade. He was itching to ask them questions. His attention went towards a sizable man down the street. He was undeniably one of the bodyguards that came to his shop earlier that day and who had marched alongside Videre in the parade. He had an inviting face as Leon walked towards him unlike what he had witnessed in his shop. The man paused and gave Leon a nod and a smile. As Leon got closer, he suddenly remembered he didn't know what he wanted to say. He didn't want to ask too many questions but he was too curious to not ask anything. The man put down his bag and stretched out his enormous hand. Leon grabbed his hand but wasn't expecting it to be nearly crushed by the man's sheer strength.

"Jooey," the man said.

"Le..." Leon stopped.

Jooey was smiling.

Of course, he already knew.

"I was wondering," Leon started.

Jooey bellowed out, "Sorry. Everyone always is wondering but you should know by now that we are sworn to secrecy." He looked around as if he were paranoid and whispered "They're always watching." Jooey let out a big laugh, confusing Leon.

Who was watching? Is this guy pulling my leg?

"If you really want to know" said Jooey, "you can always apply to become a handman." Jooey looked him up and down. "A bit scrawny though but sometimes Valencia likes to get some smart ones on her side."

"About that," said Leon. "I noticed there weren't a lot of people walking with Videre."

"She doesn't really need handmen like the other two. She isn't as needy as the other two."

Leon was surprised. "Handmaidens then?"

Jooey laughed even louder than last time. "Handmaidens! You know how much trouble we would all be in if there were handmaidens!"

He was so loud that the other men around them chuckled while picking up trash. "Why don't you apply, timemaker?"

One of the men cleared his throat to get Jooeys attention. Jooey nodded, smiled at Leon and walked down the street with his half full trash bag in hand.

That's at least a little information.

Leon turned down the street and started walking up to the hill where his house stood. He replayed the festival in his head. The magical creatures, Jaora, Vipole, and the queens of Desial were all floating around in his head as he made sure to remember every moment of this special day.

There were no lights to be seen in his house and his small street was quiet. Either Keone was sleeping or was still getting drunk. When Leon arrived at his house, he quietly crept upstairs to his room just in case Keone did happen to be home, quietly chuckling to himself thinking that he had never been the kind of adolescent to do such a thing. The full moon was shining through his window which would normally keep him up at night but with all the excitement for the day, he was glad to be off his feet. An owl hooted nearby as he closed his eyes and drifted into the sleep he so desperately needed.

TIMEKEEPER

Leon awoke with his ears ringing. For a moment, he was disoriented.

A side effect of getting older.

It must have been from the deafening drums last night. He tossed off his covers, feeling refreshed and a little guilty that most of his peers who had been drinking all night were probably still in bed and miserable. He smiled as he glided down the stairs. His grandfather, however, did not have the responsibility of running the shop like Leon. He was lying face down on the kitchen floor snoring lightly. Leon picked up a small quilt and threw it over Keone.

"Not surprising," he muttered to himself.

Leon walked out his modest cottage door ready for whatever the day was going to bring. Warm sunshine and old neighbors greeted him. The festival the day before had put him in such high spirits, it was almost confusing. Leon still felt the adrenaline pulsating throughout his body. His mind was racing and recollecting all the memories of last night's festivities.

The air did not smell like what it did last night but he was able to mentally reconstruct every scent from the fried meat to the abundance of alcoholic drinks. Mornings were generally busy but today looked to be slow. The streets were strangely quiet. No doubt, some people would not go to work today but Leon knew he had something exceptionally important waiting for him at his shop.

"Count on me," Leon laughed.

It was his signature joke. He was pleased that he came up with it all by himself when he was a mere ten years old although most people didn't find the same humor in the phrase. He turned left to make a stop at Sommer's Bakery. Normally, Keone would make breakfast but on days like this, he was glad that Sommer's was on his way to work. He opened the door and the aroma of sweet bread flooded his nostrils. The smell of chocolate, apple, cheese, and spices made his stomach growl.

"Mornin', lad," greeted Mr. Sommer. "Looks like ya didn't have a rough night unlike some of tha laddies your age."

"I like to keep a clear mind," said Leon proudly.

"I hear ye, lad. I can make pastries while drunk outta mi mind" Sommer said in a sing-song, voice obviously still intoxicated. "One apple and one raisin?"

"That, and a chocolate," said Leon.

Mr. Sommer swooped up the glazed baked goods and handed them to Leon.

"That parade was really something huh?" said Mr. Sommer. "All tha music and tha big horses. I swear they get bigger e'ry year"

"Well those war horses are always a sight to see but the other two horses were definitely extraordinary," Leon said, inciting a confused look on Mr. Sommer's face.

"Don't know what yer talkin' bout," he said as he started rearranging his pastries. "And don't worry about tha pastries, they're on me."

Leon walked out of the shop also confused.

Why would Mr. Sommer only mention the music and warhorses when there were so many more interesting things? When do people ever see a unicorn or winged horse, or even The Vasili?

Walking down the main street, he couldn't believe what all he had seen the night before. The music was still playing in his head as he timed his steps to the melodic memory. Surprisingly, the streets were clean and showed no trace of what had taken place last night. As he turned to his shop, a large man in expensive-looking clothes stood patiently in front of the red door. As Leon walked closer, he saw that the figure was Jooey. Jooey smiled and waved in a pleasant manner. He was getting friendlier with every meeting. Jooey stepped off to the side and looked around as if on watch while Leon unlocked the door. They both slipped into the dark and musty shop. Leon quickly put his pastries on his work table and opened some of the curtains. As the sunshine flooded in, timepieces and various timepiece parts gleamed, reflecting off the walls and ceiling.

"My Lady, Videre Vidal, the Queen and Protector of Desial and all of Aleria, would like to know when the... thing, will be finished," Jooey said in a friendly manner.

Did Jooey not know what the thing was or did he just say that out of secrecy?

"Soon. I just need to do a few more things. Three days at the most to get the required parts," said Leon knowing very well that it wouldn't take nearly that long.

Jooey nodded, not even asking questions of why the task would take so long.

"Do you really have to call her that?" asked Leon inquisitively.

Jooey laughed louder than Leon had expected.

"No, I don't, but I kind of like saying it." Looking proud, he continued, "If I make her sound extremely important, than as her loyal...person, it makes me seem more important too."

Her person? Maybe he just isn't good with words.

"I can deliver the piece when I'm finished."

"I will let her majesty know," Jooey beamed.

"Hey, about the parade last night," said Leon, "what was your favorite part?"

Jooey stood for a few seconds, staring at the wall then smiled. "The dancers," he said as he laughed.

"What about the unicorn?" Leon asked, anticipating the answer.

Jooey looked at him inquisitively.

"Yes, the unicorn was indeed beautiful and that horse with wings was wild, right?"

Leon let out a deep breath of relief, "Yes, it was extraordinary and very...wild."

Jooey looked as if he came to a realization. A few seconds passed as they looked at each other. Leon shifted uncomfortably.

"Well," Jooey boomed, "I must get going."

He turned and walked quickly out the door as if in a hurry.

I wasn't dreaming then. There really was a unicorn and winged horse.

Leon walked behind his desk and carefully pulled out the box he had hidden behind some of his projects. He used his master key to open the wondrous item set before him.

A relic, a myth, a legend.

So many descriptions raced through his mind. All Leon had to do was replace the jewel he had gotten from Ms. Potter. He felt a little ashamed that he had lied to Jooey. At most, it would take an hour to fix the timekeeper but he needed more time with it. He needed to study it and understand the mechanisms. If Videre had come herself under a disguise with bodyguards, it would have to be the real thing. The box was just as dusty and worn as it had been when it arrived the day before. Such important things were generally kept in better condition. Leon started straying from confidence to doubt about if this was a timekeeper or just a part of his childhood memories wishing for something extraordinary.

I might as well make it look nicer.

Digging out a rag and oil from his work table, he sat down on his stool and rubbed the top with his clear oil and a new rag. To his surprise, the box was not worn, it was just extremely dirty. As he rubbed off the muck, letters started appearing. Familiar letters from his Olde Language class started shining through. He tried hard to remember them, but the only one he knew for certain was the Olde Language version of his last name. Almost everyone in Desial had last names that could be traced back to the Olde Language.

As he cleaned off the box with more oil and another rag, images started shining through: a dragon, a horse with wings, a hawk, and a unicorn. The words and pictures seemed to be carved, then filled in with some sort of gold metal. The oil made the metal shine as if it was giving off its own light.

As Leon was fixated on the object, a small clink sounded in the entryway. The old bell on the shop door had fallen off. Keone was in the entryway staring at the bell that had just hit the floor.

"We've had to fix that for a while," Keone sighed as he picked up the bell.

As he bent over, Leon quietly put the box under the counter.

"What brings you in today, grandfather?" Leon asked, trying to act natural.

"My head hurts and the house lets in too much light."

There was no doubt he had been drinking last night. He stumbled around squinting at the worktable in front of Leon.

"That parade was really something right," Leon said.

"I only watched a little. Linwait had a card game in his shop during the parade."

"Did you at least see the horse with wings?"

"Yeah, I saw a glimpse of it towards the end but I wouldn't mention a lot about the parade to others," he said while fidgeting with the bell.

Leon was confused as to why Keone would even say that. The parade had been in everyone's head for weeks. It's not like people would forget about it so easily. Keone's fingers stumbled around on the worktable and he picked up a small gear.

"It's nice you got your parents' little dainty hands, these clocks are so hard to fix with my size of fingers."

Keone was always making fun of his grandson's small fingers but in a complementary way. It was true though. Keone's hands were large and rough and seemingly always dry. Watching Keone fix clocks made Leon cringe. His grandfather's build was more geared towards being a woodcutter or some sort of warrior.

"I'm gonna take this. I have someone who needs their time-piece fixed."

He wrapped the tiny gear in a blue worn handkerchief and delicately slid it into his pocket.

"I'll fix that bell tonight," he said groggily.

He gave a small nod and walked out the door. Leon let out a sigh of relief. He didn't know what would happen if Keone had stumbled upon his little project for a queen. Of course, there was a chance that he may not even know what it was. Right as Leon was about to pull out the box again, Jolon ran into the shop, this time without the ringing of the door bell. A big smile was plastered onto his face. He was gripping a paper in his hands. Without saying a word, he shoved it in Leon's face and shook it ferociously. The paper must have been extremely important. It was made of fine, almost cloth-like material and boasted golden edging. Leon grasped the paper that was still violently shaking in front of his face.

Congratulations. You have been accepted to take part in the selection process for handman for the Vasili of Desial. Please arrive on the tenth moon of the second season before mid-day. This year only 9 men will be selected.

Jolon had never been one to hide his feelings. He was shaking from excitement.

"What a short letter," Leon said almost disappointedly. "Well uh, good luck," Leon added, trying to be more enthusiastic, but also confused on how they had worded the date.

Jolon's smile disappeared.

"This is a big deal, Leon. Imagine living in the castle and being next to the most powerful women in the world."

The thought of it made Leon grin. He never was one for eccentricities but living in a castle might actually be nice.

"I have a shop to run, Jolon. I can't just leave."

Jolon looked around.

"Shop," he said, as he put out his right hand.

"Castle," he said, as he put up his left.

"Shop, Castle," he motioned again. "Timepieces, Queens; Bread, Steak; Boredom, Parties."

Leon smiled. Jolon was right. The city was nothing compared to the castle. The food was probably beyond anything he had ever tasted and running the shop was unfortunately boring at times. Sure, there may be a Sommer's bakery on the way to work but he would definitely not miss the dust, yelling, the musty shop, or the small house. He would much rather live in a castle, where he had so many times, imagined sitting down to eat a big breakfast at an enormous table. Ever since he was little, he imagined living in the castle just as all little children most likely did. He had remembered being in the castle once when he was young, alongside his father. All that came to mind were bright colors, lots of stairs, and nice ladies in beautiful outfits. He also remembered his mother being very upset with his father when they got back home. Something about the castle and the people inside always bothered his mother, but his father and grandfather had always taken trips to the castle to fix timepieces. Timepieces had taken a "revolutionary turn" as his father would say.

"The castle is probably different from what I remember or imagine it to be," said Leon. "I will be going up to the castle in a couple of days anyway to deliver something. I could keep you company on the walk there for your handman thing."

"Selection," said Jolon proudly. "I have no doubt I'll be selected."

His smile gleamed as he showed a full set of pearly white teeth. With a face and attitude like that, Leon believed him. They would be crazy not to choose him.

"Come over like an hour before so we have enough time to walk there."

"I'll be there," Leon said reassuringly.

Jolon wasn't worried. He knew Leon was always on time.

Jolon left the shop in the same chipper mood as he had walked in with. Leon pulled out the box from under his table. He started rubbing the box with more oil. He hated having such an extraordinary specimen in a box in such ragged condition. After a few seconds of polishing, more letters from the old language started shining through. He had seen these shining letters and words before amongst some of Jolon's family possessions. Leon had always been interested in the markings but nobody had been able to actually tell him who drew them or even what kind of metal they had used.

As Leon polished more of the box, certain words popped out at him. Light, trees, war, or so he thought. The Olde Language was a required class but not very useful. Not a lot of people in school had any intention of actually learning and retaining anything. It was considered dead as most of Aleria spoke the Viceroy language now. Leon knew he would regret not paying more attention in class. After several more minutes and another rag later, the box was gleaming to its previous splendor.

"Beautiful," praised Leon quietly to himself as he opened the box to reveal the timekeeper inside.

As he stared at the timekeeper, he realized that maybe such a piece should be handled more carefully. He took out some clean gloves from under his desk, slipped them on, and gently picked up the timekeeper. There was much power and extravagance in one simple artifact. He wasn't certain that it did what he thought, but he let his imagination roam which was slightly unfamiliar to him. From his toolbox, he took out the ring from Mrs. Potter's shop. Carefully, he removed the red jewel from the ring, which seemed a little wrong for him to do as he eyed the gleaming silver. Placing jewels in timepieces was a common occurrence that he had done a hundred times before, but this time he was uneasy and nervous. With great care, he pried the cracked gemstone out with a small delicate chisel and placed it inside of a small box. He carefully smeared bonding glue in the newly formed crevice and placed the new bloodstone inside. He smiled with relief to know that the bloodstone fit perfectly. He held his breath every time he touched the jewel and checked several times to see if there were any defects in his work before placing the timekeeper back inside the box.

He thought for several minutes on whether he should polish the timekeeper as well. It wasn't as unkempt as the box but then he started dwelling on if he should have polished the box in the first place. If Videre had wanted it to be cleaned, she probably would have seen to it herself. He had finished fixing the timekeeper but inside his heart, he had desperately wanted to find out more about it.

This is probably the last time I'll be able to see this.

He took the timekeeper out of the box again and started thoroughly examining it. The timekeeper was as big as both his hands put together. As a timemaker, he had made timepieces as small as a baby's hand and even designed one as large as a small house. Timepieces, although practical, were mainly used to show status. The timekeeper sat on the table in front of him as he stared at it. He was fairly certain his father had made this. Leon remembered every detail on the paper that he had found years ago, although it didn't match exactly, his father had a style to his work. The Minet family had customers from all over Aleria, even in Dunbar and Alflint. If there was anyone else able to make timepieces other than him, Keone, or Polne, he would definitely know about them. Many people from all over the continent had wandered into this very shop asking to become an apprentice but apprentic-ing outside of your family was not allowed.

The timekeeper had three hands; one large, one small, and one very thin long needle-like hand. They hadn't moved since Leon saw it first, instilling doubt in Leon even more and he began questioning himself as to whether he had actually re-paired what was broken. As he began looking at the other jewels, he noticed a brilliance within them that he had never seen before. In fact, the other three gems were completely un-known to him. The top one was a dark green, similar to the moss on the mountains of Dunbar Range. The gem on the bottom had a blue haziness to it. Most people liked the clar-ity to the gems but the haziness with a contrasting shine had caught his attention as it looked like streaking storm clouds contained in a beautiful rock. The last one on the left was clear. Like the bloodstone, the other three gems, he thought, might also be mined from Konis.

Konisi mountains were laced with a plethora of valuable gems so it would be no surprise if there were some types of gems that were unknown to him. All were chiseled into basic patterns which could be the work of any jeweler in Aleria for all he knew. The brilliant red color that he placed in the timekeeper matched the wood perfectly. Leon deduced that the wood came from a tree in the Desiali forest.

The Desiali forest was a great sight but could only be viewed from afar since it was banned to the public. Legends of the forest were numerous, from monsters in the treetops to strange diseases infecting all who entered. The Vasili had cut off the world from the forest hundreds of years ago, so over time, fact from fiction ceased to be. The wood was almost white and very dense with many small knots, making it almost impossible to carve or cut down. The timekeeper boasted these many knots but was surprisingly smooth as if someone had smoothed the wood and layered it with a coating.

The hands of the timekeeper didn't look fancy or peculiar like the other parts of the timekeeper. The hands were most likely made of metal mined from Desial or Reino, and were very similar to other products found in Aleria. The larger hand was shinier than the rest and Leon could make out faint engravings. It was a shame that these designs were hardly visible to the eye. Leon took out his microglass and started further inspecting the intricate designs. The small engravings consisted of flowers and curved vines with distinctive details. Leon may have been an excellent timemaker but he was no plantskeeper. He had no idea what kind of flowers he was looking at but they must have been from a faraway place. For Leon, it was quite possible he wouldn't know of such things because he had never traveled further than Reino. He had always been interested in going somewhere new but for some reason, traveling was an activity that was very much looked down upon in many parts of Aleria. A simple cultural idea had shut most of his friends and family off from the rest of the continent. Even studies in school would avoid details about other countries and even Desial's own history.

The Present is the Future.

As he examined the face of the timekeeper, Leon wondered if this was actually the creation of his father or even another ancestor. Questions started racing through his head.

Did his father make this for the Queens of Desial or for their parents? Are there more timekeepers in existence? Does Keone know that there is such a thing as a timekeeper? Does this time-keeper even work?

Maybe Leon had just fantasized about the thought of the timekeeper's magic. Maybe he had internally over-exaggerated and this is just an ornamental piece. Leon's excitement started dwindling.

Although it was nice to finally meet and even personally talk to one of The Vasili, he may have just been romanced by the idea of seeing a legendary item. Leon ran his fingers along the piece admiring the smoothness of the woodwork. He was just about to put it away when he ran his finger along what seemed to be a sliver of wood missing. Following the crack with his fingers, he started getting even more excited. The crack ran around the entirety of the timekeeper. He took his chisel and carefully wedged the tip along the crack. Slowly, he started prying little by little on all sides. Leon could feel the box separating. Gracefully and carefully, he pushed the two pieces apart with his thumbs. What he found inside was completely different than what he had imagined.

A BLESSING AND A CURSE

"What do you mean you've gone to get it repaired?" Valeria said in a furious rage. "Don't you know that's probably the most single important thing on this entire continent?"

Valeria's face was red and her voice was starting to become hoarse.

"It was broken. We needed it repaired. It's in the hands of someone very capable," reassured Videre, trying to remain civilized.

She knew her sisters wouldn't understand. A very cross Valeria paced back and forth looking like she was ready to explode. Her boots sounded heavy on the cold floor as the other two sisters remained silent for a few moments.

"Who is this capable person?" inquired Valencia, while trying to sound cheerful while stirring her cup of tea like a proper lady.

She sat in her dining chair looking as if she already knew the answer to her own question. Videre shifted uncomfortably as if she were a child being scolded.

"Leon," she said quietly. "Minet," she added as she looked at Valencia and took a deep breath.

Valeria pounded her fists on the table then stomped out of the dining hall. Valencia looked at Videre sorrowfully. Valeria reacting like this was a common occurrence, but this time was different.

"This has to work, dear sister. This absolutely must work. We can't have another mishap with the Minets. They are far too important. That family has been a blessing and a curse to us." Valencia looked at Videre solemnly. "After this, we must keep him close."

Valencia poured herself some more tea and sipped it quietly. She was thinking. Valencia always looked sad when she thought. She hated conflicts but understood what had to be done. She didn't always take Videre's side but for the most part, they agreed on most things. Being one of three was difficult at times. They fought and argued over the simplest things. However, when all three worked together, they were able to achieve greatness.

Videre looked at Valencia who was now chewing off small bits of her bread. Valencia was a very charismatic leader. The people of Desial were blessed to have her for how caring she was of her people. Valencia would take to the streets undercover to make sure things were running smoothly. She also tried to make it a point to know every single person living in Vici no matter how impossible.

Suddenly, the boulder-like doors to the dining room swung open. A very elegant blond girl stood before the two queens.

"Jaora, what a fantastic job you did," praised Valencia, "I'm sure your parents are very proud of what you've been able to do in such a short time."

Indeed, it was a small amount of time, but perhaps it would have been easier if Valencia wasn't constantly changing her mind about the colors and themes of last night's festival.

"I was told to come to see you, Your Majesty," Jaora curtsied with little balance, almost tripping with her own foot.

This girl is so innocent it's almost as if she were still in school.

Valencia smiled as if she were trying to hold back a laugh at what she had just seen.

"We were hoping you would consider a position here at the palace as head seamstress. You may either live here at the castle or stay at home. All we require is for you to be here when called and have outfits prepared in time." Jaora's mouth opened as if she were to answer but Valencia kept going, "You will be paid, of course, making more than all the seamstresses in the land. Of course, if you were to refuse, we would most likely choose one of the seamstresses already in our employ, although we feel as if…"

Videre touched Valencia's forearm and smiled.

Close your mouth Valencia, she wants this. No. She needs this.

Jaora had tears swelling in her eyes, "I would love to be of service to you, Your… Majesties."

Her next curtsy was slightly better the previous attempt. She was aglow with excitement.

"Sevete will show you to your new work quarters and living quarters if you wish to stay here," said Valencia as she motioned to the handman standing by one of the doors.

Jaora had a skip in her step as she started to turn around to walk out the door.

"Jaora, do you know a certain individual by the name of Leon Minet?" called out Valencia.

Videre was shocked by Valencia's inquiry.

I wanted this to be quiet.

"Yes, Your Majesty. I have known him for as long as I can remember. He is best friends with my brother," she gave a slight pause and saw the look from Valencia thirsting for more information. "He has his own family timemaker shop." She was smiling and blushed as though she were trying to stop talking about him but couldn't and continued, "He is a very smart person; the kind of person that can see something broken and will immediately know how to fix it."

"Thank you. Settle in and we will talk soon."

Jaora curtsied again and walked out of the room with Sevete. As the doors shut with a thud, Valencia stood up from the table still chewing her food. She curtsied, mimicking Jaora and almost toppling over. She and Videre both laughed and Valencia went on her way. Unlike Valeria, Valencia was graceful and her heels hardly made a sound on the streaked marble. Videre had a few more quiet moments to gather her thoughts until she was interrupted by a lumbering figure in the doorway.

"Jooey, please tell me some good news," Videre sighed without looking up.

"Well, he remembered everything from the parade like you predicted. Also, the lad said he would need time to get the parts. He'll deliver it himself," said Jooey as he took Valeria's seat and started wolfing down her leftovers. "Valeria didn't look to happy. She's going to be rough on the Vipole during training."

"She knows I needed it fixed. She just thinks it's better off with Keone. Tell me I wasn't crazy for just leaving my box with a person I don't even know."

"But you do know him."

"You know what I mean," said Videre as she shook her head. "Maybe I've taken this too far, but I feel as if I had no other choice."

"You didn't have any other choice unless you want to talk to Keone or go to Dunbar and talk to....her," Jooey shuttered, then he started stuffing his face with Valencia's leftovers.

Indeed. We don't want to see either of them. We had no other choice.

CHAPTER

V

CHOSEN

———————————————

We're here.

Leon was particularly sick of this reoccurring dream. Mrs. Potter was a very superstitious woman and had informed him on several occasions that it was his conscious trying to tell him something, to which his grandfather had agreed. He had never told anyone about his dreams but to them, but even so, he was doubtful she could help. She had even given him some Dunbari fruit tea which was supposed to "accentuate" his dreams or make them clearer, but the ritual got him nowhere.

Today, instead of walking to his shop, he would be walking to Jolon's house. The evening before, he had put a 'closed' sign on the red door to his shop like he did every night, but for today, it would be left as is. Leon looked at his timepiece groggily. He still had plenty of time to get dressed and eat before he needed to be on his way but he didn't mind getting there early. He smelled the pungent aroma of meat and eggs and heard the usual voices of his grandfather and Mrs. Potter downstairs. He slowly reached underneath his bed, pulling out the timekeeper wrapped in dark red silk. He carefully unwrapped the silk to reveal the gleaming box that he had beautifully and exquisitely polished. After spending a few moments admiring his work, he wrapped up the box again and put it inside his tattered delivery bag. A nicely dressed Leon walked down the stairs trying to act as if it were any other day.

"Where are you going today?" questioned his grandfather even before Leon reached the bottom of the stairs.

Leon indeed did dress a bit nicer than what he would usually wear to work and wasn't surprised that Keone had taken notice. For an old man, he was still as observant as ever.

"I'm walking Jolon to the castle today for his handman trial," said Leon, trying to conceal the delivery bag.

"What's in the bag?" asked Keone while sipping his black coffee.

"A timepiece I'm delivering this morning," responded Leon a little too quickly. Leon was bad at lying so he managed to always tell half-truths to avoid lying. He was definitely delivering a package that was, in a way, a timepiece. He grabbed a piece of bread and walked to the door to avoid any more questions.

"Can't be late!" he called over his shoulder as he dashed out through the door.

Jolon's house was somewhat close to Leon's shop. When the boys were younger, they would play in the streets in front of the shop where Leon's parents could keep an eye on them. Although Leon and Jolon's parents were friendly with one another, there were times where even at a young age, Leon could feel the tension between the two sets of parents. Leon had been scrawny and the boys would play rough. Perhaps that's why his parents kept eyes on them. Either way, he was grateful for the time he got to spend with Jolon as a child, because as an adult he had started drifting from people and putting all his effort into work, but Jolon had always stayed his closest friend.

Jolon was always more athletic than Leon but Leon had an advantage when it came to books and schoolwork. Leon was hesitant to let Jolon cheat off of him but by the time they were in life school, it had become the norm. Leon would swear that all the teachers knew about it but they didn't care enough to do anything about it.

Many teachers of Vici had been cold to the students. Grades did not seem to matter and they would never communicate with parents. Every now and then, a foreigner would observe the class making sure the teacher was up to standards. Surprisingly, the teachers would instruct like they did every day, without feeling or awareness. Leon had hated school, as did most other children. He wanted to learn more if he was going to spend an exuberant amount of time sitting in an uneventful classroom. Any questions that he may have thought of in his lessons were brought home to his parents. Playing with other children and making contraptions out of sticks and stones very well seemed more logical than sitting all morning in a damp classroom. Athletics was always interested Leon and it seemed as if the schools cared more about that, than actual education. He had great respect for those who could wield a sword or bow for their country, however, this was not the path for Leon. Leon's future was and would always be that of a timemaker. This was his so-called destiny and he was content with it. He had always had a knack for making timepieces, all the way from crafting the metals to making the internal parts. Whether it be from his ancestors or just an acquired skill didn't matter. It was what he was born to do.

Leon walked up to Jolon's gates where two guards waved him by. One was fairly new but the old man on the right had worked for Jes as long as Leon could remember. With pale skin and light hair, there was no doubt that they were from Dunbar. Seeing the Dunbari in Vici was not uncommon. Desial bordered Dunbar and the workers were paid handsomely compared to what they would receive in their homeland. Many Dunbari were large in stature and almost unnaturally agile. It was no wonder that they were favored when it came to hiring guards, yet surprisingly, he had never seen a Dunbari in a Vipole uniform. A few Dunbari women had been part of the festival as dancers.

Although on the same continent, Dunbar wasn't considered to be part of Aleria. One would have to cross large and almost impassible mountains to reach the heart of their country. Although much of Aleria had never seen a Dunbari before, Desial was known to welcome any Dunbari with open arms. Leon walked past the guards and down the long walkway to the house with either side full of fragrant and colorful blooms. The massive residence had more of an atmosphere similar to that of a palace. Jolon's house had almost every color imaginable inside and out. The flowers, the walkway, and even the windows had extravagant colors. It may have looked odd to an ordinary passerby but Leon had been there so many times that started to feel as if all houses should look this beautiful. The groundskeepers would smile and wave to Leon as if he were their old friend when he walked by. Not even halfway to the house, Jolon ran out of the front door with a smile on his face.

"Let's go!" yelled Jolon as he ran up to Leon and grabbed him by the arm.

Jolon swung Leon around to face the gate once again. The timekeeper hit Leon's leg as he was violently pivoted. Leon clutched his bag hard. There was no telling what would happen to him if it were to be damaged in his possession. He had never thought about that until now.

What if I wasn't able to fix the timepiece? How did Videre know that I could fix the timekeeper? Should I call her Videre or Queen Videre? Highness? Majesty? Why didn't they teach this in school?

Jolon saw that Leon was lost in thought as they exited his front gate. "Changing your mind about the trial?" Jolon teased.

Leon smiled back, "I never said I was going to apply."

The conversation on the walk to the castle was full of Jolon's expectations of what living in the castle would be like. He had already been picturing himself as a handman. He had a long-winded dialogue about what he had imagined the parties would be like with royalty. Jes and Jeela were no strangers to the noble parties of The Vasili, however, they withheld details from their children. The more Jolon spoke of his excitement for his new possible life, the more Leon contemplated if he would also be suited for that life. He chuckled to himself when Jolon started talking about being a bodyguard or part of the Vipole. Leon knew he would never have the strength, speed, or agility to become a handman if all of those qualities were required. He then flashed back to when Jooey had mentioned that Valencia preferred the smart ones. Jooey knew how small Leon was, yet still encouraged him to apply. Perhaps being a handman didn't always involve being strong but Leon had almost no information to what the job entailed but what he imagined seemed like a fantasy.

As the pair arrived at the first steps of the castle, other men whom Leon had gone to school with, were also walking in the same direction. He knew it was popular to apply for men their age, especially those who weren't privy to ancestral careers such as him. Stories about ladies, food, clothes, and festivities swirled amongst them. As they started walking up the stairs, Leon looked to all the different men ahead and behind them, all hoping to be chosen to serve in the presence of royalty. Halfway up the stairs, there were men walking down the steps with disappointed expressions on their faces. A confused Leon looked up to see four guards inspecting the men at the top of the steps. Manhandling their jaws and feeling their arms, they seemed to be checking to see if the hopefuls were firm-bodied. The men who had been let into the castle let out deep breaths as if they had passed the actual trial itself.

Jolon was confident and straightened out his back as he approached the guards. They were terrifying to look at. They were all large barrel-chested men that looked as if they could crush any man. The serious looks on their faces showed no weaknesses. The guards were most likely weeding out other features as well, as one man with a muscular physique was also turned away. Jolon walked up to the guards and stood up straight with his iconic smile disappearing behind a serious face. The guard who was significantly larger than Jolon grabbed his jaw and looked at both sides of his neck. He pro-ceeded to firmly grab his arm and shoulders, even turning his hands to inspect Jolon's palms. He nodded and outstretched his hand toward the open doors. Without thinking, Leon stepped up to the guard. For a second, he forgot that he was there for a different reason than all the other men until the guard motioned to the bag.

"This is a package for the...."

"He's with me," boomed a large familiar voice.

Jooey jogged up to the guard and grabbed Leon's arm as he patted the guard on the head. The guard seemed less than amused and called the next person in line.

Jooey led him through the open doors as they weaved past other guards and prospective handmen waiting in line as if they were in an assembly line. Leon eyed a short line of men waiting to be questioned by a small group of women sitting at a delicate table. To Leon's surprise, Mrs. Potter was among the women asking questions to the men who walked through the doors. As Leon passed Jolon waiting in line, a clear and confused look stared back at him. Leon knew he would have to explain later, but he had to keep up with Jooey's long strides. They walked past the table of older ladies and through large wooden doors with golden etchings. The doors looked to be similar in design as the precious box that was draping off of his shoulder. The doors had transported him into a room several times larger than his own house. Pillars with engravings held up the magnificent painted ceiling. The floor looked glazed as if it were wet and every footstep echoed in the large room. Streaks and bits of colors were strewn across the entirety of the hall as the stained glass windows left hardly anything in the room without a brilliant color and sheen.

"Welcome to the throne room," said Jooey proudly, as if it were his own room.

Three thrones sat in the front of the room on a raised platform, each one identical to the other. A cat was laying on one of the thrones with its eyes half-open as if it were annoyed that it had been woken up from a nap. Leon recognized the black cat as the creature that had been siting on Queen Valencia's saddle. Jooey cleared his throat and it then slowly propped itself up, stretched, and ran off through an open door to the side of the room. Jooey grabbed a small table next to a pillar and placed it directly in front of the thrones. Without hesitation, Leon pulled out the box, still wrapped, onto the table. As he started unwrapping, he heard footsteps nearing the open door that the cat had ran out of. A shorter dark-haired man walked through and nodded to Jooey.

"Kneel," whispered Jooey. Jooey and Leon both stepped to either side of the small table and dropped to one knee as more footsteps approached.

"Stand," a familiar voice said.

Videre.

Leon stood up and witnessed the three queens in all their splendor for the first time; all together and close up. They bore similar faces, however, only one was smiling.

"We welcome you to our home," said the one on the right. Valencia was wearing a long white dress that shimmered brilliantly. "Leon Minet, we are grateful for your time and expertise in this matter."

She bowed her head slightly, showing her silver crown with blue jewels sparkling in the sunlight, placing streaks through the stained windows. A moment had passed before Leon had realized that they were waiting for him to open the package. As he unwrapped the silk, his hands started shaking from nervousness. Jooey noticed his uneasiness and quickly aided him in unwrapping the box. Leon looked up when all the silk had been pulled off. Now Valeria also had a smile that replaced her previous scowl.

"You have certainly surprised me, Minet," she said approvingly. "To be honest, you might even surpass your father's skills," she said as she pressed her fingers into the engravings.

"You knew my father?" asked Leon inquisitively. "I do remember coming here a long time ago to meet a queen but that was when I was very young."

He stopped himself before he started rambling. Valencia and Valeria snickered while Videre looked unamused. She looked in Leon's eyes with a sad look on her face.

"To have a young boy, a citizen, come to the castle is a rarity indeed. Your father did bring you here a few times. Perhaps he knew you would be back one day."

Videre forced a smile. Leon could already tell her tone of voice was not genuine. Something was amiss and Leon did not like the unknown.

Suddenly a loud knock came from the door. Videre rushed to put the timekeeper back in the silk from which it came and stuffed it in Leon's bag. The other two queens quickly took their spot on the thrones; Valencia in the middle and Valeria on the left. Jooey shoved the bag into Leon's arms and moved the small table to where it once was.

"Enter," yelled Valencia right as Videre sat on her throne. Jooey ran up to Leon and yanked him off to the side of the room. A line of men entered the room, Jolon being the sixth. There were nine in total. Significantly less than the men that had been walking up the stairs with them earlier. Leon suddenly remembered the letter that Jolon had shown him days earlier.

This year, only nine men will be selected.

Jolon had made the final cut. Leon nodded at Jolon proudly. Although Leon knew that the Vasili conducted handmen trials every five years, the number of men that were usually chosen was something that Leon couldn't even guess. Valencia stood up regally and stepped closer to the line of men with a sort of seduction in her eyes.

"Congratulations, you have made the final stage of being selected as handmen. From this day on, you will be devoted to The Vasili and the Kingdom. You will be assigned to one of us. Upper handmen will train you in the day to day life. Every handman will be given a schedule. This will include combat training in case the need for it arises. The duties of the handmen are not to be shared with anyone outside of the people of this hall. Those who work inside of the castle are also sworn to secrecy. The period in which you will remain handmen is five years. When your time as a handman is up, you will be rewarded handsomely for your duties and may be given the option of staying for another five years or go back to your normal lives. Anyone who disobeys or who shares details about handman duties outside of the castle will be severely punished." Some of the men nodded their heads and a couple had widened their eyes as she continued, "We will now be choosing who you will be serving for the next five years. Valeria, if you would do the honors."

Valeria stood from her chair and dropped down to inspect the line of men. She embodied the likeness of a predator about to catch her next meal.

"You," she said as she jabbed her finger into Jolon's chest and smiled. Jolon smiled in return almost as devilishly as her. For him to be the first one selected probably felt like a dream come true.

"Step back," she demanded, without hesitation he bowed his head and stepped back, still smiling.

Valeria sat back down as Valencia stood and repeated the process choosing a tall dark man with curly hair as her choice. As Valencia sat down, Valeria stood again to make her choice.

"Videre hasn't chosen in years," whispered Jooey into Leon's ear, "She's just here for formalities."

Jooey must have seen the look of confusion on Leon's face as well as some of the others. Videre seemed unaffected that her sisters had skipped her turn. Valencia stood again after Valeria had chosen a large, dark-haired man named Renen that Leon had gone to school with.

Leon couldn't help but feel happy for Jolon. Jolon was obviously very dedicated and happy to be Valeria's handman. His bright toothed smile couldn't contain his happiness as if it were an aura pouring out of him. He would most likely try to stay in her service until he died or at least wasn't useful anymore.

Valencia glared at Valeria, who had clearly taken her next choice. Slowly, she stood up and started asking questions to the select few left about their lives, each man answering unwaveringly and ending with a "Your Majesty". She looked at Jooey and Leon, then toward Videre. Videre stood abruptly and stepped down to Valencia.

"I believe you have skipped my turn," she said very seriously. "Leon Minet will be my handman."

She was abrupt and stern. She looked at her sisters and said, "You may have your choice of the rest," and walked away from her lavish throne.

Valeria and Valencia looked at each other and let out a snicker with mischievous looks on their faces. Leon, on the other hand, was surprised. He wasn't here to become a handman. He was there to simply deliver a piece to the queen who had asked him for a favor. He didn't know anything about this job. He caught Jolon's eye. Jolon also looked surprised as Leon with his mouth slightly open. He gave a slight and stiff wave to Leon and smiled.

"Well, lad," Jooey whispered. "Welcome to our club."

"Come," Videre commanded as she glided past them.

In the background, Valencia and Valeria could be heard bickering about whose turn it was. As they walked down the hallways of the castle, Leon was fascinated with all of its splendor. The warm sunshine streaked through the colors of stained glass. The hall had perfect intricate designs on the walls and ceilings painted with shimmering golden hues. Their footsteps echoed in the halls drowning out the faint voices behind closed doors to what Leon had suspected were castle workers. His mind wandered to all the people who would be working alongside him.

Videre slowed down and stopped at a door guarded by a large man. The man smiled at Leon.

"Ah, the timemaker," he said in a decently friendly tone.

Leon recognized the guard as the man who had come with Videre and Jooey to Leon's shop that fateful day.

"The timemaker is now a handman," Jooey said proudly as if Leon was his own son. "Videre picked him out herself."

"Welcome timemaker, my name is Kolono."

He extended his large and rough hand out for a handshake. Remembering Jooey's intense handshake Leon, he hesitated for a moment to take it. As he took Kolono's hand, he felt the same crushing pressure and let out a grunt.

"We'll train him good," Kolono said to Videre.

"Well," she corrected. "I expect you to," Videre added as she walked through the door.

Jooey and Leon walked steadily in sync behind Videre as they walked into a large room big enough to put his whole shop into. The round room boasted high ceilings and beautiful almost life-like paintings lined the walls. The enormous windows were fitted with light pink curtains. A large handcrafted desk sat in front of the windows with neatly placed papers, pens, and envelopes as if she had been writing letters all day. A few chairs and a matching sofa faced her desk giving the feeling of a leisure room as well. She carefully took Leon's bag from off his shoulder without permission and pulled out the timekeeper. She placed it on her desk and inspected the box that started gleaming in the sunlight.

"It looks new," she said approvingly with a hint of a smile.

Carefully, she opened the box with a key she took out from her pocket and looked closely at the timekeeper.

"You did well, Leon."

Closing the box, she opened a desk drawer and locked it away with the same key.

"Come," she demanded, abruptly leaving the room.

They had walked only a little while until they came to a bright red door. She took a deep breath and unlocked the door. The room was colored in a light blue and gray with a bed twice the size of Leon's against the opposite wall. Other than the bed and a large wardrobe, the room was devoid of any other furniture. The large windows let in a tremendous amount of light, making the room feel bright and airy.

"This is your new room," said Videre somberly as if she did not want it being used. "It can be furnished to your liking. Jooey will take you to the storage area where there are quite a number of pieces that can be brought to you. Tonight, he will accompany you to your house to get your belongings. Also, you are allowed to keep working as a timemaker, however, you will be required to work on all your projects here in the castle. I will dispatch a trusted villager to stay in your shop during hours and take orders. Every night he will come to bring your requests and materials to the castle for your convenience."

Videre paused as if she had forgotten what else to say. Her face held a look of grief and pain that was confusing to Leon.

"I know you didn't apply. I don't even know if you want to be here but there is a rule that any person that is in the throne room during selections are only The Vasili, handmen, and those who are eligible to be handmen. I had to save you from...my sisters."

"To be honest, I would have never applied but I would be happy to serve my country in any way possible while maintaining my position as a timemaker," Leon said confidently, trying to be as formal and patriotic as he could.

He had meant it. His walk down the beautiful halls of the castle seemed like a familiar and comfortable place. In his heart, he knew that this was no accident.

"We will be talking soon," Videre assured him. "For now, get some furniture and your belongings here. I would also like for you to acquaint yourself with the workers and other handmen as well as Kolono and Jooey."

Leon nodded and bowed. As she turned to leave, Leon wanted to call out. He wanted to know more about what he needed to do from now on. There was a deep feeling in his heart and stomach. A feeling that was both pleasure-filled and something that made him feel queasy.

This was meant to happen.

THE CHAPEL OF THE ALERIAN SOCIETY

Leon awoke to a sunlight-flooded room that brought a sense of comforting warmth to him. There was no crowing and more noticeably, no dreams. The bed was soft and warm, making it hard for Leon to get out of bed. Even though he had been at the castle for a few days, he was always pleasantly surprised to wake in such a large beautiful room. The room was spacious but scant. The red and golden hues of his comforter reflected sunshine onto the walls as if he had paintings on his walls. Although he was directed to freely decorate, he had never had any use of anything but a place to put his clothes and projects.

Videre had approved of Leon working on his own timepieces as necessary, placing a replacement shopkeeper that would deliver his materials and supplies to the castle every day and so far the replacement had not disappointed Leon. A large flawless worktable was placed on the far wall of his room next to the window where he could work peacefully and stare at the small figures bustling on the street. His tabletop was something to marvel at. The veins in the wood were remark-able and whoever had built the table made sure it was com-pletely smooth, something that he rarely saw in woodwork so large in size. He had thought of not decorating his room with other furnishings just so the table would have its own sense of glory. Leon had no doubt that this table would have cost a fortune. He looked at its splendor, reflecting the sun's rays off the surface. Such small things delighted Leon.

As he sat up in bed, he could make out some of the people walking down one of the main streets just outside the castle walls. Only a few days ago, he had been one of those people. He wondered if the other people who had come to live in the castle also looked at the villagers in the same way as he did. A sense of power came to Leon whenever he looked out of the window that he didn't want to admit at times. He was satisfied with being invisible to others and feeling as if he was just liv-ing as a normal human. This feeling of power was unfamiliar territory to him.

Videre had not yet asked anything of him yet, which had slightly depressed Leon. He had only seen her a few times wandering the castle and when he had seen her, she was seemingly busy. Most of the time, she had not even glanced in his direction, making him feel small and almost invisible. Videre, in all her affairs, seemed to have no time to chat with him when she did glance at him. A small smile here and there was all that he had received from her. Perhaps if he would take an initiative to converse with her, then she would notice him and ask something of him; that was his job after all.

As the other handmen of Valencia and Valeria were shuf-fling about the castle running errands and doing small odd favors for them, Leon found himself wandering the halls of the immense castle trying to map everything in his head. Although he felt as if it was a strange place to be, he had decided that he might as well know the halls thoroughly since he was expected to live here for at least the next five years.

Over the several hours that he had wandered about the castle, he had related the experience to that of designing a timepiece. Everything was according to schedule, just as Leon preferred. Not only was everything run smoothly, but there was a way to things that seemed as if he were the one who directed the day-to-day operations. He was quite impressed by how the schedules were run in the castle, but of course after a few hundred years, one should expect that things would be running smoothly.

Looking at his personal calendar for the next three months, there were a few events that he was expected to attend. The calendar he had received was written in neat handwriting but scribbles from an unknown hand littered the page with small notes about certain events. Leon was appreciative of these small notes but it was almost written as if Leon were a child who needed to have detailed explanations. The Equinox Festival involving various leaders of Desial, a formal dinner in Konis, and a meeting in Isleland were the events with the most notes. Leon still was uncertain about what all these events involved and hoped that Jooey may be able to explain further what his role may be.

Sitting on his table sat a broken timepiece delivered from his shop. As it lay there, he often wondered about the timekeeper that had been taken from him after the handman trial. He had not seen it since that day and had been hoping to speak to Videre about it. Although he had a thorough examination of the item, he was still left unsatisfied. The drawing, knowing that Videre knew his grandfather, the festival, and finally being a handman; it must have all connected somehow. Leon was hardly one to believe in coincidence.

A loud knock came from Leon's door which abruptly stopped his daydreaming of Videre and the timekeeper. Without saying a word or even having a moment to answer, Jooey walked in with his signature burliness.

"You're invited to breakfast with the queen."

Leon instantly jumped out of bed and rushed to put on acceptable clothes. Jooey gave Leon at least a small sense of privacy to change while the dark husky man carefully touched the pieces on Leon's desk delicately as if the metal parts could crumble under a simple brush of his hand. The expensive fabric that Leon had been offered was delightfully soothing against his skin that had been brushing against what Jolon had called "harsh commoner fabric" his whole life. Jooey smiled and nodded at Leon as if he was approving of his outfit choice for the day. Within moments, they were walking down a long corridor just past one of the guard stations. Leon could not help but try to have Jooey give him some explanations or answers but was equally as weary that Jooey may find him too nosy.

"What's my job around here? Videre never asks me to do things like what Valencia and Valeria make their handmen do."

Jooey chuckled. "The last time Videre chose a handman was me, almost twenty years ago," he said proudly. "Videre is a very independent queen. She feels as if she doesn't need a lot of handmen like the other two."

Jooey stopped in the hall and turned to Leon. "I like you, Leon. You seem like a good lad but I would tone down on the questions. She doesn't like so many questions," said Jooey in all seriousness. "If I were you, I would just do as your told whenever that may be. If you need to know more, she'll make sure and tell you when she wishes."

The halls echoed with Jooey's booming voice. Leon wondered why it had been twenty years since she had chosen a handman. He remembered that she said she felt as if she had no choice but to choose him, but deep down, he wondered when she would choose another, and a strange feeling of jealousy started creeping through him.

Jooey started walking again, "I did that when I became handman, and now I'm basically her right-hand man," he turned to Leon and shook a giant finger at him. "You better not think you'll be replacing me," he laughed as he continued to lead the way down the hall.

Leon and Jooey walked the large hallways of the castle frequently passing ladies and handmen. While wandering the hallways Leon would sometimes run into Jolon or Jaora. Like Videre, they never had time to talk to him. Whenever Leon saw Jolon, he could tell in his eyes that there was so much he wanted to say. He would always get that look when he had heard rumors or whenever he started seeing a girl. Jolon had promised Leon that they would talk sometime soon and dramatically intrigued Leon when he accentuated the word "privately".

Leon noticed that they had been walking for quite some time. He looked around at the paintings and decorations. The wall coverings had changed into more of a duller shade of red as if it hadn't been replaced for a century.

This isn't the way to the dining hall.

Jooey smiled. He must have seen that Leon finally noticed. The pair of them turned to a small inconspicuous door close to what Leon had guessed was the kitchen as the aromas and sound of the clanging pots became more noticeably distinct. Jooey opened the door with a hidden latch and his large body had maneuvered its way into a dark and narrow walkway set before them. Glancing around to make sure nobody was around, Jooey snapped his fingers and in an instant, torches on either side of the hall lit up, illuminating the hallway and somehow making it look even scarier than at first glance. Without a word, Jooey walked down the hall comfortably with Leon a step behind. Looking around at the plain and almost crumbling brick walls, Leon instinctively closed the door behind him.

"You don't mind narrow and creepy hallways do ya?" joked Jooey. "Within these castle walls, there are many passages and corridors. Only a few of us know of these specific halls. These torches," he continued as he pointed toward the flames, "are only lit for certain people, so if anyone were to find out about the halls, they wouldn't even get anywhere because well....they can't see."

Jooey looked back at Leon and smiled as if he were a child showing a parent an intricate magic trick. As they kept walking, torches started lighting one by one. They passed other hallways but it seemed as if the torches knew where they were headed, keeping the other hallways dark.

"What if a person finds out about the halls then brings their own torch?"

"Any torches other than these will blow out," said Jooey as he touched the flame of one of the torches.

He looked back at Leon and smiled as if he were now performing in front of a crowd. Leon touched the flame of a torch he was passing and sure enough, the flame wasn't a flame at all. He had expected at least a little heat, but they were neither hot nor cold.

An illusion? Was this the work of magic?

Everyone knew there was magic on the continent but the extent of it was unknown, for most people go their whole lives never seeing anything so brilliant. A few simple tricks here and there, nothing as spectacular as a hallway made of torches that weren't made of real flames. After going down several sets of stairs and following the lights through different hallways, Jooey unlocked and opened a large iron door. As Jooey was pushing open the massive door, Leon wondered if Jooey was always this big or the handman training had transformed him into a beastly man. A bright light suddenly streamed into the hallway and all the lit torches blew out. Outside the door, Leon could hear melodies from birds and saw the sheen of almost unreal incredibly green grass. Stone walls surrounded them with wisps of vines showing off bright colored flowers of all shades.

"Welcome to the Chapel of The Alerian Society," Jooey whispered.

Leon stepped out onto the grass. This was a sight he had never seen before. The flowers were so beautiful and well-tended that it seemed as if he were staring into a painting. Leon even felt bad that he was standing on top of such magnificent grass as if every blade had feelings of their own. In the middle of the garden was a table with an overhang from a tree filled with blossoms. A lonely figure drinking from a dainty white teacup faced away from them but Leon instantly recognized her long brown hair and meek posture. Jooey outstretched his hand toward the table and nodded. As Leon approached the figure, Jooey disappeared behind the iron door from which they had entered. Leon slowly sat down on the uncomfortable white chair, as Videre sipped on a pungent fruit tea that he couldn't quite make out from scent alone. A plate with a small cream pastry had been placed at his seat and an empty teacup that matched Videre's.

"I do apologize for the delay in our inevitable conversation," Videre said eloquently. She looked calm and relaxed as opposed to the usual tension that was always written on her face. "Finding time isn't easy. I trust you have found time to work on your projects?"

"Yes, I have," answered Leon as he poured himself some tea and took a bite out of his pastry. "I'm surprised you haven't asked anything of me. The other queens seem to be using their handmen quite a lot."

He remembered the time he saw Valeria's men training in the courtyard only minutes after he had just seen them carrying her blankets in the hallways.

"I have seven handmen, including you," she said as she bit into a cake.

Leon was shocked. He only knew of Jooey and Kolono. Jooey said he was the last handmen chosen so the others must have been in her service for a long while.

"Malaki, one of my handmen created this garden for me," she motioned all around them. "He is a plantskeeper. He has been a handman for most of his life now."

"I thought handmen usually only stay for five years," said Leon.

"I don't give time constraints to my handmen. I allow them to leave when they please and so far only one has left and two have passed," she said in a somber tone. "Like all the others, I will not put any time restraints on you. I do have a favor to ask of you. All of my men know of this but it cannot be spoken outside of our circle."

Leon had been itching for this moment, "Yes," he blurted out a little too enthusiastically.

Videre smiled. She looked pleased to see him so animated. "It's something I've been working on for years. It's very complicated so I won't go too deep into all the details just yet, but I will need you to remain a handman until the plans are finished which may take a while. First, you must prepare for our trip."

"Our trip? Where are we going?" asked Leon.

"Moshny," Valeria responded calmly.

Moshny was a country far south of Desial. A very religious settlement had been established more than a thousand years ago there. Legend said that the waters of the settlement's lake would glow at night and sparkle during the day. Those who fished or even touched the lake would be banished from the country. Because of these rules, most people were intrigued by what kind of secrets it held.

"I know you don't know much about Moshny, therefore, when we get back to the castle, you will go to the library and read about the country. It doesn't have to be much, but you need to know what you're getting yourself into. I have a feeling about you, Leon Minet. You'll prove yourself. I'm most certain," she smiled briefly before sipping the last of her tea.

As soon as Leon was finished with his pastry, Videre stood up. She was wearing a simple gray dress that seemed as if a villager would be wearing the same thing. Her brown eyes locked with Leon's as her hair caught a small breeze. Leon had not noticed before, but the sun beaming onto her hair invited different colors of dull reddish and blonde hues throughout her hair. Breaking the awkward moment she quickly turned and walked to the iron door.

"Come. You have reading to do."

She didn't wait for Leon to catch up before opening the large door. As the torches started lighting, Leon had realized that this was unreal. He was living in a castle, taking orders directly from a queen, and walking into a hallway dependent on magic. A few weeks ago, he didn't even know there was a queen let alone three. He had always been disappointed in his primary education but the fact that he was one of the most intelligent in his class, and he didn't know anything about The Vasili really worried him. Even his lack of knowledge before going to Moshny was frightening.

As Videre led the way, Leon had started getting used to the feel of this passageway. He felt a sense of ease that didn't make sense to him. The walls were made of dark bricks and the floor was most certainly just packed dirt. Turning around corners and walking up stairs, he felt excited to be behind a queen as if she were bringing him to another unknown world. Leon was almost sure that this was the way he had gone with Jooey but since all hallways seemed the same, it would take some time for him to even memorize where he was going. The walls were all the same, every hallway, door, and stairs were almost identical except for some reason, he felt himself drifting toward certain doors and hallways. Their footsteps echoed and their pace quickened. Every time they would turn, the torches in the next hallway would lead them.

"The torches know where you intend to go," said Videre as if she had read his mind. "I have these halls memorized but that isn't necessary."

Leon could hear the smile on her face when she talked.

She must know I'm trying to memorize the halls.

"Forgive me. I have much I don't know," he said, hinting that he was trying to squeeze more out of her.

The torches led them to a door almost identical to the one leading into the garden. The door swung open to reveal a small man with a small gray mustache as if he had been waiting for them.

"I have been expecting you, my queen," he said as he bowed slightly and opened the door wider.

Bowing. I haven't bowed to her all today.

Leon felt a sense of shame. He had been with the queen for quite some time and hadn't bowed to her, let alone treated her like royalty. But in turn, she had not reminded Leon of such things. As he stepped into the room, a distinct smell lingered in the air as if he had been there before. Surrounding them were shelves upon shelves of books. Large, small, new, old, and even some behind clear glass, no doubt for preservation. A large desk with handwritten papers and different pens with bookbinding materials were strewn about. The small man quickly went to the desk and handed Videre a piece of paper.

"Leon, this is one of my handmen, Ezrai. He is a librarian of sorts. If you wish to know anything historical, he will have much information available, or at least can point you in the right direction," she said as she motioned to the books surrounding them. "Ezrai, Leon will need a basic understanding of Moshny before the trip."

"Before the trip, my queen?" he laughed out loud. "With the history of Moshny, this boy will need at least a week to get through just a basic understanding."

"Basic history and customs are all he will need for now."

Videre pulled a timepiece out of a hidden pocket. She glanced at Ezrai and smiled.

"I must be going."

Before she turned around, Ezrai bowed low and Leon quickly followed suit. Videre rushed out of the room through the main door of the library instead of the hallway they had just come from.

Ezrai smiled at Leon, "You look like your father. He was very fond of the books here. Read all night sometimes," he said as he started scouring the shelves.

"You knew my father?" Leon asked inquisitively.

He knew that his father would come up to the castle to deliver timepieces but it seemed as if he were here more often than that.

"Yes, Leon. Your father is known by many in this castle. I mean he was a very talented artisan so he was known all across the continent too."

Ezrai looked puzzled as if Leon should have known that his father was well known. Ezrai pulled two books from the shelves with a slight cloud of dust springing from the books.

He carefully laid the two books in Leon's hands. "One is for a brief history, the other for customs and mannerisms. I certainly wouldn't make you read the complete history of Moshny," he said while motioning to the wall of books that definitely could only be carried two at a time. "There will be four of you traveling to Moshny. If you have anything you don't understand, don't hesitate to ask. Everyone on the trip has been to Moshny several times."

Ezrai paused as he studied Leon's face and said quietly, "The resemblance is quite uncanny, almost eerie. As for your father, wait until she decides to tell you about him. Just re-member," he said in a serious tone, "no matter who your family is, you are your own person. They don't define you."

Leon couldn't make out how old Ezrai was but he definitely spoke like an elder. He imagined Exrai was a very wise and knowledgeable man. His mild manner towards Videre had also seemed odd to Leon, as if Ezrai wasn't a handman but rather her friend.

In a moment, Leon was led to the main door where Ezrai showed him the direction to get back to his room. Leon could tell that Ezrai was rushing him and was in no mood to answer any questions about his father so he had heeded Jooey and Ezrai's advice and decided to wait for Videre to enlighten him. The books that Ezrai had given to Leon were surprisingly light and looked newer than most of the books in the library de-spite the dust. The hallways in the castle were eerily as com-forting to walk through as the dark and narrow halls he had discovered earlier that day.

He had also learned that there were a few areas within the castle were divided among the three sisters. The west side of the castle was dedicated to Videre and her men. All of her handmen's quarters and her office were close to each other. Valeria had access to the armory and the training grounds on the east side. Leon had never seen Valencia's side of the castle but he had heard from Jaora that it was magnificently deco-rated.

Nearing lunchtime, Leon found his way to the staff dining room where there was a considerable amount of noise. He clutched his books and sat next to Jolon who was making a good deal of noise along with his other fellow handmen. After a few seconds of listening to their hollering, Leon picked up that they were arguing about roles for the Equinox Festival. Although everyone in the country celebrated the Equinox, Leon imagined that the feast held in the castle would be much different than the simple dinners shared with mere friends and family. Leon spotted Jaora standing in the corner with the cooks laughing at the men arguing about which drinks or tables they would be serving.

"Everyone calm down!" Jooey bellowed as he slammed his fist against a table.

Everyone suddenly stopped talking. Jooey's face showed no anger but satisfaction that he could quell such noise in a second.

"We will Lalan Antana for turns in choosing what roles to play for tomorrow night's event," Jooey declared as he pulled out a deck of playing cards.

All the bickering men stood up and circled around one of the tables in the dining room like predators about to pounce on their next victim. Jooey started shuffling the deck as their gleaming eyes stared intently.

"What are they playing for?" asked Leon moving close to Jaora.

"Servants of the night for the royalty and important people that will be in attendance for the Equinox celebration. There's a list of nine different men and women who have asked to have a personal companion for the night. Some do it because of a disability and others ask for assistance just because I think it makes them feel more important," Jaora sighed.

"No arguments. What's done will be done," Jooey said loudly and boldly.

All eyes were staring at the center of the table. All the men were tense and their hands ready to move quickly. Jooey quickly drew a card and slammed it face up on the table. The four of diamonds; nobody flinched. Jooey smiled in enjoyment. He quickly slammed another card on the table. Leon hadn't even seen the card before a tall blond handman had slammed his hand on it with three others following suit leaving his hand crushed on the bottom. The handman grinned as they took their hand off the card to reveal a three of hearts.

"Jamin," he said proudly.

There were some sighs of disappointment within the crowd of handmen.

Jaora whispered to Leon, "Jamin is a high ranking war hero. He is very old but the men talk about his amazing war stories. I heard he has broken all of his limbs. Some even multiple times and yet he lives to tell the tales of his heroics."

Jooey started slamming cards on the table again. Lanlan Antana was such an aggressive game for simple rules of slapping the special face cards but Leon reckoned that it had saved many arguments that could have resulted in injury. With five in a row regular cards, the men were starting to get antsy. Jooey looked up at Leon.

"Aren't ya supposed to be reading?" he said as he pointed towards the books.

"Yes sir," Leon said as he grabbed a freshly prepared sandwich and glided out the doorway while Jooey continued to slam cards on the table.

When Leon got to his room, he was already exhausted. History was not a subject that was in abundance in school. There was little learning material pertaining to the start of the continent or even what had happened a mere 100 years ago and Leon was excited to be able to learn more. Ezrai seemed knowledgeable and confident in the books he had given to Leon. He sat on his bed and started skimming through the pages. The writing was impressive with all the letters keeping uniform in size but definitely handwritten. Leon figured reading all of the material would take at least a day if he devoted it all to reading. He thumbed to the beginning of the book as curious as he had ever been about the history of another country.

A Brief History of Moshny
Ezrai Krono

Leon read the heading again.
"Ezrai Krono," he said aloud to himself wondering if this was the same Ezrai that he had just met.

The History of Moshny is complicated, due to the conflict of religion and beliefs held by the Kiadere and the different tribes of the region. Located in the southeastern part of Aleria, the country is south of Reino and east of Woadland. Hikari lies east of Moshny and can be seen from the shore on a clear day.

He skipped a few paragraphs that detailed landforms and terrain.

Lake Nodio is the most famous location in Moshny and has always been the capital city since its founding. The lake was discovered by an exploration party by the Dio and The Alerian Society in 104 OL. The leader of the Dio at the time was Cioto. Dio Cioto and King Konea had formed four search parties; one for the west, one northwest, one east, and one northeast. On the forty-first moon, the eastern search party had discovered the lake now known as Lake Nodio. Because of the unnatural sparkle of Lake Nodio, the leader of the party, Cipoloki, had instructed his party members not to drink from the water. They continued on until they reached the eastern coast of Moshny. Without adequate supplies or strength for making a boat to reach the islands off the coast, the search party turned to return home. On the journey home, they had reached the lake again on the sixtieth day. On the seventy-second day, three of their search crew had fallen ill. Within the next three days, they had died. Two more had also become ill. One of the men had recalled seeing the three that had died to have drunk from the lake. The two that had fallen ill later had determined that they had not drunk from the lake but the sickness had passed from the ones who had. Cipoloki made the decision to execute them within the woods now known as The Stromy. The party, due to fear of the disease spreading in the land, had made rafts and sent off the dead after lighting the rafts on fire at sunset. During the following weeks, the disease had spread to half of the party and all were immediately executed and burned without exception. Cipoloki was among the men who had fallen ill. When the party reached the Kiadere settlement, the rest of the group was sent to a separate home to make sure that no others would be infected. During the two weeks they were isolated, the remaining men had all drawn maps and stories of their travels. After the details of their *exploration were presented to the Dio and Alerian Society, The Dio decided to send settlers to the location calling the region Dio Zakatino, making sure that the residents were made aware not to even touch the waters. The settlers had made three settlements in Moshny. Kalanito, now presently Kalatov, located on the edge of the territory on the arrowhead mountains. Ziatoni, now called Kolomav, located on the outskirts of The Stromy. The last territory was settled outside of Lake Nodio. The settlers had built bridges to the island inside of the lake and became an important Dio establishment. Nodio is currently the largest city in all of Moshny.*

Some of what had been written had already been confusing Leon. He had heard of The Dio and The Alerian Society but was very unfamiliar with what or who they were. The Kiadere and the powers of Lake Nodio have been the source of many tales and legends but Leon had always been unsure of the stories. But then again, stories of winged horses and the timekeeper had also been just stories until recently. Leon's eyes felt heavy even though it was only midday. He had been picking at his sandwich while reading. Looking out the window, he started thinking about what would come to pass in the next few days during the Equinox Festival and his trip to Moshny with the queen. His bed had become warm and with the passing minutes, increasingly comfortable. As his eyes started closing, his hand released his grip on the book and it fell to the floor.

WHERE YOU INTEND TO GO

"My deepest condolences," a dark-haired Anjelika Potter touched Leon's young face. "Your parents were good people and I have no doubt you will make them proud."

Keone, already drunk, had been glaring at those who had come to pay their respects to the late Keono and Listani Minet. So many people had come and gone that Leon had hardly remembered who he had seen. After a while, their faces started blurring due to the constant tear-wiping of the young boy. Neighbors, friends, and even strangers had offered Leon their condolences, yet it had made no difference to him. It wouldn't bring his parents back to him.

Although the funeral wasn't lavish, several prominent members of the court and those from other countries had been in attendance. His father had always befriended his customers near and far. They would tell stories and jokes about Keono to lighten the mood but the peaceful face that everyone saw in the coffin was a lie.

When a royal carriage had brought Keono's body to his residence, he had seen what everyone at the funeral never did. The blood that had soaked through his clothes around his torso was still damp. Although the royal flag had wrapped him tightly to signify his honor, it could not contain the gruesome horror that had happened. The story young Leon was told by his grief-stricken grandfather was that his parents were robbed on a trip to deliver precious timepieces. His father had not survived the attack and his mother had never been found was presumed to be dead for the blood on his father's clothes were most likely from another as well. All Leon knew for certain was that someone had stabbed his father for whatever reason and his parents were no longer with him. From now on it would be him and his grandfather. The years passed and the memory of what his father had looked like had faded. Those who did remember his father, always talked about how Leon's looks and mannerisms were exactly like that of Keono. For a while, he had always resented people telling him such things. Now that his father was gone, Keone was forced to look upon Leon, reminding him of his long-lost son. It was not until a few years later when Keone had thanked Leon for keeping the memory of his father alive. Leon's burden that he had thought he was carrying was now gone and he started holding pride in the similarities he shared with his late father. The funeral, the blood-stained clothes, and the mourning eyes would always be in the back of Leon's mind whether he allowed the memories to be there or not.

Leon woke up suddenly with a jerk of his leg. The night was still and his chamber fire was slowly dying out. His attempted nap had turned into a deep sleep, taking him far into the middle of the night. There was a frightening stillness in the castle with creaking of the windows from a slight breeze. The fire cast shadows onto the uniform brick walls reminding him that this castle was his home now. The colors of the fine silks and painted walls had faded and the darkness had left the room feeling cold and unhappy. He picked up the book that had fallen onto the floor. As he bent down trying to open his eyes to become fully awake, he saw it.

Minet.

Without hesitation, he ran to the small fire and lit his bedside candle. There was no mistake. His name was inside the book. If only he could read the page with ease. Letters started blurring and mimicking other letters. There was no spare wood for kindling the fire and his small candle flickered, making it harder to see. Quickly, Leon grabbed the book tightly and ran out of his room. His footsteps echoed down the hallway sending chills down his spine. He had never wandered these halls late at night when nobody was around. The few guards that patrolled looked at him inquisitively as he rushed past them. It was just that morning when Jooey had led him to a hallway with endless light. As he hurried through the corridors, he thought about what he had just seen. His name. It could have been a coincidence that he may have family in Moshny but he had never known any family to be outside of anywhere but Desial. As he approached the hidden door, he grasped the book ever so tightly.

Is this the reason she chose me to come with her? Did she know my name is in this book?

For once, answers seemed to be in his grasp. Answers that may lead to what Videre knew about his family.

Finding the door in the near pitch dark, he felt for the latch and slowly pulled it up as not to draw any attention. He quickly slipped inside making sure it latched quietly behind him. The torches lit as they had earlier that morning. He let out a deep breath. He knew that there was a chance that the torches wouldn't light for him. Leon started walking down the lit hallway cautiously as they lit one by one down the hallway.

The torches know where you intend to go.

The torches illuminated a path that turned into another hallway a few paces down. As Leon turned the corner, he started picking up his pace. He had figured that he would sit in the hallway for the light but he realized that the hallways were leading him down a certain path. The hallways were chilling when he was by himself. He went up and down stairs and turned corners just as he had done earlier, but he seemed to be going in a different direction than before, but then again, it was to tell. The torches stopped at a large door just like all the others. Voices could be heard just on the other side. He held his ear to the door but it was so muffled that there was no point in trying. Leon held his breath as he pushed open the heavy door.

All eyes stared at him and there was dead silence. Among the figures was Jooey, Kolono, Ezrai, Videre, and someone he had not yet met. Jooey burst out in laughter and Kolono followed.

The room was brightly lit with torches similar to that of the hallway. Shelves lined the wall with books, trinkets, vials, and boxes. A large dog lay peacefully on the floor with his eyes wide open, measuring up Leon but too lazy to investigate further. An enormous hide rug lay on the floor between two large tables with maps and books sprawled across them. Leon could not explain the specific feeling that had crept up into him while he stood at the door in this particular room. There was a whispering within the walls telling him that he belonged here.

"Welcome, lad," Jooey said as he poured Leon a cup from a pungent-smelling pitcher.

The room was unnaturally silent as the cup started filling. Jooey was smiling as if he was trying to contain laughter.

"Ciansta," said Jooey as he topped off Leon's cup.

"Ciansta," they all chimed in while holding their drinks up. Even Videre and the unknown man participated.

"Ciansta," Leon said, forcing a smile.

Still confused by where he had ended up, he took a drink along with the others. Jooey had started chugging the rest of the liquid that was in the pitcher. The drink did not burn like alcohol as he had suspected but a sweet nectar dripped down his throat. The unknown man handed Jooey a small coin while shaking his head.

"Malaki," he said as he stepped forward and bowed. "It is an honor to meet you. I have heard of your talents. Such is expected of a Minet. Jooey said you would find yourself wandering in here sometime soon. I, naturally, had to bet against him," he said in a defeated tone. "Nonetheless, I'm hoping we will be able to talk more on our journey to Moshny," he smiled and started gulping down his drink.

"I'm pleased you've found yourself here, Leon," Videre said quietly. Her expression was friendly but Leon could tell she was not as pleased as she had said. "Since you have found your way by the torches, it must be fated that you came here tonight," she said as she glanced at the book in his arms. "I trust you have found something of interest about our new journey?"

"Yes," Leon said frankly as he opened the book to the page that he had discovered earlier.

Looking up at the others in the room, it seemed as if they were young children waiting for their mother to read a bedtime story. He looked down and started reading the excerpt aloud.

In the year VL 2025, King Lonie of Desial had charged Polentio Minet with creating timepieces for those of royalty to unite the new leaders of Aleria. King Lonie gave presents of goodwill and fortune among them in hopes of forging agreements in keeping a peaceful continent. The Zaro of Moshny of the time was Peter. Peter gladly accepted the timepiece but from misfortune, Peter had become gravely ill and had died within a few months. It was later deemed that the timepiece that was made for him contained a poison. The leaders of Moshny tried to destroy the timepiece but an unseen barrier had protected the artifact. The elders voted to bury the timepiece in a sacred location calling it "The Shore of Death" and had banned citizens from coming within one hundred paces of the artifact. The citizens called for Minet's head but he disappeared shortly after he had given Zaro Peter the timepiece and was never heard from his family again.

The next paragraph started with the Zaro's successor, Alexander. Leon closed the book slowly.

Had his ancestor murdered a king? Had he done it under King Lonie's orders or did he do it himself?

As Leon looked up, he was surprised to see the look on everyone's face. They seemed unaffected by what he had just revealed.

They already knew.

"Leon. There has been nowhere on this entire continent that has not been touched by treachery."

Videre motioned for Leon to stand at one of the tables as Jooey poured him another glass of what was definitely alcohol this time.

"We are gathered here tonight in memory of lost friends and family, for tonight is the anniversary of the start of Les Nettoyer. I'm sure you have heard of it, but the whole truth is something that cannot be taught in schools. The truth must stay hidden, like that story that you read about Polentio Minet. Your ancestor did not kill the Zaro on purpose by giving him that timepiece. In fact, Polentio became sick himself of the same disease that killed the Zaro. Should King Lonie had known that the materials used to make that timepiece were dangerous, he would have never charged Minet to make it. It was a simple mistake, but the people of Moshny will never know the whole truth and never will."

"Do you know the whole truth about Polentio and Les Nettoyer?" asked Leon inquisitively, trying to hold down the strong concoction he just sipped from his cup.

"I do know the whole truth about Les Nettoyer, and so does everyone here. I do not keep secrets from my handmen. I picked them to be of my service for very specific reasons. I give them all my trust in keeping the knowledge bestowed upon me as I will do with you. It may take some time, but you'll know as much as we all do someday." Videre took a paper from the table. "As for Polentio and the artifact, I don't know every-thing, but enough. This is why we are going to Moshny."

Videre handed him the worn piece of paper with timepiece schematics on it. It looked like an ordinary timepiece at first but upon closer inspection, there was something inside of the timepiece. The label said *Curian*, something Leon was unfamil-iar with. It looked as if the Curian was hidden inside at first, but then Leon realized that the timepiece was actually being powered by the unknown substance.

"We are going to Moshny to find this timepiece," Videre said with a smile.

Her smile was nothing like what he had seen before. A cer-tain glow came about her face, as if finding this specific time-piece was a mission. Even so, there was nothing but worry in Leon's mind. This timepiece had made people sick enough to die and something kept it from being destroyed. This time-piece was buried so nobody would get sick from it, yet the queen wanted to dig it up.

"Why? This is a dangerous piece, your highness. Certainly, you don't mean to dig it up yourself?"

"That's exactly what we plan to do. We will dig it up and bring it with us. I have arranged to have a box made that can safely transport the piece back to Desial."

Videre came closer to Leon. He could hear her breathing and the smell of her familiar perfume.

"This is important to us, all of us," she said nodding to Ezrai. "One thing you must swear to do is never tell anyone about what I have told you and what I will tell you in the future."

Videre's expression had changed from glowing to dark. She was serious.

"I promise I will never tell anyone," Leon said genuinely.

He was a little disheartened by the thought of not being able to tell Jolon of his experiences, but from now on, he knew his loyalties lie with the queen and to this group. Videre stretched out her hand to a chair at a small table in front of the fireplace with two chairs on either side of a small table. He made himself comfortable as she sat down across from him. Videre sat back in her chair and took a deep breath. The others in the room were talking quietly amongst themselves. The rest of the room drifted away as Videre started to speak privately to Leon.

"King Lonie united all the kingdoms on the continent. There are still conflicts and hatred amongst the countries but before the unification, there was much war and unnecessary death. Do you know of the Viceroy?"

Leon recalled the time in school when he had first heard about the Viceroys. Children talked about the stories of the Viceroys coming to Aleria and would often role-play during breaks or after school.

"The Viceroys came down from the sky in the year 1991OL. Each of them brought their own religions, languages, customs, and technology to shape each of the countries on Aleria today. Of course, there were some exceptions. The country of Dunbar remained separated from the Alerian continent. Also, the island of Alflint lying to the Southwest of Aleria was untouched by the Viceroys as the people who inhabited the island were fierce and would fight off anyone they saw as a threat. Such tales are fantastic but not always straightforward."

Unfolding a map onto the table in between them, she pointed at a region located in the center of Aleria. "This is where the origins of Aleria began. From the earliest recorded history, there was an ancient race of people, the Kiadere. They originally lived in Woadland but ventured up into Dio Filorone as their population expanded. As time went on, written language was created and the Dio and Alerian Society were formed to help keep order to an expanding civilization. The Dio were those members who kept the traditions of the Kiadere and kept records of everything that happened. The Alerian Society were nobles chosen by the people in their ever-expanding society. They kept the peace and ruled over the people with a fair hand. There was one member who stood out amongst the rest in the Alerian society and was voted to become king."

"King Konea," Leon said quietly.

"Yes," Videre smiled, pleased that he knew at least a little bit of history. "King Konea was a strong and idealistic man. By the time King Konea had become king, the small towns grew into cities and more land was needed for the Kiadere. King Konea and Dio Cioto, sent out four groups of men to explore the land around them. They were ordered to draw maps of the land, record weather, draw pictures of plants and animals, and bring back samples of what might be suitable farmland. One thing they did not expect was to find so many other inhabitants on the continent. Thankfully, almost all of these tribes were mesmerized by the Kiadere scouts and welcomed them with open arms. Within a year, the expeditions had come back from their reports and many willing settlers had been sent out to these lands. Settlers were given extra items for gifts to the tribes they met along the way which paved the roads to successful trading posts and eventually, unification under the same language and Kiadere religion. Although there have been many small altercations, the people of Aleria had generally been at peace. Until the Viceroy came to Aleria."

Valeria looked somber as she took a drink and sighed. "The Viceroy were brought to the king's court here in Desial. They had so much knowledge that they were eventually sent to different parts of the continent to teach the people their ways. One thing the king did not realize was that these Viceroy were not of one mind like the Alerians. They all held different views, religions, languages, and skills. Little by little, the Viceroy changed the regions they were sent to. The Viceroy were not only knowledgeable but grew older than most Alerians. They were soon recognized as the gods that would lead them into a new age. Slowly, the different areas started thinking like their Viceroy leaders leading to separation. The King of Aleria tried to stop the regions from changing but it was too late. After a series of events and accidents involving the Kiadere, Les Nettoyer, the cleansing of the Kiadere started. Those of pure Kiadere blood were hunted down and executed. Those who fled the massacres were welcomed in a few places in the east including Desial. Then, Polonotadere started. The entire continent was at war. Almost every region participated in several battles, whether it be to destroy the Kiadere, help them, or to help themselves."

Videre had a sad look in her eyes as she continued, "Les Nettoyer should have never happened. It would have never happened if there were no Viceroy."

Videre pulled a book towards her and opened it to the first page. Inside was a loose paper with a drawing of a woman. She had long blonde hair and light skin similar to that of the Dunbari. Her portrait was faded but the expression on her face was full of sorrow.

"I'll explain more later but there was a machine built that would help keep the continent safe just in case. This diary left gives clues as to what the pieces are and how to retrieve them. We've recovered several pieces but we still have a few more to go."

"Why now though?" asked Leon.

The story that Videre recited was unimaginable to him, but at the same time, for whatever reason, he understood.

"I want to be prepared. There are rumblings in the dark from some of my spies. We will not be at peace forever and when the time comes, I need to be able to stop it. If it doesn't happen within my lifetime, I want the next generation to be able to stop whatever is coming."

"How exactly does this machine help stop a war?"

"That, I do not know, but if they knew hundreds of years ago, I have no doubt we will be able to figure it out now."

Leon felt unnaturally tired. He felt lightheaded thinking of all the different questions that he wanted to ask but his body felt too fatigued to even talk. The amount of knowledge Videre had about the past seemed unreal.

"This timepiece created by your ancestor is one of the pieces to the machine. Each part of this machine is mentioned with clues as to where they would be. The timepiece was easy to figure out because King Lonie wanted to make sure the pieces would last long enough for someone to put them back together."

"Hence the barrier," Leon sighed as his eyes started closing.

The other voices around the room started drifting as his eyes closed and there was a vision of snow flurries that he had not seen for a while.

Come.

This time, his dream was more vivid. Colors and details started appearing and the sound of his footsteps were clear. The wind howled through the trees and goosebumps covered his skin. Finally, the woman turned around.

Mom?

MUSIC TO MY EARS

"Should we have told him so soon?" Jooey asked as he was placing Leon carefully in his bed.

The sun was rising, creating vibrant streaks through the bedroom window as voices and footsteps started to pick up outside.

"I don't want to lie to Leon," Videre said as she stroked his hair. "I want to tell him as much as I can, especially since we may need him in Moshny. We need to include him in every-thing. Besides, he drank all of the kada juice. He'll be fine."

Jooey wasn't one to worry but sometimes he would wish the queen would listen to him more. She had a strong will and it was a habit to not change her mind. He recollected bring-ing her to the timemaker's shop. Even then, his conscience had told him that she should never go there to meet with any Minets. Persistence was a strength and yet a fault with his queen. As the years passed, she became more headstrong and persistent in her endeavors to where Jooey was afraid that she may eventually lose herself. The losses she had to endure over the years were unimaginable to him, but all he could do was stand by her side as her old self started to fade away.

"We have a long day ahead of us, My Queen," Jooey looked out the window as he saw a large gaudy carriage pull up.

He shuddered at the thought of who might be in it. Many royal members and high officials of the continent were scheduled to arrive today. They were to be given private cottages at Hollow Estate which were only used a handful of times a year and they expected to be entertained during the day before the festivities in the evening. Games, hunts, and tea times had all been set up by Valencia who was well-liked among everyone who was invited to attend.

Valeria was respected as well but had also driven fear into the hearts of many. She was in charge of the armies of Desial and was gifted at her role. Her generals were all personally trained under her, enlisting them as children from parents who did not know how to handle their child's aggressions or simply could not afford to take care of a new child. She had been praised for leading and training honorable Vipole from children who would have no homes otherwise. She had sent armies to different parts of the continent fighting off uprisings and barbarian attacks, which were not numerous but an annoyance. Over the several years of peace, however, Valeria and her Vipole had grown unsteady and fidgety with the lack of fighting. She and her army were found sparring through all hours of the day in their training grounds. Providing emergency supplies and security was not enough to satisfy their hunger for what they were born and trained to do.

In Jooey's opinion, Videre had the most important job out of either of her sisters. She was sent far and wide across the continent for the needs of her country. She had traveled to almost every corner of their world, brokering trade deals, negotiating, and keeping the peace. She had a stoic demeanor and used logic to appease the leaders of all the other countries. She knew everything about everyone she had encountered due to her use of spies. Her job was always behind closed doors and unknown to most of the world.

Jooey was appreciative to Videre for the opportunities she had given him but wished she would take small furloughs and delegate her many tasks to the handmen in her service. While she would share everything with her handmen, she was also persistent in doing things on her own. This next trip to Moshny could be accomplished with just a few of her handmen and she insisted on handling the matters of state and leaving for Moshny the next day. Jooey also knew that bringing Leon to the castle and enlisting him as a handman should prove nothing but problematic to Videre. There was too much in her past to let someone like Leon into their circle, yet like all of her other handmen, he knew what he must keep from Leon.

He followed Videre down the halls of the castle to her office. She was always reluctant to handle matters of the continent in her own space, yet a few times a year such as this, it was inevitable.

"I managed to be able to shorten the list to four people today," Videre said as she started writing a letter.

Something was bothering her. Jooey looked at the letter on the side of the desk. The seal was unmistakable. It was a broken seal of The Alerian Society.

"I'm going to need you to tell Ciano to keep an eye on Lostanzo. I don't need him anywhere near the festivities."

Her hands were fumbling while writing the letter as if she could not concentrate on her words. Jooey placed his hand on hers, as she let out a deep breath. He knew exactly what was wrong. She folded the letter and took out a special seal matching that of the broken seal that was already on her desk. After sealing the letter carefully, she handed it to Jooey.

"There was a carriage this morning in the front. Would you like me to find out who came so early?" Jooey asked, trying to be helpful.

"Yes, please. And thank you for everything you do," Videre said kindly.

Videre had always had trust in Jooey ever since she had found him in the Athenian prison. It seemed like a lifetime ago. As Jooey walked down the hall, he still felt conflicted on if he should confront Videre about her recent mannerisms or if he should just stay silently by her side and see how things play out. She had started lacking in grit and confidence. She was not the same person who had saved him from the gallows all those years ago. He owed her his life and had promised to her that he would be by her side for the rest of his life. In his eyes, he was more than a handman.

As Jooey was walking towards the entrance of the castle, he heard a familiar laugh. The high-pitched squealing belonged to Queen Hania of Korona. Sure enough, Jooey found the lean Queen Hania towering over one of the Vipole who was smiling uncomfortably. Her husband King Fryderyk was standing behind her looking as exhausted as ever. Such a long trip from Korona would no doubt be tiring but having to travel with such a talkative travel companion would certainly drain anyone. Fryderyk was a man of very few words and one of the only leaders that Jooey respected. Korona was inhabited by

the strangest creatures in the land, each with their own practices and systems. The rulers of Korona were nonetheless outsiders but had successfully integrated themselves and ruled
peacefully alongside all the natives. King Fryderyk belonged
to a line of Viceroy who held their own approach to the successful ruling of such an eccentric island.

"King Fryderyk, Queen Hania, welcome back to Desial,"
Jooey said as he bowed down to a pair that was as large as him.

"I have a meeting with Queen Videre and my wife would
like to walk through the garden," said Fryderyk quietly.

Although most people wished to bask in Valencia's beautiful garden on the castle grounds, Jooey knew very well what
King Fryderyk had meant. Malaki had always admired the
plants of Korona and Videre had introduced Queen Hania to
him quite some time ago. Like Malaki, she was also an extraordinary plantskeeper. Fascinated in plants and the art of
healing, over the years she had shared her knowledge and ob-
sessions with Malaki. Every time she came to visit, she would
bring seeds with her for him to plant at the Chapel of The
Alerian Society. Fryderyk was also glad there was someone
there that she could constantly talk to, as he preferred the
company of Videre more than anyone in Desial. Being from
Korona, he had little to do with the affairs of the mainland and
welcomed the talks he had with Videre to converse on what
had been happening on the continent.

As Fryderyk and Jooey glided through the great halls of Desial Castle, Jooey had noticed that Fryderyk was tense. The
expression on his face was grim. King Fryderyk was a quiet fellow but it was odd that his face gave him away. Jooey opened
the doors to Videre's office as Fryderyk humbly thanked Jooey
with a nod.

"Queen Videre," he said as he rushed in and bowed. "I have come early to tell you of urgent news."

Usually, he was friendly and chipper with Videre but not today. Today, he took a more serious tone.

"You have been my friend for many years, too many to count," the king said as he sat down looking drained. "I fear that we will be tossed once again in a world from which we have so desperately tried to exterminate. Almost all of the members of the Koronian Council have heard rumblings and seen signs of this. We must hold a session."

Jooey was afraid of what this could mean. Sessions were only held during emergencies and the King of Korona was not faint of heart.

"You don't have to explain yourself," said Videre, pulling out a piece of paper and a pen.

Videre trusted Fryderyk the most out of any other leader in the country. She had placed spies at every court or ranking position except for at his court. Although the trust and friendship was mutual, they had maintained the facade of neutrality in public to discourage any unfriendly reactions from any other people of power.

"We will hold a session today if that is what you wish," she said as she handed the king the piece of paper and pen.

Jooey peeked at the names King Fryderyk was writing down. These were to be the fated people to be invited to the session for tonight. The only people who were to be invited were those who were called upon by the one who had called for the special session and by Videre. The list was short, meaning Fryderyk had little trust in making his information known. He handed Videre his list and after a glance, she handed it to Jooey.

Jooey knew exactly what he had to do with the list, he bowed and left out of the door in a hurry while stuffing the paper into his pocket. This was no easy job, but he was more than appreciative to be a part of plans such as this. He had access to everything and anything he needed to protect the continent from itself. Dangers lurked around every corner as if it were the destiny of Aleria to be destroyed by unseen forces.

"Jooey!" yelled a familiar voice from behind.

I don't really need this right now.

"Leon, I'm in a hurry," he paused. "Actually, I want you to join me as part of your handman duties.

I must include Leon.

"What are we doing?" Leon asked enthusiastically.

"We're going to make some arrangements for tonight's festivities. There is a young lady in town we must go visit. A very beautiful and charming young lady with an extraordinary talent and we are in need of her services tonight."

I must be careful with what I share with him.

As Jooey and Leon walked through the winding roads of Vici, Jooey felt as if he did not belong to this world as of late. He had not been to the town in days and yet, it felt like months. He was tempted to turn left and check up on the shop, but Leon's replacement, Janto, had told him not to worry. Keone was also helping out in the shop probably giving himself a small sense of purpose to his regularly boring days. They had stopped at a quaint little cottage at the end of a small road. Before Jooey got a chance to knock on the door, a young woman ran out and jumped up on Jooey to hug him.

"I've missed you, Jooey. Mother never lets me do anything."

"Well, I have some good news then, Fiora. Queen Videre has asked you to use their talents at the festivities tonight."

The girl smiled. She was breathtaking every time Jooey laid eyes on her. Her brown curls accentuated her face. Her dark eyes were soft and friendly.

"I would absolutely love to go. Equinox is my favorite holiday," Fiora said as her eyes lit up.

"That's what you say about all holidays. I'm sure the Queen will be pleased. As always, she will pick the perfect dress for you. I must go now, but I will see you tonight, my angel," said Jooey as he kissed her hand.

Fiora curtsied. Her and Jooey's gaze were so inseparable that they had ignored Leon the entire time. After another quick hug, Jooey turned back to the castle. Jooey quickly paced back up the street with Leon trailing right behind him.

"So yesterday I had fallen asleep in that room."

Jooey chuckled, "You were snoring too."

"Well I had this dream," said Leon, embarrassed, "It's actually a dream that I've had many nights. I don't know if it was the drinks that you gave me, but yesterday I saw it even clearer than ever."

Jooey stopped and turned to Leon, "Not here lad, you must tell the Queen. Tell her of any dreams of yours in private."

Jooey started his large strides to the castle and even faster this time. There was an awkward silence until they had reached Videre's office. He swung open the doors revealing a queen sitting in her chair obviously consumed in her own thoughts.

"I have talked to Fiora, she is able to attend tonight. However, there may be another matter. Tell her, lad," he jabbed his elbow into Leon.

A confused Leon sat in the chair across from Videre. Jooey leaned against her desk, waiting to hear his story.

"Well, I guess it all started several years ago. I have the same dream maybe every few days. Sometimes it's a little different but usually, it's the same thing over and over again. Last night it was more vivid than what I had ever seen."

"Tell me about this dream," said Videre intently.

"Well I'm with a woman and she's leading me through a forest of Desiali trees. It's winter and we pass by these stone monuments. She wants to show me something but it's always blurry so I don't really know what I'm looking at."

"What did you see last night?"

"Well the woman leading me was my mother. I know it sounds crazy because I hadn't seen her since I was a child, but I know it was her."

"Thank you for telling me," said Videre, as her worried expression advanced even further. "Please find Kolono. He will help you get ready for the festivities tonight."

She had her usual forced smile as if she was almost in pain faking it. Leon quickly got up and bowed as he rushed off to find Kolono. Jooey quickly took his spot across from Videre.

"Do you think it's her?" Jooey asked, "Leon doesn't know anything right?"

"I don't know. Keone is supposed to take it to his grave. Something is happening, Jooey. Fryderyk is worried and according to Malaki, so is Hania. Now, this? Promise me, you will protect him."

She looked at Jooey showing a vulnerability that he had rarely seen from her, but Jooey could not lie.

"You are my first priority My Queen, but when I know you are safe and sound, I will protect him too," Jooey reassured her.

I hope it will never come to that.

As the day went by, numerous carriages in all shapes, sizes, and colors arrived at the Desiali castle. One by one, the elite of Aleria came spilling out of the lavishly adorned carriages waiting to have servants unpack their luggage for those planning to stay at the Hollow Estate. Jolon was waiting for a particular man named Lord Licono, a wealthy man from Konis who, like Fryderyk, had been a friend and ally to the native people Neighboring lands. Jooey wasn't surprised to see Licono's name on Fryderyk's list. There was a certain tension in the air as Jooey would greet old acquaintances and the prominent members of Aleria but nothing prepared Jooey for the people he dreaded to see the most in the world, Ewan and Fyrgus Dubh. His heart started beating faster and a wave of rage started mounting as he saw the carriage that bore the flag of a yellow lion.

"Sevete, I know you can handle it from here," he said as he turned to go back inside.

Sevete nodded. As the head handman to Queen Valencia, he knew exactly why Jooey had to leave.

Later that evening in the Great Hall, tables were being filled by men and women in lavish outfits as if to show higher status to all the attendees. Roasted meats and fresh fruit sprawled across the tables in delicate designs. Patrons were chatting away and laughing with the people whom they had been thoughtfully seated next to. Finding his seat was easy for it had always been in the same place for years except for this year, there was an addition next to him. Jooey smiled thinking how interesting that a Minet would be sitting next to him but the smile quickly faded when out of the corner of his eye he saw the Dubhs. He glanced at Videre. She was glaring at them uncomfortably. It was not only from Videre but her two sisters as well. He could see the tightening in Valeria's jaw. He quickly got up and stood in front of them, breaking their line of sight to the king of Athena.

"I would like the first dance m'lady," he said as he stretched out his hand toward Valeria.

With a laugh, she threw her napkin to the ground and threw herself onto Jooey's arms. At once, the music started playing and within a few seconds, the serious faces at the table turned into joyous expressions. Jooey and Valeria were quite a scene to look at. Jooey with a kind soul had the strength to snap a man in half was throwing around Valeria who was significantly smaller but could also disable several men in seconds.

When the music stopped, Valencia stood up from her seat, and within seconds all eyes were on her.

"Welcome, citizens of Aleria. I am glad that we are able to assemble peacefully yet again on this important holiday. We have been blessed with many crops this year, enough for a year surplus and aid to the good people of Zwill. Before we get into our usual drunken festivities, let's take a calming few minutes with our talented royal musician."

She outstretched her hand to the corner of the room where Fiora, in a beautiful silver dress, started playing the harp. As everyone turned their heads to watch her, Jooey stared at Videre, who stared right back at him. He looked deep into her eyes trying to figure out what she might be thinking. During the first few moments of the song, he was sure not to break contact with her. After they were sure that Fiora's song had done its work, one by one, Jooey and Videre touched some of the patrons' temples starting with Valencia and Valeria. The melodic song drifted smoothly as everyone was seemingly in a trance, still picking up glasses to drink from and slowly eating the dinner set before them. As Videre touched Fryderyk's face, Jooey looked over at Leon.

You too, lad.

EQUINOX

Watching Fiora pluck the strings was the most mesmerizing thing that Leon had ever seen. There was a delicate art in the way that she made the string vibrate and how the tune was making him feel light-headed and sleepy. Her brown curls were soft and accentuated her face even more. Her dress was flowing as if a breeze were affecting only her. The lights in the hall started dimming but the space around her was bright. Everyone else was fading away until it was just him and her in the Great Hall. Suddenly, Leon felt pressure on his temples and he was transported back to where he was before Fiora had started playing. Jooey pulled him up by the arm.

"Let's go, lad, we don't have all night."

Leon looked around at the rest of the attendees. Jolon was staring at Fiora while Leon was being dragged away. A handful of other people at the banquet were walking through the open doors while everyone else was seemingly in the same trance that Leon himself was in.

"What was that?" asked Leon as they walked quickly down the hall.

"Fiora has a great talent, you've witnessed that yourself. She'll probably be able to play for I'd say half an hour until she starts complaining about her fingers."

"So Fiora has magic?"

Jooey laughed, "Aye, something like that."

The scattered group walked down the hall toward the dining room. Ezrai and Malaki drifted toward Leon, Jooey, and Kolono.

"Do we know what this is about?" whispered Ezrai.

Jooey shook his head, "When Fryderyk called for the meeting this morning, he looked almost terrified."

"Hania is really worried too," added Malaki, as he looked around. "Why isn't she a part of this meeting?"

Jooey frowned, "You know her. If she were in attendance, it would probably send her into a panic."

After all of the attendees entered the dining room, Kolono quietly shut the door behind them and the people that had been called upon all respectively took a seat around the dinner table. Leon only recognized the three queens and Videre's handmen who did not have seats but were standing against the walls as if to form a barrier. Leon stood next to Jooey who was blocking the entrance next to Kolono. When everyone was well situated, Videre stood up.

"This session has been called upon by King Fryderyk. As always, we do not have much time," said Videre then extended a hand toward Fryderyk, who then stood up.

"Good Evening. I have called this session in regards to serious rumblings of which I have heard throughout the forests of Korona. The Koronian Council have spoken of an unnamed group, prying into our affairs with spies and sabotaging daily operations. The Silics of Korona have also discovered many plants that have been harvested in the Forbidden Forest. These plants are considered very dangerous in capable hands."

"So you called a meeting because of plants," scoffed a white-haired woman.

"The Silics and Jaborskis have also tallied up missing members of our society totaling up to twenty-eight. They have mostly been young ones."

Fryderyk's eyes filled with tears.

"I have also heard rumblings within our country and in Alflint," said a blond-haired dark man. "There have been plundered trade routes and stolen food. This is not the work of mere thieves. We have placed security along our borders. Even wagons sent at night and along small paths get ambushed yet the decoys are always left untouched."

"Do you think you have a spy among your trade stations?" asked Videre.

"I am certain of it. Usually, it is a matter to be handled on our own but if Korona has trouble with spies and sabotage, I fear it may not be a coincidence. It may be best to work collectively to perhaps gain more information."

A small woman stood up and cleared her throat, "The Alerian Blood Clan."

The group looked confused as some of them muttered the name, trying to recall if they had heard it before.

"Would you mind being more specific, Ana?" asked Valeria.

"The Alerian Blood Clan," she repeated. "My men intercepted a letter that looked suspicious. It was written in the Olde language, but it talked of the operations of The Alerian Blood Clan."

"Why has this not been brought to our attention," roared Valeria with a fit of remarkable anger that Leon had never seen before.

"We did not know if this was relevant but it did talk about....children and plants. I am truly sorry Queen Valeria. You must know we get many suspicious letters every week. It would be chaos if we followed every lead from every letter we read."

"What made this letter suspicious in the first place?" asked Valencia in a calming voice touching Valeria's forearm.

"It was sent by a really ragged looking zanianbird that looked as if it had a hole in its wing. I personally had seen it many times and well, it piqued my interest."

"It cannot be a coincidence if it mentions plants and children, especially written in the Olde Language. It would be quite difficult to decipher for most people," said Ezrai as he gazed at Anabar who looked down, trying to break eye-contact.

"We will do what it takes to investigate this threat," said Valencia. "I ask that all of you take the necessary precautions and investigate in your own area as well. We also need to do this privately. We do not know if we can trust the other leaders in this matter. All reports should be directed to Anabar and let us use the regional scribes for this task. We must return now and please be careful."

Valencia bowed as the others stood up. As members of the meeting approached the door, Kolono raised his hand, while in somewhat of a trance. A gust of wind blew across the room and Kolono lowered his hand. Kolono and Jooey slowly opened the doors and they briskly walked back in the direction of the Great Hall, whispering to each other about their plans for this new threat. They slipped into the Great

Hall where Fiora was still playing and everyone was seated where Leon and the rest of the meeting members had left them. As the participants who returned situated themselves, Videre nodded to Fiora and the melody ended abruptly. Valencia stood up and started clapping, prompting the other meeting members to clap as well. Within seconds, everyone in the Great Hall had started clapping and talking amongst one another as if half an hour of their lives hadn't just passed by. Jooey looked at Leon and smiled.

"That's how we do things around here, lad. King Fryderyk," Jooey motioned to the large man who had spoken first in their meeting. "He is the king of Korona. His Viceroy ancestors wished to be far from the other Viceroy and found themselves on the island of Korona. Most people haven't been to Korona but everyone knows there are some strange people and creatures there."

"What kind of creatures?"

"People who are basically half tree and half human, people who have horns on their heads and even fairies," Jooey laughed. "You'll have to see them with your own eyes to believe it. The Viceroy who ruled there are well known for keeping the peace among the different creatures that live there. They have created a system where each group gets their own voice and makes rules collectively."

"So King Fryderyk doesn't have all the power?"

"No. In fact, his main role is to settle arguments, but the Queens of Desial hold him in high regard. He is very intelligent and well mannered unlike most other rulers on the continent," he said as he glared at an old man sitting on the other side of the hall. "Queen Hania is his wife sitting next to him. She is a lover of strange creatures and was excited to marry

Fryderyk partially because she would be able to live amongst them. She's a prolific plantskeeper and treats Malaki like her own son. She always comes bearing seeds from Korona as gifts and every time she visits, they always record the progress of the Koronian plants and how they fare in our own climate. She can also talk your ear off, which is why Ezrai avoids talking to her. That man," Jooey motioned to the blond-haired man who had talked about the trade routes, "That is Valencia's brother in law."

Leon was in shock. How could he not have known that Valencia was married? Although he had been enlightened in the past few days, he had this sinking feeling that he had no idea what he was doing here and why Videre had brought him to the castle. He started doubting that Videre would follow through and tell him everything she knew.

"Valencia is married?"

Jooey laughed, "Yes, to the charming young advisor to the king of Zwill. He should be here by the end of tonight, I believe. We received a zanianbird this morning informing us that his carriage had broken down on the way here. We rarely see him, but there are rumors that he is going to be living here in the near future and act as an ambassador. He is definitely quite the character and I'm sure he'll make quite a presence in the Desial."

"So why did Valencia marry an advisor and not a king or prince? Isn't that usually how it works?"

Jooey laughed, "Lad, you got so many questions," then he leaned in and whispered, "That's something we have to talk about later. Anyways, the one right there," he said, pointing at the one who had talked about intercepting the letter, "Her name is Anabar. She resides in Woadland. She may be small but she used to be a fighter for a group of rebels. The rebels had good intentions; typical robbing the rich and giving to the poor. After things started getting sour with their group, she defected and pleaded for forgiveness from Valeria herself. Valeria, being the kind of person she is, decided that she would forgive Anabar if she were a worthy opponent. So naturally, that day, they sparred in the courtyard. Anabar was bested but I guess Valeria was impressed enough to pardon her. Over the years, Anabar has proved her loyalty by quashing rebellions. She is an important asset for our current situation."

"Who is that?" asked Leon discreetly pointing to the old man that Jooey was staring at earlier.

Jooey let out a deep breath while he looked as if he were trying to compose himself.

"That's King Ewan Dubh of Athena and sitting next to him is his brother, Fyrgus. It's best you don't talk to them, now that I think about it."

"I can tell you and the queens dislike them."

Jooey laughed as if a dark cloud had disappeared.

"Dislike is such a kind word, lad. What they have done to my queen and Calan is unforgivable, may he rest in peace."

"Who is Calan?"

"Calan is, or was, King Ewan's son. He would have made a fine king that one. I'm sorry but some things must not be said in public. We will get a chance to talk about, well, everything."

As time flew by, Leon had seen more this night than possibly in his whole life. The dresses that most of the women were filled with intricate designs and enough jewels to fill Mrs. Potter's shop. Men were dancing elegantly which is something that Leon was never privy to, as the men in the city usually danced when they were drunk and were far less graceful.

Then, it hit Leon. He was in the presence of the most powerful people in the world. Politics in Vici was discouraged as people went on living their lives without meeting anyone in actual power, yet here he was. Leon was a fly on the wall and this was nothing but intriguing to him. Perhaps that's what made him a great timemaker. He wanted to know the inner workings of everything. He wanted to know how strings were pulled and how everything interconnected. Jooey and Kolono were having the time of their lives, dancing with everyone they saw in sight. Suddenly, a familiar dress blocked his view of the dance floor. Fiora was standing in front of him with an outstretched hand and a bright smile.

"I would love to but I'm not that great," Leon said embarrassingly.

"Don't worry about it," she said as she circled around his table and forcefully pulled him out of the chair onto the dance floor.

They spun around and around gracefully. His feet moved as if he had been practicing for this day his whole life. Never in his life had he danced like this yet his feet seemed to know exactly what to do.

"This dance floor is magic," Fiora whispered and laughed.

A few weeks ago, Leon would have laughed at such absurdity but now he was questioning whether she was joking or if it was really magic. As her curls bounced with every step they took, he felt as if the world were slowing down. Maybe this was what he had experienced during her performance earlier. The colors started becoming more vivid and her dress was flowing ever so elegantly. He felt a hand on his shoulder and everything became normal again.

"I need to dance with this charming young man at least once tonight," Valeria said, smiling at Fiora.

"Of course, Queen Valeria," said Fiora, right before she was swept up by Jooey.

Leon's feet started moving with Valeria's. Valeria, one of Aleria's most talented warriors, was as graceful as all the other dancers. Her grip tightened around his hand as the music changed. She pulled him close enough so that he could feel her chest when she drew her deep breaths.

"My sister trusts you. I do not. Videre is blind to who you are and you must not take advantage of her. You have a great opportunity to set things right for your family's sake and I will be right here watching you. If you hurt her, I will not hesitate to hurt you."

She pulled back and smiled as if she didn't just threaten Leon, bowed, and started dancing with Jolon. Leon was shaken. She had mentioned his family and setting things right but he had no idea what she had meant. The bright and joyous celebrations had turned into a dark and dismal affair. He made his way up to the queens' table and bowed to Videre who hadn't danced at all.

"I'm feeling rather tired. I think I must call it a night."

"I hope you had fun tonight and learned some things of value. We will talk more on our trip," she smiled at Leon, but was visibly distracted and worried.

Leon knew why she looked so gloomy. There was a threat on the horizon. He knew her well enough by now to sense that she was already thinking of solutions or plans for the current problem. Leon said his goodbyes with nods to his colleagues before exiting out the large Great Hall doors. A few castle workers were wandering down the halls. Servers with empty food trays were leaving and servers with trays full of finger foods were entering the Great Hall.

"Tired of the festivities?"

Leon turned around as a black-haired man came out behind the shadows.

"Do I know you?"

"My name is Lostanzo," he said with a deep bow, "and you must be Leon Minet."

"You know who I am?"

"Of course, boy," his voice slithered as he got closer. "You look just like your father."

"Don't harass the boy," came another voice from behind him. "Ciano," the other man said with an outstretched hand.

As Leon shook his hand he noticed his eyes were so light, they were almost white. Ciano laughed.

"I'm not blind if that's what you're thinking. It just runs through my family. We are both handmen to Queen Videre. I suppose we are the last to meet you since we've been away on official business. We also didn't go to the ball because, well, Lostanzo is not very social if you haven't noticed and I'm tasked to keep an eye on him," he said, clearly annoyed that he had to babysit rather than to partake in the festivities.

"We are to go to Moshny in a few days. Are you coming as well?" asked Leon.

"Yes, we will be accompanying her highness. I hope to learn more about you during our travels."

Something about Ciano made him feel comfortable as if he was already friends with him. He had a friendly smile, but Lostanzo, made Leon feel unsteady as he received a deadly glare.

"So why exactly are you a handman, little Leon?" inquired Lostanzo.

"I'm not sure. She just chose me, I guess," Leon answered truthfully.

"There must be a reason though. Are you like your father?"

Ciano grabbed Lostanzo's arm, "Sorry Leon. Now you know why we couldn't go to the party. You must be tired and we have a long journey ahead of us. I would suggest you get as much rest as you can."

Ciano bowed slightly still gripping Lostanzo's arm and disappeared back into the darkness where they had appeared. As Leon started walking back to his chambers, he started thinking about the handmen in Videre's employ. They were definitely different from one another but he couldn't figure out what they all had in common. He could feel himself drawing closer to each and every one of them, even Lostanzo. He seemed to be in league with them even though he had just met them. Leon also couldn't get over what had happened with Fiora. She had everyone under some sort of spell, even Leon. He kept thinking about the meeting that took place right in the middle of a festival and Valeria's threats. Leon had had so many unnerving thoughts in the last few days but tonight was so bizarre that it had left Leon unsettled.

I may not even be able to sleep.

LADY KAYLE

"We will leave during supper," said Videre intensely.

Her plans were always to be on schedule. Whenever things did not go as planned, Videre was not one to be trifled with. Her handmen understood this all too well.

"I trust Ciano filled you in with what happened during the session," said Videre to Lostanzo.

"Yeah, but I'm still upset I wasn't allowed to go to the party and give Ewan Dubh a piece of my mind," said Lostanzo disappointedly. "Did you tell the boy everything? It seems to me, he doesn't have a full understanding of why he's here with us."

Lostanzo was never one to shy away from the tough and uneasy questions. In fact, Lostanzo seemed all too happy to watch someone squirm from being uncomfortable.

"Leon knows what he needs to know for the time being. There was a time when none of you knew who you were until I found you. Leon is the same. We need to give him time to figure out who he is."

"And what about who his father was," asked Ciano, taking Lostanzo's side.

Videre glared at the two of them and puffed, "There will be a time and place for that. We must focus on making sure he finds himself first."

Suddenly, the doors to the dining room opened. Leon walked in, stunned to see all of Videre's handmen gathered in one room.

"Please," Videre motioned to an empty chair with food and drink already set in front of it.

As Leon sat comfortably in his chair with the aroma of fresh food before him, Videre started talking about the upcoming trip to Moshny. A look of excitement saturated her face. There was a bright cheeriness in her voice accompanied with a serious resonance.

"We will leave during supper when we can go unnoticed. We don't need any unwanted attention. If anyone asks, even my sisters, we are going to Moshny to visit Seymon, which is technically true anyway. I've also decided that because of our new found information, we will all be going as a group."

"I'm guessing since we're trying to avoid people, we will be staying out in the wilderness?" shuttered Ezrai.

"Unfortunate," teased Jooey with a chuckle.

Ezrai was comfortable around his books in the library. In fact, despite his natural dark complexion, his skin tone had gotten lighter over the years from his dismay for being outdoors.

"I'll protect you," Kolono said as he slapped Ezrai's small frame a bit too hard.

"I hope I don't have to remind you about not telling anyone outside of this room of what all goes on here," Videre said as she glared at Leon with even more seriousness.

"You have my word," Leon said with a little bow of his head.

Lostanzo laughed and Ciano hit him in the chest. Poor Ciano was always trying to keep Lostanzo in line, however, it seemed as though Lostanzo liked the attention. Although fully matured, Videre sometimes felt as if she was their mother. Most of the handmen she had chosen, were orphans such as Leon. Videre had always had a hand in their chosen path in life. Most everyone who knew about the handmen she picked would always wonder if she had always chosen the broken or lost men. She had never been overly strict with them but would make her displeasure known whenever they had disobeyed in any way. In the end, she always knew they would be loyal as if there was a spell binding them to her.

Videre took one last sip and stood up as the rest of the table followed suit.

"Prepare your bags. We meet right before dusk at the stables. ONE bag per person," Videre stressed as she glared at Kolono.

"He has issues with weapons," whispered Jooey to Leon.

Without another word, Videre left the table with Malaki and Ezrai right behind her.

As the doors slammed shut, everyone sat back down and Lostanzo leaned back in his chair. He smiled at Leon as if he were a cat ready to pounce on an unsuspecting mouse.

"Have you read up on your trip?"

"I have a little," answered Leon as if he was being investigated.

"So you know of Polentio?"

"I know he made the timepiece for the King of Moshny"

"The Zaro of Moshny," Lostanzo corrected almost as if he were annoyed at Leon. "You should very well at least learn some of the words in the country you're going to visit. Even though a king and the Zaro are no different, one must know to call the King of Moshny, Zaro, especially if they find out you're a relative of Polentio." Lostanzo's annoyance all of a sudden turned to a worrisome gaze, "That's something that you may not want to happen actually."

Just a moment ago, Leon had felt that Lostanzo was giving him a hard time, but it seemed as though he was now trying to help Leon, confusing him on where they stood with each other. A long silence overtook the hall. The castle workers' feet could be heard outside of the doors as the handmen were left eating quietly. It was eerie to Leon as he was used to the constant chatter of Videre's handmen. There was a silent chill in the air until a dark, handsome man stormed through the doors. He had a beaming smile that looked genuine to the fullest. His clothes were made of fine cloth and his small, but muscular physique could hardly go unnoticed.

"Good morning, friends," he exclaimed as he sat down in Videre's chair.

The man started grabbing the uneaten food off of Ezrai and Malaki's plates and stockpiling it on top of Videre's plate. He looked up with his light brown eyes at Leon.

"Ah, Leon! Valencia had spoken of you," he said as he started stuffing his mouth with fresh fruits.

Leon felt uncomfortable that this unknown man had heard about him, which was becoming a common occurrence now.

"Kinobi is Valencia's husband," said Jooey appearing to be entertained by watching Kinobi eat. "I'm a bit confused why you're eating in our dining room and not of your wife's."

After a few mouthfuls, Kinobi drank Videre's leftover coffee and leaned back comfortably in the chair.

"Sevete has this weird thing called 'making sure his queen eats the healthiest possible food' and it makes me sick," he said as pointed at Jooey's bacon, "That's why I come to this dining room for breakfast. I also hate going to Valeria's dining room because they're a bunch of savages."

He sighed and looked out the window as if something were on his mind yet he did not speak.

"Did you get here this morning?" asked Kolono.

"No, I got here late last night. I was awake all night and haven't eaten yet," he said as he winked at Lostanzo.

Lostanzo shifted in his chair uncomfortably as Jooey and Kolono snickered.

"How is it down there in the south?" asked Ciano.

The cheerful look on Kinobi's face disappeared.

"I heard all of you were present for last night's meeting. I decided that I need to be here to support Valencia in any way possible if things turn out as bad as it may seem. There's a hidden force somewhere, I can feel it. Videre will figure it out soon I'm sure of it."

The tone of his voice was hopeful as if he knew that Videre could stop any threat that may come. He started eating again as Ciano sighed deeply.

"We don't want another Polonotadere."

"Woah, slow down Ciano," Jooey said concerningly. "Polonotadere will never happen again."

At that moment, one of the doors swung open. Sevete and Jolon with a look of excitement on their faces were grinning from ear to ear.

"My Lord, you have been summoned to a duel by her highness, Queen Valeria," Jolon said with great enthusiasm.

All eyes were on Kinobi. He paused and seemed to contemplate the demand.

"He can't possibly duel Valeria. She'd destroy him," whispered Leon to Jooey.

"Tell my lady that I will duel her if she beats me in chess," he said with a large grin.

The excitement disappeared from Sevete and Jolon's faces. Leon figured Valeria would probably have beaten Kinobi in a fight but it was apparent that Valeria had enough common sense to choose her battles. As the disappointed handmen closed the doors behind them, Kinobi continued their previous conversation.

"Polonotadere will most likely never happen again, but I'm afraid this may be as destructive if we do not act quickly. We have kept the peace for so long that people have forgotten our core values."

At this point, Leon was confused. Polonotadere was taught in school, but only briefly. So briefly, in fact, that all Leon knew was that it was a war that happened long ago. Nobody seemed to recognize that Leon did not quite understand how serious these threats could be. Kinobi continued on about bandits, mysterious letters, and missing children. There was a seriousness in their conversation that Leon didn't completely understand. After a while, a large demeaning cook had chased off the group in preparation for lunch placements.

"Get your stuff ready," said Ciano to Leon as they walked down the halls of the castle. "And remember, we have a one bag limit."

Ciano walked off with Lostanzo, both of them obviously concerned and most likely whispering to each other about what they had just heard. Questions raced through Leon's mind as he walked to his room. Every question was a piece of the timepiece, he just didn't know how all the answers fit with each other. He still had not finished the book of Moshny and was itching to learn more.

Since Leon was to leave on a long journey, he started working on the timepiece that sat on his desk since the day before. Removing some pieces and replacing them was muscle memory to him. He did so carefully, at to not to disturb any of the other pieces. He had gotten into a routine where Janto would come at night to deliver any orders or requested pieces from the shop and Leon would send a messenger when the pieces were finished. He quickly packaged up the finished timepiece and took it to a messenger to deliver to Janto.

When he had come back to his room, he started packing his things into a bag. Not even halfway through, he realized that he didn't know what to bring. He had been provided many new clothes to be worn for all different occasions. Once, long ago, he had traveled to Reino. Reino was a large country right next to Desial but the trip to Moshny would take at least four times longer. If they were traveling on horseback, it would take at least a week he thought, as he tried to recall a map of Aleria. Little by little, he started filling up his bag until it was nearly bursting.

He looked at the timepiece that he had just completed on his work desk. He didn't want to admit to himself that he had not really missed being in the shop fixing timepieces. He was comfortable here in the castle and had already mentally prepared himself for being in this position for at least the next few years. He had several hours of reading to do until he would have to leave for the stables. As he made himself comfortable in his bed with the book in hand, he caught a glimpse of the city outside. This was the city he was born in and he had rarely stepped outside of its borders. A part of him was excited to travel to a foreign land, but he was still wary of what was out in the different corners of the world. He opened his book from where he left off before he had fallen asleep.

Moshny is famed for holding The Great Games of Aleria in the northern part of the country. The weather in the northern part of Moshny stays at a comfortable constant throughout the year with an extraordinary abundance of sunny days. Lake Nodio, is a famed vacation destination where members of high classes and royalty often spend time shopping for luxuries and staying at expensive cottages. Peasants and lower class people are not allowed to live on the Island of Lake Nodio and resort to living in Nodia which surrounds the lake.

Leon put the book down and grabbed his notebook and pen off of his nightstand. He decided to write down everything that intrigued him just in case he needed to reference it later on. He scribbled down a few notes and started reading again.

The Stromy is the largest forest in Moshny. Some tribal villages from before the Olde Language Era remain inside the Stromy. With the Alerian Tribal Pact (Kianomoso) of OL 120, Moshny has limited the amount of people who can live in The

Stromy to preserve the indigenous ways of life. After a founda-tion of trust was built when Kianomoso was made, the indige-nous tribes of Stromy started trading regularly with the people of Aleria, and slowly integrated within certain societies in Moshny.

Leon was a little overwhelmed. He had heard of the Alerian Tribal Pact but he didn't know that it had been so long ago. He scribbled down the word 'Kianomoso'. He remembered read-ing and learning about The Stromy but hadn't ever heard of indigenous tribes living inside the forest. He had heard of the indigenous tribes in Desial but have never laid eyes on any of them. Keone had always told him stories of different tribes of Alflint and Korona looking completely different than the Ale-rians to which he was accustomed. He wondered if the tribal people of Moshny were also different or looked similar.

The largest, most relevant tribe is Chukrofi (Ciokolopi in Olde Language). Located at the mouth of The Stromy River, they were discovered by the first search party of the Dio and The Alerian Society. Cipoloki, the leader of the eastern search team, took to them quickly due to their friendly nature and similar sound-ing name. The Chukrofi had welcomed the foreigners with open arms and readily traded with the Kiadere. They had also taught the Kiadere to harvest and plant the seeds that grew native in Moshny. The Kiadere gladly accepted any knowledge from the Chukrofi however the climate in the native land of the Kiadere did not support most of the plants from Moshny.

Leon started writing in his notebook.
Kiadere, "The People of Magic".

The Kiadere were deeply embedded in Alerian history. The most powerful and influential people in all of Aleria. The only places that the Kiadere didn't touch were Korona, Dunbar, and Alflint. The fall of the Kiadere was confusing as there wasn't much information about them. The only thing Leon knew was there was some sort of argument leading to a world war between the Viceroy and the Kiadere, Polonotadere. The Viceroy, knowledgeable in many different ways, had effectively defeated the Kiadere. There had been rumors that there were survivors forced into hiding. What they looked like, or where they had hidden was completely unknown to Leon. Whether they had escaped to nearby islands or fled past the Dunbari Range to the frigid land of Dunbar was a mystery.

He was a little perplexed on how to pronounce the Chukrofi. Since the Olde Language had been dissolved, effectively replaced by the Viceroy language and regional Viceroy languages, translations of ancient languages were confusing. Although the Olde Language was slightly similar to other neighboring territories such as Dunbar and Alflint, he wondered if the Olde Language was similar to those of the tribes also. He thumbed through the other pages with more details about the tribes of Moshny. Most seemed small and unimportant. He scribbled some more in his notebook before continuing on.

The land of Moshny is covered in lush vegetation, as the weather throughout the country is agreeable and not harsh unlike many of the other countries. With an exception to the Zankanto, the country is mostly flat land with a few rolling hills. Fruit trees grow naturally in the Zakatino providing a significant amount of the country's food and income. Residents are limited to a basket of fruit a day per family and the rules are strictly enforced. A special government unit run by Moshny, cares for these natural trees and monitors the daily limit.

Leon scribbled in his notebook again. A compass rose this time. Zankanto for the West, Zamano for the East, and Zakatino for the South. He left the North blank. The days of learning the Olde Language had long gone, leaving only fragments in memory. The Olde Language was still prevalent in names, certain cities, and regions, but the spoken language was probably extinct.

Leon's stomach growled. He had not eaten lunch and was getting hungry again. Since they were to leave during supper, he figured that he should probably eat before his trip. He wasn't sure if he had read enough to satisfy Videre and Ezrai's instructions. He shoved the book with his pen and notebook into his already overwhelmed bag.

As he walked down the corridors to the staff dining hall, Leon thought of all the words he knew in the Olde Language. He wished he had kept all of his notes from primary schooling because he now knew what importance it may have actually held. Leon was quite certain that Videre and the other handmen knew the Olde Language more than he did. They obviously knew more about other topics as well such as Polonotadere and even his ancestor, Polentio Minet. He thought of Lostanzo's warning earlier.

Maybe I should come up with a different family name, just in case.

"Leon!" shouted a familiar voice. "Where are you going?" asked Jolon as he caught up to Leon.

"I'm going to go eat some lunch."

It was nice to have a friend in the castle. Although Leon didn't sign up for being a handman, he was glad to be there. However, Jolon looked a little tired and not so bright-eyed as of late.

"Why do you look so tired?" asked Leon worryingly.

Jolon laughed, "I'm always up late in the night and always training. I'm hoping to become one of Valeria's Vipole."

Although his eyes had dark circles underneath he had a cheerful look on his face. Jolon certainly had been training. Leon could see that he had been getting bigger. His veins had started bulging just like Vipole. There were also several visible bruises and cuts on his arms.

"I feel like I was born to be Vipole, and Valeria certainly has noticed me," he said proudly.

"Do you like being a handman to Valeria," asked Leon, hoping to gain insight on what it might be like to be a handman to someone else.

"I love it, but it's hard work. I'm tired all the time but I can feel myself getting stronger. Valeria is...," he let out a long whistle then whispered, "kind of crazy but in a great way."

"How is working for Videre?"

Leon so desperately wanted to tell Jolon everything about what had been happening but he knew everything that had happened was to be kept a secret. He looked at his best friend who looked like he hadn't slept in days and felt embarrassed. Being Videre's handman had been easy. He had kept up his work from the shop and hadn't been requested to do anything but to read and pack a bag.

"It's been fine. We plan things and..."

Leon couldn't think of anything he could tell Jolon.

"That's fine," Jolon laughed, "I've been sworn to secrecy as well."

Leon had felt relieved that Jolon understood. Maybe when he returned from his trip to Moshny, he could tell Jolon about it since the trip probably wouldn't be a secret anymore. As they reached the dining hall, Leon had an uneasy feeling while looking around at all the other handmen and staff. Everyone was sworn to secrecy to the outside world, but now Leon understood that they were sworn to secrecy to their respected queens. Looking at Jaora eating quietly across the room, Leon wondered if she too, had secrets to keep. The regular staff wasn't assigned to a queen, but they all had specific duties and could be called upon by anyone of status in the castle. Jolon and Leon grabbed a dinner plate with stacks of delicacies and started moving towards Jaora.

"Hi boys," she said in a cheerful manner as the two men sat down.

"This BOY is about to be promoted to Vipole," laughed Jolon.

"I will make sure and tell our parents how successful you've become," teased Jaora.

"Have you made any friends?" asked Leon.

He had noticed that Jaora was always sitting by herself and worried about her transition to this life.

"I have actually," she said in a friendly manner. "Lostanzo is extremely kind and I would call him a friend."

"Okay? Do you have any female friends?" asked Jolon protectively.

"I wouldn't necessarily call them friends. I would say more like co-workers."

She leaned over the table, looked around, and whispered, "Valencia put me in charge of some of the girls who have been here for a few years and I don't think they like it."

Leon felt bad for Jaora. She had always been one to avoid conflict. Putting her in charge of other staff members seemed as if there may be a target on her back. Also, Lostanzo befriending Jaora was odd to him. There was no doubt that she could attract any kind of man. She had beautiful long blonde hair and eyes that changed anywhere from green to hazel to blue. Her silent and docile demeanor was an invitation for anyone to take advantage of her. Leon decided to keep an eye on Lostanzo for the time being.

"I think they'll warm up to you," said Leon reassuringly. "We just need to get into a routine."

"Thank you, Leon. That settles my nerves a bit," Jaora said while blowing on her hot tea.

The rest of the conversations consisted of the new and exciting events, as well as gossip from around the castle. Time flew by and Leon felt comfortable joking and conversing with Jolon and Jaora as if their lives hadn't changed dramatically. After a while, Leon glanced out the window. He had nearly forgotten that he had to meet everyone soon. He quickly got up and made up an excuse for a meeting during supper. Running down the halls, he seemed like an idiot. He was never late. Running into his room, he grabbed his bag and ran out the door. Right outside the door, he stopped and looked at his bag.

Someone went through my bag.

He felt his notebook deep within his bag under his clothes. Something told him to go back and search his room but he did not need to be late. Terrified, he continued running toward the stables.

Who would search my room and why?

Finally, after almost knocking over a statue, he turned the corner to the stables, where everyone was waiting for him. He panted hard as Jooey and Kolono laughed softly.

"Just in time, lad," whispered Jooey. "I don't know if you remember but this was supposed to be secret. Ya can't very well keep it a secret when you're running like a madman."

Jooey was right and everyone had a chuckle, which made Leon feel better.

Nobody's angry at me.

"Someone went through my bag," Leon blurted.

"Good," said Videre. "I told Lostanzo and Ciano to sort through your things to make sure you've packed well. They replaced a couple of clothes with a coat. You'll need it."

It got cool at night but not nearly enough to wear a coat.

Malaki came from the shadows with a horse in hand. Seven other horses followed behind him. One horse, he recognized right away. It was the horse that Videre was riding on in the parade. Looking at it up close, he felt a sense of calm but also was confused. He could have sworn he saw wings on her horse before.

Noticing the confused look on his face, Kolono whispered to him.

"That's Lady Italych. I'm guessing you've already seen her. We have to hide the wings in public."

The other horses looked similar but in all different colors. They were slightly different in size too which made sense when Jooey and Kolono swung their bags over the two largest horses. For a second, Leon had felt bad for Jooey's horse but then had noticed the sheer bulk of its barrel and flank and figured the horse did not have a hard time lugging Jooey around.

Ciano grabbed the reins of two horses and passed one to Leon. Everyone looked at Leon as he grabbed the reins and started touching his horse. She was gentle and passive. As he stared into her eyes, it seemed as if she stared right back and for a moment he could feel a connection. Ciano took Leon's bag and fastened it to the saddle.

"We don't have all day," said Videre impatiently as she swung on top of her horse.

"Lady Kayle is her name," admired Ciano. "I knew she would take to you quickly."

When the group finished tying their luggage to the saddles, they headed out toward the setting sun. The air was crisp and small pink and purple wispy clouds scattered the horizon. Instead of following the main roads leading through Vici, they had traveled out toward the opposite direction through a series of tunnels and small paths through patches of trees. Along with her handmen, Videre was wearing plain clothing as to not attract any attention. The only thing that Leon figured would catch a person's eye were their horses. The elegance of Leon's horse was unimaginable. It truly was a royally bred horse, unlike the ones that he had always seen in Vici. The saddle was made of fine materials and more comfortable than most dining chairs he had sat on. Lady Kayle's mane was silky like the other horses and the shine from their coats reflected in the disappearing sunlight. She was a brilliant white with large brown spots. He looked around him at his companions, riding in perfect unison. They were lined up in pairs with Videre and Kolono in the front. Leon was riding next to Ezrai, who was on a dark and small-framed horse. Behind them were Malaki and Ciano, and in the back rode Jooey and Lostanzo. The group rode in silence until the sun's rays had disappeared completely. The clouds that were once wisps had turned into rolling storm clouds. In a few minutes, heavy fog covered the ground. Videre came to a halt and dropped off of her horse as the rest of the group followed suit.

"Put on your coat," said Ciano as he unpacked his bag.

Without hesitation, Leon pulled the coat out of his bag. Ezrai leaned over and unbuckled Leon's saddle. A large gust nearly toppled Leon as dust got into his eyes. The fog and darkness hid what had happened but after a few moments of adjusting his eyes on the horses, Leon finally saw it. All the horses stretched out their wings nearly hitting their riders as everyone started re-buckling the saddles. An awestruck Leon stood still as Ezrai smiled and put Leon's saddle back to its original position. Leon could hear faint chuckles from his companions but he didn't care. When Leon had laid eyes on Videre during the Grand Festival, he admired the beauty and magnificence of her horse with wings. Never in his life would he think that he would be riding his very own winged horse. Lost in his own thoughts, Lady Kayle nudged Leon with her nose and looked at him as if beckoning him to climb back on. He quickly mounted her as he felt awkward that there were large wings now almost touching his legs. Ezrai smiled as he leaned over Leon and buckled a loose strap around his lap.

"Hold on," he said loudly as the wings of their horses started beating.

As Lady Kayle lifted gracefully off the ground, Leon's stomach dropped. The fog swirled as the horses, in unison, ascended higher and higher until they were all above the dark clouds. The air was chilly and wet as the wings started beating slower. The atmosphere was peaceful and quiet as the clouds below glistened in the moonlight. The elegance of the ride would have put Leon to sleep if his heart wasn't beating so hard from the splendor of the current setting. Stories of magic and childhood fairytales were nothing compared to experiencing the real thing.

He remembered his grandfather reading a story in the timepiece shop about senrima, the horses who could fly a thousand miles. All of a sudden, he again flashed back to his shop. He felt comfortable there before being a handman. It was his livelihood, his family trade, and what he did best. The thoughts made him self-doubt whether he really did belong there. Maybe where he really belonged was by Videre's side along with the men that she had chosen to be her handmen. The castle never felt uncomfortable to him. In fact, he felt more at home in his large room in the castle now than he did in his small childhood room that had been a comfort for his entire life.

His stomach started turning again. The senrima had started their descent into the haziness below. They had dove down so fast that Leon now understood why Ezrai had strapped him in earlier. He felt himself gripping the reins even harder as he was hardly touching the saddle. While diving through the thick clouds, Leon felt as if he had an odd smile on his face. He was uncomfortable, but at the same time, he was thrilled about the adventure that had unfolded. Diving faster and faster through the clouds, the haziness started fading and he started making out the scenery below. To his left, were the shimmering waves of the ocean and to his right, crops and small trees littered the landscape. Leon marveled at this picturesque setting as the senrima started leveling out and slowing their descent. Smoothly, they started gliding and within moments, they had touched the ground silently as to not disturb the night. Right when they landed, they started trotting again as if nothing had happened. The saddle, still strapped to Lady Kayle's frame, exposed her lustrous wings. As they neared a forest, the horses slowed their pace. One by one, they strolled down a small path within the dense trees until they came to a small clearing. A pit for fire was already set and the group started unpacking and taking saddles off the senrima without saying a word. Without tying up the senrima, the creatures all made their way to the outer edges of the circle and laid down around the group as if they were forming a ring of protection. Without much conversation, everyone started pitching their tents and unwrapping blankets from the saddle-bags that were already equipped on their senrima coming out of the stables. Ciano helped Leon with his tent, as Leon was quite noticeably struggling.

"Videre always makes sure we have all we need on our trips. This is your first trip of many more to come. We don't always travel with senrima," Ciano looked at the senrima sleeping only a few paces away. "Unfortunately, we have to hide their true nature from the world."

Whispering to each other as to not disturb Videre who had already entered her tent, they said their goodnights and disappeared inside their own tents. As Leon made his way into his tent, he was surprised to find it quite roomy and comfortable. The ground seemed softer than what he had imagined when he wrapped up into his blanket. The events of the entire day had worn Leon so much that he instantly fell asleep.

MISS RAYNE

The sun had just come up and the leaves from the canopies scattered bits of sunlight throughout their camp. Videre was always the first one to wake as she had always been a light sleeper. Slowly, she crept out of her tent, as not to make a sound to wake anyone. She needed time alone here. As the leaves rustled in the wind, Lady Italych's eyes slowly opened and watched Videre tiptoe out of the clearing. Videre looked back and shook her head at Lady Italych who closed her eyes once again. There was a slight ocean breeze as there always had been in this forest. As she walked barefoot through the thick woods, she retraced her steps that she had taken so many times in the past. As she got closer to the noise, the wind started picking up and the smell became stronger. She was walking so fast that she felt as if she were almost running to the place that she had longed for the most. Her heartbeat rang through her chest as she finally arrived.

The waves of the ocean beat against the cliffs. Water sprayed, throwing glistening crystals high in the air. With the forest behind her and the sea in front, she wanted to meditate to prepare for what was coming. The air suddenly turned chilly and orange leaves whirled around her.

"You must be prepared," a figure said, coming out of the shadows in the forest.

"I don't even know what I need to be prepared for," she said without turning around. "All we have are whispers. King Fryderyk is scared and I've never seen him like that."

"If there is another Polonotadere, you know what you must do."

"Why do you think I'm going to Moshny? I've been preparing everything since you left."

"Good," he said quietly as his footsteps crept closer. "The Alerian Blood Clan is coming. Anabar and Fryderyk are in danger if anyone finds out that they have found anything. You must also keep all the leaders of the region close, especially the Dubhs."

Videre tried to touch his hand but there was only wind flowing through her fingers. A tear rolled down her cheek as she imagined his red hair and gleaming smile, details that had slightly faded from her memory. The air warmed as the green leaves swayed in the sun and as she could hear the crashing waters below.

"Your Majesty," called Jooey from afar, "We have to go."

She took a deep breath and wiped her tears before turning around. In his hand were her shoes, knowing very well she had snuck off without them. Videre smiled slightly at Jooey as if to show her appreciation for his caring demeanor.

"My lady, this is a nice place and all but," he paused, trying to be sensitive, "this is not a place where you should dwell. We all have a point where we have to move on."

Videre stared at Jooey with sad eyes. He knew exactly why she had come here and she knew he was right. She needed to focus.

The Alerian Blood Clan. Where have I heard that before?

To her sisters and to Anabar, it was a name that they had never heard before. It was understandable that they weren't as worried as Videre. When Videre was younger, she had spent many days in her room entertained by her books. As she started traveling around the continent with her father, she learned the way that her father had dealt with the leaders of other countries. Even at a young age, she had found out that trades and negotiations were better than bribery and manipulation, although they were never off the table. Her father had expected her to remember every name she came across. There was one place that her father had taken her that she would always find herself wandering back to for information and this specific place was now on her list of where to go after Moshny. She must find out more about The Alerian Blood Clan.

When Videre and Jooey had gotten back to camp, they found the rest of their group already up and strapping their bags onto their respective senrima. Kolono, being a fast worker had already finished his and was almost done with Videre's luggage. Knowing that they needed to leave soon, she looked back at the trail and wished she had just a little more time.

Two by two, the group started their journey again, with the saddles neatly tucking in their senrima's wings. Going downhill from the woods, they crossed a large river and in the distance, they could make out a marvelous estate.

"If only," Ezrai sighed.

"Maybe next time," Kolono laughed.

Ezrai turned to Leon who was riding next to him. "That's a Royal Chateau. This one is Reino Chafo Chateau. It takes many days for people to get from one country to another, even by carriage. These chateaus were made for people of importance to be able to stay during their long journey."

"The chateaus were made during my father's reign," added Videre. "He was irritated that face to face diplomacy between leaders was rare just because nobody had wanted to travel for so long for a meeting. The creation of the chateaus along major roads made it so the trip would be as comfortable as possible, therefore opening more personal communications between countries."

"Yes, there are dozens of Chateaus placed in convenient spots all around Aleria, such as this road that goes through Moshny AND Desial," Ezrai said in an annoying tone indicating that he was still upset about camping in the wilderness.

Everyone, even Videre laughed. She was always entertained by the quirkiness of her handmen. Each one had different talents and personalities. Ezrai, unlike most of her handmen had been with her for almost her whole reign. Like Videre, Ezrai had a passion for books and learning. His special talent was with his knowledge of history. This made him invaluable and almost even sacred in these times that the world now had been plunged into. If Ezrai had little knowledge on a topic that was relevant, Videre knew very well that within a week, he would be well versed and able to cite anything that may be helpful. Ezrai's family had always had a comfortable life working for The Vasili. Just as his father was the Vasili Historian, he was also destined to be one. At a young age, he was assigned to Videre as her father saw that she would make use of Ezrai, unlike her sisters.

She glared at Ezrai looking longingly at the chateau as it passed in the distance. Ezrai may have grown up with commodities and luxuries but this was a time where they had to be uncomfortable for the sake of the future of Aleria.

Riding on a path with a full view of the ocean, Videre could see faint landmasses in the distance. Rigid rocks in the ocean, barely big enough for a few trees created uneven ripples in the waves. Beyond the small islands lay larger islands with lush vegetation. Hikari, like Korona, was considered part of Aleria, yet strayed from the affairs of the mainland. Not much was known about Hikari on the mainland, as they were not open to many strangers.

The group continued to the south until they came to a bustling town called Ciolon's Point. The harbor was hosting several ships of many different sizes and colors. People from all different countries and lifestyles were scurrying through the streets in seemingly smooth conduct. Looking back, Videre saw the look on Leon's face. He looked delighted to see the spectacle before him. She had no doubt he had never seen so many different people all at once. Now it wasn't uncommon for citizens to go their whole lives living in the same house let alone stepping outside of their country. If only Videre could change the culture of the continent to be able to travel without fear of the unknown, but it was too late for her to change their mindset. What had been done in the Treaty of Aleria was already set and she wasn't particularly confident in changing the minds of the leaders to reverse it.

There was a loneliness in the air whenever she traveled by herself, which is why she always brought some of her handmen with her. Not only would Jooey insist that she kept a bodyguard with her at all times, but she actually enjoyed the company of her handmen. With the exception of Leon, all her handmen knew the truth. The truth of Aleria was difficult to keep, especially from her sisters. Her father had told her everything from such a young age and she had to shoulder the burden for so many years before bringing handmen into her service. Although it took many sessions and drinks of kada juice, she finally got to a point where they knew almost as much as she did. Unfortunately, some details had to be kept from Leon for the sake of his own safety and mental health.

Poor Leon was never supposed to be a handman but maybe it's destiny.

Reaching the outskirts of town, people stared at the magnificent horses that Videre and her handmen had strolled in on. Their coats were glossy and all of them started stepping in unison as if the senrima had made their own pact to show off to outsiders. Lady Italych certainly had a mind of her own and the others followed suit.

Although Videre knew that people had been staring at them, she was quite certain that nobody would recognize her with her hood pulled up in a drab-colored cloak. Passing through the city, she took in all of the sights and tried to recollect what had changed from the last time she was there. It had been almost a decade and things had certainly changed. Buildings had been replaced, roads had been repaved, and the crowd appeared more diverse. This time around, she clearly saw more Hikarians and Dunbari walking the streets of Ciolon's Point.

Ciolon's Point was named after Ciolon, a resident merchant of Reino, who was tired of going to certain cities to get his goods around the east side of Aleria. Establishing a trading post and harbor town in between Reino, Moshny, and Hikari, he was able to convince people to trade directly by centering the merchant meetings where it was easily accessible to all three countries. Establishing the harbor also brought more trade from Desial and eventually Dunbar. Inns and theaters were established on both sides of the cobblestone roads for housing and entertainment for the merchants who were weary from their travels. For the number of people in the city at any given time, it was relatively clean and peaceful. Ciolon, sick of the rowdy merchants he had met during his travels, had made sure there were some rules in place. The merchant community was so tight-knit that banning certain merchants who chose not to follow rules were easily enforced.

The hoofbeats of the senrima on the cobblestone roads clip-clopped in unison. On the horizon, a magnificent view of ships paraded the harbor. Flags from almost every country could be seen including the red and black raven of Dunbar and blue turtles of Alflint. Seagulls circled around the boats as men unloaded crates and barrels for trade. Pubs and restaurants were filled with merchants chatting away as Videre and her group headed to the outskirts of town. On a hill up an older road sat a large house with a tower next to it. As they reached closer, Videre saw a man peacefully sitting in a rocking chair on the porch. He nodded at the travelers and quietly went inside as they dismounted their horses. Videre gazed at the house in wonder. For so many years, it had stood here against all adversity looking exactly the same as she first saw it all those years ago.

"Welcome," shouted a woman from another room as the group had entered the house.

The house was filled with shelves of all kinds of trinkets that always gave Videre a sense of comfort. Miss Rayne Kaner was a great collector and keeper of all things and materials.

Walking along the beach with Videre, Rayne would pick up rocks and tell the young princess all about what type of rock she was holding and how it was made.

Back then, Miss Rayne had such great curly brown locks that all the women in town were jealous, leading them to create rumors about wig-wearing and even ridiculous hair magic. Her thick eyelashes and high cheekbones certainly caught the attention of many eastern Alerian men. Videre was mesmerized by Miss Rayne but not in the way that others were. The knowledge that Miss Rayne had in her head was intriguing to Videre. She spoke with such elegance when explaining the world to Videre as if she knew everything about all that surrounded them. One summer, Videre's father had sent her to Miss Rayne's house to learn everything she could. Books had been a favorite out of all of Videre's past times, but at Miss Rayne's house, she was taught almost entirely by Miss Rayne's lectures and explanations.

Visiting a few times as an adult, Miss Rayne's home was where Videre had first met Lostanzo. Lostanzo, being a nephew of Miss Rayne's, had run away from his home and made his way to Ciolon's Point to become a student of Miss Rayne. He had a burning desire to learn more about the world and his family. From the first time Videre had laid eyes on the quiet boy, she knew that he had what it took to be one of her handmen. From their very first conversation, she had realized that there was a deeper part of him that nobody would be able to bring out, other than her. Without telling him her true identity, she and Miss Rayne had convinced him to go to Desial with her to start a new job, one that would be fulfilling his destiny.

Lostanzo looked around the room with a gigantic smile, one that Videre wished that she would see more often. Miss Rayne, walking out of her kitchen, took one look at Lostanzo and started tearing up. She ran up and hugged him, which was a side of Miss Rayne that Videre had loved the most. Almost all the professors and teachers that Videre's father had hired for his daughters were cold and drab but Miss Rayne was different. She was full of life, excitement, and joy. Videre would laugh at the thought that she and Lostanzo could ever be related. Her hair had turned gray and the wrinkles on her face became clearer to see but she never lost her liveliness or energy. Constricting Lostanzo tightly, she looked at Videre and nodded.

"Thank you for bringing me this boy," she said as Lostanzo blushed. "It has been so long and he's one of the only ones left in our family."

Shortly after Lostanzo had run away from home, his family had died from the plague, extending his five-year handman position into a voluntary lifelong job. Lostanzo's family was of great wealth and had left much to him, including the Rayne Mansion, but Lostanzo never wished to go back to live there. Valuables were kept in a safe place and the house was looked after. Even though he had many offers for the purchase of his childhood home, he had always refused. Over the years, they had stayed in the Rayne Mansion when traveling, using it as their private chateau.

"I have the piece you requested," Miss Rayne said as smiled and led the group to the next room.

She pointed to a wooden box that was set on her dining table. There was nothing special about this box that anyone could see, but Videre knew. In all of Miss Rayne's genius, this was no ordinary box. Miss Rayne handed Videre and Lostanzo each a necklace with a key on the end. As Lostanzo draped his necklace around his neck as Videre took her key and unlocked the box. All of her handmen inched closer to see what was in it. She slowly lifted the lid and to everyone's surprise, the box was bare.

"Perfect," she said quietly with a smile on her face. "How much do I owe you?"

"Nothing, my girl," Miss Rayne said in a serious tone. "I want to do as much as I can to help you and my country."

Miss Rayne stared at Leon, visibly making him uncomfortable. Videre's heart started pounding and she made sure to take deep breaths to not show any weakness.

"You're not Keono," Miss Rayne said as if she remembered that he was gone.

"That's his son, Leon," chimed in Lostanzo, as if he already knew what she was going to say.

"The resemblance is outstanding," she said as she inched closer to inspect him.

Leon, still uncomfortable, held his ground.

"Perhaps, you will be just like him," she said with a smile as she started backing off. "He was an intelligent boy. I will be excited to see you in the years to come."

"Thank you, ma'am. I don't know much about my father though, he died when I was very young."

Videre and the rest of the people in the house went silent. Her heart started pounding and her mind went to deep unknowns that she had wished would stay hidden.

"His passing will not be forgotten in our community boy," she said as she stepped forward and grabbed his hands. "And what fine hands you have, you must make fine timepieces also."

"I've been told by my grandfather that they've surpassed my fathers," Leon said jokingly, although it was true.

"Keone! What a fine man! Tell me, is your grandfather still of this world?"

"Yes, healthy as a horse. He still gets rowdy."

Miss Rayne let go of Leon's hands and ran out of the room. With a confused look on his face, Leon caught Videre's eye.

He has questions.

How stupid Videre felt for bringing Leon to Miss Rayne's home. Of course, she would recognize that face. His face was almost an exact replica of his father's. Her hand was shaking and she started feeling lightheaded. She would have to explain it all to Miss Rayne in private. She hadn't told Miss Rayne everything that had happened the past several years, but she must have heard about everything that had happened. Miss Rayne came back with cookies and looked at Videre inquisitively as if she were thinking the same thing.

"Please, come sit for a while," she said, leading them into another room with several sofas and chairs. Miss Rayne had always been one to meddle in affairs and hold secret meetings. The fact that Ciolon's Point was on the border of Moshny and Reino and was a declared independent city, such meetings continued unnoticed by both countries. Although not illegal, the Alerian Guard still had enough power to be able to interrupt such meetings and charge the members with absurd crimes.

"I have arranged for you to meet a young man by the name of Jakoba at the edge of the Stromy. From there, he can lead you to The Shore of Death."

"Is there anywhere specific we need to meet him?" inquired Videre.

"Jakoba will find you," she said with a big smile. "He is the best tracker I've ever seen; of course, other than you," she said to Ciano.

"Have you heard of the Alerian Blood Clan?"

Miss Rayne's smile faded as Videre's tone became serious.

"I have, but I don't know much about them. I assume since you're asking, you'll be stopping in Hikari for more answers."

"Yes, I figured if I could find any information, it would be there."

Miss Rayne leaned in, "You need to be careful, my dear girl. From what I know, The Alerian Blood Clan has been around since the beginning of written history. If it's true that they've resurfaced, I'm scared of why. There must be some reason why they've come back and most likely have a plan in motion. What have you heard?"

"Fryderyk told us that there have been at least 28 missing children. I've also been told in private that many more have been missing all across Aleria by members of The Alerian Society. The Koronian Council has also noted many dangerous wild plants and herbs have been harvested in large quantities. Stolen goods and money missing from the treasuries in Konis and Zwill indicate that there are spies within the government. I have Anabar leading the investigation and she is in charge of hiring out other trusted investigators in all the regions. Kinobi..."

Miss Rayne raised an eyebrow. "Kinobi is trustworthy, but unreliable and inaccurate"

"Yes, he knows that it's not always accurate, but we don't have much to go on. Right now, he's keeping most of it from

Valencia. If Valencia finds out, she may tell Valeria, and we all know the kind of unpredictable things she does."

"Have you talked to the members of The Alerian Society?"

"I have reached out to a trusted few, mostly scribes. I sent a letter yesterday to The Dio but I have planned to go to Hikari after our trip to Moshny. I would like to keep the item here while we are there."

Miss Rayne had a large smile on her face. "I would absolutely love to babysit the item while you are gone."

Videre laughed, "I knew you'd like that. It'll only be for a day, maybe two.

"I'll also write some letters. I am intrigued and I'm quite certain you might need me."

Miss Rayne had always been self-confident in her many abilities and talents. Some might say she was even arrogant. She sipped her tea, almost looking as if she was royalty. Her mannerisms could rival that of nobles. How much Videre would love to have her at court as opposed to some of the others who were obligated to be there just because of their blood relations.

"Miss Rayne," chimed in Ezrai. "I would love for you to come to peruse through my library sometime."

Jooey started laughing as some of the others joined in.

"I would love to look through it, Ezrai," Miss Rayne said to a red-faced Ezrai. "It has been a good while since I've been to Vici. I have missed all of you."

"Aunt Rayne," said Lostanzo quietly. "Much has changed since we last saw you."

"Yes," she looked at Leon, "I am curious, but maybe another day. You all should probably get moving if you want to make it to The Stromy by nightfall."

While getting ready to leave, Videre put Lostanzo in charge of holding the wooden box crafted by Miss Rayne. Ordering all the handmen to prepare the senrima, she stayed behind for just a moment.

"That boy is Keono's son?"

"Yes"

"Keono and Listani, yes?"

"Yes," Videre answered annoyingly.

"My condolences, I heard about Calan not too long ago and I have been too preoccupied to come visit."

"Thank you," said Videre quietly.

"Things get better over time. Life hasn't necessarily been easy for you but you have made the lives of this country infinitely better."

Miss Rayne always had a way with words. She was like a mother to Videre when she had nobody to lead her in the ways of womanhood. Her father knew exactly what he was doing when he had assigned her to Videre.

"Thank you for everything," said Videre with a tear in her eye. "I'll see you in a few days."

OLD SCARS, NEW SCARS

After a day of riding, nightfall was approaching as the group neared a forest which Leon assumed was The Stromy. The tree line was impressive as if it were a tight formation of soldiers going into battle. The dark trees sported higher branches than any tree that Leon had ever seen. His stomach growled as the only food they had eaten were snacks that they had brought for the trip and Miss Rayne's cookies.

Living at the castle has definitely spoiled me.

Leon wasn't necessarily poor growing up. His family had kept their business alive with diligence and hard work. He started contemplating his perception of The Vasili after staying out in the woods with Videre. He didn't know much about the other kings and queens but he was slowly starting to realize that Videre, even with her comforts within castle walls, had put herself in uncomfortable positions to make the continent run smoothly. This mission and everything that she had been planning could even save the world and nobody would ever know the hand she had in such matters. Even Valencia and Valeria had their own specialties and were keeping the country afloat. He had envied The Vasili before, but now he felt sorry for their troubles and understood that they deserved all they have.

Watching Videre in front of him, he daydreamed about what went through her mind. Her long brown hair hypnotized him as he tried thinking about the questions he needed answers to. He looked at Ezrai, who seemed to be noticeably more comfortable than he was the previous day. They rode in silence but what had really caught Leon's attention was the confidence on everyone's faces. They looked as if they knew exactly where they were going and what they were doing. Leon seemed to be the one who's only job was to follow their lead.

They're keeping secrets from me.

He had felt it from the very beginning but their meeting with Miss Rayne made it more evident. He could see that Videre was holding back information and that she was trying to limit her words in front of Leon. He always knew Lostanzo was keeping things from him but now he could tell that all the handmen knew things he didn't.

Leon was hopeful, but he knew that he may never really know everything that the other men knew. Although Videre had promised that one day, he would be on the same footing, he had no way of really knowing. They knew his father but he had no idea how or to what extent. The other handmen seemed to know his life story, yet he knew almost nothing about them. Even trying to guess their age was nearly impossible.

For them to know his father meant that they were probably adults when Leon was a child. Videre had a certain look on her face whenever his father or almost anything from the past was mentioned. It was also the same look she had when she looked at the Dubhs during the Equinox Festival. Joey had mentioned that they had done something to her but it still remained a mystery.

Such bureaucracies seemed trivial when he was living in Vici as an ordinary citizen but once he became handman to Videre, he had started worrying more and more about the other kingdoms and politics. Videre had her hand in everything, and for him to be one of her personal attendants, it was imperative that he knew everything he could to assist her.

As the sun started disappearing down into the horizon, it became harder to see what lay before them. They were nearing the towering trees of The Stromy and started trotting up the last hill before reaching the forest. The senrima seemed weary as they started nearing The Stromy. The whole time, they had traveled in unison but now the senrima were walking out of step and the tension was noticeably high. Their tails were swishing fiercely and they started squealing.

Leon glanced around as everyone in the group looked concerned as if this had never happened before. Ezrai was next to Leon trying to calm his senrima down with a fretful expression. With every second, Videre and the other handmen looked more panicked. Lady Kayle started spinning as if to search for which direction to run in. There was a terrible sound beneath their feet like the crackling of a large fire. The senrima were visibly in distress, trying to fly off with their saddles still strapping their wings to their body. As the senrima started running, Leon suddenly felt the same drop in his stomach as he did when flying with Lady Kayle.

He had been engulfed into certain darkness where he could only see whirls of dirt glimmering in the moonlight. Plunging into the darkness below, Leon heard a great snap that echoed all around him. The wind nearly knocked him off of Lady Kayle and her outstretched wings thrashed about. His grip on the reins tightened so much that his short fingernails had started digging into his palms. After a few more moments, her wings had stabilized right before landing mercilessly on the ground below. Leon was dazed and his heart was pounding sending sensations throughout his body. Taking a moment and loosening his grip, he slowly slid off of Lady Kayle's broken saddle who was panting from undue stress, he looked around him in confusion. His eyes started adjusting with the small amount of light being let in by a hole above him. It looked to be a large cave with several different tunnels leading to this one cavern. Still unable to see clearly from the dust, he could feel liquid pouring down his right side. Looking above him, he couldn't find a trace of stalactites but could hear dripping throughout the cave. Judging by the hole in the ceiling, he determined it wasn't nearly large enough for Lady Kayle to fly up and maneuver through with outstretched wings. Leon's ears started ringing as if it were a delayed reaction to the fall. Leon took a few deep breaths after coughing the dust out of his lungs.

As the dust settled, he noticed worn blankets and a rusted shovel lying on the ground.

This cave must have been used at some point by someone, which means there is an entrance at the end of one of these tunnels.

Leon thought to himself, yet it seemed as though someone was putting the thoughts in his head. His ears were still ringing as he tried to concentrate on a solution to his current situation.

You need to find a way out.

Adrenaline was pumping through his body, but instead of panicking, Leon was thinking calmly.

First, are you hurt?

Leon looked around his body before touching the moisture on his arm and on his side. He realized that blood was dripping down off of his fingertips. He took off his shirt and noticed a big gash on his shoulder.

Wrap it to stop the bleeding. The saddle should have something to help.

Leon grabbed the pack off of Lady Kayle's saddle and started rummaging through it. His eyes were quickly adjusting to the darkness, almost as if there was a light in the cave. Pulling out a scarf, he wrapped his shoulder while looking over Lady Kayle for any injuries that she may have sustained. As he was looking her over, he noticed that it wasn't only the moonlight aiding his vision, but it was Lady Kayle who was letting off the light. Her brilliant sheen had started glowing ever so lightly, enough to be able to see more clearly throughout the cavern.

With his wound tightly wrapped, Leon looked carefully around him. Five separate tunnels surrounded him, all of them looking nearly identical. Looking at the walls, some of the features of the cave looked as if it were dug and not natural. There were hints of paintings and writings on the walls that looked as if they had been there for centuries. As Leon took a closer look, he could tell that they were written in the Olde Language and the Viceroy Language but were so worn that he wasn't able to read any of it. The pictures looked familiar as if he had seen them before, but his current state contributed to his foggy mind.

Follow the moon.

Leon looked up, there was a streak of moonlight shining on the cave wall behind him. Looking forward, he grabbed Lady Kayle's reins and started trudging along cautiously. The echoes of the steps were frightening as Leon followed his instinct to keep going in the direction of the moon.

That's right. We were following the moon. Perhaps there's an exit in The Stromy and I can find my companions.

Leon's conscience seemed to have a mind of its own as if it knew better than him. Lady Kayle walking by his side felt comfortable and the way she walked reliably next to him made him feel safer. Looking around, he concluded that there definitely used to be people who used to dwell here for quite some time. There were elaborate and indecipherable drawings both painted and etched onto the dark walls. He passed bits and pieces of pottery and clothing inside the tunnel. He could hear wind either from the hole above where he had fallen through or perhaps from the end of a tunnel. As he kept walking, he started hearing something else other than their footsteps and the wind. A scurrying sound was coming closer and closer.

Is someone here? No. It's a rabbit. A rabbit? It is really a rabbit?

Leon felt like he was losing his mind. There was no time to argue with himself when something was coming right toward him. At the far end of the tunnel, he saw a small fleck in the darkness. With a similar glow to that of Lady Kayle, it came closer and closer but hardly grew in size. His first hunch was correct, with two long ears, he could make out the small figure. The white rabbit came closer and closer and stopped only a few paces away. The rabbit stood up on its hind legs with its nose twitching in the air staring directly at Leon. After a few moments, the rabbit turned and slowly started hopping back from where it had come.

Follow the rabbit.

Picking up his pace, Leon and Lady Kayle started following the small and ominous rabbit. Once in a while, it would turn and glance at the two followers and then would continue down the tunnel, as if to make sure that it was being followed. Leon kept trying to think of if he had ever encountered any bizarre situations since before becoming a handman. He was not one to admit that his life before this was boring, but compared to the last few days, he could confidently say that his previous life had been dull at best. Learning new things every day, he had seen so much and learned more than he ever thought he would in such a short amount of time. Even to be in such a large ancient cave system would have been unimaginable to him a mere week ago.

If only Videre would tell me more. She's hiding something from me. No. She's helping you. In time she'll trust you more.

Leon started wondering if the lack of air in the cave was making him hallucinate. His ears still had an ever so slight ring still and he was following a glowing rabbit with his glowing horse and kept arguing with himself. Perhaps he lost too much blood or hit his head during the fall. Then he saw it. Such a sight lay before his eyes and he let out a deep breath of relief. In front of him was not only a rabbit but a woman glowing in the moonlight.

Videre.

She smiled and stood patiently as Leon picked up his pace. Never had he been so happy to see his queen. Reaching the end of the tunnel, he noticed three other figures behind her; Ciano, a young boy, and an overly large dog. The hum in his head stopped and his mind became clear again. Sure enough, he had exited into a thick area of The Stromy. The trees were swaying in the wind as the rabbit stopped at the feet of the boy for just a moment before hopping off into the woods. The large wire-haired dog next to the boy stared at Leon as if it were waiting for him to talk.

"Very good," said Videre as she smiled at Leon and Lady Kayle. "We should get back to camp," she said after a quick turn.

It seemed as though Leon being in an unknown cave, had not phased Videre. Ciano looked at him and smiled as if he knew something that Leon hadn't. The young boy next to him followed Videre like a lost puppy. Walking quickly to keep up with Videre, Leon all of a sudden thought about his arm. It definitely needed tending as he felt warm blood starting to reach his fingertips again. As they arrived at the camp, not far from the exit of the cave, he saw a look of relief on Jooey's face that Leon had not seen in on Videre or Ciano's expression. In the background, he could hear chatter between Videre and the boy. The boy was clearly getting on her nerves as her face had a look of annoyance. In that moment Leon chuckled as the resemblance that the annoyed look on Videre's face to that of Valeria's was almost identical.

"Jakoba," Ciano whispered to Leon. "He's the one that Lady Rayne had sent to aid us. He desperately wants to become Videre's handman but she says he isn't old enough."

"He tries to negotiate more than the men of Konis," laughed Kolono.

"Most likely Videre will agree to him being a handman when he turns of age," chimed in Ezrai. "She is right about not letting him join so young. Especially if there is a threat on the horizon. All handmen are obligated to fight in any conflicts."

"Yes, but this lad is talented. He could be a great asset in a battle," said Jooey as he took a ladle full of soup from a communal stew pot. "It's not like it's uncommon for some handmen to join while they're still young."

"We shouldn't talk of battles," said Malaki softly as if he were remembering something. "Too much blood."

"Speaking of blood," Ciano motioned to Leon's arm.

Malaki quickly got up with an intense look on his face and ran to his tent to retrieve a small bag. In almost no time, Malaki had unwrapped Leon's makeshift bandage and started wiping the wound. Wincing at the stinging pain, Leon had determined that this wound was significantly bigger than he had previously thought. The blood had stopped dripping and started oozing out of the wound but after a little bit, Leon felt a little lightheaded. He struggled to stay awake as Malaki started pulling plants and vials out of his tiny bag. It seemed as though all the things Malaki had been pulling out of his bag couldn't possibly fit. Barking out commands to everyone, the whole camp seemed to move effortlessly to help with anything he needed. Malaki was always so mild-tempered that it had shocked Leon to see him so demanding. Fetching hot water, grinding up herbs, putting pressure on the wound was all smoothly run as if the group had been through this many times before. Even the young boy had started helping.

Time seemed to slow, as he watched every single person perform a duty. Everyone except for Videre. She had sat by Leon and held his hand. A sign of affection from Videre was rare to Leon, even to a handman. She rubbed Leon's hand while speaking jumbled words to Malaki. Malaki's response at first seemed as jumbled as Videre's words but Leon recognized the phonetics and sounds. Delving deep into his memory in his Olde Language class, he tried to make out the words but they had been speaking too quickly for him to understand.

I thought the Olde Language was dead.

Malaki forced a cup of tea into Leon's hands. "Drink"

The tea was sweet with a bitter aftertaste but Leon's reaction was not as bad as Videre's as she looked like she was going to regurgitate after even looking at the tea. After a few sips, Ezrai took the cup from Leon as Kolono forced Leon's arm to stretch. With a sharp needle and thread, Malaki swiftly started stitching Leon's wound. To Leon's surprise, it didn't hurt nearly as much as Malaki cleaning the wound. He watched as Malaki's fingers danced with the needle. In and out, the needle penetrated Leon's skin with ease and in just a few minutes, Malaki had finished sewing and washing the wound. Videre, who had been gripping Leon's other hand, had let go and let out a sigh of relief.

"We have a long day ahead of us tomorrow," she said quietly before turning to her tent.

Leon was not new to her apathetic tendencies. He had felt like these moments were the only moments where she actually had shown care towards him.

Jooey slapped Leon on the back and laughed. "Welcome to our club, lad. Now you got a nice little scar for the stories to tell the ladies."

The next hour consisted of his companions comparing scars accompanied by the stories of how they got them. Jooey and Kolono had a massive amount of scars that Leon had never noticed. Kolono's injuries ranged from a chicken attack to falling from a cliff.

"I have heard that her highness had a large scar on her stomach," blurted out Jakoba.

The whole group turned silent. The eeriness of the still night that only moments ago was cheery and uplifting, had hinted to Leon that Jakoba may have mentioned something that he shouldn't have.

"Queen Videre had many scars also, even that one on her stomach that you have mentioned," Malaki said quietly. "It's unfortunate that the wound never healed completely."

"May I ask what happened?" asked Jakoba, a little more carefully after reading the tone of the group.

"She was stabbed," said Lostanzo aggressively, "from someone who was banished. In my opinion, that person should have been removed from this world."

"Why wasn't he killed for stabbing the Queen," Leon asked.

Jooey let out an odd chuckle.

"Lad, the audacity of your question," Jooey continued to look cheerful.

"SHE was under a spell. That, combined with a crime of passion, Videre couldn't bring herself to make the order," said Lostanzo glaring at Jooey and Kolono.

"I'm sorry, I have no idea what makes this funny," said Leon.

"Don't mind them. They're immature," said Malaki with an annoyance that Leon had never seen from him before.

"It's just a weird coincidence," Jooey said in a more serious tone. "Videre was injured very badly. We all saw the damage it did. The worst injury I've ever seen. Malaki basically brought her back to life."

Although the air seemed a little lighter with Jooey and Kolono's little impulses, Leon could tell that the rest of the group had not completely moved on with the event. Maybe they were keeping the details from Jakoba but a part of him knew that they were being overly cautious with Leon as well. Leon looked over at Jakoba. A young boy with a dog that probably weighed more than him. He was perhaps an orphan too by looking at the raggedy clothes and dirty appearance as if he had lived in the wilderness for quite some time. Leon thirsted for more but he abhorred being rude.

Who was the one who stabbed her? Where is that person now? Who put her under a spell and why?

"You'll learn more in time," said Jooey as if he knew that Leon was thinking of questions that he so desperately wanted answers to.

It had been annoying Leon that they had been keeping secrets from him. He had been told to wait but he was running out of patience. He felt as if he were a child again just like when Keone would tell him that he would learn in time.

"My Queen is a very strong woman," said Malaki admirably, "But there have been many things that have happened to her in the past. I can't even imagine carrying all her burdens by herself. That's why we, as her handmen, have a very important job. While Valeria and Valencia's handmen run errands or are used for, well, despicable things, we support and help our country as much as we can. We are always there by her side without unwavering loyalty. We pledge our whole lives to Videre with very good reason. Each one of us is destined to be here with her, even you."

Leon thought of what his life would be like from now on. He knew most handmen stayed for five years, maybe more if they were allowed, but Videre's handmen went by different rules. These men had been with Videre for who knew how long. They have obviously been through a number of situations that Leon could never imagine. She was a queen, but to them, she was their world. They would sacrifice their lives for their queen, but for what, Leon didn't know. They were bonded to her, maybe even addicted. He had thought about what Videre had said to him in Malaki's garden. She had asked him to stay with her until her mission was finished but he was unsure of what the mission actually was or when it would end.

The air was chilled both by the weather and the mood of the handmen. Jakoba, Leon figured, was just as information-hungry as him. He could see Jakoba forcing himself not to ask more questions. Leon, however, figured that he would be around these handmen enough to slowly get more knowledge from them. He thought about how Malaki had talked about such dedication to Videre and how they were different than the other handmen.

"You said that they do despicable things," said Leon. "Valencia and Valeria's handmen."

Kolono, Lostanzo, and Jooey roared with laughter, while the others sighed as if they didn't want to discuss it.

"Perhaps you can ask your friend Jolon what Valeria makes him do," laughed Kolono.

Leon had never asked in detail what all Jolon was doing for Valeria but he also knew that he was sworn to secrecy as well. He had already seen that they had been running around errands for the queens and sparring on the training grounds. He always had a weird feeling about the type of person Valeria was and their laughter had almost confirmed Leon's perception of her. In a flash, he remembered what Videre had done for him that first day as a handman in the audience hall. She had told him that she picked him to save him from her sisters.

Perhaps she meant to save me from Valeria's indiscretions.

The moon was high in the sky and after a few passing yawns, the handmen started turning in for the night. Videre had been in her tent throughout the whole conversation but Leon wondered if she was awake and eavesdropping on what they had been saying about her. Slowly creeping to his tent that had already been set up, he was stopped in his tracks by Lostanzo's voice.

"I have been with her highness since I was an adolescent, even younger than you. I will tell you right now that all the handmen and I are sworn to protect her, even from you."

Leon was shocked at the tone in Lostanzo's voice as he sounded as if he was threatened.

"We're on the same team, Lostanzo."

"You think that way, but things happen. Things we cannot explain or understand. Feelings and allegiances change. I, for one, do not trust your family, which is why I can never trust you."

Leon sighed, "You always talk about my family as if we're cursed and I don't know why. I don't know much about my family and it seems like you all know more than me."

"Lostanzo, go to bed," said a quiet voice behind Leon.

Lostanzo immediately bowed, glared at Leon for a second, and angrily stomped to his tent.

"You must forgive Lostanzo. He has been with me for a very long time and has experienced too much of what I have. You'll gain his trust sooner or later"

"Lostanzo keeps talking about my family. I know it sounds ignorant but I wasn't told anything about my family as a boy. I hardly remember my parents, and the only grandparent I know is Keone. Jolon always talked about visiting his distant family members in all parts of Aleria and that's something I never had."

Videre sat down. She had a worried look on her face accompanied by bags under her eyes as if she hadn't slept in days. Leon had never seen her like this. Usually sitting straight and regal, she was hunched and weary sitting next to the campfire. Only a little bit ago, she looked fine, but he could see bags under her eyes and discoloration in her flesh. Leon sat close to her but far enough away to look at her bodily expressions. She looked at him with sad eyes.

"I lost something that day," she said as she lifted her night shirt slightly to reveal a large scar on her stomach. "It was no ordinary sword. It was a tainted sword. I could feel it deep down in my blood like poison was surging through my entire body. Malaki is an expert on poisons and said it was something that he had never seen before. After months of research, he finally found out what the poison was from. Queen Hania who is somewhat of a plant fanatic like Malaki had identified the plant that grew in Korona in a few patches around the island."

"So it's a poisonous plant? Why don't they just eradicate the plants?"

Videre laughed, "That's the thing. The plant is not poisonous but at the same time, it is. You see, Malaki started studying this plant and started injecting it into snakes, birds, cats, and other animals. The only animals that it affected were rats. After a while, we decided to test it on people. You'd be surprised at the number of people who are willing to test a poison in exchange for monetary compensation sent to their families. A few hundred people we tested a small amount on, not enough to seriously hurt them, but enough to see the effects. We concluded that the poison only worked on a few of the subjects, which means whoever had given the sword to the woman who stabbed me, knew that I would have a reaction to this poison."

"Who was it?" asked Leon inquisitively. "The person who stabbed you. Maybe you can trace the person who put her under a spell."

Leon," said Videre as if she were talking to a child, "This happened many years ago. My handmen have explored every angle to this problem and came up with nothing. All we found out was that the sword was made from ore in the heart of Aleria, the location of the start of our known civilization. The mine with this ore was closed hundreds of years ago, so it's an ancient sword but that's all we know."

Videre glanced at her saddle with a long sword hooked on the side.

"You kept the sword?"

Videre smiled, "It's actually a pretty nice sword and not too heavy, so I kept it despite the opinions of others."

Leon started understanding Videre's personality the more he talked to her. Although she kept a strong outward appearance, he could tell, especially during this moment, that she had endured much pain throughout her life. Now, he understood. Videre indeed would eventually tell him everything, she just needed time maybe not because she didn't trust him but because she had to be comfortable with telling him. His previous angle about getting information from Jooey was wrong.

"This poison, or should I say, these plants, are the ones that have been harvested in Korona."

"That's why Fryderyk was so worried. He knows about the poison."

"Yes. That is why we must step up our efforts in finding out what this Alerian Blood Clan is doing. I am assuming that they are behind these missing plants and in turn behind what happened to me."

Her eyes looked heavy as she smiled at Leon.

"I hope your wounds heal quickly," she said in a friendly tone.

Leon had nearly forgotten about his shoulder as he didn't feel any pain.

"Malaki is a great healer," she said as she stood up and smiled. "I owe him my life and now you owe him an arm."

Leon smiled as Videre walked to her tent. He looked up at the moon that was shining so brilliantly in the sky. The night was peaceful and his adrenaline rush had faded. He thought about when Malaki had been stitching his wound and how the handmen were working in unison. It had opened his eyes to the kind of family he was now a part of. He thought back to when Videre and Malaki were speaking in the Olde Language. Although he could not make out the words, he understood the syllables and familiar pronunciations. The other men probably also knew what they were saying. He wouldn't even be surprised if Jakoba could understand everything that they were saying. He pulled his notebook from his bag and started writing all the words he remembered in the Olde Language.

I'll show her I am just as worthy as everyone else.

BRING THE BOX

Jooey soaked in the morning sun before anyone had woken. He had slept soundly after eavesdropping on Leon and Videre's conversation late into the night. Although he was worried that Videre would tell Leon too much for his own good, Jooey was relieved to know that she had controlled herself in how much she had actually told Leon. Knowing Videre, he figured she told Leon just enough to put the issue of her scar to bed. There was no room for error with Leon. Although he looked docile and calm on the inside, there was no telling what he may do if he found out what had all happened that very fateful day.

Jooey looked up to the sky, sitting in front of a pot of boiling water to make some tea for his companions. The air was crisp and the campfire still had some glowing embers from the previous night. The wood here burned differently. With all the travels to other countries, Jooey sensed that he was more perceptive than most people. Of course, part of his purpose in life was to protect Videre. He had no choice but to be preceptive.

There were two large birds flying overhead, seeming to circle the camp. Jooey looked at them in wonder.

"We're in the clear," said a small voice behind him.

The birds gracefully swooped down to Jakoba's feet as he let out distinct whistles. He tossed some bread crumbs which they joyfully accepted and they took off again with elegance similar to that of the senrima. Within a moment, the birds were already high up in the sky over the towering trees and circling once more. One by one, the handmen started coming out of their tents to sit by the fire, pouring hot tea into their cups. Climbing out of her tent, Videre wrapped up in her shawl, as the air was starting to get chilly this time of year in the morning. She sat down next to Leon as Kolono handed her a cup of hot tea.

"Let's see your wound," she said to Leon, still looking exhausted.

Leon put down his tea and took off his coat and shirt. Malaki unwrapped the bloody cloth to reveal a wound that was hardly visible as if it had been healing for months. Malaki looked pleased with his work as he cleaned off the crusted blood and applied a small bit of paste on top of the scar.

"Beautiful job, Malaki, as always," Videre complimented.

Malaki blushed. He was definitely talented. From the time he had stepped into Videre's life, he had grown so much in the ways of healing that he quickly surpassed any healers in known history. He had relentlessly studied and experimented to make his craft perfect. Ezrai and Miss Rayne were happy to find him any information that he needed to succeed, and now he had grown bonded to Queen Hania who had given him so much to work with. Videre was as proud of him as his own mother would have been. He had not been able to save his mother who had also been a healer but she had made sure to get him into Videre's care before she had passed. She knew if there was anyone who could give Malaki the tools he needed to be the best in Aleria, Videre would see to it. Although Videre was hesitant to let a child into her care, she had done it before and was easily convinced that he would be of great service to her.

Jooey looked at Jakoba who seemed to be enjoying his time around the other handmen. Jakoba was still a child but he probably was about the same age as Malaki when Videre had taken the young healer in. Maybe with a little more debate, she might actually let the boy be a part of their group.

Kolono and Jooey started packing Videre's horse. The metal of the longsword clanked against Lady Italych. Such a sword was plain and not suited to be at the side of a queen but it had kept Videre hidden in plain sight. Although her senrima looked to be noble horses, her plain sword and clothes had turned strangers away from the notion of who she actually was.

As soon as Videre had finished her tea, everyone was ready to be on their way. With no senrima to ride, Jakoba was forced to sit with Ezrai, who was also small in stature. The large dog stayed by Jakoba's side as they started their trek through The Stromy with Ezrai and Jakoba now leading the way.

"Do you know why we're getting an item that supposedly can kill people?" Leon quietly asked to Jooey so Videre couldn't hear him.

Jooey smiled. He was starting to get to know Leon a little more and had been growing to like the man more with every day that had passed. At their first meeting, he had thought of Leon as someone too young and inexperienced to help Videre shoulder her duties but he started realizing that the young man was ambitious.

"It's a puzzle piece. A piece of a puzzle that Videre has been trying to decode for years. I'm not the one you should be asking, because I know almost nothing. That is one thing she won't fully share with anyone but Ezrai."

"Why only Ezrai?"

"Because Ezrai already knows."

"Because she told him?" Leon asked in a very confused tone.

"Ezrai's family members are historians. They have served the Vasili for hundreds of years. Like your trade, his family passes down the knowledge to their children, and their children become historians whether they like it or not. Fortunately for Videre, Ezrai does like it. Without these historians, I'm afraid history and the stories of the past would be lost forever. Stories such as this puzzle she is after most likely had been passed down from his father."

"So if it's such a secret, who told Videre?"

"I guess her father told her shortly before he passed, but she already knew some of it from snooping around. I never met the man because it was quite a long time ago, but I've heard stories. He was the one who picked up the pieces after Polonotadare. Brave and kind, he was. Apparently, he and a couple of Viceroy were researching something and left notes and diaries that help her. The writings are sealed in a chest in the Videre's research chambers."

"Is that the same place where we had that late night meeting?"

"Yes and no. That room is our meeting room. There's a hidden door in that room that leads to the research chambers.

That dog that was in the meeting room guards the research chamber. Alpha is his name. Fat, lazy, and spoiled but I reckon if he senses anyone snooping around, he can get vicious."

"Have you been into the chambers?"

"Only a few times. She rarely lets us in unless she has to show us something important. Like the tunnels in the castle, she can pick and choose who gets to go in."

Jooey looked up. The birds silently circled overhead. He looked toward Jakoba leading the way. He had a good feeling about him. The young boy was innocent now but still had a fierceness to him, but Jooey knew all too well that people can be unpredictable in tough situations. Although their job seemed relaxed, the lives of Videre's handmen were not as simple as it seemed, such as going to a different country to pick up perhaps the most dangerous artifact known to all of Aleria.

He glanced at the box on the back of Lotanzo's horse. It wasn't very large. He wondered how big the timepiece was, as they were all different in shape and size. He hadn't looked at the drawing long enough to determine if there was any evidence as to how large it was. They didn't fully understand the timepiece, yet Videre had trust that this box would actually house it safely. Miss Rayne was a genius but he didn't like how Videre has complete trust in her. Videre always had a plan and it always went smoothly. Almost always.

Ahead of them was a small village on the shore in The Stromy. The waves rippled on the dark sand of the beach. The huts were almost primitive, lacking basic necessities of those in a more civilized world. It looked quaint and peaceful as villagers wandered around with baskets of fruits and fish. The canoes, docks, and huts were built with dark wood that matched the forest surrounding them contrasting the light-colored wood of the Desiali forests. Small canoes lined the shore and were anchored into place by posts driven into the ground all spaced exactly the same distance apart. This was definitely a fishing village, not from the sight but mostly from the smell. Stopping abruptly, Jakoba swung himself off the horse and walked to Videre as everyone gathered close.

"This is the village of Poshany," he said as he pointed to a large hut in the center of the town. "I already talked to the elder two days ago. He said to do our business quickly and leave everyone be."

Videre nodded and tied up her senrima to a nearby tree. Everyone followed suit except for Lostanzo. He kept his senrima by his side with the box from Miss Rayne still tied to his saddle. Slowly and cautiously, they trekked down a small hill in The Stromy leading to the small fishing village. The villagers were smaller than what Jooey was used to. Even though he was a head taller than most people back in Desial he was even taller compared to the indigenous tribes of Aleria. It was one of the biggest markers between different races of the people of Aleria. With all of Jooey's travels around the continent, he had taken mental notes of the differences between the people of different tribes and areas. Those who live in Alflint were also smaller compared to those on the main continent. Viceroy descendants were known to have certain features such as the red hair in Athena, and the light skin and bright eyes of Moshny.

The people of Dunbar were also easy to spot. They also had extremely light skin and most of them were as large as Jooey. In the Alerian games that took place every four years, Dunbari were almost always the winners for anything strength and size-related. Their people spoke a variation of the native Olde language and isolated themselves from the main continent of Aleria. Jooey had the pleasure of accompanying Videre a few times to the frigid north but the weather was quite a challenge for Jooey. Dark-haired and dark-skinned, Jooey was quite different from the other men in Dunbar and had made him popular in the villages that he would visit. His Olde Language had a slight accent, making people even more interested as they didn't have very many visitors from the main continent crossing the Dunbari Range.

The people of Korona, from what Jooey had seen, were hardly people at all. They were more like human-like creatures, but to Videre, she had treated them all the same, noting no differences between them. All the indigenous tribes of Korona were vastly different and their history unknown. No writing systems were established until the discovery of the island by the early Kiadere explorers. The cultures on the island were extremely different which was intriguing to Jooey. Although the island was a fraction of the size of the continent, most of the tribes lived in harmony despite their differences. They had strict borders in their regions and visitors from another tribe would always respect the rules and customs of those territories that they were currently in. The Viceroy, in later years, had introduced the new language to the people of Korona and had made life a lot simpler for them. Instead of learning the language of all twelve tribes to effectively communicate with each other, they had switched to a system where they would communicate with each other in the Viceroy language while retaining their native language.

As Videre's group walked through the town, gazes were set upon them but everyone kept quiet and attended to their tasks. An older man walked up to them quite briskly with a smile on his face.

"Lady Videre, it is pleasure to meet you," he said as he bowed quite formally.

"You must be Chief Kalo Palo," said Videre in her usually friendly tone that she used during talks with foreign leaders.

Although he was a little rusty with his Olde Language, Jooey knew that Kalo Palo meant Large Quiet. Looking the Chief up and down, Jooey could tell why he was called large but with his shining personality, the Chief looked like he wasn't quiet at all. The chief's beard was impressively smooth as if he never missed a day to comb through it. It was hard for Jooey to guess anyone's age nowadays. He looked old but the way the man carried himself was like that of a robust young man.

"The artifact, this way," Chief Kalo Palo said as he turned and walked towards the shore. Walking quickly down the shore passing the canoes, they came closer to a small and old looking shed.

"I not know why this made fusses. The people of Moshny swear if we get close, it most definitely make people sick but it is like old myth to me. We have no bad luck with it," he turned to Videre and his expression changed to a more serious gaze. "I am curious. Why you want something that they say is dangerous?"

"We want it for research purposes. We have the best scientists on the continent and it is a quite intriguing artifact. I do have one request though," she said quite sternly.

"Yes, you don't want Moshny to know you take it," he laughed. "I have heard stories of the….relations between your two countries when it was made. I will not speak of this for you. I am respecting what you and Desial do for tribes of Aleria and for Kiadere."

Videre nodded in approval. Indeed, she had done much for the tribes of Aleria, ensuring that they were able to preserve their traditions after the time of Polonotadere.

"Here," he said as he stopped at the door of the shed. "I will not going in but you can do what you need to. You do it quickly so to not be suspicious if anyone come."

The Chief bowed and walked away in a hurry. Looking at the shed, Jooey felt an uneasiness pulsing through his body. Lostanzo's senrima was skittish and Jakoba's dog was whining and refusing to get closer. If Jooey knew anything about animals, it was that they had a sense about things like this. The Chief had ensured that there was nothing bad happening to the people in his tribe but he knew that the story of Polentio was historically true. Ezrai's family would not put any foolish falsities in any of their records. He looked back at Videre who had an excited expression on her face. Her ambitions were getting in the way of her usual caution. She had changed over the many years that Jooey had known her and was starting to doubt her decisions. He glanced at all of the other handmen. Worried expressions dominated their faces as if they were feeling the same uneasiness.

"Let's be quick about it," she said as she unstrapped the box from Lostanzo's senrima.

Entering the shed, it was uncomfortably dark and musty; no doubt the humidity from the ocean had contributed. There was a hatch in the floor accompanied by a rusty lock. Videre, Jooey, Kolono, Leon, and Ciano entered the shed leaving no room for anyone else as they surrounded the locked hatch. Jooey looked around for perhaps an instrument to break open the lock. Without hesitation, Leon bent down and inserted a key hidden in his pocket. Much to everyone's surprise, the key turned smoothly and the lock unlatched as if the rust was there for show.

"What was that?" asked Ciano in an extremely confused tone.

"It looks just like the locks that are used for our timekeeper boxes. I always carry the master key," said Leon as if he were confused himself.

Leon carries the key to the hatch leading to the deadly weapon that his ancestor made? Interesting.

Kolono carefully opened the hatch and looked down. An ancient-looking ladder went down to the pit below. Only able to make out a few feet down, there was no telling how deep the pit was. Videre inched closer to the edge trying to make out any signs of a bottom. Jooey prepared himself to grab her in case she slipped and fell. It was no issue to Jooey as this had been his job since the day he joined her. Preparing for the worst was instinctual now. Videre took a step back and nodded to Kolono.

Kolono sat down on the dirt-covered floor and closed his eyes. Taking deep breaths, he looked as if he was almost asleep. Visibly confused, Leon stared at Kolono.

This will have to be explained later.

Jooey knew exactly what was happening with Kolono but never had to explain it to anyone before. His chest moved up and down with deep breaths and his eyelids flickered. After a minute of silence, Kolono opened his eyes and stood up.

"I would say it's about thirty steps down. The ladder is un-stable though. It would be smart not to go down it ourselves."

Jooey sighed. He peeked down the hole then looked at Videre who nodded to him.

"The lad?"

Videre looked at Leon. She knew exactly what Jooey was worried about.

"We might as well. We'll have a long talk tonight," Videre smiled as if she had no choice.

Videre was right. Leon would have to learn sooner than later and perhaps he could learn about himself in the process.

Jooey stood by the opening of the hole. He could feel his pulse running through his veins and in his heart. He couldn't possibly be scared of a dark hole, yet he knew what he was feeling was real. Looking at Leon, he smiled and summoned deep within him, the monster that lurked in his soul.

In a moment of focus, he had come out. Choono had lived deep within Jooey since he was born but it wasn't until desperation that drove him out into the real world. The large ghostly figure that had just appeared to come out of Jooey's body, bowed to Videre and then smiled at Leon. As expected, Leon's face had drained of color and his eyes opened wide as his jaw dropped. Although Choono almost never had any words to say, Jooey knew exactly what he would say to Leon if he could.

"Ta-da," Jooey said quietly and quietly laughed along with Choono.

Choono looked down the hole and without hesitation he started climbing down the decrepit ladder. The ladder creaked beneath his feet signaling to Kolono that he was right. Although Choono had the physicality of Jooey, he weighed much less with the same amount of strength as his master. Jooey concentrated on what Choono was doing and navigated him down through the darkness. His eyes and ears were focused entirely on Choono which came easily with practice. He had nearly mastered being able to fight independently with Choono by his side trying to let go of control and letting Choono fend for himself.

In his earlier days, it was Valeria who had actually taught him how to use his ability to the fullest. She had taken countless hours to help train and teach him in her style of fighting, although he knew very well that he would never be equal to her. Training with Valeria was completely invigorating to Jooey but his loyalties lie with Videre. He would often think back on when Valeria had begged Videre to let Jooey join the Vipole. Giving Jooey the choice for himself, he had not hesitated to stay in service of his one true queen, Videre.

Feeling Choono's senses, Jooey closed his eyes so as to not be distracted by anything else while guiding Choono down the ladder.

We should be there soon. Surely we've gone down thirty meters.

Suddenly, he felt Choono's feet touch the ground. With a sigh of relief, Jooey smiled and nodded at Videre, who he could tell was tense the whole time. Kolono took a small vial with a clear liquid inside and opened it with a push of this thumb. He dropped a small tablet inside, closed the tube up again, and shook it until there was a soft glow. Looking down the hole, he dropped it. The tube showed a preview of the hole in the ground while descending in the direction of Choono. The ladder indeed did look ancient and the hole dug in a rushed fashion as if they didn't care if it collapsed or not. Standing at the base, Choono looked up, and with a graceful swipe of his hand, he caught the vial, illuminating the space around him. With hardly enough room to move around, he spotted a small box conveniently in plain sight. Tucking the box under his arm, he started making his way up the ladder again.

Going up was a little trickier than going down. The ladder was creaking just like it had before but this time he had a hindrance. If he had the use of both of his arms he could distribute his weight evenly on the wooden steps. Steadily climbing the ladder that creaked with every step, Choono finally reached the top as everyone relaxed. He took the small box and quickly by instinct put it inside of Miss Rayne's box. His heart started beating faster and pains ran from where the box had been touching his arm. Feeling sick, he bowed to his queen and went back to where he came from. His body fully absorbed inside of Jooey within a moment and Jooey also felt the same pain that Choono did.

"Do you feel that?" asked Leon who still looked as though he was in shock.

"Yes, This is exactly what I expected to happen. That's why we brought this box," said Videre in a worryingly but pleased tone.

"Thank you Jooey and Choono," she said gratefully and grazed his cheek.

She quickly grabbed the box and walked out the door as Jooey looked at Leon.

So much explaining to do now.

"I promise, I'll tell you," Jooey said to Leon quietly as they exited the shack.

Everyone including Jakoba huddled around the box that Videre had set on the ground.

"This, my fellow men, and boy," she said looking at Jakoba, "is a piece that may be one of the most important artifacts in our world. It was built by a timemaker but inside is a rare piece, salvaged from the wreckage of the Viceroy Transport. According to Ezrai's wonderful research, this material is not found anywhere else in Aleria. Unfortunately, certain people cannot examine and study it since it makes them sick."

Videre stared at the box looking like she desperately wanted to open it.

"We will have Miss Rayne examine it when we make our trip to Hikari."

"Hikari," Ezrai smiled, "I didn't know we were taking such a trip."

"I decided it was time to confront The Dio and perhaps gain information about The Alerian Blood Clan."

"Are you sure we need to be that drastic? Can't we just write a letter as usual," asked Lostanzo, visibly distressed.

"I wrote a letter before we left, but I wouldn't have received the reply yet. I don't want to wait any longer and we're somewhat in the area anyway."

"I want to have some of you take this to her right away, just in case," she said almost nervously as she looked around.

There was nobody in sight, but Videre was one not to take chances when it came to one of her puzzle pieces.

"Who is the area scribe?" she asked Jakoba.

"My great uncle," said Jakoba proudly. "He lives maybe halfway between here and Lake Nodio. He will be so excited to see you milady," he said as he bowed trying to impress Videre.

The men chuckled softly as Videre nodded to him in approval. "Maybe you are ready to be a handman after all."

As Videre and her men walked back to where they had left the senrima, Jooey had an uneasy feeling. He looked back at the box now tucked into a blanket and latched to Lostanzo's saddle. His arm was still hurting from when Choono had been carrying it. It was unfortunate that he felt the same pain as Choono when he returned inside Jooey.

Such a dangerous item should not be taken so lightly.

THE KIADERE

Leon couldn't believe what he had just witnessed. They were on their way to where they had left the senrima as if it were another beautiful day to go riding. They had traveled half of the continent on flying horses but that was nothing compared to what he had just seen. He replayed the event in his head over and over again trying to make sense of it all.

They had been in the small building just moments ago. Nobody batted an eye when another figure came from Jooey's chest. Jooey didn't even wince when this person named Choono came out of him. And Choono wasn't even a person. Leon could feel certain energy from Choono but didn't know what. He had so many questions and his head was spinning.

What exactly was Choono? How did he come out and go back into Jooey?

"Where are we going next?" Leon asked, trying to keep his composure.

"In the direction of Lake Nodio to talk to the area scribe," said Videre without turning around.

Videre strapped the box to Lostanzo's senrima once again. She paused for a moment and started walking toward where they had left the senrima. She immediately started picking up her pace while the others followed suit. Leon felt as if he were in a small army marching towards battle. Jooey tapped Leon on the shoulder revealing a big smile when he turned around.

"We'll talk more about it when we set up camp for the night. Perhaps this time, we may actually be able to go to an inn since it is getting chilly down here."

Jooey was right. The weather was drastically different. Leon had noticed that the people they had seen in Moshny wore furs and heavier clothing. He knew winter was still a while away in Desial but perhaps the seasons were different in the southern part of Aleria. Satisfied with Jooey's reassurance that they would talk about the day's events, he started asking more questions.

"What's an area scribe?" Leon asked enthusiastically.

Although he was annoyed at everyone for hiding somewhat important things, he always felt satisfied with the answers they gave him instead of waiting around for explanations.

"Aleria is broken up into many areas. Each area is assigned a scribe by The Alerian Society. The scribe's main purpose is to record anything from births, deaths, sicknesses, anomalies, and things of the sort," said Ezrai.

"So the scribe just keeps records for the area?"

"Yes," Ezrai looked at Leon curiously.

"What?"

"I'm waiting for you to ask me what The Alerian Society is."

Leon smiled, "What's The Alerian Society?"

"I'll tell you after we meet the scribe."

Jooey and Kolono roared with laughter as Ciano patted Ezrai on the back.

"I love it when you surprise me like that. Your nose is always in those books. It worries me that maybe you've lost your sense of humor."

Leon also laughed. It was nice to see Ezrai come out of his shell. After a short walk through the forest, the senrima gleefully nodded to their riders as to appreciate their return. Mounting Lady Kayle, he looked at the box that had been strapped tightly to Lostanzo's senrima. He feared the artifact but he was also deeply intrigued. Leon had instinctively unlocked the hatch as if he was destined to be there to uncover it. Also, the feeling that he got from being around it was nauseating. He could feel it deep within his heart and head as if he could feel it killing him too, just like it did with the Zaro of Moshny.

Riding up and down small hills and past fruit trees that were dropping a bountiful harvest, they came upon a run-down cabin. It was quiet and meek, hardly large enough to be called a house. Jakoba, who had led the way, quickly swung off the saddle and ran inside. Within moments, an old frail man hobbled out of the door motioning for everyone to come inside. His robes were drab as if he had worn them for decades. Judging on his appearance, Leon figured that he was nearing his time of death. Bowing deeply, he smiled and grasped Videre's hand.

"My queen, it has been many years since I have seen someone as important as you. Your father was a curious man and a great leader. My name is Cal."

"You knew my father?"

"Yes, my lady. He was my commander and to this day I will always regard his descendants as such. I'm too old now to fight, but I find that being part of The Alerian Society helps me serve your family as long as I shall live. In fact, my young grand-nephew here says his dream is to become a handman of yours or maybe even a handman to one of your sisters."

Videre smiled as Jakoba blushed. "Your grand nephew, no doubt, has what it takes to be a handman. I, myself will guarantee that if he does make it through the handman trials, I will see to it that he serves under me. I cannot waste such talent on my sister's trivialities," she said jokingly.

"Thank you, my queen," the scribe bowed again as they all entered the house. "I hope you don't mind, but I do have my sub-scribe here with me. Sometimes my memory and eyes fail me and he has already been accepted by the council to take my place whenever I choose to resign."

As they walked into the scribe's house, Leon could smell a faint but recognizable scent that he could not quite put his finger on. The house was dark, only illuminated by a few candles but somewhat cozy. Colorful blankets were strewn on the chairs that had been prearranged to seat the visitors. The floors creaked as they walked quietly to the chairs set in front of the scribe's desk. On the far end of the room, Leon saw what appeared to be the same statue of the cat that he had seen in Mrs. Potter's shop. Videre sat in the chair closest to the desk as everyone found a seat, except for Jooey and Kolono, who took their respective spots on either side of the entrance. The sub-scribe was gleaming, standing behind the scribe's desk. He was a middle-aged man and wore plain clothing similar to the scribe. There was a stillness in the air as the old scribe sat down in a creaky and ancient chair.

"I would like to introduce myself," said the sub-scribe standing up straight. "My name is Tomas, I am the sub-scribe in the area. I am very pleased to have finally met you. Many scribes never get to meet any of the true kings or queens of Aleria."

Videre, halfway embarrassed, bowed her head slightly in appreciation. Leon was no master of politics but he assumed such talk in the public eye of Moshny would definitely welcome a death sentence for Tomas.

"What are you in need for, my queen?" asked Cal.

"I need to know about any records you have on the artifact of Polentio."

Cal leaned back in his chair, "What you know is probably all that we know. The artifact was crafted by Polentio Minet at the request of your father as a gift to the Zaro of Moshny. The Zaro was a selfless man but also was quite a collector of beautiful objects. To make it more precious and of intimate value, the King also commissioned the timepiece to include parts from the wreckage of the Viceroy transport. Of course, neither your father nor Polentio knew that there was an object inside the timepiece that was supposedly lethal to the Zaro and select people."

"Select people?"

"Yes, not everyone in contact became sick. In fact, it is a little confusing. It seems as though the sickness started a while after it was in the Zaro's possession. At first, they thought someone may have been poisoning the king and some of his men, but after deliberate investigation, it would be almost impossible to single out and poison certain members of the palace since all the food came from one kitchen. They also ruled out diseases, otherwise, they would have spread outside of their quarters and throughout the country. The timepiece was said to glow at night and sometimes was hot to the touch. Sure enough, when they buried the timepiece, their symptoms slowed down. Although it's not proven, they blamed your father and Polentio for trying to kill the Zaro."

"Has the timepiece been disturbed or has it always been in the hole?"

"Nobody has any intention of trying to retrieve the timepiece. Rashan Kaner, I believe, is the one who sealed the door."

Kaner? As in Miss Rayne Kaner. That can't be a coincidence.

"The key was also made by a good friend of his," Cal said as he opened a book that Tomas handed him. "Chen Fraer."

"The Fraer locksmiths," Leon blurted out.

The Fraer locksmiths were the ones who had also made the lock for Videre's Timekeeper. This was definitely not a coincidence.

"Yes," Cal smiled. "They are said to be great locksmiths. Rashan Kaner and Chen Fraer helped the Zaro lock up the timepiece in that hole. You know of the Fraer family? What's your name?"

"Leon," he said cautiously as he recalled Lostanzo's warning about letting the people of Moshny know his true identity.

"Minet," Videre added.

"Ah, I see," said Cal as his eyes lit up. "I assume you are Keone's grandson then?"

"Yes," said Leon slightly surprised.

It now hit Leon that his grandfather may have been more popular than he thought.

"Have there been any sicknesses of the sort reported in the area?" asked Malaki.

"The tribe is a little secretive about their affairs, yet we have convinced them to help keep records of their families. It seems they are all healthy."

"Actually," Tomas chimed in, "There was Freddy"

"Ahh yes, Freddy moved to Lake Nodio after he started becoming ill. I know he is a printer now but he grew ill at a young age in a similar fashion to the historical accounts. I believe his parents and brother still live in the town. The chief and I persuaded his parents to have the child leave the area just in case it was indeed the artifact that had been making him sick."

Thomas brought another book from a bookshelf to Cal's desk. This one seemed to have been sitting for a while as a dust cloud sprang forth from its cover.

"We store records from their doctor," Cal said as he flipped through the pages. "Freddy was a curious one indeed."

"Why would you say that," Videre asked.

Cal looked up from the book. "We do not speak of such things usually, but Freddy's family are natives but he was born with almost black hair and the blue spots."

"Are you saying that his real father is Hikarian?"

"Either Hikarian or Kiadere," Tomas said in a hushed tone.

"The doctor of the village told them that it was uncommon but not impossible. The mother however looked like she knew."

"Are there any other mixed races inside that town," asked Malaki.

"No," said Cal. "That tribe, in particular, are very insistent on keeping their blood pure."

"Do you know exactly where he is now," asked Videre.

"I think there is only one printer in Moshny. Someone there should know where it is."

"Thank you," said Videre abruptly as she stood up. "We must be on our way now."

Cal stood up slowly and bowed with discomfort as his body creaked. With almost a slight rudeness, Videre nodded to the scribes and quickly dashed out the door. One by one the hand-men thanked the scribes before exiting. Lostanzo took some coins out of his pocket and handed them to both of the scribes before leaving. Jakoba tried to follow the men but Cal grabbed him by the arm.

Upon exiting the house they instinctively mounted their horses and followed Videre without a word. After a while of silent riding, Videre came to a halt and dismounted. The hand-men followed suit. She stared at the box on Lostanzo's horse.

"It never made the tribe sick."

"It must be Viceroy blood," chimed in Malaki.

"Yes, somehow their blood must be different. Which means that this could potentially be a weapon against them. All of you must vow to never speak a word of this."

Jolon pounded his chest and kneeled in front of Videre. The others followed suit, leaving an awkward Leon standing for a second until he copied the others.

"Kolono, Lostanzo, and Ciano," Videre said harshly, "Go to Miss Rayne's house and tell her everything. Make sure she studies it thoroughly. We will meet you there, after our travels. Ciano, you can keep track of where we are if need be. Lostanzo, make sure nobody can follow you."

The three men bowed and without a word or hesitation, they turned and rode off on their senrima.

"There is an inn down the road, My Queen," said Ezrai hopefully.

Videre let out a short laugh as if she hadn't just been as serious as she had ever been. Ezrai let out a sigh of relief.

"Yes, we can go to an inn tonight," she said as she looked down the small gravel path that lay ahead of them. "There's no use in being secretive. We will be visiting the Zaro tomorrow."

There was a chill in the air as Leon could see storm clouds rolling in. Lighting filled the sky and thunder rolled in the direction where the three other handmen had headed. Worry started to fill Leon's head as he had now grown close to every member of the group. He had randomly thought about why Lostanzo had taken interest in Jaora. She was attractive and nice, but Jaora seemed without a doubt too enthusiastic and bright for the dark and mysterious Lostanzo. His mind had wandered in circles until it came to what had happened earlier that day. A sight that he had nearly forgotten from the excitement of their travels. Anxiety had started setting in and Leon couldn't contain himself.

"Is anyone going to tell me what happened today?"

Jooey in his classic sense had let out a roar of laughter. "I had nearly forgotten all about that!"

Videre looked back and nodded to Jooey as if giving him approval to explain. Jooey took a flask out and gave it to Leon. As Leon swallowed the sweet juice, he recognized it as the drink that was given to him when he was in Videre's study.

"Let's ride and talk," Jooey said as he swung his heavy legs on his senrima.

Videre rode out in front of them as if she didn't care if she was part of the conversation or not.

"A long time ago, there were these people called the Kiadere," Jooey said as they started following Videre at a slow pace.

Leon had limited knowledge about the Kiadere even with his assigned reading. They were the reason for Polonotadere and the target of Les Nettoyer, the genocide that had happened long ago.

"The Kiadere were the smartest, kindest, strongest, most handsome people in Aleria."

Malaki shook his head as he smiled.

"Many people loved the Kiadere because they were so awesome."

"OK, enough with that", Malaki laughed.

Jooey looked at Malaki as if he were annoyed with him for interrupting his masterpiece of a story.

"The Kiadere means people of magic in the Olde Language. That's because they are. People of magic, that is. Many Kiadere do not have abilities but there are a few pure-blood Kiadere still left today."

Leon was shocked. He had heard about the cleansing, the mass genocide, but he had never been taught the outcome. To his surprise, there were still Kiadere left in the world.

"So you're saying, that you are Kiadere and you have magic," asked Leon cautiously as he might have been extremely off in his prediction of where Jooey was going with the story.

"Lad," Jooey said matter-of-factly, "Don't you know we are all Kiadere?"

Malaki smiled at Leon in a giddy manner.

"The Queens of Desial only choose Kiadere to be handmen."

Leon didn't know what to say. He didn't know if he was surprised or horrified. A race that he had figured was extinct was in fact still alive. Not only that, but he was surrounded by them. A few moments in silence and Leon came to the conclusion that if Videre indeed, only chose handmen who were Kiadere, then why did she choose him.

"Yes," Videre said as she turned around and stopped. "You are also Kiadere. Your parents were both of Kiadere blood. Pure Kiadere are rare these days."

"Don't look so shocked, Leon," said Ezrai as they started riding along the road again. "It's really not a big deal. Not unless there's a cleansing going around."

Malaki and Jooey laughed as Ezrai looked pleased that he had said something witty again.

"A little more than three hundred years ago. The Viceroy came to Aleria," said Videre as she interrupted their laughter, "They were revered as Gods. The knowledge that they were able to share with the people of Aleria was utterly fantastic. They were from another time and place. A place where they had greatly advanced knowledge. You see, the Viceroy came to Aleria in what we call the Viceroy transport. It was unlike what anyone had ever seen. It crashed in Reino and that piece in the artifact was a part of their transport. It was taken by my father and hidden from the world at the direction of one of the Viceroy. That particular part in the timepiece is not of this world but of theirs."

"That doesn't tell me anything about what happened with Jooey," Leon said.

"Indeed, lad, it doesn't. Long story short, the Viceroy were threatened by the Kiadere because some of us still have special abilities, such as what you saw earlier. Choono, is my other half. He comes out when I tell him to and does what I want him to do. Usually."

"So everyone has another half?"

Jooey chuckled, "Not at all actually. Although the diversity of these abilities are limited, there are many different abilities that the Kiadere are prone to. For example, Malaki can heal anything that is living at a rapid pace."

Malaki smiled and looked at Leon as if expecting him to thank him again for fixing his arm. Leon had thought that maybe Malaki had used his quick and precise skills to help his arm, but he had noticed that there was no pain at all and the mark had almost completely disappeared.

"Kolono," Jooey continued, "Also has another inside of him, Kialo. Kialo usually can't be seen or felt. Kolono can use Kialo to scout discreetly which has its advantages and disadvantages. Only a few of us are able to see Kialo."

"Why is that?"

"Kialo and Choono, have their own minds too. Kialo only shows himself to those that he completely trusts. Everyone among us is able to see him and you will gain his trust soon enough."

"I don't have any abilities," said Leon disappointedly.

"You have to find yourself, Leon" reassured Ezrai. "Being the Desiali Historian was destined for me by my family. I was trained ever since I was young to use my abilities in service to the Vasili. Most people, such as yourself, don't know about who they really are."

"What ability do you have?"

Ezrai sighed, "I can see the past. Only through the eyes of my ancestors, that is. That's why it's important for me to travel and stick with Queen Videre. One day my offspring will be able to see this very conversation we are having."

"That's why Jooey says you know more than everyone else."

"Precisely. I'm not too fond of it myself as I can recall horrors, but my ability makes me best suited for my job. I just wish my queen didn't travel so much," he added loudly so that Videre would definitely hear. "My brother has the same ability as me but she chose me for some reason."

"Probably because your brother is one of the most annoying people she's ever met," chuckled Jooey as Malaki nodded in agreement.

"Ezrai is a wonderful travel companion if you ignore the whining," teased Videre.

"Thank you, my queen," Ezrai responded to the backhanded compliment. "There is much you don't know," he continued talking to Leon. "There is also much that most of us do not understand. The past is frightening but I've slowly been more open to reading and understanding the past. It is no easy task though. Reading the past takes much effort and drains me for a while. I try to write everything I can about what has happened so eventually we'll be able to share our knowledge with all of Aleria."

Leon all of a sudden felt a deep sadness within him. "I left school at the top of my class, yet I feel as if I don't know anything. I didn't even know that the Kiadere still existed. I know you told me about them before, but I must admit, I was really tired when you told me and maybe have forgotten a bit."

Videre let out a big sigh. "The Treaty of Aleria is one of the most shameful things that we have ever agreed to. It was the only way to peacefully stop Polonotadere unfortunately. You see, when the Viceroy came to Aleria, they had so much knowledge. To share this knowledge, the King of Desial had sent the Viceroy to all corners of Aleria to help teach the people in all the regions of the continent. Instead of uniting the people through common knowledge, quite the opposite had happened. The Viceroy were of many cultures and languages. They taught the people in their own sense and the continent divided. It also didn't help that the Viceroy did not seem to age as fast as the ordinary people of Aleria. The Viceroy, with no help at all, became self-proclaimed kings and queens of their assigned region. When war broke out, almost all of the countries became established with their own claimed territories. Alliances started forming and some of the Viceroy routed armies in every direction. For years, Polonotadere raged on. Among the mass hysteria, the true king of Aleria formed a council that brought together the Viceroy once more and established the Treaty of Aleria. Putting a stop to the war, he gave up power to much of the continent and divided the continent into different countries, where laws could be made under the new rule of their respected Viceroy. One of the stipulations of the treaty was to keep much of the knowledge about history, Viceroy, and even the Kiadere from the new generations. So much damage had been done during the war to bring Aleria back to its previous state. The best they could do was to make sure it was never talked about in the future. To enforce the law, there is a separate education council the makes routine checks to all the schools on the continent to make sure that every country complies with the treaty. There's also the Alerian guard who enforces compliance, for the so-called safety of the continent and its people."

"So they're trying to erase history so people don't know that the Viceroy started the war?"

"Exactly," said Ezrai. "It is unfortunate that people would try to erase history. It doesn't matter if you like it or not, it's something that happened and cannot be changed. The

Viceroy were greedy people. People who had never held real power in their hands until they came to Aleria."

"Why do they not teach about the Kiadere?" asked Leon.

"The Viceroy thought the Kiadere to be dangerous because of their use of magic. If people know that the Kiadere still exist then that fear will eventually come back again. You have to realize that in order to silence history in schools, we put in a clause that the Kiadere are to also be left untaught."

"So the Kiadere themselves, are the ones who didn't want others to know about them."

"Precisely. It is for our own protection. Before the Viceroy, pure-blooded Kiadere children were taught at home or sent to specialty schools to help them excel in their abilities. Now, we must hide any Kiadere children from the world. There are some of us left, but most do not know their own potential. Not only that, but now there are so many mixed children because people do not know about Kiadere. We may simply just die out."

"Do you need to be a full-blooded Kiadere to have abilities?"

"Yes, although there have been stories of a few people who are mixed yet hold some abilities."

"Maybe that's why I don't have any abilities," said Leon disappointingly.

"Lad," said Jooey. "You're definitely a full-blooded Kiadere.

Leon couldn't imagine his parents being Kiadere. An ancient race that he thought was extinct was alive all along. He couldn't even imagine Keone being a Kiadere; some mythical race of people in the blood of an old inappropriate man. Looking at the brutish Jooey and the scrawny frame of Ezrai, Leon deduced that Kiadere can look and act like anything. Leon's mind wandered as it always did with so many possibilities.

They had walked up to the inn and had already started unloading their senrima.

"Our journey is done," said Videre quietly. "We cannot talk of such things in public."

"There is so much more I want to know."

"There is so much that we all want to know. Even I don't hold all the answers. I promise I will tell you all I know as I also strive to know the answers of the past as well," said Videre softly and eloquently.

Leon bowed slightly to the queen so as to not attract any attention. There was a certain air about her when she talked to Leon in particular. She was genuine and caring with him, leading him through the world like she was his mother. Ezrai looked at Leon with meaningful eyes and crept up beside him as the others were walking in.

"Listen, Leon. I know you want to know more. I don't blame you, but it will take some time. Until then, you must have faith in Videre for her to eventually show you the way."

"I do have faith."

CATHERINE, HEIRESS

Videre's long brown hair flowed in the wind as she led her men to Lake Nodio. She could see her breath in the icy air of the early morning. She was pleased to have stayed at the inn at Ezrai's constant imploring. Although the beds were not as cozy as the castle's, she agreed that it was much better than sleeping outside. She could feel Lady Italych yearning to fly off to their destination. If only Kiadere, senrima, and magic were normal again, she would be more satisfied with the world. So much hiding had drained her to where she had become desperate. There were few days in her life where she had forgotten what kind of world she was living in. However, those days of happiness had come and gone while sorrow and duties had taken their rightful place in her life.

"Did you mean what you said to Cal about Jakoba being a handman?" asked Ezrai.

"Of course. Jakoba has great potential. He is also from a prominent and loyal family."

"I meant the part about you taking him instead of your sister. Wouldn't he be well suited with Valeria?"

"Yes he would, but to be fair, so would Jooey and I wouldn't give him up to my sisters."

Jooey blushed, "Thank you, my queen. To be honest, I don't know what kind of things Valeria would do with me if I were in her service. She can be quite intense."

Videre laughed, "Yes. I feel bad for Valeria's handmen at times."

Leon sported a worried look on his face.

"Don't worry about your friend, Leon. My sister takes very good care of her handmen. She just takes things too far with them sometimes."

Valeria had always had a hunger for three things. She could eat as much as any man, she would fight better than any man, and she had eyes for many men. She was, in Videre's eyes, a conqueror of men. Ever since they were little, Valeria would get into fights with noble boys while Valencia gambled in the back rooms with maids.

Young Videre was always found in the study reading a book or reviewing affairs of state. Although politics didn't fascinate her as much as her father had wished, she always found the political dealings amusing as she could see exactly what tricks her father was up to. Ignorance, jealousy, and stinginess among the Viceroy had gotten her father into many advantageous political dealings. Like a mental map of the many trading crossroads of Aleria in her mind, she was able to see how the pieces connected together. The players in this game of power had no idea what lengths one would be willing to go through to keep the peace and to help Aleria thrive. Back channels would not be needed if Aleria had stayed as one unified continent.

Videre remembered one day when she started complaining about the Viceroy, her father had quietly sat at his desk and started writing on a fresh sheet piece of paper. Later that day, he handed her the handwritten page. On it, was a list of all the benefits that the Viceroy had brought with them. Keeping the paper in her possession, Videre always reminded herself of her true mission to carry out what her father started and to keep the peace in her continent. As for her sisters, they had even less interest in politics than Videre. Valeria, always with a hot temper and the skills of any man, was to oversee the army, to either keep the peace or to defend the country in case of another Polonotadere. Valencia was always interested in the people who surrounded her. She liked the comfort of knowing that people respected her. Most of all, Valencia loved to be loved. As triplets, the girls could not be given a preference for the crown. Their mother, who had died shortly after childbirth, had made their father promise to split the responsibilities of the crown among the three of them.

As the young princesses grew, they were taught, trained, and certified by the best within The Alerian Society. War heroes had turned their eyes to Valeria, who had tremendous skills with any weapon and against any foes. Viceroys had brought new ideas of psychology and charismatic training which was bestowed upon Valencia. Videre's father had personally taken her under his wing as he was the most prominent figure in his field. There were a select few members of The Alerian Society that worked with her, but when she became older, he realized that she had grown to be more gifted than any other and handed her to Miss Rayne. Back then,

Miss Rayne was a relatively unknown alchemist who vowed to teach her all the knowledge she had to offer.

"What do you mean too far?" asked Leon.

Videre smiled as if Leon should already have known.

"You've seen my sister, yes? You've seen that she's not with any man."

Leon with a sudden realization on his face looked embarrassed.

"But you aren't either."

A shock went through Videre. Of course, Leon had become more comfortable with his choice of words, as not anyone but her handmen would ever speak to her like that.

"My Queen will choose someone when she feels ready," said Jooey quite harshly. "Of course, I've always been ready to be that man," he said as he took Videre's hand and bowed.

Videre and Jooey laughed while Malaki and Ezrai smiled and rolled their eyes. Jooey always knew how to make her smile. His light spirits and quick humor had always had a well-balanced relationship with her occasional darkness. Even though he had only been her handman a fraction of the time that some of the others had been with her, he had no problem blending in with the group and rising to her second hand.

"Ah, I never answered your question lad," laughed Jooey as if he remembered something significant.

"To be fair, there are a lot of questions," said Leon embarrassingly.

"The question as to why Valencia had married an advisor instead of a king."

"Because the kings are of Viceroy blood and she wants to keep the Kiadere blood pure for her children."

Ezrai laughed hysterically as Jooey looked offended.

"Why do you even ask me questions when you can figure it out yourself," Jooey said disappointedly.

Malaki started laughing along with Ezrai.

"Just like your father," Jooey said under his breath.

Malaki and Ezrai stopped laughing and stared at Videre.

"How well did you know him," asked Leon.

"We all knew Keono very well," answered Ezrai rather quickly. "Lady Kayle also knew him very well," he said, motioning to Leon's senrima.

"Your father was smart, kind, and knew his duties well," said Videre softly.

She looked at Leon, puzzled that he looked confused.

"My boy, I thought you've already figured out that he was one of my handmen."

"I thought about it, but I wasn't quite sure," Leon stammered.

Videre laughed. The way Leon responded to such things made him look so innocent.

"Why did he leave your service," asked Leon.

"I told him to leave. He was destined for much bigger things."

"Like the timekeeper."

Videre smiled. She looked at Leon proudly. "I can't tell if you know all of our secrets or you just feign ignorance."

"I think I'm piecing things together slowly. So you confirm that it's a timekeeper," Leon said excitedly.

Videre smiled even more. "Leon, you looked inside didn't you?"

Leon smiled embarrassingly. "I did," he said as he bowed for forgiveness.

"I'm not surprised," replied Videre. "But you are wrong. Your father didn't create the timekeeper."

She could tell Leon was so sure of himself. She also saw that she had just defeated his hopes of his father making an object of legend. Although she had bent the truth about the object, she knew that for now, Leon must not know the whole truth. Someday, he would figure everything out. For now, if she led him down that road, there would be many more questions that shouldn't be answered quite yet.

Nearing the edge of Lake Nodio, Videre could see sparkling reflections on the horizon shining from the sacred waters. There were many beautiful sights in Aleria but Lake Nodio was among the most accessible places one could go to witness such grandeur. Lake Nodio's waters had an illusion to it as if millions of silverfish were darting about just below the surface. Although there was a law in place forbidding those to drink from the lake, it seemed almost impossible to even touch the water with steep cliffs on all sides of the lake.

Nodio was located right in the center of the Lake with equally steep cliffs. The city could defend itself from any attacks which was proven effective during Polonotare as a large bridge was the only way in or out of Nodio. The bridge that Videre had crossed only a handful of times in her life was made of stone was said to be unbreakable. As they took the horses across the bridge, it was evident that the bridge could hold a hundred more of them. The ripples of the water beneath them reflected off the castle that stood in the center of the island. Videre had always wished to fly Lady Italych over the lake for it must have been a beautiful sight.

All Eyes were on Videre and her men as they reached the gates of the city. The guards gave a slight bow as they let her through in acknowledgment of knowing exactly who was in their presence. The streets were filled with vendors and people in a similar fashion to Vici putting Videre feel at ease.

"Printer?" she asked a young boy who was staring at them.

The boy pointed behind him and said, "Duva Kubarkta."

With a nod and a smile, she handed him a small coin which he was most excited to receive and she headed toward where he had pointed. It had been a while since Videre had studied the language of Moshny. Unfortunately for Videre, her job was a lot easier if she learned the languages of all the regions of Aleria and the outlying countries. Miss Rayne had taught her a few basic languages and The Alerian Society had provided her with tutors in almost every other language. Although Videre didn't retain all that she had learned, she felt comfortable enough to communicate in another language if need be.

Looking around the streets, she glanced at street signs but also couldn't help but notice the people in the streets. Although Moshny was known for giving free food to their people, Videre could not think of much except for the sad state that they were living in now. Even the poorer of Desial looked better than the people of the most prosperous city of Moshny. Videre knew better than to intervene in the affairs of how the Viceroy leaders run their countries, but she always had a strong urge to change their practices. She stopped outside of a wooden building with a large green sign with the word "pitchatnik". Even the air outside smelled of ink.

"I thought we were going to see the King of Moshny," said Leon.

"Yes lad, but remember what Cal said," said Jooey, "Videre is like you. She needs to have all of her questions answered."

As they entered the printer's shop, it seemed cluttered as pages were hung up to dry and clipped to strings strewn all across the room. Videre remembered when she had first seen the printing press in action. The forming of wooden blocks and transferring the images onto paper had seemed practical to print large volumes of the same prints. The Viceroy had told the people of a faster way for printing, yet the press seemed sufficient enough.

"Can I help you," asked a small-framed man who stood in a doorway to the back room.

"Are you Freddy from the Ciokolopi clan?"

"Yes, madam. How do you know my birth name?"

Videre forced a friendly smile. "I won't take up much of your time. We are friends of the tribe and are trying to do some research into childhood illnesses in the area. I want to know about your illness when you were young and how you became well again."

Freddy sat down on a nearby chair with ink stains all over his hands and even some on his face. His face was round and his long black hair was tied back.

"My mother insisted I move to Lake Nodio when I was a child. She knew a printer that needed an apprentice and without question, he took me in. I've been here ever since."

"What about getting rid of your sickness," Malaki chimed in.

"Well, there was a lady who gave me herbs and would heat parts of my body. Salakina, I think was her name."

Videre knew that name and her heart started beating faster as she turned to Malaki.

"How long ago was this?" demanded Malaki abruptly.

"Maybe twenty years ago," said the man in confusion.

Videre pulled Malaki back and thanked the man for his answers. She knew the fire he had in his heart although it was rare to see. Malaki was almost in tears as he most likely had not heard his mother's name in years.

"It's not her," Videre said quietly to Malaki as they stood outside the printer's shop.

Ciano had sworn that he watched Malaki's mother die with his own eyes only a few weeks after she had given the boy to Videre.

"Could it be you have a family member with the same name?" asked Leon.

Almost everyone in Aleria except for the Viceroy named their children similar to their own name. It was not uncommon to have one child with the same name although it was ever so confusing.

"I never had siblings. But then again, I don't really remember anyone except for my mother."

It was unfortunate that many Kiadere families had been split apart during Polonotadere. Videre had hoped she could start reuniting the Kiadere families but it was nearly impossible when the Kiadere were in hiding, not to mention that many younger Kiadere had no idea who they actually were.

"Don't worry Malaki," said Videre as she touched his arm. "We will find out who it is."

"My Lady," a loud voice boomed.

A light-skinned man as large as Jooey was staring at them. He was wearing light armor with a tone of red and a symbol in yellow. The Dubh's also had similar colors but a very different design. She much preferred her countries silver and purple as she had always hated the colors of yellow and red together.

"The Zaro has been waiting for you," he said as he turned away assuming that Videre and her men would follow.

The man in armor led their group up the winding road leading to the palace. All eyes stared at them in wonder, even though they were not dressed for such attention. Videre's plain clothes were worth several times more than the drab dresses worn in the streets by the Nodians. Moshny didn't have an overwhelming population nor were they lacking in exports, yet Videre was confused on why there was so much poverty in the nation.

Walking up the palace stairs was even more tiring than back at her castle in Vici. Although Videre was not in bad shape, she was soon huffing and puffing as her legs grew weary as she was still drained from the night when Leon had fallen into the cavern. Without a word, Jooey swooped her up and started walking up the stairs, showing everyone how superior his strength was. Videre welcomed the rest especially from the long rides and lack of sleep but she was not at all amused. Scowling at Jooey's face, she stared at him until they reached the very top and he set her down. With a devious smile, he bowed low to her for everyone to see. She wanted to slap him but Videre knew how to keep her reputation as a calm and loving queen. She narrowed her eyes at Jooey who obviously knew what she was thinking and thanked him for his help. The group of villagers at the base of the stairs looked at Videre in awe.

Quietly, Videre and her handmen entered the palace of Moshny and walked down a long empty hallway with large framed portraits on either side. Every few steps held a pedestal with a piece of art clearly not worrying about what would happen during an earthquake or if a rampant child were to find themselves inside the hall filled with expensive and fragile items. At the end of the hallway stood two guards posted on either size of enormous blue doors leading to the throne room. The Zaros' of Moshny spared no expense in showing off their success with the world.

The blue doors were pushed open with ease as streaks of different colors shined on their faces. As they approached the throne, it looked different than what Videre remembered it from the last time she was there. Unlike the thrones of other countries, the one of Moshny changed frequently.

"Wait for his Royal Majesty here," the guard demanded before he marched back through the blue doors.

The throne room was a magnificent sight indeed. The windows had been stained with figures of the Viceroy history commissioned by the first Viceroy leader of Moshny himself. Animals, buildings, and people, not of this world were painted on the windows, confusing anyone who did not know anything about Viceroy history.

As an avid student of the history of Aleria, Videre had also had a special interest in Viceroy history. When she was a young girl, the Viceroys were still establishing their own respected countries through trial and error. The thinking of the Viceroy greatly differed from that of her father's rule. Laws that made no sense had been passed. New religions, ideas, and occupations started forming bringing a new, yet partially destructive age of enlightenment to Aleria. The Viceroy seemed to overcompensate for their hand in Polonotadere. Ignoring Polonotadere was no easy feat for Videre, as the Kiadere had suffered to an incredible extent to which the people of Aleria would never know due to the Treaty of Aleria.

After a while, an old man hobbled slowly toward Videre. With a jewel-encrusted wooden cane, he smiled and bowed his head ever so slightly.

"Queen Videre," he said ignoring the handmen. "I have longed to see your face in these sacred halls for quite some time."

Videre forced a smile knowing very well that he knew she wished to stay far from these halls as much as possible.

"It's as beautiful as the last time I was here. Speaking of beautiful, I would love to greet Princess Catherine."

The man's smile disappeared, delighting Videre slightly.

"Yes, of course. The Zaro and Zarina are to have dinner with you later today. The Zaro is busy at the moment but I'm sure he will make time for any conversations you may have during dinner."

"And will you be there at dinner, Lord Sergey?" Videre asked in a slightly condescending tone.

"I am afraid not, for I have matters to attend to," Sergey bowed his head again. "I am wondering how you arrived though, Lady Videre. I have reports that you had come from the West and not the North."

"Yes," Videre said abruptly. "As you know, the tribes of The Stromy make the most beautiful bead necklaces and my sister absolutely loves wearing them."

Videre pulled out a bead necklace that she had brought with her just in case this specific question was asked. Lord Sergey was meticulous on details. Spies were everywhere and she could not risk the leaders of Moshny finding out that she had just taken one of their artifacts out of the country.

"I see," said Sergey cautiously. "The natives are great workers. It's too bad they are stuck in their traditsii"

"I believe that their traditions keep the soul of Aleria alive."

Sergey laughed, "That is the type of thinking that holds us back from enlightenment. It has been very nice to talk to you again. Perhaps we will see each other soon. You are welcome to roam the castle grounds until dinner. I trust you remember where the dining room is."

Without a moment to let Videre respond, Sergey hobbled through a small door by the throne.

"We should wander the grounds," said Videre as she headed to another door on the opposite side of the hall.

Although she had told herself to not let Sergey get into her head, the image of his broken frame was floating in her mind. His snarky voice was enough to make her want to scream. There were many people she considered as an enemy to her country and Sergey, without any proof, was one of them. She knew not of anything terrible that he had done, but his way of thinking would eventually open the door to great atrocities.

Like most advisors, Lord Sergey had Zaro's ear. Although Zaro Seymon was a greedy and gaudy man, he at least tried to be a decent ruler. Lord Sergey would sway his actions ever so slightly and would take credit for anything good that ever came from the kingdom. Poor Lady Catherine was young, but not naïve. Videre had only met with her a handful of times, but she enjoyed the princess's company. A brilliant young woman with a bright future as the Zara of Moshny was being overshadowed by Lord Sergey.

After zipping down the halls with her handmen at her heels, she pushed open an enormous set of doors exposing a large sitting garden. Blue trumpet flowers were intricately weaved on an arched trellis at the entrance of the garden. Videre looked back and smiled at Malaki who was in awe of the sight of the magnificent garden. His face hadn't changed much from when he was a boy and his smile reminded Videre of those days.

In the middle of the garden was a table and chairs similar to what Videre had in her garden in Desial. On the opposite side of the table was a girl in a white gown with long blond hair shining in the sun. The girl was so focused on her sketchbook that she hadn't noticed her visitors. Without invitation, Videre walked quietly toward the girl and sat across from her. When the girl looked up, she shrieked in excitement.

"Queen Videre," she said with tears in her eyes. "I have missed you so much. So much has happened since we've last talked. Father says I'm to marry Prince Hans of Konis," she blurted out rather abruptly.

"That's wonderful," said Videre reassuringly. "Prince Hans may be a bit younger, but I've heard good things about him from Kinobi. Not only that, but he is most likely one of the wealthiest men on the entire continent."

"That's great and all, but I haven't met him in person," she said as she started crying.

Videre understood all too well the burden Catherine had to shoulder in a potential marriage match. A childhood accident had scarred the right side of her face. Without the scar, Princess Catherine could easily be one of the most beautiful royals in Aleria. The Princess had always been locked away and out of view from her father's shame, and a veil covered her face when making public appearances. With a few sobs, Jooey walked up to the princess and kneeled before her.

"Princess Catherine, we've met before when you were younger. Like my queen, I am excited for your rule in the future and am looking forward to working with you and your people to strengthen our alliance with Moshny."

Videre smiled at Jooey's sincerity. He knew exactly what words to say to any lady. Jooey kissed Catherine's hand and the other handmen followed suit. Even Leon, who had never seen any other royalty other than in Desial, had thought of something to say and also kissed her hand as if he had done it several times before. Jooey's quick thinking put Princess Catherine in higher spirits. So high that Videre had noticed a sparkle in her eyes when looking at the handmen.

Poor girl rarely talks to men outside of the servants of her palace.

"You have a magnificent garden," admired Malaki.

"Thank you. I rarely leave the palace so I have much time on my hands to garden."

"Maybe next time we will be able to discuss some of your plants."

Videre laughed, "Malaki can talk about plants all day."

Catherine's eyes lit up, "I love plants. I know it sounds weird but there's some sort of power in knowing that you can grow something so magnificent from a small seed. All plants are beautiful in their own way."

"I would love for you to come to Desial and see my garden," said Malaki gleefully as the handmen snickered.

"Catherine," said Videre quietly as she grabbed her hand. "I need you to be a vigorous leader. There may be trouble in the near future. You must make your own way in this world and rule gracefully, as I know you are able to do."

"My friend," said Catherine, "If only I could be as good as you in foreign politics, maybe I could be taken more seriously."

"Don't worry about that, dear. I will take care of the foreign politics for you and find you a suitable advisor if you wish."

"I would prefer someone from," Catherine leaned in and whispered, "The Alerian Society."

"Of course," Videre smiled then also lowered her voice, "But please be careful what you say. I don't trust that relic of an advisor your father has."

Catherine giggled, "He is pretty relic-looking, that old fart."

Talking to Catherine was refreshing. Although significantly younger than Videre, she felt as if they were the oldest of friends. Videre had set her mind to sway Catherine in ruling Moshny as she thought was best, but Catherine with such mindfulness like her own did not need to be convinced. Videre was certain she would be a great queen for Moshny someday, and hopefully a greater ally for the days to come.

"Your highness and Lady Videre," called a servant from the door. "Dinner will be served soon."

"Are all your handmen attending?" asked Catherine enthusiastically.

"If you wish for them to come," said Videre.

"It would delight me to have such...men joining us," Catherine said as she blushed.

All of Videre's handmen smiled as they had been flattered that they had caught the attention of The Zarina. Catherine quickly stood from her chair with her sketchbook clutched tightly to her chest and ran to the door.

"I must change my clothes first," she yelled behind her.

Videre heard some snickering behind her coming from the handmen.

"Is there something you want to share," she said curiously.

"Nothing, my queen," said Ezrai, "Except for that Malaki seems very fond of the princess."

"Now calm down Ezrai, we all invite princesses to talk about plants all day in our gardens," said Leon jokingly.

Jooey roared with laughter and hit Leon on the back. "This lad is fitting right in!"

Malaki was blushing. He was never one to talk to girls. Videre normally would join in on teasing Malaki for liking a princess, but she had other things on her mind such as the dinner that was about to take place. The air in the garden was warm unlike that outside of the castle. Even with the warmth of the beautiful surroundings, Videre felt uneasy. Routine visits to different kingdoms were part of her duty but with a new threat on the horizon, she was unsure of who she could trust. Someone as dim as the Zaro of Moshny surely could not plot against Desial but Lord Sergey was another string in the web of politics, a string that Videre desperately wanted to cut.

Only a short while later, Videre found herself sitting at the opposite side of an enormous table across from where she assumed the Zaro would be sitting. Her handmen had already been seated along with Catherine who was pleased with the view at her royal dinner table. Starting conversations with all the handmen, Catherine had quite a distraction. Videre leaned toward Jooey who was sitting next to her.

"We need to convince Zaro Seymon to restructure his government. Lord Sergey has too much power."

Jooey looked around before answering. "I'm also sick of that old man. I wouldn't doubt if it was his idea to prepare the marriage of Catherine and Hans without their meeting. Poor girl is shunned by her looks and they don't know her potential."

Catherine was chatting away with Leon, Ezrai, and Malaki when the doors to the dining room opened. Immediately, everyone except Videre stood up and waited for the Zaro of Moshny to take his seat. Taking his time to his chair, he smiled and waved as if he were addressing a crowd of people in the streets. His long blonde curls bounced against his jewel-encrusted clothes.

The difference between the way Videre carried herself was significantly different than that of Zaro Seymon. She did not need to be loved or recognized in the way that Seymon did. Her power came from the shadows and back-door dealings. The Zaro's power came from him riding in a carriage down the streets and tossing out small coins totaling only a small percentage of the taxes that he had gathered the previous year. In a way, he reminded her of Valencia.

"I have been expecting you, Lady Videre," said Seymon as he sat down and motioned the others to sit.

"I am sorry, I have been delayed in my rounds to the other countries."

"Ah yes. I have heard about Calan."

Videre was sick of people talking about Calan as if it were her identity. She smiled back politely keeping the fire inside of her.

"There are many reasons for my delays but this meeting will be swift as I have not much to offer this time around. My first question is about the marriage between Catherine and Prince Hans."

Catherine choked on her food as her father's smile disappeared.

"Prince Hans is a perfectly respectable young man. As you know, Catherine is my only heir and Prince Hans is third in line for the kingdom of Konis. After my death, she will rule Moshny with Hans."

"I understand the logic of such union but I do not understand the logic of keeping her from meeting Hans first."

With a slam of his fist on the table, his face turned red. "Have you seen her? What do you think I should do?"

Videre smiled and looked at the princess, who now had tears filling her eyes. "Catherine has much to offer as a wife, a ruler, and a future mother. I know you're a kind father who is concerned with her well-being and for her future. If Prince Hans does not wish to take her because of her looks, which would clearly be the only reason, he does not deserve her."

Zaro Seymon let out a deep sigh and sank into his chair.

"I have tried protecting Catherine since the accident. We still don't know who was responsible so you understand why it's difficult to trust anyone."

"Trust has nothing to do with your hesitation. I will personally see to a more than suitable match for Catherine if Prince Hans refuses her. Please let them meet face to face first before plunging them into a marriage."

The Zaro bowed his head. "I will expect you to keep your word then."

Catherine let out a breath of relief and smiled at Videre.

"I have also come to talk to you about the trade route to Zwill and Konis."

"Yes, we've had problems with shipments being ransacked somewhere around the borders. They are mostly fruits and vegetables but we have paused the shipments until we can figure out what's happening to them."

"Who is in charge of these shipments?"

"Lord Sergey is in charge of the shipments."

"Forgive me, Zaro Seymon. I know our government is run very differently than that of yours and your father's but who all is in charge of running the country other than you and Lord Sergey?"

"It is only us. Sometimes I do let dear Catherine arrange public appearances and festivals."

"I understand that there is a level of control that you wish to have in regards to running Moshny, but there is also much that one man cannot do on his own. Perhaps you would be open to having a council or board that may help lighten the load of your rule."

"Lord Sergey says if we delegate, then we won't know what's happening with all aspects of Moshny."

"I will admit, it is a bit terrifying to put others in charge of certain roles, but when you get someone very capable of doing that specific job, it makes everything run so smoothly. I have so much that I have put on very capable people and now I'm able to enjoy a beautiful life. I hardly have to do anything and the people love me."

The Zaro's eyes lit up. "I think that's a brilliant idea, but I don't know where to start."

"I will have our Board Chairman draw up a plan for you. You are always welcome to change and modify it as much you see fit."

Zaro Seymon smiled and thanked Videre, something that she had rarely heard from him. As materialistic and greedy as he was, Seymon was open to suggestions. Videre knew exactly how to twist his mind just like she knew Lord Sergey had been doing for years. She flashed back to the tactics that her father used to use on certain people similar to Zaro Seymon.

Proud of herself for convincing Zaro Seymon of accepting her help, Videre was high in spirits until she saw it. Just a small motion out the corner of her eye. Catherine joyfully talking to the handmen and gracefully touching Leon's hand. Although for a mere second or two, Videre suddenly felt uneasy. Something deep inside her told her not to worry about it, but she could not help but feel as though Leon must be protected. A motherly instinct or juvenile jealousy caused her to speak out abruptly and rather loudly.

"Zaro Seymon, I beg you to send guards with the shipments to Zwill and Konis. They are a great source of your wealth and you are their main provider in food. With guards, they will most likely not be ambushed. I have already ordered some of my men to take up posts along the route for safety."

"Have there been other attacks on trade routes?"

"There have been some new troubles along some of the trade routes. Most likely from mere bandits that decide to take advantage of unprotected merchants. We are all working hard together to eradicate the petty thieves."

"Well then, I must agree to reopen trade. They do provide us with a good amount of capital as you say."

Videre continued the evening flattering Zaro Seymon and listening to the entertaining conversations that Catherine had to offer. All the while, she could not shake the feeling of protecting Leon whether it be from the past, outsiders, or from herself.

MY DEAR JES

Valeria opened her eyes slowly with a yawn. The sun had yet to rise and her fire was still going. She looked at the body next to her and smiled as she stroked his hair.

Such innocence.

She pulled his arm off of her and quietly got out of bed. She picked up her clothes off the floor and slipped them on in the warmth of the fire. For a moment, she knelt in front of the fire and prayed for the souls that she had lost. It wasn't a common occurrence for her to pray but the fire sometimes reminded her of the cremated bodies that had once stood by her side.

Quickly and quietly, she exited her bed chambers. There were no guards at this queen's door like every other queen in the world. She had always lived among her Vipole taking up a room that was similar to theirs. In case of an attack at night, nobody would know which chamber was hers, due to the identical doors and the lack of guards. She thought it was an ingenious plan to which Videre had agreed to partially partake but Valencia was stubborn. Her greatly carved doors caught the attention of every passerby. The two guards always posted at her door gave her chambers away. Videre, on the other hand, had put Kolono's chamber on one side and Jooey's on the other with a secret door leading to her room in case of an emergency. It was understandable. Videre didn't have the same abilities to protect herself like that of Valencia and Valeria.

The halls were quiet and the morning air was chilly. Most everyone in the still morning had not even started to wake. There were a few guards in the halls who bowed to Valeria when in passing. Her footsteps were quick and light, just like what her teachers had taught her. Although most of her training had involved heavy weapons and archery, she was exceptionally skilled at close hand-to-hand, swift combat. She loved the element of surprise and had mastered the movements to where she could sneak up on anyone. The rush that she felt during a fight was starting to fade as recently. There was only training and nothing substantial to fight for. She had been itching for a war.

"Your Majesty," said a hushed voice behind her.

She turned to find Limono next to a column as if he appeared out of nowhere. She was not the biggest fan of the doctor. His dark curly hair, for some reason, annoyed Valeria as she would have a very specific daydream about cutting his precious locks from time to time and watching him cry.

Valencia had hired him as staff to help alleviate any mental tension that the workers in the castle may have. After the incident with Videre, Valencia had started worrying about what kind of stress and problems the handmen had to face. She also assured her sisters that if anyone was able to find any traitors among them, it would be a doctor of psychology.

"Harry did not come to his session last night," he said sternly. "Your men are strong but they also need to keep a balanced mind and that cannot happen when they do not show up to sessions."

"Perhaps Harry feels as if your sessions are a waste of time," Valeria said with a fake smile.

"Your Majesty, there is a delicate balance between the body and mind. I am only here to help your men."

"I will tell Harry to come to your sessions," she said meaninglessly as she walked away. "If he wants to," she yelled over her shoulder.

She never liked the fact that her men would tell Limono their personal feelings. Psychology was a broken art to Valeria who would prefer settling any grievances by fighting her way out of them. It was the honorable way according to her war teachers, but according to her father, it was the brute's way. She had never been close to her father like Videre had been, but at least she shared some common ground with her. Valencia was quite the opposite. She had to have the latest fashions, no matter how uncomfortable. Her dresses and frills had to be perfect when she would have tea parties and luncheons with ladies of other courts and noble families. It almost made Valeria want to vomit.

She entered the training grounds to see that a few of her men were sitting around putting on their training gear. She was always happy to see such men up so early in the morning. The men bowed to Valeria as she sat on a stool and crossed her arms.

"I was thinking some of us should go to Dunbar to train. We should be able to fight in all sorts of terrain and weather. My sister told me the Dunbari Queen had made a new war center in their capital. It supposedly has advanced weaponry and large training grounds. I am quite excited to see it."

"Your Majesty," said one man. "I would absolutely love to accompany you to Dunbar."

"I also would like to go," said another man. "Perhaps we can strengthen our friendship with their country by means of military acclimation instead of these fancy politics."

Valeria smiled. She was pleased with her men for having the same mindset as her. Most of her Vipole had been with her since they were mere children. Videre and Valencia were both opposed to the practice but it worked well for Valeria. She motioned to a light-skinned man who was putting on his worn gloves. He quickly walked to Videre standing up straight with a smile.

"The doctor told me you weren't going to his sessions."

Harry shrugged. "That guy gives me the creeps and I feel like he's not really helping. I just sit there and talk about my day or my feelings."

"Look Harry, I'm not going to force you to go," she said with a smile anticipating that that's what he was going to ask her.

"Thank you Queen Valeria," he said with a relieved smile, "I mean I've already fallen asleep when he was talking to me. It was quite embarrassing and I really didn't want to see him after that."

Videre laughed and shooed Harry away. He was the youngest of the Vipole. She had rescued him from a fight in the streets of Isleland. After learning that he had no father to speak of and a mother who was slowly losing her mind, she had offered a large sum to his mother to bring him home with her. Valencia had scoffed at her but Videre could feel the boys' strength and had agreed that it was the best for the boy.

"Queen Valeria," whispered a black-haired man from a crack in the door, obviously intimidated by the Vipole inside. "Breakfast is ready."

Valeria loved breakfast. In fact, she loved all meals, especially the ones at festivals and banquets. She quickly got up to leave and then threw a small knife at one of her old Vipole. Catching it with one hand without flinching, he smiled.

"One of these days, I'm going to lose an eye to this."

"I think an eye patch would suit you well, Jaime," she said as she laughed and caught the knife that had been tossed back to her.

The sun was slowly starting to peek over the Dunbari Range in the distance. Multiple footsteps echoed in the halls as staff started their normal routines for the day. Opening the dining room doors Valeria grunted as she saw that Valencia and Kinobi were already seated and eating.

"Good Morning, sister," said Valencia in her normal friendly manner.

Without answering, Valeria forged a smile and sat in front of her plate that had a considerable amount of food.

"Did you sleep well?" asked Valencia, trying to make small talk.

"I slept extremely well," said Valeria suggestively.

Kinobi snorted as Valencia got red.

"You are a shameful woman, Valeria. You need to leave those men alone."

"I have no husband to share my bed with and I don't see how it's any of your business," said Valeria in a snarky tone.

"Queen Valencia," said Sevete from the doorway.

In his hands was a tray of letters. He walked quickly to the table and set down the tray. All the letters looked slightly different but all had the same unmistakable seal.

"There must be thirty of these," said Valeria as she thumbed through the tray.

"Did these all come in today?" asked Valencia.

"Yes, Your Majesty. Normally, I would give these to Videre but she isn't here."

"Well just give them to one of her handmen," said Valencia.

"They aren't here either, Your Majesty," said Sevete in a confused tone.

"All of them?"

Sevete sighed and nodded. He always hated to be the bearer of bad news and it showed. His calm demeanor was not something that Valeria liked in a man as talented as him.

"Where the hell did they go?" asked Valeria, still rummaging through the letters.

"Moshny," said Kinobi looking like he wondered why Valeria and Valencia didn't know.

"I'll keep them until she gets back," said Valeria, stacking the letters nicely.

She knew that if the letters were to go into Valencia's hands, then who knew when Videre would get them. Valencia was never one to remember things as she was generally only worried about her schedule. Valeria could see that Kinobi would sometimes be frustrated by her ways but they really were a nice pair.

Valeria had long ago considered marrying Kinobi, as he was one of the only Kiadere nobles that Valeria could stand. At the time, Valencia was betrothed to his cousin, but before they had even started planning the wedding, he had died from a heart complication. After Valencia's period of mourning, she had looked to Kinobi to carry on the Kiadere line without knowing Valeria's intentions. Although Valeria was decently upset, she figured that she would do well in life without marrying and having children. She had all that she needed from her Vipole anyways.

"Why are they all in Moshny?" asked Valencia.

"Something about meeting with the Zaro," replied Kinobi.

"That's strange. Usually, Videre doesn't bring everyone with her during her trips. Did Leon go to?"

"Yeah, as far as I know, all of them went with her. I'm surprised you didn't know."

Valeria laughed. "We never know what the other is doing."

She started gulping down her juice louder than usual just to annoy her sister. It was true. The sisters were so out of touch with each other more than anyone ever knew.

"I don't like Limono around here," she said suddenly after remembering his annoying voice so early in the morning.

"Limono does great work with the people of the castle," said Valencia reassuringly.

Valeria was scarfing down her food like a mad man. She could tell that Valencia was disgusted but Kinobi was thoroughly entertained by the sight.

"It's a slap in the face for us to have to share feelings with a man who thinks he's better than us," she said with her mouth full of food, knowing that it would get on Valencia's nerves.

"Then ignore him and let the men talk to him as they wish."

"Fine. But if he gets in my face one more time, I'm breaking his arm," said Valeria as she swooped up the letters and walked from the table while chewing.

Looking through the letters as she was walking in the hallways, she felt a sense of worry. All the letters were addressed to Videre and all were bearing the seal of The Alerian Society. It was rare to get letters from The Alerian Society but this was unprecedented. Perhaps Fryderyk and Anabar's warning was part of a much bigger plot than Valeria previously expected. Without thinking, a smile spread across her face. If there was to be a war, she was ready and more than willing.

As she walked to her office, she spied a tall elegant blonde-haired man pacing back and forth in front of the door. His stature was easily recognizable even under all the colorful clothing.

"Jes," she said joyfully almost running toward him.

"My Lady," he said with a deep bow. "I would like a word in private."

Valeria smiled enticingly as she unlocked the door and let him in.

"What's the reason for your visit today?" she asked as she sat on her desk and set the letters down next to her.

Jes sat down in the chair in front of her desk. His blue eyes sparkled just as they did all those years ago.

"My son is doing well, I presume."

"Your son is doing extremely well. I've been debating to promote him to Vipole."

"Don't jest with me Valeria. You only promote to Vipole after several years of service and if they pass the trials."

"He's been training with me, Jes," she said matter-of-factly. "He has great intuition and works extremely hard."

"I hope training is the only thing you're doing with him," Jes said harshly.

Valeria laughed. Jes knew very well what it meant to be a Vipole. His concern as a parent was something that she expected. Almost all of her Vipole had no parents or at least parents who hadn't cared for them. For her, it was easier to make soldiers from men without families.

"I don't want Jolon to become Vipole."

Valeria's smile quickly disappeared.

"Jolon is of age where he can choose. You should understand."

"I understand very well, My Lady. There are rumors within The Alerian Society. I cannot lose my only son."

"Jes," she said quietly, "You promised me your firstborn. It would be a shame if you broke your promise."

"He was to be a handman, not a Vipole. The only reason why I had to make that ridiculous promise was because that was the only way I could leave the Vipole.

"But we had fun, Jes. You were one of my best. The power deep within you is envied by all."

"Why do you think I haven't taught my children? The power in them is so destructive. I'm scared that if Jolon loses control, he may regret something."

Valeria sat next to him and took his hand. Jes had always been softer than most of her Vipole but worked hard to prove his spot among the men.

"You never lost control. I will make sure that Jolon won't lose control. I train him every day and I observe him carefully, just for your sake. Videre should be back soon and I can make sure he finds himself the peaceful way."

"No," blurted Jes. "If he is to find himself, it'll be with you."

"Videre is the best at what she does and you know that."

"I understand that, but Keono was my friend. After what happened to him, I cannot trust my son with her."

"It pains me that you think of my sister in that regard, but I will teach Jolon myself if you insist," she said as she gripped his hand. "Only for you, not because I don't have faith in Videre."

"I would also like to have you watch over my daughter."

Valeria laughed. "Jaora is such a sweet girl. It's unfortunate that she hasn't found herself yet."

"She has," said Jes a little apprehensively.

"You can't hide her true self from us Jes. Videre knew the first time she saw her. Why do you think Videre hired her?"

"Jaora said that Valencia hired her because of the work she did on the dresses."

"Sometimes, I don't know if you're joking or serious," she said. "Videre knew the potential that Jaora had, so she convinced Valencia that Jaora had surpassed her mother in her abilities."

Jes looked down. "I apologize. I've tried to hide her true nature all these years. You never know what will happen to people like her."

Valeria laughed. "I just think it's funny how you thought Videre wouldn't see her true nature."

"Keep an eye on Leon too," he said quietly. "I know he's in the service of Videre."

"Why do you have an interest in Leon?" asked Valeria inquisitively.

"I took Leon under my wing when his parents passed. He is like my own child. He is just like Jaora and Keono."

Just like Jaora and Keono? It can't be. Videre didn't tell us.

"Of course," Valeria smiled. "I'll keep an eye on the boy."

DIO SECRETS

After a good night's rest in the magnificent palace of Moshny. Leon awoke feeling refreshed. Staying the past couple of nights outside and at a common inn on his journey across Aleria certainly made him realize how blessed he was. The comfort of his surroundings quickly disappeared as they found themselves on the road once again. With a few gifts from Zaro Seymon, they departed early in the morning to the east. According to Jooey, they would be flying on their sen-rima once again at night. The night before with Zaro Seymon and Princess Catherine had opened Leon's eyes to how things were run between countries. He had started to understand the deeper connection that Videre had with other leaders throughout the land.

Riding through the countryside of Moshny was refreshing to Leon. The chilly air accompanied by the rolling hills and bright green grass was something he wasn't used to, but seemed like it could be familiar. Riding alongside his queen and her handmen was invigorating. He had felt that he had already been accepted as a member of the group, especially since Lostanzo wasn't present. Being exposed to politics and secrets came easily. So easily in fact, that he questioned how far he had come in just a matter of weeks.

With the ocean in view, he heard it again. The sound that he had heard in the cave on the edge of The Stromy. The ringing in his ears was unmistakable. Before he could tell anyone about it, the noise disappeared. Videre looked back at her men and she slid off of Lady Italych, as they reached a small cliff with the waves of the ocean crashing beneath.

They had been riding for quite some time since late morning. Instead of talking during their ride to the ocean, they had traveled in silence. Leon had learned to let Videre ride in peace when she had a certain look on her face. Leon had started understanding her expressions and the moods that accompanied them. Eating the sweets that were provided to them by Princess Catherine, Leon admired Videre from afar. She was looking out into the distance from which they came as if she were waiting for someone. Her brown hair flowed in the wind and her breaths drew deeper and slower as the brilliance of the light around her shone in sparking hues.

"Come sit with us, My Queen," offered Jooey, snapping Leon back into reality.

With a face of appreciation, Videre sat with the four men around a campfire that Jooey had started.

"We made great progress, but who is this Board Chairman you were referring to?" asked Ezrai.

"You're my Board Chairman," Videre laughed.

Ezrai laughed too, "I guess I'm to make this new government plan for Zaro Seymon."

"Yes. Don't worry Ezzie. Just put together a mix of what the other countries do for their government and send him an outline."

Ezrai's face flushed. "Yes, My Queen."

"I was impressed with how easily he accepted ideas for a new government," said Leon.

Videre smiled, "This is my job, Leon. If I couldn't get through to the leaders of Aleria, we would most definitely be at each other's throats. I have my own tactics for people like the Zaro. First, I used Catherine as a premise to seem confident in his one and only heir. Recognizing that Catherine would be a good ruler would put the Zaro at ease knowing that Catherine would have a strong ally. I also offered to lend a hand in finding a suitable match for Catherine just in case, making it seem as though there were many matches available when in fact there are hardly any that I can think of, but I will deal with that when the time comes. The next step was to feign ignorance. I knew exactly how their government was being run and how it was mostly Lord Sergey making the calls. Skipping a common step, praise, I immediately went to bragging. Someone like Zaro Seymon needs more. He wants people to love him. He wants a beautiful life without the work. Although a small lie, I knew how to form my words to where he became jealous. Then, I offered a helping hand from my Board Chairman. Such a man didn't exist of course until now, but working together with Ezrai, he would never know. I also added the fact that he could change any of the plans to fit his own needs. This was to reassure him that I wasn't trying to undermine his politics. Of course, a man like the Zaro will probably keep to the plan if there is no interference from Sergey."

"Sergey needs to be dealt with," mumbled Malaki. "He is undermining the princess and I wouldn't doubt if he tries taking over."

"Which is why Catherine must have a suitable marriage. Unfortunately, Prince Hans is one of the few that can actually help secure her spot on the throne. Zaro Seymon is getting older and we must be prepared for a transfer of power."

"What's that?" asked Jooey looking in Malaki's hands.

Malaki turned the paper around revealing a picture of a flower that was obviously given to him by Catherine.

"I was looking through Princess Catherine's garden and saw a flower I had never seen before. She said it was from the land of the Viceroys. She drew a picture of it for me and gave me some seeds so I can plant it later."

The flower was indeed nothing like Leon had seen before. The petals were plain and almost bowl-shaped. Catherine had added a splash of red paint and her small signature at the bottom dotted the "i" with a heart.

Malaki, completely unaware of what she may have been hinting at, started talking about the flowers that looked similar but had the smallest differences. Leon listened attentively as did the rest of the group while he envisioned the fun Catherine would be having to listen to such rambling.

The day wound down and the sun had started setting as everyone made preparations to fly once more, but this time, across the ocean. Leon's heart beat faster as he rubbed Lady Kayle's side. In just a short time, Leon had to have complete trust in each Lady Kayle. After what had happened in the cave in The Stromy, he knew that Lady Kayle would protect him. As he mounted her, he felt the familiar rush of the wind as her wings took flight into the darkening sky.

Collectively, the senrima soared together once again through the thick clouds. Like before, Leon felt such power and freedom on top of the clouds and he fell into a trance. The wings of the senrima had slowed, the stars sparkled like Mrs. Potter's diamonds and the cold air didn't bother him during the few moments of bliss. After a while of flying through wisps of clouds high above the thick clouds, he started seeing beautiful lights in the distance dancing in the sky. With the clouds disappearing slowly, he could make out hues of red and purple lights that looked as if a stream were crossing in the sky. Below them were dotted lights from the street lanterns of small villages on a group of islands far from the mainland. Without warning, Lady Kayle and the other senrima dove down toward a small island with few lights.

Once again, Leon felt the enormous pressure in his chest igniting memories of dreams long ago where he had fallen through the sky in a similar fashion. Gripping Lady Kayle's reins, he looked up at the lights in the sky wondering if his father had also taken the same path before with Videre. The fact that he had left his beloved country, met other royalty, uncovered an artifact, and now was looking at the beautiful skylights of legend appeased Leon for now.

He had recalled hearing stories of the skylights from his father. He said that the Hikarians look up to the skylights and pray. What religion they followed, Leon had no idea. Looking at the skylights, he could see why praying to them would make sense as they seemed to be mythical and majestic in a spiritual way.

Feeling and hearing the rush of the wind, Leon gripped the reins tightly until they had landed on a dark cobblestone street. Few people were in sight and had seen them coming down from the sky but barely batted an eye and went about their business.

"We should have kept Lostanzo with us," said Jooey looking at the sky while dismounting his senrima.

"We needed Lostanzo with the box. We don't need as much cover here in Hikari," said Videre looking around trying to find her sense of direction.

"I think it's this way," said Malaki looking to the north.

"Zakalan," said Ezrai.

"North," answered Leon confidently.

"They say Alerian will die out with the new generation," said Videre as she started walking north. "I do, however, appreciate that the Viceroy languages have an expanded vocabulary."

Their footsteps echoed eerily in the small village on the Hikarian island. The village looked old and almost decrepit as if a small gust of wind would be able to do significant damage.

"This city is called Nanoto. It means 'to live' in the Olde Language," said Ezrai. "Here, we don't have to hide away," he said motioning to the senrima who Leon had just noticed were still unbuckled from their saddle strap with their wings clearly visible.

Videre had no hood on when passing the villagers and some would stop and bow in recognition. Leon was astounded how the people of this small village across the ocean could recognize a queen of Desial while her own countrymen couldn't. Stopping and boarding their horses at a clean and unused looking stable, Videre led the men to a nearby tavern and sat at a table situated in the center of the room. Without ordering anything, a young man brought food and drinks to them. The people at the other tables bowed their heads slightly when Videre would look their way.

"I don't like it here," said Malaki quietly as he took some food from the center of the table.

"Nobody likes it here, lad."

Before Leon could open his mouth Videre started explaining to him as if she knew the questions would start again.

"Nanoto is a safe haven for people like us. It's masked as an old creepy town for our own safety."

"So everyone here is Kiadere?"

"Mostly everyone, yes. It is also a safe haven for The Alerian Society and The Dio."

Leon had just realized that Ezrai had never given him the explanation to what The Alerian Society actually was. Ezrai also looked like he just realized and started explaining.

"The Alerian Society was made more than two thousand years ago since the beginning of record. The Alerian Society was sort of like a council of men who governed over the Kiadere and after many years of exploration and trade with native tribes, they governed over all of Aleria."

"Except for Alflint, Dunbar, and Korona," Videre added.

"The Alerian Society and Dio, in fact, ruled together," said Ezrai.

"The Dio?" asked Leon, vaguely remembering the name.

Videre continued the explanation. "The Dio is the religious part of the old ways in Aleria. They believe in bonding with nature and using powers for the good of humankind. The leader of The Dio is simply called Dio. Right now, Dio Cioto is the head of The Dio. His son, Poloto, is Zien Dio. It means second Dio. Zien Dio takes over as head of The Dio when Dio dies."

Videre winced as her words seemed jumbled and looked as if she confused herself.

"The Dio also believe that the Kiadere came on a boat from the skies and landed in Aleria in a calling to unite the natives of the land," said Ezrai in a quavering voice.

Videre looked at Leon sorrowfully, "When Les Nettoyer happened, the pure blood Kiadere, The Dio, and The Alerian Society were all hunted down. Even children had no place in their world. With a few Viceroy allies, we were able to save some Kiadere from harm as long as they hid in plain sight. The only way someone could tell if you were really a pure Kiadere would be if they saw you using your powers or if they knew your age. You see, the Viceroy can live to around three hundred years which is one of the reasons why they were worshiped. The pure Kiadere also live to that age, but the natives of Aleria live to about eighty years old. It's a significant difference, which is why Kiadere were revered so much before the Viceroy came."

"Most people on Aleria, however, are mixed with Kiadere and the natives. Their life spans are usually about one hundred fifty. So if you want to hide as a pureblood Kiadere, you have to make sure nobody knows your true age," said Jooey. "I don't know much about the age range of the Dunbari, Alflintians, and of the Creatures of Korona. It's amazing how we've been at peace with them for so long, yet they remain partially isolated from us."

"I did hear of a species on Korona that can live up to six hundred years," blurted an excited Malaki with food still in his mouth.

"Aye, The native species of Fitzroya Forest of Korona," said a loud and deep voice next to them. An older man with magnificent robes smiled at the group, after a long bow toward Videre.

"Zien Dio Poloto, it's been a while," said Videre politely.

"Queen Videre, I must say I was surprised to receive your letter. It's been years since a Vidal Vasili has come to our quaint island. I see you have brought the finest handmen," he said as he looked at Leon.

"This is Leon Minet," Videre said cautiously.

"Of course. He looks just like his father. I have heard of your talents, Minet," Zien Dio Poloto said optimistically.

An embarrassed Leon quickly thanked him, stirring up an uneasiness inside of him. He looked at Videre who was looking right back at him. She could see what he was thinking, he was sure of it.

"Please," he said as he extended his hand toward the back of the building.

Leading them through a twisted tunnel similar to the tunnels at the Vician castle, Leon questioned what he had gotten himself into. Just like the torches in Desial, they lit up mere seconds ahead of them. Upon reaching a large and seemingly heavy door with several locking mechanisms, the man strained as he opened it. Inside the large doors seemed all too familiar.

"Welcome to Kiadere's cavern, lad," whispered Jooey.

Leon had flashed back to the cave that he had fallen into on their way to The Stromy. This cavern, however, was immense and modern. He could imagine the whole city of Vici fitting into the cavern. Buildings and houses had been built inside which seemed impossible. Leon had no doubt that all of her handmen had been here before because there was no look of shock or excitement on their faces. Zien Dio Poloto led them down a narrow road until they reached a beautiful purple and silver mansion.

"Nobody has been inside since the last time you were here. I hope it is accommodating enough for you and your group," Zien Dio Poloto said as he looked at the house with pride. "I must get going now. Dio Cioto will be expecting you at the temple tomorrow," he said and left down the road from which they came.

The inside of the house was as magnificent as the outside. Flowers in vases were intricately designed and placed in all areas of the house. The main room was large and lofty, offering overstuffed seating around an oval table. Almost everything was made with purple and silver hues, representing the colors of Desial. Although Leon never really minded the national colors, he did feel that the decor was a bit overwhelming. Like adolescent boys, Jooey, Malaki, and Ezrai ran upstairs to claim their room.

"There are seven rooms here, don't worry," laughed Videre as soon as Leon finally understood what was happening.

After finding an empty room, Leon started getting ready to go to sleep to put an end to a travel-filled day. The fireplace in his room was already lit and burning in a similar fashion to the torches in the castle hallway. Leon had always known the stories of magic but the past few days had opened his eyes to the possibilities of the world. The bed was just as comfortable as the one back in the castle. Although he had never been here before, h felt oddly safe and started dozing within moments of pulling the covers over him.

Come.

She grabbed Leon's hand once again.

Mom. Where are you taking me?

She stopped and turned to look at him. Her face was clearer than ever, but now they were not in the snow in Desial. They were outside on a hill. A city in a valley lay beneath them with small twinkling lights.

You need to know about your past. You need to help your queen. It's your destiny.

Her hand slipped from Leon's. The monuments that he had seen in his dreams before were also in this location. Although different stones, the writings on the stones were written similarly. He could feel the sea breeze and hear noises from the village below. The dream was almost as vivid as reality.

You are the key to her plans, but you cannot trust her completely.

Leon awoke abruptly. Keone had always told Leon to be wary of his dreams and to tell him if they ever changed. Both Keone and Mrs. Potter believed that dreams were a hidden part of you, speaking to yourself but even as the dreams became more vivid, he couldn't understand any deeper meaning to them. Why Leon kept seeing his late mother was beyond him. The fire crackled as fiercely as it did when he went to sleep.

Unable to go back to sleep, Leon's stomach begged him to go down to the kitchen as he only had a few mouthfuls in the tavern. Slowly tiptoeing out of his room so as to not wake any others, he could feel his stomach rumbling. On his way to the stairs, he saw Videre and Ezrai sitting on the sofa conversing. Heeding his dreams warning, he decided to stay on the stairs and listen to their conversation. Closing his eyes he strained to hear their exchange.

"I don't like what you're insinuating," said Ezrai. "We are at the heart of The Alerian Society and The Dio. You are their one true queen."

"It doesn't matter right now. Even Miss Rayne would agree with me."

"So what are you going to say to them?"

"Only the partial truth. We will ask them for information about The Alerian Blood Clan. Nothing about the artifact and definitely nothing about Jessica Henderson."

"I was really hoping that either The Dio or The Alerian Society would be able to help us. They have the resources we don't."

"We can always ask for help but it would have to be in the form of another reason. Dio Cioto is getting old. We must be ready for a change in power here also, and I still don't know enough about the Zien Dio. He has the Marciella ability and I worry. There are only a handful of people with that ability and I wouldn't trust any of them no matter how well-intentioned it is."

"I understand. I wonder if there's any news on the artifact."

"Ciano updated me a few hours ago. He said Miss Rayne had been working on it all day."

"What do we tell Leon?"

After a short pause, Videre sighed. "We'll tell him the truth. In small bits anyways. Ezrai, you must dig into the past soon. We're running out of time," she said as she stood up.

Leon quickly got up from his listening post and stealthily ran back to his room.

"Go to the library while I visit with Dio Cioto. I expect we won't be here for long," said Videre as they walked to the large temple in the middle of the cavern. Leon was groggy from the night before. Between the conversation that Videre had with Ezrai and the dream of his mother's warning, his head was still trying to make sense of it all.

"Of course," Ezrai said, changing directions and quickly walking down another street.

Upon closer inspection, Leon noticed the buildings inside the cavern were not old and run-down like the ones outside. Leon couldn't help but wonder how such a city was built inside of an enclosed space and when they had been built. Looking at the ceiling and the pillars of the cavern, he could make out faint etchings and drawings similar to that of the cave near The Stromy. There were also more people in Kiadere's cavern than in the town outside and almost everyone who passed, bowed to Videre. Videre almost completely ignored the people of the cavern as if she was unhappy about being recognized. They were headed to the center of the cavern towards a building that towered all the other structures in the area. As they came closer, Leon recognized the man standing in the middle of the road.

"Dio Cioto is waiting for you, your highness," Zien Dio Poloto said cheerfully as he ran up to her. "We are so glad you have come to visit us as our true leader of Aleria."

"Would you mind if Malaki stayed here?" asked Videre looking at the magnificent garden that surrounded the building. "He has a thing for gardens."

"Oh yes, my Queen. Our gardens here are truly a sight as our lights in the cavern do not come from the sun."

Leon looked up once again. He can't believe that he hadn't noticed it before. There indeed was no sunlight or even torches for that matter. It was bright enough to be dawn but there was no source of light. Leon realized that it was dark as night when they had entered the cavern so there must have been some magic that allowed the time of day to be in sync with that of the outside world. Such a wonder seemed to be impossible, yet all too familiar.

Malaki bowed to Zien Dio with a smile on his face before waltzing onto a brick path into the gardens. The outside of the temple was built with plain stone and wooden doors, but walking into the temple was very different than what Leon had expected. The floors were made of a hard stone that was glimmering with gold and silver specks. Lining the halls were marble statues of different men and women. The ceilings were high and arched and their footsteps echoed throughout the temple warning everyone that there were visitors among them. Leon had gotten used to Jooey looking around almost nervously for threats even though they were entering into what Leon assumed was a safe place. Walking through the empty and eerie hall, they came up to a large table with a lone man sitting seemingly uncomfortable, engrossed in a large book.

"Come sit," he said without looking up.

In an uncomfortable manner, Videre took the seat opposite of him while the two remaining handmen stood behind her. After a few moments of waiting for the bearded man, he closed his book with a loud thud that had also echoed through the great hall.

"Forgive me for not greeting you properly," he said remorse-fully. "If I stop reading the section, I'll soon forget it. Get me some water, boy"

Zien Dio Poloto sighed and turned back to where they came from.

"You wrote to me, my dear."

"Yes. I have heard rumblings about The Alerian Blood Clan. I was wondering if you know anything about them."

"The Alerian Blood Clan, I'm afraid, is just a silly little name for anyone who is against the Kiadere and the Viceroy. All I know is that they have never been large enough to form an organized group to do any sort of damage. May I ask how you came about the information?"

"We have an intercepted message. Of course, I would have to recognize any threat seriously no matter how small, but I remember hearing about them when I was young, right here in these very halls."

"You are right, we did talk to your father about them. I was only Zien Dio, but Dio Kirine deemed it not necessary to pursue them any further as we see them as no threat. What exactly was in this intercepted message?"

"I'm not sure as I didn't see it personally. It talked of missing people and plundering trade routes."

She didn't mention children and plants. Does she really not trust Dio that much?

"Why would they be against Kiadere and Viceroy?"

"Because according to them, they are not of this world. Viceroy came in a flaming iron dragon and had unnatural wisdom. The Kiadere came on a boat from a foreign land and possessed unnatural powers. I am disappointed that we are slowly dying out. Now that we have gone into hiding, many more Kiadere are mixing with the natives. Abilities are now few and far between. I fear that my children will live in the last generation of Kiadere. We never ruled the people with iron fists like the Viceroy, yet we have fallen from power and are the ones being persecuted," said the old man, starting to look angry.

"There are more of us than you think. I hope to bring back many more generations of our kind."

The old man smiled, "I would trust nobody other than you to keep that promise. I sincerely hope the people of Aleria can see how good it was when we had common values instead of all the separation we have had since Polonotadere."

"Do you have any information about the Alerian Blood Clan? In your library, perhaps?" asked Videre faking a small smile.

"Unfortunately, they have always been just a rumor. I believe we don't have any written records of them. I can send in a request to a librarian. It may take some time, but we can send a message if anything is found in our records," said the Dio gracefully.

Videre stood up rather abruptly, "I'm afraid we must get going. I have some appointments that I must keep. Please send a message to the library and I hope to receive a letter from you in the near future."

The old man stood up from his seat slowly and bowed.

"I am very glad to see that the Minet boy is your handman," said the man staring at Leon. "He is destined for great things."

"Yes," said Videre almost proudly with a smile.

"Your Majesty," yelled Malaki as he came running toward her when they stepped outside into the gardens. "I was given some rare seeds from a woman who runs this garden," he said, as he motioned to an elderly woman across a few rows of colorful flowers.

Videre smiled, "Go get Ezrai then pack up our things at the mansion, we will be leaving shortly."

As the men followed her orders without question, Videre turned and walked toward the woman. Videre's fist tightened and her heart beat loudly as her ears were filled with a distinct and familiar ringing.

"Malaki was young, but I was not. How do you expect me to keep your secret from one of my handmen."

The elderly woman bowed as tears filled her eyes. "I have my reasons for not retrieving the boy. I was being hunted and when his mother had gotten sick, I knew it was by their hand. They threaten to destroy our family line and we had no choice."

"Are you going by his mother's name?"

"I did treat a few people in need and gave them her name. It was the first name I could think of. The people who were after me think I'm dead and this sanctuary keeps it that way," she said as she looked around nervously. "Please be careful, something is coming. The Dio has ordered me to make a certain concoction. He will not tell any of us of what is happening," she said, discreetly giving Videre a small vial filled with liquid.

Videre took a deep breath, still angry with the elderly woman, "He saved my life once. I will repay my debt by not telling him. I will, however, summon you when I feel the time is appropriate so you can tell him yourself."

THE LOVE FOR YOUR QUEEN

Navigating their way out of the Kiadere cavern, Leon was brought back to the cold desolate village once again. The buildings were as run down as he had seen the night before. More people walked the streets, staring at Videre and her handmen with small whispers amongst them. A young girl ran out from a house and offered Videre a small bouquet of hand-picked flowers.

"Save us," she said quietly with tears in her eyes.

Without a word, Videre took the flowers and patted her on the head as she continued on. Leon thought such a cold reaction was unwarranted but after seeing her face, he could tell Videre was keeping in her true feelings. The senrima made a loud ruckus when setting their eyes upon their riders. Familiar comforts of the castle had also affected them in the dreary stables.

"We have to take the ferry to the next island," Videre said sorrowfully as she looked at Lady Italych.

"We should pray for safety first," said Jooey looking upon a nearby hill.

Leaving their senrima in the stables, the four of them trekked up the small hill. As they neared the top, Leon felt uneasy. He could make out the etched monuments that were in his dreams. Another few steps and he looked down the hill to the valley that lay below them.

"I've been here before," he said out of breath, struggling to keep up with Jooey's long strides.

As they reached the top, he was sure that this was the place he had seen in his dreams the night before.

"You've never been here before," said Videre confidently.

"I've seen this place in my dreams," said Leon walking around the stone monuments trying to find the exact spot where he was standing in his dream. "I have dreams of these monuments. This is the first time actually seeing them with my own eyes. Last night, I saw these stones. Usually, the stones are covered with snow and in a forest."

A worried look came over Videre's face. "Are you sure you've never seen these other than in your dreams?"

"What was the dream about?" asked Ezrai curiously before Leon could answer.

"It's usually just me at the stones or walking around them. I'm usually with my mother."

"I thought your mother had passed," said Ezrai visibly confused.

"She did. I don't know why I dream about her. My grandfather said that dreams were a part of me speaking to myself."

"So you remember what your mother looks like?" Ezrai continued as if he didn't believe Leon.

"I didn't really remember until I saw her face in my dream. What exactly are these stone monuments?" asked Leon, trying to get off the topic of his mother.

"They're ancient relics called Solano Zintoya" said Ezrai confidently. "These were built by The Dio long ago and engraved with stories of the lands and certain prayers. There are several monuments all over Aleria."

The letters were made mostly of straight lines and hardly any circles or curves like the alphabet he was used to writing. The classes in school never taught the students how to write in the Olde Language although there were still many places where the Olde language could be seen like on the streets of Vici. They were taught to write the pronunciations of the Olde Language in the Viceroy alphabet.

"What do they say?"

Ezrai smiled as if he had been waiting for someone to ask him.

"This one here talks about the skylights and the legends surrounding them such as the different colors meaning different patterns in the weather that's to come. And this other one talks about the natives and what kind of ships they built. Our ancestors wrote these to not lose sight of the history of the land. Unfortunately with the new generation not being able to read the language, it will most likely be lost."

"We must get going," said Videre annoyingly. "We have a ferry to catch."

She quickly trekked down the hill and Jooey followed after he had a short moment of prayer. Leon couldn't describe it, but there was something wrong with Videre. She had the same look on her face as his grandfather when he mentioned his dreams. He was sure that she would be in a foul mood on the ferry.

Retrieving their senrima from the stables, they found their way to a small ferry with only a few people on board. Without saying a word, the men and their senrima followed Videre onto the rocking boat. Within minutes of boarding, the ferry had left the dock. Leon had never been on a boat this large before. A few times, he had been on a canoe and a fishing boat, but this was something entirely different. The blue-gray waves rocked the ferry ever so slightly, as the strong ocean breeze had a distinct smell to it. The waters glimmered and the sky was nearly cloudless as if he were in a painting. The ride would have been more peaceful if it wasn't for Jooey.

"I've always hated the sea," said Jooey almost hurling on the side of the ferry.

The senrima were equally restless. Leon could tell that Lady Kayle was itching to fly instead of riding on a boat across the small stretch of ocean. He reached into his pocket and felt for the small stone inside. Before descending down the hill of the Solano Zintoya, Leon had noticed a small glimmering stone at his feet in the same location of where he had been standing in his dream. The stone was no ordinary stone. It was the jewel that he had taken out of Videre's timekeeper and replaced with the Bloodstone from Mrs. Potter's shop. The fact that it was here in Hikari, in a place that he had only seen in a dream, could not have been a coincidence. Although it made him sick to his stomach, he kept this secret from Videre after the warning in his dream. As the ferry reached the dock of the next island, Leon could tell that Videre was becoming even more nervous than Lady Kayle. She had been pacing back and forth on the boat in seemingly deep thought. Jooey, Ezrai, and Malaki also seemed to be nervous but only because of Videre.

"I would like to make this visit short," said Videre as she stepped off the boat. "We need to get to Miss Rayne's house tonight."

As they stepped off the boat, a group of older men slowly walked up to Videre. All of them bore robes and bowed in unison to Videre.

"Queen Videre," said the oldest of the men, "My name is Sakazaki and we welcome you to Hikari. My men will take your horses to the royal stables. Please follow me."

This Island of Hikari was vastly different than at Nanot and Lake Nodio. The streets were neatly made with stones of irregular shapes that fit together intricately. The buildings were made of raw-looking wood and roofs that looked like stacked clay cylinders that had been cut in half. The streets were busy but eerily quiet unlike that of Vici and Moshny. There was a strange peace that he felt while walking through this city.

The people of the streets stared at the men who were escorting the Desialians and their senrima. Leon figured the people revered the men in robes but had no idea who Videre was. The people of Hikari were most likely under the same law ensuring the absence of information about the leaders of the other countries. He did feel more at peace with the men in robes leading them than he did in Moshny when the intimidating guard had led them.

He could see that they were headed to the large castle that stood atop a mountain in the middle of the city. He expected to walk up another set of stairs leading to the castle but to his surprise, there was a contraption unlike what he had ever seen before. A set of several large ropes lead up to the top of the mountain from where they stood. The ropes were wound around a large wheel with two horses attached to it. On the ropes, were benches on which to sit. Leon knew what was about to happen and he was not excited. His trust in foreign structures had waned ever since he had fallen into the cave at The Stromy.

Videre and Sakazaki sat together on the first bench as the attendant started driving the horses, moving the large wheel. Slowly the seat started moving up into the sky. Without stopping the horses, the handmen had to time themselves to take their seat on the benches. The ride was favorable and smooth unlike what he had thought. However, he would rather ride Lady Kayle up to the top of the mountain. He was grateful for an experience he never knew existed, even though he was hesitant. He looked at the bench ahead of him. Jooey had sat by himself, being so large, there wouldn't be much space for anyone to sit by him. Behind him were Ezrai and Malaki in a deep conversation with worried looks on their faces. Leon was not sure of what to expect from the rest of this journey. He had already had quite an adventure meeting Miss Rayne, going to Moshny, and meeting the head of the Dio.

As the bench kept crawling up into the sky, he was in awe by his view. He could see distant islands and small ships on the sparkling ocean. He was also able to make out the main continent in the distance and wondered if he was looking at Reino or Moshny. The increasingly strong blowing wind sent shivers up his spine when the bench rocked. He gripped the bench and started taking deep breaths. Looking back, he could tell that Malaki and Ezrai were so engrossed in their conversation that they hadn't noticed at all.

Upon landing, they were greeted by Hikarian women in long flowing robes of different patterns and colors. Their hair was put up into intricate buns with perfectly placed flowers and small trinkets. Their white faces and bright-colored lips smiled and bowed to Videre as they were standing in a line to the entrance of the castle. The base of the castle was built on top of large gray stones serving as a foundation. The white castle boasted many stories, looking more like a tower, getting smaller with each level. The top-level had sliding doors leading to a balcony with a red railing. Standing on the balcony were three figures looking down at them, too far away to see their faces. Walking inside was as impressive as the outside. Tapestries lined the walls donning paintings of people and mythical creatures. The stories depicted on the tapestries were as foreign to Leon as the castle was.

"Senrima," whispered Ezrai, pointing to one tapestry. Several figures of horses were painted on a tapestry across the room flying high above the wisps of purple and pink clouds. The number of colors inside of the plain white castle was mesmerizing. The robes of all the people inside were also like tapestries of flowers and creatures. Even the suits of armor were elaborate with small metal pieces fitted together perfectly, just like the stones at the base of the castle and the roofs of all the houses. Going up one floor, they came to a large audience chamber. Unlike the first floor filled with beautiful paintings, the room looked plain and dull. To Leon's surprise, they did not stay in the audience chamber but went up to another floor. This floor was all white with gold accents adorning everything from the table to the ceilings. A short table sat in the middle of the room covered in different, meats, fruits, and vegetables. The sight and smell caused a great rumble in

Jooey's stomach as his face turned red. At the opposite side of the table were the three figures that Leon had seen outside on the balcony. He recognized the Emperor as one of the members of the meeting that King Fryderyk had called during the Equinox Festival. On the right, was an older woman with gray stands in her black hair that Leon had recognized as an attendee at the festival. On the opposite side was a younger man that looked to be Leon's age. They were dressed in plain robes and were sitting on the ground with large cushions. Videre smiled as she bowed and sat on a cushion across the table from the emperor.

"Please," the younger man said to the handmen, motioning to the empty cushions around the table.

Leon sat next to the woman rather uncomfortably as he wasn't used to sitting on the floor to eat. She smiled slightly as he sat next to her.

"I am Princess Midori. This is my father, Emperor Hideki, and my brother, Prince Aoki. It is nice to finally meet you."

"You know who I am?"

"Yes. Your grandfather had made us a magnificent time-piece that sits in our ancestral room. I have also heard of your work."

"I am very glad you have come, Lady Videre." said the emperor, interrupting his daughter. "You have only met my son when he was young."

"Yes. It's been a while. He takes after his beautiful mother," she said, smiling at the prince.

"Prince Aoki is at the age where he must get to know the ones who rule the lands west of Hikari. When I leave this world, Prince Aoki must be able to rule peacefully alongside the other countries just as you have done with yours. My father held the Kiadere people in high esteem which is why they are granted asylum here. There is no doubt that they are extremely beneficial to us as well with funding and their special talents. I have, however, heard rumors about the group that wishes to eradicate them and I worry that they may come to our country to find them."

"Have you heard anything else?" asked Videre intently.

"That group called Alerian Blood Clan. I have talked to Dio Cioto but he tries to convince me that it is nothing. I did learn from an old merchant that they have resurfaced but claims he knows nothing beyond that. I know you will be truthful with me in your findings."

"I have heard of the whispers of this supposed group, but I don't know much about them yet myself. I have a few people who are digging deeper into the matter. You are right to worry. If they are targeting Kiadere, your country and mine will be the first ones they will come to. I promise I will keep you updated with any news. As a precaution, I will send word-of-mouth messengers instead of written messages."

"You are practical, Videre. It is a shame that you share your crown with your sisters. Tell me, if one of you has a boy, then will he become king?"

Like Lostanzo, the Emperor was not one to shy away from such questions.

Videre let out a deep breath. "I do not know. We had talked about it a long time ago but have not brought it up since. I guess when the time comes, we will discuss it again."

"I know your sister, Valencia, married a Kiadere nobleman. You and your other sister have yet to marry. I assume Valencia will be the first one to bear children, producing an heir to the throne. This makes me wonder if you and your sister will marry into Viceroy lines to strengthen alliances. It would make sense for Lady Valencia to rule Desial while you two would become queens of another country within Aleria such as the Viceroy custom. I have heard that you wish to keep the bloodline pure but if your sister already has done that, then it would leave you and Valeria free to pursue others such as a situation like Prince Calan."

"You are right, Emperor Hideki," she said in a sad tone. "That would make the most logical sense. As with our custom, we must have a full-blood Kiadere on the throne. If my sister and I were to marry outside of our people to Viceroy, we may have a chance to strengthen our alliances. We wouldn't have to share the throne and we would be queens of our marriage countries. Perhaps we will not marry or bear children at all," said Videre as she laughed almost nervously.

"I do not give advice to other Viceroy, Lady Videre, but I give you advice. You must think about what is good for you. Do not worry about your sisters, their heirs, and their politics. Worry about what you may achieve in the future by the decisions that you make now. I urge you to consider my son as a match for you. I will be gone soon and he needs a helping hand in the messy world we live in."

Videre had a shocked look on her face. Leon couldn't believe he had just heard. He looked at Prince Hideki, who stared down at the table. He noticed the ever so familiar ringing sound in his ears when the table went silent.

"Emperor Hideki," said Videre quietly. "I am grateful for your offer. As with any offer, I will keep it in mind as I have many things to tend to before I tend to myself," she bowed her head then looked at Prince Aoki. "I hope no matter what, we will end up forming a friendship so we can work together in the future. I do look forward to having you visit Vici so we can get to know each other better."

Prince Aoki, who was certainly embarrassed by his father's forward nature thanked Videre. After a few moments of awkward silent eating, conversations started again. Rumors, experiences, and political talk occupied them until the sun had started going down. Leon kept looking at Videre throughout the dinner, carefully listening to her words. He had never thought about what troubles came with the three queens sharing a throne. Kinobi was married to Valencia but he was not called a king. Leon could not help but think about what would happen if Valencia indeed bore an heir. Videre said that they had discussed it but he thought they would have figured out what that would mean for them by now.

After the dinner of surprisingly agreeable foreign foods, they retrieved their senrima from the royal stables which looked to be even more elegant than the royal stables of Vici. Lady Kayle looked impatient as Leon strapped his bag onto her saddle. He had grown quite fond of her since the first time he had taken flight with her. She acted like she had known Leon her whole life. Unfortunately for Lady Kayle, they had to embark on a ship once again to get to the mainland. Leon could tell Videre was more stressed on this boat than on the last. She took deep breaths as she clutched a letter in her hands. Looking around, Leon noticed that the other men were looking nervous as well.

"Is she going to be ok?" Leon asked Jooey quietly.

"Let's hope so. When she's not ok, well, let's just say it's not good for any of us."

"Would you like to sit and see what I found?" said Ezrai, pulling papers from his bag. "I wanted to be far enough away from Dio to show these to you."

"Did you steal these?" whispered Leon.

Ezrai looked at Jooey sternly when he laughed.

"Ezrai never steals. He borrows things to be permanently stored in our library."

Videre's eyes lit up as she grabbed one of the papers and sat down in front of the men.

Ezrai smiled. "I didn't get a chance to read them but I figured some may come in handy. I do regret tearing out the pages but I did notice there were some other pages that had been torn out."

"That's quite concerning. Either someone is looking for something and committed a crime such as yourself or The Dio want to hide something."

"I know this may seem like a silly question," chimed in Leon, "but isn't The Dio on our side?"

"The Alerian Society is, for the most part. The Dio should be, but I have never known their true intentions. They have their own secrets that they do not share. The Alerian Society is made up of the Kiadere all throughout Aleria and work together. The Dio is centralized in that cavern and has few members. A long time ago, The Dio had much sway in politics. Very few times did they clash with The Alerian Society but when the Viceroy came, The Alerian Society wanted to be at peace but were cautious. The Dio, however, wanted to imprison them. They had a fear of these people from another world and said they would create destruction and seek the removal of the Kiadere. Many members of The Alerian Society laughed at the idea, but sure enough, The Dio was right. When Les Nettoyer happened, The Dio had ordered the Kiadere to fight back as opposed to The Alerian Society who encouraged Kiadere to hide while trying to make peace. The only reason why Desial stands is because The Dio and The Alerian Society agreed that the Kiadere must hide in Desial and fight within their own country."

"But I don't exactly understand why the Viceroy wanted to remove the Kiadere?"

Ezrai shrugged. "The Kiadere and the Viceroy were considered to be gods. They outlived everyone. The Kiadere had their powers, and the Viceroy had their knowledge. It could have been jealousy or fear, but what sparked Les Nettoyer was an angry boy and killed one of the Viceroy's sons with his ability. The Dio was set up mostly to make sure that we all stay one with the world. When we stay balanced, we can control our powers. Anyone who did anything bad with their abilities would be punished harshly so we lived in relative peace. Before the Viceroy, The Dio ran a home for people who could not control their abilities. They would either get rehabilitated or The Dio had the ability to strip them of their abilities. The Viceroy, for some reason, believed that The Dio were giving people their abilities and drove them out of Aleria and into hiding. One thing led to another and the Viceroy leader of Athena declared war on the Kiadere saying that they were too dangerous to live in their world. While a good majority of Kiadere fled and hid from the world, few of them fought back using their abilities, which made the situation even worse. Some Viceroy saw the error in their ways when they realized that The Dio was there to help and made alliances with the Kiadere. Other Viceroy leaders made an alliance with Athena thus starting Polonotadere."

"I think I found something," whispered Videre as she stared at a paper intently. "The Alerian Blood Clan used to be called Aleria Ila Kinlani ."

"Aleria blood children?" said Jooey. "That sounds a little creepy but it still doesn't ring any bells."

"There are medical notes here but it's hard to translate. It looks like a more native ancient dialect. The only ones I know for sure who can read this are the members of The Dio. Perhaps Miss Rayne can dig up someone that would be able to translate."

"I can translate," said Ezrai taking the papers from Videre, "but it will take time."

"Yes Ezrai, we know you can do book stuff but can you do stuff like this," Jooey quickly scooped up Videre in his arms and lifted her high above his head."

Roaring with laughter, Videre's bad mood quickly disappeared. Leon was unnaturally happy that Videre had such an intimate bond with her handmen. He wondered if Jolon had the same kind of relationship with Valeria as Videre did with Jooey. Now that he thought about it, he had no idea what exactly Jolon did for Valeria. Leon didn't even know what he did for Videre. All of a sudden, he felt as if he had no meaning.

Videre herself had told him that the only reason she had chosen him to be a handman was to save him from her sisters. Even so, it seemed like a strange coincidence that his father had also been a handman to Videre. He started delving into his unknown relationship with Videre. His father had been close to all of them no doubt. His ancestor had made a timepiece for a Zaro commissioned by Videre's father that they had just dug up illegally. The people that he had met along their trip all recognized him yet he had no knowledge of the outside world. He looked at Videre's glowing face who was dancing with Jooey. She moved so gracefully that her dress flowed with the wind as the non-existent music played in the background. Her unkempt hair flowed through the wind with as much grace as her. Jooey, even as the big brute that he was, danced gracefully while towering over her. Once again Leon could see the colors from her body shimmering and moving slowly around her like fireflies in the summer.

"Ciolon's Point," yelled a man in the front of the ship.

Videre and Jooey stopped and bowed toward each other as if they had been dancing at a ball. Videre's mood seemed to have changed and for some reason, Leon could feel it. He could feel her happiness, sadness, and anger. Looking at her other handmen, he wondered if they could also feel it.

"She's my special person," whispered Jooey to Leon.

"Like you love her?" asked Leon, trying not to let anyone else hear.

Jooey let out a big laugh. "We all love her, lad. She is our Queen, our leader, our protector, and our savior."

Picking up their luggage and unloading their senrima from the boat Jooey yelled to Videre, "I love you."

"I love you too, Jooey," she said as she turned around and laughed.

CHAPTER

XIX

JESSICA HENDERSON

"It's quite fascinating actually," said Miss Rayne. Videre and her men had arrived at her house right after sunset. "I am also fascinated about your trip that Ciano has been telling us about."

"Well, I'm assuming you know more about my trip than I know about your discovery."

"So you don't want to tell me about your thoughts on the marriage proposal from the emperor? Very well."

Miss Rayne's smile was as devious as Videre remembered. Her constant teasing of the girl and flirting with various men was something to almost be admired because it came so naturally.

"I can tell you one thing. The box I had crafted for you definitely helped you out. This artifact is made out of a Viceroy material that is poisonous to our bodies if not stored correctly. I'm guessing Polentio had no knowledge of this material and that's what made everyone sick who was in contact with it. The boys told me about that young boy in the village who had the same symptoms. For some reason, it doesn't seem to affect the natives. That boy's father is most likely a Viceroy if this had made him sick. I don't know the long-term effects on Kiadere so I urge you to take precautions and leave it inside the box."

"My Queen," said Ciano quietly.

"You can say it out loud boy," said Miss Rayne. "We have no secrets here right?"

Ciano sighed, "Leon was eavesdropping on you and Ezrai at the mansion in the cavern."

Videre looked at Leon intently, waiting for him to explain himself.

"I heard you talk about how we aren't able to trust The Dio and about someone named Jessica Henderson. I swear I was just going downstairs to get something to eat."

"Jessica Henderson," said Ezrai, "was probably the best Viceroy of them all. She fought to protect the Kiadere and to preserve our customs and traditions. Because of this, she was chastised and rejected by almost all the Viceroy."

"We aren't purposely keeping this information from you, Leon. You have to realize that understanding these things takes time. We will talk about her when we're back in the library. We have so much material there to help you learn more about everything"

"Thank you for understanding," Leon said quietly.

Videre could tell he was just being polite. He thirsted for more just like his father which eventually led to his untimely death.

"Well, if we can stop this love fest, I would like to get to sleep or either get the senrima and go home," said Lostanzo annoyingly.

Videre glanced at Lostanzo. "Watch your mouth."

Lostanzo apologized with a bow before storming out of the room. Lostanzo didn't always have such a temper but he had been through so much with Videre that he had started changing over the years. He had grown more protective and cautious to a point of paranoia.

"He wasn't happy about letting Leon travel with you," said Miss Rayne quietly to where only Videre could hear. "He is scared of recurring events."

"I promise," Videre said back just as quietly, "Leon is not his father. This is our chance to get things right."

"I still do not fully trust Jessica Henderson's findings. Ettore started going crazy towards the end. Do you really think we can trust his contributions?"

"We have no other choice."

"It's not just that, Videre," she said as she grabbed Videre's arm tightly. "You know I have a personal investment into the well-being of Leon."

"Forgive me, Miss Rayne," said Jooey trying to remove the obvious tension. "We haven't eaten for a few hours and a big boy like me has to eat."

Laughing in her signature tone Miss Rayne nodded and sent one of the workers out to get the group some food from town. The men had their own fill of entertainment while they waited for their food as Jooey, Malaki, and Ezrai recounted all of their travels with the handmen that had been absent from their journey.

The trinkets all over Miss Rayne's home always were a joy to look at. Paintings were hung all over the walls of people and places all across Aleria. She had commissioned drawings of the creatures of Korona. Along with dozens of sketches, were specimens and artifacts to better understand the world's secrets. Items from Alflint and Dunbar also lined the shelves of her house. Videre was fully convinced that Miss Rayne had more knowledge of the people in Aleria than anyone else. She had also trusted with all her soul since she was a young girl.

"Tell me about the proposal," begged Miss Rayne sitting with Videre on her extravagant overstuffed chairs after shooing the handmen away into the other room.

"It wasn't much of a proposal. It was more the Emperor trying to convince me to marry his son."

Miss Rayne looked at Videre intently as if she was urging her to continue.

"He must have thought about it for a while. It is understandable that he would want someone experienced to take over the throne with his son. Unfortunately, his customs won't let his daughter on the throne. He had his son late in life. So late, that he has had little time to teach him about politics. He was right about one thing though. Valencia is married and will most likely have the next heir which makes Valeria and I almost worthless to the throne of Desial. It would be wise for us to marry to strengthen alliances instead of staying and co-ruling Desial. But if we do that, then our pure bloodline will be gone."

"Although I disagree with you on marrying to strengthening alliances, I do understand." Miss Rayne took Valeria's hand. "My sweet girl. There was a reason why your father groomed you. In his eyes, you were to be the one true queen. It's in your Kiadere blood. You have the blood and the power of King Konea. The fact that you have to co-rule makes me sick. Your mother, rest her soul, was not a politically savvy woman like your father. If there happens to be some argument between who is the sole ruler of Desial, you know where my allegiances lie."

Videre looked around and whispered, "Don't talk of such things, Miss Rayne. It would be considered treason."

Miss Rayne sighed, "I have been through so much, dear girl. An insurrection and so-called treason is nothing to me."

"I most likely won't bear an heir anyways according to Malaki," said Videre. "Prince Aoki is very handsome though. He is so young that perhaps I may shape his politics. His father is also one of our loyal allies, which is something we need right about now."

"Queen Videre, Miss Rayne," called the returning servant. "Food is ready."

The dinner was full of various different kinds of food that Videre had missed. If she wanted to, she would be able to eat anything she liked at the castle, yet to be on the safe side, Sevete had devised a way to have food that was inspected and from trustworthy sources come to the Vasili's dinner table. Although Valencia's right-hand man was a pain, the only thing it seemed like he truly cared about was the well-being of the Vasili.

"How did you know I spied on them?" asked Leon bluntly out of the blue.

"That's my ability," replied Ciano without missing a beat. "Anything you see, I can see. Anything you hear, I can hear. Anything you think, I know."

"You know that little buzzing in your ear?" said Jooey. "That's Ciano, hanging up in your noggin."

"Yes, like when you took a tumble into that cave. Jakoba sent a rabbit in there to lead you out because I knew exactly where you were."

"So, is your ability unlimited?"

"Almost," said Ciano proudly. "When I meet someone and talk to them for a bit, I can dive into their mind as long as I remember who they are. I tend not to do it a lot because, well, it makes me nauseous. Every mind is different. Some are quite strong and have the ability to recognize that something isn't right. Those minds can clam up right away and things become quite hazy. Minds like yours are so young and easily intruded upon," he smiled knowing very well how demeaning he sounded.

Leon looked annoyed. He had the same look of annoyance on his face that his father and grandfather often sported. Miss Rayne saw it too as she smiled.

"Leon," she said gleefully, "We haven't had much time to get to know each other. I would very much like to speak with you more sometime."

"Perhaps, you can visit us in Vici sometime soon," said Lostanzo. "I'm sure there will be some people you recognize and miss."

"Boy, I have no problem slapping an adult," Miss Rayne joked, "But I do want to visit. It has been a while since I've been to Vici."

Videre loved the genuine smile on Miss Rayne's face, but she often wondered how much more time Miss Rayne had. Videre had pondered giving her the timekeeper because if anyone was able to make a difference in the world, it would be Miss Rayne. Keone certainly would approve if Videre had handed Miss Rayne the timekeeper to extend her life. For all she knew, Keone hated Videre and blamed her for Keono's death.

"Did you know your grandfather used to live close to here?" asked Miss Rayne to Leon.

Leon shook his head, "My grandfather doesn't tell me much about his life. Was he a trader?"

Miss Rayne laughed, "Keone and Polentio were timemakers such as yourself, of course. They had a shop in town. It certainly was a strategic place for their craft."

"You knew Polentio?"

"Aw yes, Polentio was a fine man. Your great grandfather. Always friendly and knew how to convince people to buy two small timekeepers. One for each hand, that is. And on good days, he could convince someone to buy one for each of their family members."

"Miss Rayne," interrupted Videre. "If you find any information about the Alerian Blood Clan, I would prefer you to come in person. I do not trust zanianbirds anymore."

"Of course. I have already sent a message to King Fryderyk with my intentions to travel to Korona and hopefully get all the accounts of what's been happening with the children and the plants. My guess is that things like this are happening in every country; they just haven't been noticed. The government under Fryderyk is managed well."

Eating dinner with Miss Rayne brought back a feeling of warmth that seemed to have left her soul many years ago. Polonotadere was before Videre's time, but she remembered when Aleria had to pick up the pieces of the broken country. People were starving, poor, and helpless as new governments tried to make their own laws and ways of life. The culture was nearly destroyed, leaving shattered bits throughout the continent with only a few daring to piece it back together. New cultures accentuating vanity, popularity, and selfishness started rising rapidly. People had started relying on their governments for leadership and support. The idea of hard work to become successful had been drained and the children were devoid of any real knowledge. The good people of Aleria used to live in small and cohesive communities tending to their own and trading freely without restrictions. No matter how much good came from the Viceroy, Aleria would never be a free world with them in it.

"Someday, Aleria will be free of the Viceroy," said the young girl with long brown hair.

"And who says that?" asked Miss Rayne, obviously entertained.

"Jessica Henderson. I heard my father talking with her. With certain powers, they may be able to fix all of it."

"And let me guess, your ability had something to do with it," laughed Miss Rayne.

Miss Rayne had a long apron on, stained with grease from one of her latest projects. Her neatly combed brown hair seemed to never get messy no matter what project she was working on, unlike Videre's.

"Do you think it's possible? Ettore said it could be."

"Ettore has lost half of his mind, dear. Jessica Henderson is of sound mind but is too optimistic. Instead of changing the world without Viceroy, your father has decided to change it by helping them. Perhaps this is the best way to bring peace to Aleria."

"My father says there will never be peace," said a loud familiar voice behind them.

The boy, slightly older than Videre had been helping Miss Rayne with her projects. His father had entrusted him to Miss

Rayne to possibly help him tone down his rowdiness by keeping him busy.

"I'm going to help Videre get rid of all of them," he said as he spit on the ground.

A furious Miss Rayne slapped him upside the head and made him clean it up before washing up for dinner. Their dinners were always hearty as Miss Rayne believed a full stomach led to a good mind. Dinner conversations were always lively with information about anything and everything that was accessible through Miss Rayne's mind.

Videre had always thought of this house on the hill as her home and Miss Rayne as her mother and by being here, she had also gained a brother. Miss Rayne never made Videre sleep at a certain time, but would always expect her to wake up when the sun rose. Before bed, the young princess had made a habit of looking up at the stars and sometimes the lights of Hikari that were visible on a cloudless night.

"Did Jessica Henderson find anything?" asked the boy sitting next to her.

"I'm not sure. It's hard to hear them through the walls. Someday we'll sneak in there and take a look at their journals. I know she writes everything down."

"Does Henderson and your dad have... a thing?"

Videre laughed, "Jessica Henderson is a Viceroy. I don't think my father would ever."

"I want to go to Vici with you next time you go."

"We should ask Miss Rayne. It would be nice to have a friend in Vici."

"You don't have any friends there?"

Videre looked out past the rolling hills without answering. She had been hidden away. The people she knew most about were the Viceroy and the other leaders of Aleria. She was groomed to be a queen, not a girl who would be able to play with friends on her days off.

"I wish Jessica and Ettore could live long enough to figure out how to remove the Viceroy," said Videre in a sad tone.

"How would they just simply remove the Viceroy without destroying everything they've done."

"I don't know, but Jessica said Aleria could return to what it was before the Viceroy came," said Videre, staring far past the shore to the lights in the sky.

"I should make a timekeeper for them," the boy said as he pulled out a drawing from his pocket.

Videre smiled as she looked at the paper, "It looks different than last time. This stone is new," she said pointing to a dark stone.

"Yes, that's a dark bloodstone. Legend says that it draws in love to whoever wears it. I thought about what makes a person whole, and their heart is an important piece of them," he said as he folded the paper and put it gently back into his pocket. "I want to finish it completely before I show my dad."

They sat together in silence for a few minutes watching the flickering lights of the stars and the trading port below them.

"Will you make me a promise?" she asked quietly.

"Of course," he smiled.

"Help me in the future with Jessica, Ettore, and my father's plans."

"Of course, my future queen," he said as he stood up and bowed like a prince.

Videre laughed. She was easily entertained as most of her days were filled with studies.

"And make us both a timekeeper."

"I don't want one," he said as he puffed out his chest. "I don't need to live that long. It'll take the fun out of life. But I will make one just for you, Videre."

"Thank you," she smiled, "I'm lucky to have a friend like you, Keone."

FIND YOUR WAY HOME

"Videre has been asking about the Alerian Blood Clan," a familiar voice said.

"She knows nothing and is grasping at straws. The Dio will not help her and The Alerian Society is too busy with their own troubles to worry about a petty rumor."

"Videre has heard the name before. She is not easily satisfied. We must do something about her."

The other name scoffed, "We cannot do anything about her. We need her and her handmen to further our purposes."

"We must speed up our process. Now that Calan is out of the picture, she will be able to focus on her true destiny," said a woman.

In the corner of the next room was a man with long hair who had been housed there for years. How many years he had been there was almost uncertain. He had a cushion for a bed and rusty bars were the best decoration of his cell. Beams of light shone through a small tunnel that was only big enough for a small cat to fit through. His throat itched as it had for years. He could see the shadows of feet shuffling on the other end of the long tunnel.

If only he could scream out, someone would know he was here. If only Ciano could see through his eyes. He had been in a cell for years, although not always the same cell. He had been moved around a few times, mostly during the night. Each cell was different yet the same. The same metal that kept him from the world had its slightest differences. Rustiness, shininess, the smell of death. It overloaded his senses when he was brought to a new location but to anyone else, it would be the exact same metal bars. He had tried starving himself to relieve himself of the pain and suffering nearly succeeding once. During the past couple of years, he had made every effort to remember everything he heard outside of his cells so he could finally relay it to his queen when he got the chance. If anyone were to do something about these monsters, it would be her and the other two queens of Desial. He had pledged his life to her and he was determined to keep that promise.

"I think he's still hiding things from us. He has no use to us if we are at our limit," said the woman.

"He will be used as a bargaining chip if we do indeed run out of information."

"A bargaining chip?" scoffed the woman, "So he can tell them what had happened?"

"We are cautious and we have someone with the ability to wipe his mind. Don't you worry about that."

The man strained to hear but the voices were so muffled he could hardly make out what they said. He had always been blindfolded when coming in contact with his captors. They were smart and cautious, so much so that even he admired their practices. Anytime they were in close proximity, they would start whispering, most likely so he wouldn't be able to recognize their voices. The only face he had seen, belonged to a large guard with a heavy purple scar on his eye who came to blindfold him from time to time.

"Take him to extraction again. We need to know more about Keono."

The guard's familiar footsteps came closer, echoing throughout the underground cell. As the doors to the cell creaked open, the prisoner thrust his hands in front of him knowing very well that he would not be leaving without being shackled and blindfolded. The guard had long sleeves and gloves on as did everyone else who came in contact with him. The prisoner wished that one of these days, they would forget and expose one of their hands but it had never happened.

They knew very well what he was capable of with just a touch, but he had figured out exactly what they were capable of with a tremendous amount of pain and deprivation. He would try to scream out during their sessions but his vocals would never work again. The scar around his throat would often itch, reminding him how degraded he had now become. Walking up the stairs, he could imagine where he was. He figured that he was being taken out of an abandoned building during the night as to not alarm any villagers. The previous location where he spent most of his captivity was also underground but there were no noises outside like at this new cell where he currently resided.

Slowly going through the motions, the guard shackled and blindfolded him. Walking up stairs and passing through various doors, the prisoner was always alert. For however long he had been in their hands, he had always tried to make out any details he could. Musty smells and drips were all that he could sense in this particular location. Quite some time ago, he had various cell mates. They all seemed to understand that he could not speak back so he heard of their life stories and respond by making noises on the bars or tapping his feet. Communication always was by a tap for yes and two taps for no, but it was nice to have some other souls around. He tried to make out why they had been captured but none of them had any similarities as if the prisoners were at random. He knew exactly why he had been imprisoned by this shadowy group. They needed the information that he had, but from what he could tell, the other prisoners had no such knowledge.

He was shoved in the back of a creaky wagon that he had always dreaded. As the wagon started moving, tears came to his eyes. He could not help but give up the memories of Videre. He had wished so many times that Videre had not shared with him as much as she did. He was being forced to give up everything he knew about her life. Now, they expected to extract memories out of his mind about Keono for a reason he couldn't think of.

The wagon started racing down a stone road. He could hear nothing other than the wheels as they were so loud, it was almost deafening. The constant lack of noises in his cell seemed to have a devastating effect on his ears whenever he heard something loud. He frequently took off his blindfold while in the wagon, looking through a crack that he had become fond of. He was always sure to put it back on when they stopped. Peering through the largest crack, he saw moonlit trees but nothing else. They were in a forest but which one, he was not able to tell.

I could be almost anywhere.

There were indeed no structures that could help him identify where he was. The moonlight shone inside of the crack as he leaned back and sighed. The trips in this wagon were always different. Sometimes he heard the ocean, and other times he could smell the desert. He had been to every corner of Aleria with Videre but he had given up trying to map where he may have been long ago. He longed to be back in the castle again. Videre and the other handmen were all that he had of this world. He regretted making fun of the other men for being too comfortable inside the comforts that the royal family had to offer. He was always out in the wilderness or other countries on official business for Videre. He was the best scout and spy that she had and she utilized him from the very moment she had saved him. He often wondered if he had been replaced by anyone of similar talents or abilities. Instead of back when he would depend on his excitement and adrenaline, anger and vengeance had taken hold of him.

Then he saw it. Just a sliver of metal. This creaky old wagon had been falling apart all these years and his tolerance for the deafening noise had paid off. He quickly pulled the metal from the seams of the ceiling. Sure enough, it was a nail that had come loose. Thinking quickly, he tried picking the lock of his shackles. He had only picked a lock a few times in his life before and wished he had asked Lostanzo how he was able to pull it off in a matter of seconds. Even Keono might have known how to pick locks effectively. All of a sudden, the wagon started slowing down and rounding corners.

He was out of time. He looked outside once more. There were buildings and lights in the distance. Beyond that, there was the reflection of the moon across the water and the faint purple streaks of light in the sky. His eyes narrowed to focus on what he was seeing. For once, he knew exactly where he was. As the wagon slowed down, he put his blindfold back on and wanted to scream out at his failure to escape.

"Come," said the guard quietly as he yanked on the prisoner's arm. Although the guard wasn't necessarily mean to him, he could have been a little more gentle at times.

"Sorry," the prisoner mouthed as he took the blindfold off and quickly pierced the guard in his eye with the nail.

The guard screamed out in pain and clutched his eye which had started bleeding profusely. The prisoner swiftly took the keys from the guard's belt and started running. He knew where he was and he knew exactly where he was going.

FIND YOURSELF

"Pack your senrima, Leon," whispered Kolono.

Leon awoke with a startled fright. Looking out the window, he could see that it was early in the morning as soft fog covered the ground. The night before had opened his eyes to the type of family he had gotten himself into. The connections between Videre and her handmen were all different. Like parts of a timekeeper, he started labeling every member the same way as he had labeled the intricate parts of his timepieces. She trusted Ezrai with all her secrets. With Malaki, she trusted with her life and well-being. Jooey was there to stable her feelings. Kolono was to be a protector along with Jooey. Ciano was her spy and Lostanzo was the boy she was attached to. Although a moody boy, she could trust him to get anything done for her no matter what kind of task she requested. Figuring out everyone's role wasn't difficult, but what Leon hated most, was that he had no idea what his role was. Videre still did not trust him and he was still useless. One thing was for sure, they all loved her.

"Where's the box?" asked Leon looking at Lostanzo's senrima outside of the window.

"Miss Rayne convinced Videre to leave it here," answered Kolono. "We must get going if we are to reach Lucia by nightfall."

Quickly picking up his bags, he headed downstairs where the rest of the men were waiting. Videre was in deep conversation with Lostanzo and Miss Rayne as Leon quietly went outside with the other men who started packing their bags onto the saddles.

"Where is Lucia?" Leon asked Kolono.

"Lucia is in Reino. We'll be spending the night there tonight. Videre has spent too long away from the castle on her own business. Trips like this must be secretive and short. People like Valencia are very curious as to what Videre does."

"Why does it matter? Videre is the one in charge of foreign affairs. It makes sense that Videre would be on trips to other countries."

"It's not that," said Ezrai. "Many years ago, people started to support her as the one true queen of Aleria. Valencia went a little berserk. There was a big fight. It was a mess for about a year before things started getting back to normal."

"Videre did mention the fact that Valencia may have the first child making him the heir to the throne."

"Videre is destined for the throne," scoffed Lostanzo walking up to his senrima. "Heir or not."

"Keep your thoughts quiet, Lostanzo. We never know who's listening," said Jooey in all seriousness.

Videre exited Miss Rayne's house and without a word, mounted her senrima and started riding. Her expression was filled with worry and perhaps a bit of sadness.

Leon felt a wave of worry coming over him. He had never thought that Videre wished to overthrow her sisters. She had never mentioned anything of the sort. Valencia seemed to be the face of the throne but what would happen to Videre and Valeria if their sister were to have a child. Leon wasn't well versed in the affairs of the throne but he was sure that having three queens was something that had never happened before. As they started riding north, Leon's mind started to wander even more through all the possibilities.

If Videre were to claim the throne for herself, then who all would support her?

He looked around at the men surrounding her. They would no doubt fight for their queen but Valeria also would play a big role. Valeria could side with one sister or they would all three fight against each other. If they were to fight, there would be no doubt that Valeria would have the upper hand with her Vipole. He started thinking about Jolon and how he would have to fight his friend.

"Tell me," Videre said unsuspectingly as Leon didn't notice that she had slowed down to ride next to him.

"They say you're the true queen of Aleria."

Videre laughed, "Sevete says the same to Valencia and your friend probably says the same to Valeria."

"Why do you share the throne? Wouldn't the firstborn be the one who takes the throne?"

"My mother gave birth to all three of us on the same day. It's not like they kept track of which one of us came out first. Unfortunately, my mother died shortly after. Before she died, she made my father promise to raise us all equally and to split the throne. He devised a plan where we would take separate roles that were fitted to our personalities and abilities."

Videre looked at Leon inquisitively and smiled, "You haven't asked about my ability."

Leon smiled back, "I know. I actually would like to figure it out on my own."

"You are so much like Keono," said Videre in a sad tone then quickly rode up to the front of their line by Lostanzo.

Lostanzo looked back at Leon with almost a scowl on his face making Leon feel uneasy.

"Don't worry about him," said Ciano, taking the spot next to him. "Lostanzo feels betrayed and he gets moody all the time. We've all been a target. He has always had a wave of deep anger inside of him and sometimes he lets it show a little too much."

"It seems like it's always toward me."

"You have your father to thank for that," said Ciano. "Lostanzo and Keono were very close. Keono, like us, had sworn allegiance to our queen and loved her as we all love her. One day, Keono..." he paused trying to find the right words. "Keono hurt the queen unintentionally because of his actions. I'm sorry, Leon. It's not my story to tell. Lostanzo acts cold toward most people but I suspect more so toward you because of your father."

Leon was surprised. Lostanzo wasn't mad at Leon. He was mad at Leon's father and taking it out on him. He started feeling bad for Lostanzo. Without knowing the details, he could feel Lostanzo's pain. He did also understand Ciano's hesitation to tell Leon what had happened to Lostanzo and his father. Whatever pain that Lostanzo had, he knew that Videre must have felt the same pain. Perhaps this was his time to make things right. Leon started feeling as if he had a place among them, however small it may be.

The air was cold, like when they had traveled to Moshny. Leon had traveled to Reino a few times before as a young boy with his grandfather and also with Jolon's family to buy dyes. The landscape was fair and similar to Desial. Rolling hills and farms dominated the lands as they trotted down small stone roads. They had gone unnoticed passing through small villages when they came upon a large house as the sun was starting to go down towards the horizon.

The perimeter wall was made with stone with creeping orange flowering vines. The gardens were meticulously cared for and the hedges were cut perfectly seeming like nothing was out of place. The house was of particular elegance to where it could match the beauty of the castles that Leon had seen. A man in an old-fashioned suit came out to greet them as if he had been waiting for their arrival. He bowed low and steady as if he had been bowing his whole life.

"Queen Videre, Master Lostanzo, I welcome you back to Kaner Residence."

Master? Kaner? That's Miss Rayne's last name.

"Good evening, Charles," said Videre while dismounting her senrima, "Thank you for accommodating us. I know the boys are hungry."

Lostanzo walked up to the man and hugged him tight and laughed. Such a sight was rare to see for Leon. Even seeing him with Miss Rayne had questioned what he knew about Lostanzo.

Walking into the house was as beautiful as walking up to the large wooden doors. The foyer donned the largest staircase that he had ever seen in a house. The shiny dark wood of the staircase and the floors matched the dark green walls. A great chandelier hung in the middle of the ceiling bringing a sense of cozy elegance to Leon. Lostanzo walking in kicked his shoes off as if he were a young boy just getting home from school.

"This is Lostanzo's childhood home," whispered Ciano. "Charles was indebted to Lostanzo's parents and when they died, Lostanzo made a deal with Charles to care for the estate and he could reside here as long as he lives, which looks like it may not be much longer."

Ciano was right. Charles looked frail and old. He walked in a crooked and almost tiring manner. He could tell that Charles was struggling to carry himself upright.

"What will Lostanzo do when that happens?" asked Leon quietly so Charles wouldn't pick up on their conversation about his impending death.

"Well that'll be a surprise, I guess. Although handmen have a five-year contract, we have been with her for much more than that. After your father died, Lostanzo vowed to be with Videre his whole life. Whether he actually will, is beyond me. It is nice for him to have this place though. It's our home away from Desial for when Videre needs to get away or when we're out traveling."

Leon noticed Videre lying comfortably on the couch with her shoes off reading the papers that Ezrai had stolen from The Dio's library. Jooey lifted her legs, sat down, and put them on his lap. Leon noticed that she didn't wince, as if Jooey's behavior was second nature. Many times on this trip, he had forgotten that she was the queen and they were her loyal servants. Videre's handmen did not act at all like any other handmen or servants that he had seen. As other handmen and people in the castle were bowing and displaying extreme politeness toward the queens, Videre's handmen seemed to be more comfortable addressing her in the fashion of a normal person. Leon felt a strange happiness inside of him knowing that he was not only a handman, but one to Videre. Seeing the comfort that Jooey and Videre felt with each other stirred up a jealous emotion within Leon. He longed to be that close to her as if fate was calling him ever so nearer.

"Upstairs, third room on the right," said Lostanzo with a calm tone while walking past him.

Leon smiled, genuinely happy that Lostanzo was being nice to him. He walked up the enormous staircase glancing at the pictures on the walls. Pictures of Lostanzo's family were grand and majestically painted. A painting of a young Miss Rayne caught his eye as she looked wonderfully magnificent. He all of a sudden wondered if she had ever been married. Such a beauty like her must have had a husband. His eyes trailed to the right of a painting of Videre and Lostanzo. Her bright red dress was unlike what he had ever seen her wear, as she almost always wore plain clothes. There was a difference in this painting. It was as if the painting wasn't painted at all. Everything was crisp and as if he were looking at the real thing.

"I remember that painting," said Ezrai sneaking up to Leon. "It was right after the plague killed off his family. He was so upset although he hardly showed it. Lostanzo was quite new to the handman role at that time. She promised him that we would be his family. She had commissioned a painting of just the two of them to remind him that whenever he left her service, he could still consider her as his family."

"Ciano told me that Lostanzo promised his life to her."

"We'll see about that," Ezrai laughed. "I am the only one who is legally bound to her my whole life. The rest of you are free to go when you please after the contract is over."

"Videre talked about two others who were in her service other than my father? What happened to them?"

Ezrai let out a deep breath. "Ciyo was from Korona. He died from the same plague as Lostanzo's parents. He was only in Videre's service for a few years. The other was Lo. Lo was as faithful as all of us. He was on an assignment to Soro and disappeared. Ciano was unable to find him and we have no idea what happened to him. You should get settled, then come down to eat some supper."

Glancing at the painting one last time, Leon made his way to the room to which Lostanzo was referring. This was un-mistakably his father's old room. Parts of timepieces were placed neatly on a beautiful work table. Several timepieces were hung on the walls looking exactly like some of the draw-ings that Leon would occasionally stumble upon in his father's old books. He sat on his bed that already had his bag on it. Charles must have brought in his bag unnoticed. Although this was Lostanzo's home, he felt comfortable as if it were his own home in Vici. Unpacking his bag, he noticed a letter neatly tucked into his bag with his name in it. It was unsealed but when he opened it, a piece of paper and a sealed letter with his grandfather's name had dropped out. Puzzled, he started reading the neat handwriting.

Dear Leon,

I was overjoyed to have met you. Like your grandfather and your father, I expect you to do great things for your Queen and country. Although we have had only a short time to get to know each other, I will make it a point to visit you in Desial. Please de-liver this letter to your grandfather.

Best Wishes,

Rayne Kaner

A smile ran across Leon's face. He was surprised, yet delighted that Miss Rayne had slipped him a letter. Although he hardly knew her, she seemed like someone he would be able to trust or depend on if anything were to arise. Perhaps it was Videre's thinking that was rubbing off on him, but he started making a mental list of those who he could trust. He was so tempted to read the letter that she had intended for his grandfather but it was neatly sealed.

"And then the Emperor basically begged her to marry his son!" exclaimed Jooey when Leon had arrived in the dining room. The men were casually eating a variety of foods that Charles must have prepared himself. All the men laughed as if the proposal was a joke. Even Videre was smiling.

"It caught me by surprise. I would have thought his son would have the courage to ask me himself," Videre said as she shrugged.

"This Alerian Blood Clan," started Charles, "I have heard of them before."

The room went silent as Charles looked confused as the faces of the handmen all expressed seriousness.

He continued, "Well not really heard of, but read in a book."

Charles rushed out of the dining room as everyone was bewildered that Charles knew of something that might have been helpful. Leon quietly grabbed a plate and started loading it with food, trying not to be the one breaking the awkward silence.

Charles returned with a leather-bound book in hand as Lostanzo's eyes lit up.

"Where did you find that?" asked Lostanzo. "I looked for that everywhere."

Charles shrugged. "I found it hidden underneath his desk. It most definitely was hidden and I happened on it by chance. I only read a few pages, but I'm pretty sure I read the name somewhere in the book."

Charles handed the book to Videre, who looked extremely grateful for any leads she may discover. She clutched the book tightly as she thanked Charles and walked out of the doorway. Slowly, the men started up again with their stories and jokes. Leon was having a fantastic time but in the back of his head, he desperately wanted to know what was inside of the mysterious book.

After a while of eating and enjoying themselves, it was time to wind down. Charles had informed them that he expected all the men to be present for breakfast at sunrise. Satisfied with the filling meal, Leon headed to his assigned room that he was pleasantly comfortable in. Looking at his notebook, he regretted not writing down his travels thus far. So many things had happened that he hoped he would never forget.

He started writing down the places they visited and the people he had met. Trying hard to remember every name of every person along the journey, there was a sudden knock on his door. Putting down his pen and paper, he hoped that someone could help him later with all the names. When he opened the door, he was surprised to see Videre. She held a small flickering candle in her hand and smiled.

"It's late so we'll make this quick," she whispered, then turned and walked down the hall.

Without hesitation, Leon followed her closing his door quietly. He found himself tiptoeing after her wondering if it was necessary to be quiet. Quickly and quietly, Videre led him downstairs and through a hidden door in the kitchen going underground. The air was musty and dust covered the stairs as if Charles had never stepped foot inside. Descending even deeper, Leon's heart beat faster. Videre glided down the stairs until they reached another door that looked vaguely familiar. As Videre opened the door, he could see a once dark room slowly lighting up with the same torches in the passageways of the Desiali castle and The Dio's tunnels. As the torches lit, Leon saw it. The familiar sight of the cave that he had fallen into and The Dio's cavern. The writings and drawings on the walls were unmistakable. Videre put her candle down and sat on a rug on the floor while motioning for Leon to sit across from her. Leon uncomfortably sat down facing her, trying to look as confident as he could.

"There are many of these caves and tunnels throughout Aleria. They were commissioned by my father when the Viceroy came to this world. He did this in secret with only a handful of his trusted friends. He was worried about what might happen to the people of Aleria and assigned prominent Kiadere families to these caves. The one in Hikari is natural and was assigned to The Dio. This one was built for the Kaners as they were a prominent family in The Alerian Society. Stocked with food supplies, he ensured the protection of hundreds of Kiadere during Les Nettoyer using of these caves. When Les Nettoyer led to Polonotadere, the fighting distracted the opposing armies long enough to rescue all the people who had hidden in these caves. The writings and drawings are protection spells although I can't say if they actually helped in any way. This cave housed the Kaners and a few others, including Polentio."

"So my family and Lostanzo's family were hidden in this cave together?"

"Yes, this is an important part of your history, Leon."

She took his hands gently in hers.

"Close your eyes and clear your head."

Leon closed his eyes, slightly scared of what she was going to do. He tried clearing his head but it was almost impossible. Memories of their travels and him imagining his great grandfather in these caves kept floating around in his mind. Finally, all he could see was black and all he could think about was breathing. An image in his mind started forming. He was in his shop working on a project. After a few moments, he saw it clearly. The timekeeper that Videre had entrusted to him. The jewels were neatly placed in their respective spots except for the red bloodstone in his hand. Leon distinctly remembered this moment in his shop.

Videre must be digging through my memory.

His mind became clearer and the images became much more vivid as if he was reliving the moment again. He saw himself place the stone in its spot, exactly as he did before. Leon remembered what happened next, but this time, something was different. The stones had started glowing and barely visible lines started connecting the pieces together. The inscriptions on the box also started glowing faintly but only for a few moments. He opened the timekeeper and saw what was inside. A single leaf, so green as if it had just been plucked from a tree. Unlike when he looked at it in his shop, the veins of the leaf were glowing red in a similar fashion as what he just saw on the outside of the timekeeper. A few strands of hair were wrapped around the stem of the glowing leaf. What was magnificent about this leaf, was that it was somehow floating in the box. No matter how tempted Leon was to touch the leaf, he respected the sanctity of whatever he saw and let it be. Unlike the box with the fading glow, the lines on the veins of the leaf kept glowing.

"That's enough," said Videre as she broke hands with Leon.

"I didn't see that glow before," said Leon.

Videre smiled, "Leon, I didn't see what you did. What I was doing was far beyond showing you mere memories. We will continue our sessions when we get back to Vici. Once every few days should suffice to find yourself."

She quickly got up and picked up her candle. Without another word, Leon followed her back upstairs, itching to know more. The memories were his own but they had been different. He had not seen the glow before but he was confused on why he needed to remember the moment to see them. He also didn't understand why he was only able to see them when Videre was there. He was starting to think that she had an ability that was able to read minds, but she had clearly explained that his theory was wrong. He walked quietly behind Videre back to his room wondering the whole time what she had done to him. She opened his bedroom door and walked in with him. She took his hand gently and sat on his bed, pulling him down to sit next to her.

"You have the same special abilities as some of your ancestors, which is a rare sight to see. Many children can inherit either of their parent's ability or a recessive ability that hasn't appeared for generations. Your family has been very important to Aleria and I have no doubt that you will be even stronger than any of them."

Videre smiled as she gripped his hand tight. Standing up, she gently kissed Leon on the forehead sending a tingling sensation down his spine.

"For the future of Aleria," she said softly, before bidding him goodnight.

The next morning, Leon felt unnaturally refreshed for staying up so late. He glanced around his room wondering when they would be able to stay in the mansion next. Eating breakfast was as enjoyable as ever, since Lostanzo was in such high spirits. Many plates full of different scrumptious foods covered the kitchen counters as the men formed a line with their plates in hand, grabbing whatever they craved. There was so much food that Leon doubted that Charles did this all himself.

"We are grateful for your service," said Videre, politely handing him a small coin purse. "We will be on our way shortly. Please ready our senrima."

Videre had a pleasant way of words when showing gratitude, yet the tone she frequently used with her handmen and those close to her could be harsh and unapologetic. She could be taken as rigid to others who did not know her well, but Leon had seen the softer side of her which gave him a sense of comfort. Although it had not been very long that he had started in her service, he knew that her true intentions had always hidden in deep crevices of her personality. He stared at Videre as she ate her food quietly among the ruckus that the men were causing.

"Did she take you to the cavern?" asked Ezrai quietly as he sat next to Leon.

Leon nodded hesitantly. Ezrai seemed to be in on Videre's plans. If anyone were as secretive as her, it would definitely be Ezrai.

"I assume you saw things you haven't seen before," said Ezrai.

"I saw something from the past, but it was different."

Ezrai smiled almost deviously, "You're on your way to finding yourself."

"What exactly does that mean?" asked Leon, recalling that Videre had said the same thing to him.

"You probably unknowingly use your abilities from time to time in small quantities. Historically, Kiadere parents had the duty to teach their children how to use their abilities. It's easiest for parents to teach their children because usually, they have the same abilities since it's inherited. If parents failed to extract the abilities, then the Dio would take the children under their wing and teach them. Now, we hide in fear of our abilities so many Kiadere don't find themselves. The practice is quickly becoming a dying art in our culture. We see Videre as our parent guiding the way to finding ourselves. My father taught me, as was his duty to the Vasili. Lostanzo's parents helped him, but it was Miss Rayne who developed his true potential. Ciano naturally found himself which is very rare. He actually never sat down with Videre for guidance."

"So everyone else has... sat with her to find themselves?"

"There were a few things Lostanzo was able to do after sitting down with her. I, myself, continuously sit down with her to retrieve memories which is hard work. I can see my ancestors' memories. I can go back as far as I want but after several hundred years, the memories become hazy. Together, Videre and I have gone back about a thousand years but we must push for more as most historical written records were destroyed by the Viceroy."

"I understand that it's important to know our history, but how important is it to go that far back? It won't change the future."

"Videre has hope that we will be able to find something important. I don't know what yet, but I must admit, I am as curious as her. After every one of our sessions, I write it down. We recreate historical records but of course, we are very limited in what we can see since it's only from the perspective of my ancestors."

"How many times will I have to sit with her to gain my true potential?" asked Leon, secretly wishing the events of last night would happen more often.

Ezrai shrugged and then walked off to get more food.

The images in his head gave him a sense of power that he had never felt before. The power must be what Ciano feels when he sees through others or when Kolono and Jooey let out their other selves. He thirsted for more. He had to put his trust in Videre that she would give him the tools he needed to finally find himself.

TEA PARTIES

"What a bore," exclaimed Valencia as she tossed a book on her bed.

"It doesn't really matter if it's boring. It matters that you know what's inside," said Kinobi as he thumbed through some of his paperwork.

"Yes, but this stuff is suited for Videre, and I don't have time for it anyway," she said as she pulled off her covers.

"It's still helpful," said Kinobi while shaking his head.

"Ugh. Who even cares about the politics of Alflint?"

"You should. Probably because we have a trip there in the near future and it would be helpful if all the queens knew about what they were getting themselves into."

"I'll just have Videre tell me all about them beforehand," she said as she opened the door to call in Jaora and her hairdresser, Paula.

Jaora and Paula had been waiting outside of Valencia's chambers for at least half an hour waiting to be called in. Valencia had planned a special tea party in the Royal Gardens with some of the noblewomen throughout Desial. Valencia stood on her fine Dunbari rug and posed for the two ladies to dress her.

"You can't just depend on Videre for information like this," Kinobi said, as Jaora started dressing the queen in a silver dress.

The dress hugged Valencia's curves perfectly, as expected. The fine fabric draped on her shoulder flowed as if Jaora had breathed life into the material herself. Valencia was pleased that Videre had convinced her to take on Jaora as a seamstress. Although the Vanirisi talent seemed worthless to most, it was of great use for Valencia.

"I doubt Valeria has even read up on Alflint. She's probably training that new boy toy of hers."

Kinobi cleared his throat and pointed at Jaora who was too busy strapping Valencia's dress to notice. Valencia shook her head. Valeria seemed to always make some sort of mess.

"I'm excited to hear all the gossip. It's been a good few months since I've seen the ladies," Valencia said as Paula was braiding her hair.

Kinobi sighed. Valencia could tell that she annoyed him in matters such as this. She was not one to be interested in any country other than her own. She was also not interested in anything that had to do with fighting or soldiers. Her one focus was to make sure that her country was prosperous and the Kiadere lines would not die out. It just happened to be that the best and most effective way to see to that was to hold luxurious tea parties and wear beautiful dresses. She loved every moment of it.

"It looks perfect on you, Your Majesty," said Jaora as she bowed.

"Yes, it's perfect. Thank you. You may leave," she said in a friendly tone.

"Perhaps you would like to accompany me to the tea party?" Valencia asked sweetly to her husband while Paula was finishing her hair.

"Isn't the tea party for women?"

"Yes, but you can accompany me to my seat then leave."

Kinobi laughed and shook his head. Valencia knew he would never do it but she had hoped that one of these days, she could show off her handsome husband to the ladies.

"I have these to escort," Kinobi said as he waved his papers. "I still have a job to do, you know."

"Of course," Valencia sighed as the hairdresser finished her hair.

Kinobi got out of bed and kissed Valencia on the hand.

"Simple braids look beautiful on you, My Lady."

Valencia smiled as she looked at the timepiece by her bed. She was already late but didn't mind. She knew the party wouldn't start without her. As she walked down the halls, she felt marvelous. She loved a good party and her spirits had been almost exhaustingly high ever since Kinobi had returned. Although he still had work to do in other countries, he would be able to live with her for most of the year. He fit in perfectly with Valeria and Videre also, as they seemed to despise many men of the country if they were not their own handmen.

Handmen and castle workers bowed deep to Valencia as she smiled and nodded to each and every one of them. The sun was shining in the gardens and the air was warm and crisp. Making her way down the stone steps and into the gardens, she saw a group of ladies sitting at a large round table already settling in with their gossiping. To Valencia's satisfaction, her handmen had not yet passed out cakes or poured any tea.

As she moved closer to her seat, the ladies stood up and bowed low, all with a large smile on their face. They were grateful to Valencia for such formalities, no doubt taking them away from what Valencia imagined were boring lives. She sat down as the other ladies followed and a nearby musician started playing soft melodies in the background. Her handmen started pouring tea and passing out brightly colored and perfectly round cakes.

"How are you, Lady Vaniriso? I saw Jes was here in the castle not too long ago."

"I am well, Your Majesty. Jes just wanted to check up on the children. He worries so much."

"How is it having two of your children working in the castle?" asked an older woman.

"It's amazing really," said Jeela. "I must admit I think Jarine is a little jealous."

"Jarine would also be welcome at my court if she wasn't married," laughed Valencia. "You have fantastic children. Even Valeria speaks highly about your son."

"Thank you," said Jeela quietly and sipped her tea.

"Yes, I am hoping Fiora may also marry soon," said the older woman trying to chime in.

Her hair had turned gray long ago. Living separately from her husband, Lady Funa had always itched for more meaning in her life. She cared so much for their daughter, Fiora, but Valencia was sure that Fiora would never marry. From what she knew, Fiora was rarely let outside of her house. She was sure that Fiora was only able to go out when she was summoned to the castle. Poor girl almost never even got a chance to have very many friends. Long ago, Valencia had extended a hand to Lady Funa to have Fiora become a permanent worker of the Desiali castle but she had quickly refused, citing the dangers of the outside world. It was a well-guarded secret that she was from a high-ranking family. Valencia often wondered if the women at her gatherings knew of such things. Although they were part of a prominent family, Valencia could not help but feel uneasy about Lady Funa. Something about her demeanor made Valencia decide to keep her close. Sometimes she would still try to persuade the old woman to let Fiora live with the Vasili, not for parties but for a bad feeling in the pit of her stomach to try and rescue Fiora from an unknown threat.

"Fiora is still young, Lady Funa. She should have time to grow up and have tea parties such as we do," said Anjelika Potter, who was sitting next to her. "I have heard that Lady Chisa's daughter wants to marry a boy by the name of Colin Williams. He is said to reside in Athena and is supposedly very handsome with brilliant green eyes."

"I have never heard of this Williams family in Athena," said Jeela.

"Neither have I, but Lady Chisa swears that he is one of the most handsome men in the country," the Angelika squealed.

"Speaking of handsome men, I have seen you hanging around Keone Minet, Lady Potter," said another woman deviously.

Jeela laughed, "Keone Minet is a handsome man. Very intelligent and humorous as well. We don't blame you."

Valencia smiled. She loved it when rumors started swirling. She looked at Anjelika who was bushing but sitting tall and smiling as well.

"From what I hear, Leon Minet is an excellent handman to my sister."

"Wasn't his father also a handman to her many years ago?" asked Lady Funa.

"Yes, he was," smiled Valencia.

"Poor boy. His parents were fine people. I sometimes wonder what ever happened to them," said Lady Funa in a tone that rubbed Valencia the wrong way.

"From what I know, it was bandits trying to rob them," chimed in Mrs. Potter. She smiled at Valencia, "Leon is a fine young man. I have no doubt he will be of excellent service to you all."

Mrs. Potter had a unique air about her. She knew the right things to say to anyone. Of course with her ability, it was understandable.

Changing the subject off of Leon, Valencia and the ladies kept gossiping and laughing throughout the afternoon in the gardens. Her handmen kept filling up their cups with aromatic teas and fetching cakes. Valencia loved her group of women but her sisters didn't know her true intentions. They thought her to be a silly girl who loves parties and gossip but Valencia was much more than that. This was her version of politics. This was her time to shine.

As ladies started leaving to get back to their own lives, Valencia felt refreshed. However, her work had only just begun. The handmen started cleaning up as she watched them with joy.

"Take all the leftovers to the kitchen. You may have what you like," she said waving her hand.

Kinobi had been waiting for her to finish up on a distant bench. Combining all of his work, he gracefully walked across the garden and took Jeela's chair.

"How was your party?" he asked as he sat next to her, taking a bite out of a cake that had been left.

"Very informative. Do you know Lady Chisa?"

"Of course. She's a distant relative. Why?"

"Her daughter wants to marry an Athenian boy. His name is Colin Williams."

"I've never heard of the surname."

"Aren't you concerned? Lady Chisa cannot have a powerful Kiadere line die out because of her daughter's whims," said Valencia, clearly annoyed. "Lady Chisa doesn't hold Kiadere tradition. I know she hasn't told her daughter. This Colin Williams is most likely a native or mixed. That marriage will not happen."

Kinobi laughed as Valencia pouted.

"I have something I must do now. I'll see you at dinner," she said and kissed him.

Valencia walked proudly down the hallways of the east wings of the castle, smiling and greeting everyone in sight. She would think back to her father telling her that her smile could light up a room. There was no doubt that Videre was his favorite, but he had treated Valencia like a true princess, buying her sparkly dresses and fashionable shoes for every tea party that he had let her have with her noble girls.

"Queen Valencia," a familiar voice cried out.

"Anjelika, I was hoping to talk to you afterward," said Valencia when she turned around. "I must get to Valeria's side if you'd like to accompany me."

Mrs. Potter linked arms with Valencia like a young school-girl sharing secrets. Valeria always liked that about Anjelika. No matter how much time they spent apart, she would always be her best friend.

"I don't like her," Anjelika said softly. "Her air is wrong. I don't know what it is. I only see it a few times here and there, but it's always hanging around her."

Valencia knew exactly who she was talking about.

"I know, Anje. I can sense it too. I'm trying to convince her to let Fiora stay with us but she's always refused. She says its too dangerous."

"That's the thing too. I can almost never see Fiora's air."

Valencia stopped. "How often does that happen?"

"I do but rarely and usually among Vipole."

Thinking of Fiora being similar to any Vipole was laughable.

"I wonder if she doesn't have anything because she's always locked up," Anjelika pondered aloud. "That actually makes a lot of sense. No experiences of the outside world can do a number on a person's soul."

"Poor girl. Some people take the Kiadere legacy too lightly but Lady Funa is quite the opposite."

Still walking arm in arm, Angelika also started up again with a smile on her face.

"Jeela's air changed drastically when you mentioned Jes in the castle."

Valencia laughed, "Of course it did. I thought you'd enjoy that. This is my stop. I'll see you later, Anje," she said as Mrs. Potter bowed and walked away.

Valencia quickly went up to a plain-looking door and knocked vigorously. Pressing her ear to the door, she could hear rustling inside and kept knocking.

"Open the door," yelled Valencia, not caring who all could hear.

The door swung open revealing a tall blond man. His hair was messy and he had bags under his eyes.

"Valeria had asked me to straighten up her room today and then I'm to go to the training grounds," said Jolon as is he had rehearsed his lines.

"Of course," said Valencia, not hiding her sarcasm.

Jolon shrugged, knowing that Valencia could see right through him.

"Walk with me," she demanded as she spun around, heading toward the training grounds.

As they walked down the halls of the east wing, she could see why Jolon was attracting so much attention from Valeria. He was tall and had a muscular physique. Valeria was predictable with men, unlike Videre. He was young, vibrant, and innocent. Valencia could tell that he strived to please. She had noticed an overwhelming change in his appearance as of late. His muscles had visibly gotten larger underneath the fresh cuts and bruises.

"Do you know the Chisa family?"

"Yes, Your Majesty. My mother often makes dresses for their family."

"I heard their daughter is an extremely beautiful girl," she said as she smiled.

"She is beautiful as many other women in Desial are."

"I heard that she fancies you. I just thought you would want to know," she said as she smiled at him.

To Valencia's surprise, Jolon didn't seem to care.

"Queen Valencia!" yelled Sevete as he came running toward her from the training grounds.

A small group of Vipole ran past them in a hurry. Jolon and Valencia instinctively ran towards the commotion as heavy boots made almost a deafening noise on the marble floors. Valencia was still wearing heels from the tea party and tried to run in discomfort. All of a sudden, an extremely large cat appeared next to her, and without a moment's hesitation, she swung on top of it. The cat made swift leaps and bounds past the other men. As she looked back, Jolon had stopped running and stood with his mouth open.

No time to explain to the boy.

A small crowd was huddled on the floor, as the moaning that she had heard just a few seconds ago turned into screams of pain. Swiftly, Valencia dismounted the large feline.

"Move!" yelled Valencia as she shoved one of the men.

An older man was writhing in pain on the ground groaning and clutching his hand. Valeria ran up behind Valencia and gripped the man's hand to take a closer look. The cut was shallow but was bubbling. She could see the veins in his arm turning a dark purple as he gritted his teeth. She looked back at Valencia with a look of fear. They had seen this before.

"Where the hell is Videre?"

MIND, BODY, SOUL, HEART

Saying goodbye to Charles and Lostanzo's estate was always depressing to Videre. Although she paid for the upkeep on the estate and ensured Charles had a comfortable life, she could not help but worry. The estate held so many treasures and memories that were important in unlocking the mysteries of the past. If she had it her way, she would retire from being a queen and live the rest of her days in this house.

Breakfast was filling as usual and she thought about using it as an excuse to not ride out quite yet. Charles had already brought their senrima onto the cobblestone road in front of the mansion and was waiting to help them be on their way. As they slowly started packing and mounting their senrima, Videre caught Leon staring at the walls surrounding the estate. Motioning to the men to continue forward, she kept Leon in the back to talk to him privately.

"Tell me, Leon. What did you see?"

"The glowing. I can't see it now but I saw the faint glow just a moment ago."

"You mean like the ones on the box of the timekeeper?"

"Yes. They were almost exactly the same as the ones on the box and the walls of the caves," said Leon as they started riding.

Videre was pleased. It didn't take long for Leon to start seeing the true world all around them, but it also worried her. She didn't know if Keone had passed on the tradition of teaching him or if he had naturally been this fast. Although, it was wonderful to see a Kiadere find themselves naturally, she knew that they were more prone to lose control, especially with the type of Kiadere that Leon was fated to be. On the other hand, it was exciting to see that Leon may one day surpass his father.

"What else did you see last night?" asked Videre intently.

When she sat down with a Kiadere, she could feel the powers harnessing in her subjects but unfortunately could not see what was in their mind.

"There were glowing lines on the timekeeper and the box. The leaf inside the timekeeper too. They were different colors but I could feel the pressure from it. The lines...made sense. The way the timekeeper works; it's starting to make sense to me."

Videre was sadly not as knowledgeable in timepieces and the timekeeper as she wanted to be. For some reason, it was one of the subjects that she never had to learn about.

"The inscriptions on the walls of the mansion are for protection just like on the timekeeper. It's written by a powerful Kiadere who only makes himself known when he is needed. Unfortunately, his family was the most wanted by the Viceroy because their inscriptions could protect us. He was one of the people who could effectively protect us and our secrets. He is long gone now and I'm quite sure he has no more family to carry on the tradition."

Videre could tell that Leon was fascinated. He had just learned some of the biggest secrets of the Kiadere and was soaking it all in even without the kada juice.

The journey back to the castle was to take all day but Videre wished it would take even longer. She wanted more time to herself with her handmen. She wanted to be around those who understood her and who would be willing to help her achieve great things for their kind. Unfortunately, her life was to be part of the Vasili. The happiness she would feel with being queen was overshadowed by the sadness of all the pain that she had endured. The only person truly bound to her was Ezrai. She had tried encouraging the other handmen to go live their lives, but they were always right by her side. They gave up their lives to reach her selfish goals and she loved them for it.

The sun was high up in the sky. It was warmer in Reino than in Moshny. Videre always hated to pack for travels because the weather was so different in most of the regions of the continent. The worst of all were the trips going through Moshny, Woadland, and Zwill. She took at least a day or two to readjust to the climate even if her meetings with the leaders didn't take very long. She didn't like change but she did appreciate the changing customs of each country. She held a strange sense of pride that she knew the customs and mannerisms of any country she visited. She didn't understand why, but she got a sense of power from being able to blend in with any culture as if she could disappear and live out her days among the people of any country.

I hope Valencia and Valeria are reading up on Alflint.

Videre already knew the sad truth. They didn't care. They left all the foreign politics to Videre. She felt like it was retaliation for getting so much attention from her father. Her mind wandered again to Valencia bearing an heir. It would be messy, but even if she did want the throne to herself, she always thought that it would be easy for her to gain the endorsement of all the foreign powers. She forced the thought from her mind as such speculation was a slippery slope.

"Drink," said Jooey, motioning to a nearby stream.

The group followed Jooey's lead and led their senrima to the calm cold waters that they seemed happy to drink from. Videre looked toward the west to the mountains that separated the east side of the continent from the west. Just on the other side of those mountains was Athena. She knew that she needed to add Athena on the rounds for political visits, but even the thought of it tired her. The leaders of Athena revered their own traditions but also pushed for advancing mankind.

Convincing other leaders in joining them in Les Nettoyer, the Kiadere had been sworn enemies despite The Alerian Treaty. After some time, the memories of the past faded and Athena had brought technological advances to the world, making them a prominent country. New ways of building, infrastructure, farming, and many more everyday applications had been made easier by their dedication to research and the willingness to share their knowledge. They had been so close to unification not very long ago and it all changed over the course of a summer. Now, she looked at the leaders in disgust instead of holding them in high esteem for what they had done for the continent.

"Remember that one time?" Jooey laughed as he put his arm around Videre.

She smiled at his gleaming face as he stared at one of the mountains. There had been a handful of times where they had traveled through the mountains instead of taking the valley between Moshny and Woadland. She knew exactly what he was talking about. Jooey's face had become weathered over the years. He had been stressed from her endeavors. His expressions of worry were more numerous as of late. She could tell that he had started becoming more protective of her, whether it be from other people or from herself. She found herself telling him not to worry frequently but now was starting to question her own choices.

"I remember," she said with a smile. "We've been through a lot since then."

He stroked her hair and whispered, "You need to slow down. You have all the time in the world."

His face became serious and sad as he walked to his senrima and made sure his saddle was secure before swinging his lofty body on top of the large animal. Videre understood what he meant. Every once in a while, he begged her to slow down. He told her she had time, but it was not in her nature. She wanted things done quickly and efficiently. She didn't want to take her time. She needed to change the world and she needed to do it as quickly as possible.

Kolono brought Lady Italych to Videre, completely satisfied with the cold water that had flowed from Choson peak. Taking one last look at the mountain, Videre and her men started following the country road once again. The sun was still high in the cloudless sky. Reino, like Desial, was dominated mostly by farmland. Although the country itself was large, the population was a fraction of what it was in other countries. Farmers and ranchers worked the large fields and were caught staring as Videre and her handmen passed by. The people of Reino were hardworking and almost entirely governed themselves by living in small communities mostly consisting of only a few families.

The government had little to do with their affairs. Videre almost envied them. The people of Reino had so much freedom and the ruling family had almost no hand in their lives. If it weren't for their strict laws on the restriction of foreign immigrants, she suspected their population would have grown like wildfire. If there was anything she knew about the people of Aleria, most of them simply wanted their freedoms and the chance to live their lives without any intervention. If only all people were decent and good people, this could be easily accomplished. This was the way of the old Kiadere government. Back then, the Kiadere had certain families with specific abilities in charge of the security of citizens. The Dio had been in charge of regulating the Kiadere abilities which proved effective for centuries. Meanwhile, the people lived out their lives in almost complete freedom. Now their world was in chaos. Although most did not see it, Videre could see all too easily with every trip that she took.

"Something is coming," whispered a distant and familiar voice.

Tell me.

"I don't know. You need to take care. Something big is coming. You're all in danger."

I need you to tell me more.

There was no response.

She looked back expecting to see his red hair but he wasn't there. Instead, she saw an image far off in the distance and stopped her senrima. She squinted as the figure came closer with amazing speed. After a few moments, she saw that there was a man speeding on a horse toward them. Within a moment, Jooey and Kolono with both swords drawn positioned themselves in front of Videre but still allowed her a view of what was coming. The horse had a blue blanket adorned with roses under its saddle; the Rayne family emblem. There was only one horse left in the stables of the Rayne Mansion and she had seen it this morning when they had left. The light mane was also unmistakable. It was Lostanzo's family horse except it wasn't Charles on that horse. Her heart pounded as the horse got closer and closer without losing any speed. The man's face was gaunt and his hair was long and unkempt. His clothes looked familiar as if he had gotten them out of Lostanzo's closet.

"Identify yourself," yelled Jooey in a loud, demanding voice.

The figure started slowing down but did not speak back. He stopped the horse several paces in front of them, unmounted, and ran as fast as he could toward Videre. His weak frame was evident as if he had just learned to run, almost stumbling several times in the process.

Videre couldn't believe her eyes. She dismounted and ran out past her personal guards and embraced the man who almost knocked her over. Jooey and Kolono let down their swords in confusion. Together, Videre and the man fell down to the ground as he had clearly exhausted himself. Videre grasped his face with her hands, inspecting him in wonder. She stroked her thumb across the scar on his throat.

"Can you talk?" she asked quietly.

He shook his head with tears filling his eyes even more. Videre hugged him as he tried to touch her hand.

"Not now, Lo. You must rest first."

Videre had never imagined that Lo would come back to her after all these years. He must have escaped whatever captivity he was in and found his way to Lostanzo's mansion shortly after they had left. He was thin and frail unlike when he had gone missing. Always agile and athletic, Lo was the best spy she could ever ask for. The things he saw were quickly and efficiently reported to her. He loved his job and Videre made sure he was never stagnant because of how ambitious he had always been. She looked up to Ciano who was also in complete shock. Ciano took a deep breath as his eyes glazed over. Within a few seconds, he snapped out of his trance.

"I can't get through. I can feel him but I can't get through. Someone must have closed his mind."

"Were you underground?" asked Videre

Lo nodded.

"I could be that you couldn't feel his presence before because he was underground."

"I never thought I'd say this, but I think I need to sit down with you. Perhaps I am not at my fullest," said Ciano in defeat.

"Yes," Videre agreed, holding Lo tightly as a mother would with her son.

A long silence fell upon the group for a brief moment before Videre got up with Lo.

"You need to eat and drink," said Videre. "We're close to the next town and soon we will be in Vici, then you will go straight to bed and we will resolve this in the morning."

Her tone would take the role of their mother from time to time. Although she had desperately wanted them to be treated like equals, she was the one holding their plethora of personalities together for one common cause.

Lo nodded and bowed low to Videre. She was grateful but also worried. Lo had been gone for almost twenty years. Whoever had him wanted him alive and Videre knew why. The incredible power that Lo had was a double-edged sword for her. She was also concerned about Ciano. He had come to find himself naturally and was extremely proud of it. Not only that, but now there was an issue of perhaps being able to close one's mind to Ciano. Wielding such power may have devastating consequences, especially with a threat on the horizon.

Making their way to the next town, they had found a small familiar diner to eat at. The sloped roof was unmistakable as the outside was painted a different color every time Videre passed through this particular town. Reino was known for its prized inks and dyes stemming from all sorts of animals, minerals, and plants. They had long kept their sources a secret and brought in much foreign revenue from the sale of such luxuries. She had helped facilitate a trade agreement between Jes and Jeela and the dye-makers. That was another thing she admired about their government. Private sources were able to trade freely without the watchful eye of the leaders of the country.

Although the food wasn't as satisfying as the meals at Lostanzo's house, Videre did not care to eat as she was so engrossed in watching Lo eat.

"Be careful, Lo. You don't want to overeat," said Malaki while checking his pulse.

A concerned look engulfed Malaki's face which did not suit him well. Everyone could see that Lo had been starved and tortured. Lostanzo's clothes draped over him like sheets as various scars were visible. His fingernails were grotesquely misshapen and his hands showed slight tremors while picking up his food.

Malaki inspected the line on his neck. "Were they meaning to kill you or were they wanting to silence you?"

Lo looked at Malaki and put a finger up to his lips.

"So the people who did this knew how to cut your voice but not your life," said Lostanzo.

"Did they extract any secrets?" asked Ezrai bluntly.

Lo looked defeated as he nodded his head. Lo stopped eating and pointed toward Leon.

"That's Leon," said Jooey. "Keono's son. He is our newest handman."

Lo looked at Videre and pointed to her. Videre completely forgot about when Lo was last at the castle. She shook her head and smiled.

"We will have to fill you in once we get back home," she said as she tried to hold in her tears.

The others started talking to Lo about all the things that had been happening while he was gone. They talked about the changes in Viceroy rulers as well as things that had been happening in Desial. He had not heard of the marriage between Valencia and Kinobi and Jooey managed to slip a little bit of information about his infatuation with Fiora into their conversation. Videre started relaxing once the men had started making Lo smile. His eyes that used to be sharp and full of intensity were now tired and sad.

The sun was starting to go down as the group had lost track of time talking to Lo. Riding off to the north, Lo rode next to Videre the entire trip to Vici. She could feel his calm aura as they got closer to the castle that he had called home for many years. Videre frequently looked back at Kolono who still seemed like he was in shock. Kolono and Lo had been child-hood friends in Athena. In fact, Kolono refused to go with Videre unless she had agreed to take Lo with her also. She would never regret that ultimatum after seeing the kind of man that Lo grew into.

"Your Majesty," greeted a young handman that was assigned to the stables for the night.

"House this horse with the senrima," said Videre pointing to Lostanzo's family horse.

The senrima who had always had a tight bond had accepted the horse as their own, recognizing that Lo was also one of their own. Walking up the tower stairs with Lo, she kept looking at his face and how much it had changed after all these years. It was remarkable how much older he looked compared to Kolono. She wished nothing but peace for Lo who had obviously been through trauma, but she was impatient for all the information that he had to share and also what he may have unintentionally shared with his captors.

She walked Lo to his room that had remained unchanged for the entire time that he had been gone. His clothes were still neatly folded and hung in the wardrobe and his belongings and various trinkets were still inside of his desk. Once a year, on his birthday, Videre would order a maid to go dust his room, but other than that, it was left untouched.

Lo grabbed Videre by the arm over her sleeves.

"Tomorrow, Lo. Show me tomorrow after you've rested."

Videre placed her hand on his shoulder and hugged him goodnight. Headed to her quarters, she noticed her handmen with the exception of Leon, in a tight huddle in front of her office. Rolling her eyes, she opened the door and let them all in. She sat at her desk and waited for someone to start speaking.

"We can't trust him," blurted Ezrai.

"Are you serious?" interjected Kolono. "He came back to us. We don't know what he had to go through to escape."

"He might have been let loose. This could have been their plan," said Ezrai calmly.

"We don't even know who they are," said Lostanzo.

"Whoever it is, they know what they're doing," said Ciano. "All this time, I only tried finding him a handful of times. They must know how to get me out of his head and keeping him underground probably didn't help either."

"Not to mention what they did to his throat," said Malaki.

"What's your professional opinion of his condition," Videre asked Malaki.

"He is obviously weak. We should give him a chance but I definitely recommend keeping him close, just in case someone tries to contact him. Right now, he needs our support for his mental health."

"I hate to say this, but should we take him to see Limono?" asked Ezrai.

"No," Kolono said suddenly. "I don't trust that man. He knows everyone's secrets."

"I must agree," said Malaki. "There is a medical healing and psychological healing. I can take care of medical and I think we all know Lo enough to take care of his mental state. Besides, we all know Lo is of strong mind."

"I must agree to that," said Ezrai wearily. "Perhaps we should consider keeping his return a secret."

Videre sighed, "I think that would be wise."

"His room is next to mine," said Lostanzo. "I'll keep an eye on him."

"Everyone, get some sleep," said Videre to her handmen. "We've had a very unique and extraordinary trip. We must act as if nothing out of the ordinary has happened."

The men all stood and uniformly bowed to her before exiting out the door. Poor Leon who had already gone to his chambers probably didn't understand how important this was. Lo needed to also be informed of all the things that had been happening since he was gone, but Ezrai was right. He couldn't be trusted just yet.

"Wake up, Leon," said Videre quietly.

Her fingers were running through his hair as she was sitting on the side of her bed. Disoriented for a few seconds, he realized that he was sleeping in his bed at the castle. His mind could hardly keep up with where he had been waking up for the past several nights. Her fingers were still rubbing through his dark coarse hair making Leon slightly uncomfortable with how close she was getting. The moon was shining through his window.

"I'm sorry but I need something from you," she said softly as she pushed him to the other side of the bed and slipped under his covers, and faced him. "I need you to swear your allegiance to me. Not just for being a handman but your mind, body, soul, and heart. I need you to do it."

"I swear that I am yours," said Leon without hesitation, but also feeling even more uncomfortable.

The words had gracefully poured out of his mouth. Videre smiled and closed her eyes and fell asleep almost instantly.

WINSTON

It was a dreary and cold day. The clouds had dominated the sky for almost a week. The ground was constantly wet as the skies brought a steady shower to this part of Aleria. The rain was much needed but Winston knew that if the weather continued, they would have to start digging trenches to drain certain parts of the city. Some homes were in danger of being swept away by mudslides in recent years. There was only the sound of rain as most people stayed indoors during this weather. The farmers in the surrounding villages welcomed the rains, but it was beginning to prove detrimental. He opened the door and peeked outside, seeing only a few people strolling down the streets. The clouds in the sky looked thinner than the previous day yet were still dark. He sat on a small red chair on his porch after wiping off the wet drops that had found their way under the overhang of his roof. He had enjoyed sitting outside of his door, breathing in the fresh air, but recently, the dust from the road in front of his house had irritated his lungs. At least with the rain, he was able to sit outside and breathe comfortably, hardly noticing the stray drops that hit his face. Today was the first day of the month and he was always sitting on his porch patiently waiting at this exact time of day.

"Do you want some hot coffee while you wait?" asked his wife, peeking her head out from the front door.

"No. It shouldn't take much longer," he said, looking around impatiently.

Winston looked at his timepiece. Tindo was late.

He's never late. Perhaps the rain slowed him down. That would be a first.

Winston sat waiting while his wife had started on his lunch. This was unlike Tindo. If there was anyone more reliable than Winston, it was Tindo.

"Sara, I need to go to the market. Do you need anything?" he yelled behind him.

"Yes, actually," she said as she ran to the door. "I forgot to get some cream last time."

He smiled, got out of his chair, and kissed her goodbye. He tried to conceal his anxiety as he peeked at his timepiece while walking out into the rain. Almost ten minutes had gone by and no sign of Tindo. Something was wrong. He had inadequately prepared for his short trip to the market. With quite a few thoughts running through his head, he had not even contemplated bringing an umbrella or boots. He had hardly noticed that his feet were now soaking from the puddles that he had not even attempted to avoid.

Something is wrong.

He could hear a few voices up ahead at the market, but instead of keeping to the road, he veered off down an alleyway. The roof of the buildings on either side of the alley had a slight overhang although the rain had already soaked through his clothes and shoes. A small, narrow set of stairs on one of the buildings led him down to a blue door. Usually, this door was locked, requiring a secret code to get inside, but he could make out that it was cracked open. Winston knew better than to go through the door. He quickly and quietly ran up the stairs. Thoughts were running through his head as he walked with great speed back home, trying not to look like a mad man.

I need to get home. Where is Tindo? Why was the door open? Do they know who I am?

He knew he had to get home. He needed to protect Sara. They needed to leave this city.

He burst through the door screaming for his wife. Terrified, his wife looked at him with big eyes.

"We have to leave."

"Winston, what happened?"

"We have to leave now," he screamed as he grabbed a box from under his bed.

Sara's eyes widened. She never knew what had been kept in Winston's box, but she knew that it was important enough to where that would be the one thing he would bring with them.

He ran out the door, with the box tucked under his arm and Sara's hand grasped tightly in his.

"Where are we going?"

"To the stables," yelled Winston almost out of breath.

They ran quietly down the street, looking like an old couple who desperately wanted to get out of the rain.

"Winston. Where are we going?" Sara asked in a louder voice.

Winston looked back at her with an unmistakable panicked look on his face.

"Vici"

PURPLE SICKNESS

Videre woke up feeling refreshed and with a new perspective. She wouldn't have to worry about Lo. Lo was strong and fearless. He had come back to her after all these years. After all the torture, he found his way back to her. She knew he would shortly begin requesting that he start back on his missions. Of course, she would refuse until some time had passed, but an unusual excitement filled her as she thought about how much Lo could be utilized in the coming months. For now, she would continue on her path with Leon, just as his father had done with her. She had a feeling that he was the key to the solution. Watching Leon inside the shed in Moshny proved to her that this was indeed the chosen path for both of them. All of these recent distractions were minor and could be easily dealt with. There was one person she needed to visit to solidify her suspicions.

She looked over next to her. Leon was sleeping soundly. His black hair was exactly like Keono's. Quickly she rolled out of his bed and slipped into the hallway coming face to face with

Jooey. He was standing in front of the door, arms crossed, obviously waiting for her.

"I saw you come in here last night," he puffed.

"Calm down, Jooey," she said as she started walking down the hall. "Nothing happened. He swore allegiance to me last night and then I fell asleep."

Jooey grabbed her by the arm. "I hope you know what you're doing. I don't know all the details of your and Ezrai's plan, but I cannot risk what happened last time."

Videre touched his chest. "I'll be careful. I promise you."

She looked into Jooey's eyes. She saw something that she rarely saw from him; the look of fear.

"Videre," yelled a familiar voice down the hall.

A large man was stomping toward her angrily.

"Oh boy," whispered Jooey. "I'll see you later."

Jooey bowed his head and walked quickly out of the line of fire.

"Come into my office, Keone," she said as she opened her door begrudgingly.

Keone had not visited Videre in years and she wished that when it finally did happen, he would have at least come in good spirits.

"That boy is not your toy," he said as he sat down.

"Where is this coming from?" Videre asked trying to remain calm.

"You went to see Rayne," he said as he waved a letter with the blue seal. "You took him to see her."

"She didn't say anything, Keone."

"I know she didn't, but that boy isn't ready yet. He's not ready to fill his father's shoes. I absolutely do not approve of what you're doing."

"There was a time when you supported my endeavors."

"I still do, but it got my son killed and Leon is at risk. This really cannot be the only way through this."

"This is the only way," Videre yelled and slammed her fist into the table. "Leon is protected. I will never let anything happen to him and you need to understand that."

Keone's angry face changed suddenly. He leaned back in his chair and let out a loud laugh. "I know I have a temper but you need to stop bottling yours in."

"I'm a queen," Videre said quietly, grateful for the broken tension. "I can't be like you."

"It's a shame that you weren't some regular Kiadere girl."

Videre all of a sudden remembered why she needed to talk to Keone.

"Listani," she said abruptly.

"What about her?"

"He has dreams with her in them."

"Yes," Keone said calmly. "But they're always the same. I make sure of it."

"You knew he was having dreams?"

"Yes," he replied annoyingly. "I don't even know if it's her. He says it's the same dream over and over again and a woman is leading him."

"Things have progressed. He's seen her face and the dreams have changed. She's talking to him. He even picked something up from a location in one of his dreams."

"What was it?" asked Keone looking even more worried than Videre.

"I'm not sure, but it was small enough to put into his pocket. He has no idea that I know."

"This is dangerous, Videre. You have to do something."

Videre stood up and started pacing. She never knew a time like this would come. Listani probably didn't know that Videre would find out.

"That's the thing. I don't know what to do. Maybe we should let things play out and keep track of his dreams."

"You should have executed her when you had the chance."

Videre was shocked. "This is your daughter-in-law. How can you say that?"

"She killed my son and she nearly killed you. You let her get away with it. Exile is not a proper punishment."

"Exile is a proper punishment. She has been denied to see her child grow up as I have been denied to see mine."

Without a knock, the doors to her office swung open.

"There's something you need to see," said Kinobi.

"I'm in the middle…"

"No," he said calmly as he turned around.

Videre rolled her eyes as she and Keone both started walking out into the hallway. Jooey, Lostanzo, and Ciano were already waiting in the halls. She did not like to be hurried so early in the morning but something about Kinobi's face had worried her.

"What's going on?" she asked Lostanzo.

"I'm not sure, but they fetched Malaki early this morning."

The halls were unnaturally quiet as guards started looking at Videre and whispered amongst themselves. Kinobi was several paces in front of Videre and did not turn or talk at all. His footsteps were light and quick, almost unnaturally so. Kinobi led the group through the halls of the east wing before stopping in front of Valeria's office doors guarded by a few Vipole.

As the doors opened, she saw her sisters talking to some of the Vipole in hushed voices. Malaki was kneeling on the floor with his medical bag in front of the sofa in Valeria's office. His face looked tired as he was using a stethoscope on a large man laying on the sofa. All eyes turned to Videre as she slowly walked towards the man. Sir Jaime, one of the oldest Vipole in Valeria's service, looked to be drained of all color. His heavy breathing crackled as his eyes opened and looked at Videre. When she saw it, she felt sick to her stomach.

Videre was not one to shy away from hardship or uncomfortable situations but this was something different. She could feel this in her veins and in her soul. Something that had left her body long ago had also left its imprint on her mind. She now looked at Sir Jaime and could not help but feel like screaming out to him. She knelt next to him as he looked at her with bloodshot eyes. Sir Jaime knew that he was now experiencing the pain that she had felt many years ago. Lostanzo, who was standing in the doorway, ran out into the hallway while Jooey started talking to Valeria. Keone, just like the old days, commanded Jolon and the other Vipole to stand back out of the doorway for privacy and closed the doors.

"When did this happen?" asked Videre while inspecting Sir Jamie's arm.

"It's been a day," replied Valeria.

"I would like for you to enlighten us on where you were. If you and Malaki were here yesterday..." Valencia paused as tears rolled down her face.

"We need to take him to the infirmary," commanded Videre.

"Videre, I would rather him stay here in my office," said Valeria with a shaking voice.

"No, Videre's right. He needs to be in a sterile environment and where Malaki and the nurses can treat him effectively," said Valencia, almost breaking down.

"Jooey, bring the cart," demanded Videre, trying to stay calm.

With a nod of his head, Jooey ran out of the doors into the direction of the infirmary. Years ago, Videre had moved the infirmary to the East wing due to several sustained injuries that the Vipole endured throughout their daytime training. Although Valeria never thanked Videre for the wise decision, she had always been silently grateful.

"Sir Jaime, do you have any family that you would like to come to visit?" asked Keone.

"Keone," he said in a whisper but could not continue.

Videre could see his pulsating veins and his slow heavy breathing. She could sense that Sir Jaime was in so much pain, but as one of the commanders of the Vipole, he would not show any weakness.

"You're doing alright. Drink up," Malaki said with a smile holding a cup to the man's lips.

Videre saw the tea that Malaki had made for the soldier and felt her stomach turn. Many times, she drank the pain-reducing concoction to a point where she would feel sick even looking at it even though the taste was bearable.

Jooey came running in with the cart that was so rarely used due to the stubbornness of injured Vipole. Sir Jaime immediately started trying to get up out of his indent on the sofa. Keone and Jooey quickly helped him to the cart, laying him down as if he were a frail old man. A man that only a couple of days ago could beat almost anyone in a strength contest was now so crippled that he couldn't even stand on his own.

"Who knew I'd die before you, Keone," he muttered with half a smile.

"You ain't dying Jaime. Just think of it like the old days when you drank too much at the pub," Keone reassured him.

Sir Jaime started laughing but it was quickly interrupted with a fit of coughing.

The blood hasn't come out yet. We still have time.

Jooey and Keone started pushing Sir Jaime on the heavy cart. Videre looked at Keone in wonder at how old but strong he still was. With a deep sadness she could not feel anything but upset about what had come between them. Her best friend with whom she shared her deepest secrets was now almost a stranger who now bore resentment toward her.

"Malaki has gone through this before. He is sure to make you better," assured Videre while rubbing Sir Jamie's arm.

As they pushed Sir Jamie quickly to the infirmary, he tugged at Valeria's arm. She leaned over to kiss him on the forehead, but he pulled her close and whispered to her. She let go of the cart and stood in the hallway with a dismal look on her face. Running down the hall were Ezrai and Lo, who looked to be in shock, but not as much as Valencia and Valeria.

"Lo?" said Valeria as she ran up and inspected his face. Her fingers brushed through his long hair and then trailed to his throat.

"Who did this to you?" asked Valencia, but Lo was still staring at Sir Jaime who was now also looking back at Lo.

"I'll have to ask that you all stay outside the infirmary. We don't need to be getting it dirty," said Malaki, trying to keep a friendly smile on his face.

It was the same friendly smile that he always had on when he was about to treat someone who had little hope. Videre knew that smile all too well. The doors of the infirmary swung open as Malaki himself pushed them with his cart. Inside, Videre could hear the frantic chatter of the nurses that were stationed there.

"Is anyone going to tell me what happened to Lo?" asked Valeria.

"We were going to get to it this morning," said Videre.

"Who did this?" asked Valencia again.

Lo shrugged with a sad look in his eyes. He opened his mouth and covered his throat signaling to Valencia that he couldn't speak.

"I see," said Valeria as she cleared her throat and gestured to her office.

Both Valencia and Videre with grim expressions walked toward her office.

"You stay here and update me," Videre whispered to Lo as he nodded.

"I'll go say hi to my grandson," said Keone. "I don't miss being here in this wretched place."

As Keone stormed off, Jooey started walking back to Valeria's office with her.

"Queens only," demanded Valeria, obviously talking to Jooey and Kinobi.

Videre suddenly realized how long Lo had been gone. He had not been there to see when Videre had gone through the same sickness. He had not seen the purple veins and blood-shot eyes. She inched toward Lostanzo as her sisters waited for her in the doorway to Valeria's office.

"You need to show Lo what happened. He needs to know what happened," she said as she looked at Lo, "With everything. Gather everyone into my office. I'll be there shortly."

Lostanzo nodded hesitantly. She knew it would be painful for him to relive the memories but Lo needed to understand.

"I would like to have Ezrai with us for the record," said Videre.

"Yes, I believe we must," said Valencia.

Videre let out a deep breath as they all walked into the office and shut the doors behind them. Ezrai sat on a chair in the corner as Valencia and Videre sat in the two chairs in front of Valeria's desk. Sitting at her desk, Valeria carefully pulled out an object from a drawer. Unwrapping the red cloth around it, she brandished one of her prized throwing knives.

"We were just messing around," she admitted in despair.

Videre carefully took the knife by the handle. She could see there was a slight discoloration to the blade.

"He must have cut his hand on it."

"You wouldn't have even noticed something was wrong with it," said Valencia reassuringly.

"My question is, was this poison meant for you?" asked Videre. "You could have easily cut yourself with it."

"That's precisely what I was thinking. I don't even know how it would have gotten there or even when. I carry it around almost all the time."

"When do you not have this blade on you?"

"When I bathe and sleep. I even carried it to the Equinox Festival," Valeria said in a defeated tone.

Videre quickly wrapped up the dagger neatly back into the cloth.

"Should we tell the handmen to keep their eyes open or should we keep it a secret?"

Videre sighed. Valeria was right. The handmen may be useful when it came down to trying to figure out who may have poisoned the blade, but on the other hand, it may have been a handman who did the deed themselves.

"Keep it a secret. We don't need the culprit to be on guard," chimed in Ezrai from the back of the room.

"Agreed," said Valeria quietly.

"I'll take the dagger to Malaki so he can determine what we're dealing with," said Videre with a glimmer of hope.

"Before I forget," said Valeria.

She pulled out a box of letters from under her desk. Each one was written on different parchment but bore the same unmistakable seal.

"This all came in over two days' time," said Valeria.

Videre was confused. The Alerian Society communicated mostly by word of mouth but if something was urgent, they had to send letters by zanianbird.

Putting the wrapped knife carefully in her pocket, she started opening some of the letters and skimming over them. Each one was as disturbing as the last. Ezrai quickly joined her with an equally concerned look on his face.

"I know both of you don't know much about the affairs of state or the traditions of The Alerian Society but there is one tradition that has not died out yet," said Videre quietly.

She kept opening and skimming the letters until they had gone through half of them. After quickly picking up the letters and returning them to the box she handed the box to Ezrai.

"If an Alerian Society member dies, then the Vasili must be notified," said Ezrai.

"These are all death letters?" Valeria asked in shock.

"Most are, some members are sick and are foretelling their coming death," Videre said.

"We have to notify everyone in The Alerian Society."

"And do what?" asked Videre. "Many of them have already died from the sickness. They're being hunted down. There must be someone out there with a list of names of the members."

"That's impossible," said Valencia. "We're the only ones with the list. Even The Dio doesn't know who all is in The Alerian Society."

"Then we have a spy in our midst. There's a traitor in this castle," fumed Valeria.

Videre flashed back to Lo. She was sure Lo had never seen the list so it wouldn't have come from him. He also hadn't been in the castle to poison the blade. It make Videre even sicker to her stomach that she was even thinking about her own handmen being traitors.

"This has been a long time coming," Videre said calmly. "The plants that had been harvested in Korona that Fryderyk warned us about, the petals are what the poison is derived from. The leaves contain the cure."

"Ok, that's good news. We just ask Korona to give us some leaves," said Valencia.

"Valencia. All the plants were harvested. That's why Fryderyk was so worried. Only us and the Koronians know of the poison. We kept it a secret last time it happened."

"There must be some plants or seeds somewhere. We'll just have to go look for them," said Valencia almost enthusiastically.

"I'm afraid that that's our only option as of right now," said Videre.

"I'll take care of warning the rest of The Alerian Society," said Valencia seriously.

"I can send my Vipole to scout for the plant. Please have Malaki get me a drawing of it or any information as soon as he can."

Videre could feel the immense danger that was now in her pocket. Ezrai was there with her for many nights watching over her as she had to overcome the sickness and a simple cut from the blade would be all it took.

"What happened to Lo?" asked Valencia sternly.

"I don't know. He must have escaped and found his way back to us. I'll be sitting down with him later and hopefully, we can get more information."

"I don't like this Videre. Sir Jaime has the sickness and now Lo is back. It cannot be a coincidence."

"Lo is a faithful handman. You know that," she snapped.

"I have no doubts he is, but remember what happened with Listani. The same could happen to anyone in our service, especially the weak-minded."

Before exiting the office she looked at Valeria who was on the verge of breaking down.

"What did Sir Jamie tell you earlier?" asked Videre.

"He asked me to end his pain."

RIPS

____

The sun had started rising as Winston and Sara had hardly stopped since the day before. The rain had dissipated and the cool air started drying their previously soaked clothes. The horses that they had taken from the stables were meant for this one purpose. They had been bred specifically for this emergency, yet Winston could feel the horses slowing down as their panting had slowly turned into wheezing. He knew these horses all too well. Valeria had made sure that they would most likely run to their death before failing The Alerian Society.

"If only Tindo were here," panted Sara.

She looked exhausted. Their old bodies were not meant to ride on horseback all night. Their entire bodies ached, but the adrenaline running through their bodies kept them going. Sara was right. Tindo would have gotten them there in no time. Winston was unsure of how far his ability would have taken them but he definitely could have cut the travel time short. Winston's arm was increasing in soreness from clutching the box He knew that he didn't have to grip so hard but he was not willing to take that chance.

All of a sudden, he saw something only a few paces in front of him. It was unmistakable. A rip in the world. The circle had come out of nowhere. The view of the countryside was now interrupted by a large circle with a view of dark fog. The rip was big enough to swallow both of the horses. The horse was still running straight, unaware that something was about to engulf them. Winston, with quick reflexes for an old man, had turned the horse sharply to the side. As he passed the rip, he could see no depth to it. He also noticed that as he passed, he was the only one riding now.

Sara was gone. A part of him knew that Sara would never be able to turn as sharply as him. She had disappeared through the rip and had made her way into the fog. As he took deep breaths to keep himself from screaming, he saw a glimpse of something in the sky in the distance. Another rip in the sky that he had not noticed had spewed out two figures, a horse and a person. Falling through the clouds, he knew what had happened. This was the same as Tindo's ability. Tears rolled down Winston's face as he closed his eyes making sure to not look towards the crashing sound of bodies hitting the ground. This was his job. This was a sacrifice he would have to make for his queen and country. He shook uncontrollably as he rode away even faster from the rip that had now disappeared.

It was Tindo's ability, but not quite the same. He could make out a faint blue outline on the rip for the mere second when he had seen it. He knew very well that Tindo's rips had a golden hue to it. He was also unaware that anyone had the same ability as Tindo. Yet again, he had never even thought to ask if Tindo knew of anyone else with such ability.

Winston's heart was hurting. From the lack of sleep, adrenaline, and now the unfortunate death of his wife, he could feel his body was starting to shut down. He had only taken the road to Vici a few times in his life and wondered how much further he had to go. He looked around nervously again. He knew they had to have seen him coming to make the rip in the world. Nobody had been following them. Perhaps they had been waiting for them all along, knowing that this is exactly where they would have been headed. Perhaps, whoever was behind this, knew that Winston would take the box and would react exactly as how he did. Perhaps, this was his fault. Maybe he overreacted and the events led Sara straight through the rip in the world.

Sorrow and guilt filled his body as he found it even harder to breathe. Then, he saw it. The purple and silver flag of Desial flowing elegantly in the wind at the top of a pole. Winston pushed his horse even faster. Without complaint, the horse pushed through the wheezing, knowing exactly where to go.

The rushing wind became almost deafening as it started beating into his ears. Suddenly, an enormous bird was flying next to them as if it had come from nowhere. The wings were easily longer than Winston's horse and the beating wings were so powerful, the wind was now almost pushing him off of the saddle. He had heard about these beasts in children's tales but had never seen one in real life. As if the bird had telepathy, the horse had slowed to a stop and the bird seemed as if it was beckoning Winston to climb on. It brandished a small cloth-like saddle as it leaned closer to Winston. The old man looked at the castle, which was now visible in front of him, and took a deep breath as he slid off the horse.

Without warning, the bird screeched and the horse had tumbled down to the ground. An arrow was deeply embedded in the horse's leg from behind. Winston still could not see anyone on the horizon as he tried to determine where the arrow originated from. With the box still tucked under his arm, he quickly climbed onto the bird and before he even felt comfortable on the saddle, the bird took off. The rush of wind had hit Winston in the face so hard that he was disoriented for a second. As soon as he opened his eyes, he could see that he was higher up in the air than he had ever been as his stomach churned. He had been on his fair share of towers and mountains but nothing had prepared him for this view.

He looked down to see the horse still struggling, but also in the distance he could make out three figures, one with a bow. They had stood still, perhaps given up, now that he was in the safety of the massive beast. All of a sudden, he saw one of the figures making motions with their arms. As the figure's arms went up, the bird swooped down at an alarming pace. Winston closed his eyes in fear of perhaps the bird had been struck by an arrow and was now falling to their deaths, but the bird steadied. He opened his eyes again as he saw another rip in the sky appear.

They're trying to swallow us too!

The bird avoided the rip more gracefully this time by flying over it. Several more rips appeared with the same blue hue as the bird zipped past them as if this were a common occurrence. Winston looked down at the figures. They were barely visible and once they disappeared out of sight, the rips in the sky had stopped.

The castle was getting nearer every second and Winston could make out soldiers posted on top. He had never in his life thought that this would ever happen. Plans were in place that he had previously scoffed at, but now he knew for sure that Videre knew exactly what she was talking about.

The bird swooped down and landed on top of a flat section of the roof of the castle. Two guards ran up to them and helped Winston off of the saddle on the bird. Gently, they escorted him down the stairs. As he started descending, he took one last look at the bird that had just saved his life. He wished he could tell the bird to bring back Sara, but there was not time for that. He held his box with both hands as the guards walked him through a series of hallways and stairs.

As Winston passed several workers in the castle, he wondered what he looked like. They all seemed to be staring at him, but then again, he probably looked suspicious carrying a box, being escorted by guards, and being soaking wet and most likely extremely dirty. They had quietly led him to the office of Videre. He had been here before years ago when she had entrusted this special mission to him. He had carried out her orders dutifully but it had come at a great price.

"I can take him from here," a loud voice boomed from behind them.

Kolono unlocked the office door and waved to the guards to leave. Ezrai was right behind him.

"Winston," said Ezrai in shock as he looked at the box. "What's the meaning of this?"

"I'm afraid, it has begun."

TIMEKEEPERS

Leon woke up as the sun flooded his room. He was glad to get back to the castle again in the comforts of his old room. Videre was no longer next to him and he thought that maybe last night had just been a dream.

He looked over to his work table that had been left untouched. Leon had been waiting for this since he left Hikari. He quickly got out of bed and grabbed the stone from his pocket. It was a clear dark red stone and the cracks inside shined ever so brightly. Putting it on his desk, he pulled out a small box from under his bed.

Videre had only asked for him to replace the stone, never to give it back with the timekeeper. When he picked up the stone in Nanoto, he thought it impossible that someone would have taken it from his room and left it in a place where he could find it. He took a deep breath and opened the box.

Laying inside was the stone that he had taken out of Videre's timekeeper. Leon was shocked and his heart beat harder. He compared the stone from the box and the one he had just pulled from his pocket. The stones were the same cut, but the cracks inside were definitely different.

There's another timekeeper.

www.ingramcontent.com/pod-product-compliance
Lightning Source LLC
Chambersburg PA
CBHW051501150726

47997CB00001B/65